FOWL

A NOVEL IN THREE ACTS

PLAY

STEVEN LEIGH MORRIS

FOWL PLAY
A Novel in Three Acts

Steven Leigh Morris

ISBN 978-0-99069665-0

First published in 2016 by Padaro Press
An operating unit of Morling Manor Music Corporation
Los Angeles, CA

Cover and interior design: designSimple.com

PADARO PRESS
padaropress.com

Fowl Play starts at a small Los Angeles theater and ends in a forest, and in between, Steven Leigh Morris spins one of the most oddly compelling tales of obsession, midlife crisis, and exurban anomie I've read. Though it defies genre, it's a kind of love story, and a kind of family drama, and definitely a kind of satire. Its gimlet-eyed view of Hollywood — of the dilapidated, ephemeral neighborhood where actual people live, not the factory where collective dreams are churned out — occasionally put me in mind of Waugh's *The Loved One*. But this novel's strange alchemy of galline gallantry, theater criticism, and haunted Russophilia is a distinctly Morris-ian brew.

——Rob Weinert-Kendt, *American Theatre* editor

Fowl Play is dedicated to the memory of Monica B. Morris.

INTRODUCTION

This novel attempts to interweave my two great passions in life: the theater and barnyard poultry. The people in the former seem, for the most part, to know what they're doing and why they're doing it. The creatures in the latter don't give such things a moment's thought, and for that, they also deserve respect. Both thespians and barnyard poultry live in the moment, or in moments, fleeting moments, When a theater production is concluded, it's concluded. The same can be said of a chicken. All that's left are memories and vapors. In the theater, and on the farm, these are obvious truths. Less so for us striving and staggering about in alternate worlds, often cruel and violent worlds filled with tedium and humor and rage and giant swaths of love, struggling to fathom the purpose of it all. It is from that struggle that this novel was written. Thank you to all the dear people who helped shape it.

ACKNOWLEDGEMENTS

I would like to acknowledge the contributions of Martha D. Ludlum, Cathy Carlton and Judy Proffer in the creation of this novel, and to Laurie Ochoa for when, as the new editor of the *L.A. Weekly*, created a column on local idiosyncrasies, and chose my essay on hatching and rearing chickens in Hollywood to launch that column. Around that time, she suggested I write a book on this theme. I'd also like to thank the Los Angeles theater community for being a perpetual source of inspiration, rumination and entertainment. They know what they're doing, and why they're doing it.

TABLE OF CONTENTS

PROLOGUE: THINGS WE DON'T KNOW WE DON'T KNOW

Dusk. Those ambient colors in the sky tell the world below that nothing lasts. Some hues may linger, but nothing lasts. This is the song of twilight, just before streetlights shine and headlights wink.

The sun, having scorched Los Angeles into triple-digit temperatures by 2 p.m., was now slipping out of sight behind the prop houses and television studios that pepper Hollywood. Seth Jacobson studied the barely registering speedometer of his dented Honda Civic as he nervously inched west along Santa Monica Boulevard. Seeing that he was crawling forward at a mere four miles per hour further triggered anxiety. His stomach churned.

Glossy new towers of condominiums and office buildings lined Sunset Boulevard to the north. Seth had plenty of time to survey the urban redevelopment given his torpid pace. Any other time he might have been interested in inspecting the newness of the city he called home, but on this particular evening, the lack of any significant forward momentum presented a particular challenge because, as lead drama critic for the alternative weekly newspaper L.A. Observer, he was due for an 8 p.m. curtain. It was now 7:41, and he was about a mile away. He understood that in this molasses traffic, nineteen minutes wasn't nearly enough time to traverse the remaining mile. His hands turned clammy.

Meanwhile, the odometer was on the cusp of clicking over from 99,999 miles to a milestone 100,000. But at this rate, that clearly wasn't going to happen anytime soon.

After rolling forward about three triumphant feet, Seth braked to a halt once more. He knew that the publicist over at the Hudson Theater was waiting for him with some anxiousness, and that professionalism mandated that he show up on time and not make a spectacle of himself, either by absence or tardiness. Besides, Seth was a member of the Los Angeles Drama Critics Circle, and word spreads fast in any local theater community, even in a city as large as Los Angeles — especially in a city as large as Los Angeles.

As part of an idiosyncratic L.A. tradition of outdoor movie screenings in a graveyard, the cause of the traffic cluster was a showing of *Invasion of the Body Snatchers* at a very popular screening series located, appropriately, amidst the tombstones and vaults of Hollywood Forever Cemetery: permanent home to Rudolph Valentino, Charlie Chaplin, the DeMille and Talmadge families, Douglas Fairbanks, Tyrone Power, and countless other representatives of Hollywood's Golden Age. Seth felt a vein in his neck pulse as he watched the logjam of traffic trying to pass through the cemetery's ornate gates on Santa Monica Boulevard and into its now constipated parking lot.

"Why didn't I just take Fountain," Seth grumbled to himself, catching a glimpse of his face reflected in the rear-view mirror. Dark circles under his eyes were beginning to bulge. The spider-web of lines extending from the edges of his eyes appeared more pronounced due to a silver-sparkled stubble of a beard. "How did that happen?" Seth mused. "Only yesterday I was young." He hadn't been eating well or sleeping much of late. Though he was reasonably fit for being nearly fifty, stresses from all kinds of congestions in his life were taking their toll.

Seth was not only the drama critic of the *L.A. Observer*, he was also on staff as the theater editor, meaning that in addition to his column, he also assigned shows to a team of reviewers and edited their eight or nine short "capsule" reviews that appeared in the paper each week. Having been with the *L.A. Observer* for almost twenty years, Seth was known within a certain, circumscribed theater circle, and he told himself that he was an advocate for "truth and beauty." On good days, he believed this to be true.

The sky was now darkening into a gorgeous, blood-rich crimson.

Seth inched by *carnicerias*, discount clothing stores and medical marijuana dispensaries, taco trucks, wooden billboards capped with bird-deterring propellers, a squalid stretch of dusty cement and shanty-like shop façades that gave so much of Los Angeles the appearance of a third-world city. This particular stretch contained the storefront theaters of what the consortium of businesses known as the Hollywood Media District had labeled "Theater Row."

Seth watched an intrepid cyclist whiz through the millimeters of vacant space between the left-side mirrors of one lane and right-side mirrors of the other. The cyclist wore a helmet and a lurid blue-and-gold Spandex outfit bearing the insignia "UCLA." To avoid crashing into the rear of the 704 Rapid bus that had just suddenly braked, the cyclist careened to the right, bolting directly in front of a stopped Camry before resuming his bird-like trajectory along the thin ribbon of asphalt adjoining the sidewalk. The cyclist looked back at the traffic he had just passed and caught Seth's eye.

That's arrogant, Seth thought.

Yet Seth also felt a pang of empathy after the cyclist, his torso twisted so that he was still looking backwards, plunged into a gaping pothole. No stranger to biking himself, Seth imagined what UCLA must be enduring as he watched the helmet drop several inches and saw the cyclist jolted from his saddle. Seth cringingly observed UCLA coasting while straddling the crossbeam until he was able to extract himself from that humiliating position, probably suffering from a lingering ache in his testicles as he continued darting west.

As UCLA slipped away into the sunset, Seth now had time to reflect on his own momentum. What really was the point of these arduous passages through Hollywood's grid-clogged arteries? What was the point of his job? It was more than a job, it was a "calling," he told himself. So what if the L.A. *Observer* lacked the reach and influence of the L.A. *Times*. The scrappy weekly that employed him still had its own following. The readers were loyal to the paper, and he was loyal to them.

Just past the cemetery's congestion of cars and trucks, the traffic started to flow, which in Hollywood on a Saturday night meant moving from a stall to a sustained roll of up to fifteen miles per hour. At exactly 7:57, Seth crossed the intersection of Santa Monica Boulevard and Hudson Avenue where the theater was located, but he saw no available parking spaces. Those legendary "parking angels" in Los Angeles? The ones that make a parking space appear when you needed it most? Nowhere to be found.

Nor was there a soul on duty at the valet station in front of the theater: no doubt they all were busy parking cars of other equally frantic theater patrons. He lurched up Seward Avenue, past warehouses and water-stained stucco duplexes with iron window bars, beyond Lexington and Fountain avenues, three long blocks north, almost to De Longpre Avenue when he finally spotted an opening on the left between a beat-up Toyota Tercel and a shiny new Prius. Seth spun a three-point U-turn, and spent approximately ninety seconds wedging his Honda into the available sliver of a parking space. Stepping out into the night air, Seth clicked the remote and the car snapped locked. He took a deep breath, checked for the pen he hoped he'd stuffed in his jacket's side pocket, and sprinted for the theater.

The wind on his face enlivened him and Seth heard the clump of his boots landing on the sidewalk in swift succession. His breath heaved as he approached the boulevard. He almost crashed into a woman walking her Chihuahua. He barely noticed a pair of lovers making out in front of a hedge, and caught a glimpse of a tranny hooker in bright green hot pants and stiletto heels. He or she puffed on a cigarette while posing on the corner of Seward and Santa Monica and clutching a golden purse.

As he expected, Darla the publicist was waiting for him on the street outside the theater. Darla shoved a black folder containing a press release and a program into his eager hands and guided him swiftly into the lobby. From there, Seth was passed like a relay baton to the theater's house manager. She, in turn, told Seth that because the show had *just* started, she would be unable to allow him in through the audience seating area, which was now darkened. Instead, she would need to guide him into the hall through a safer entry, to usher him through the maze of hallways interlinking the venue's four intimate theaters. En route, they passed a young actor in a 1940s gabardine suit. He paced nervously in one hall, awaiting his entrance for a production of Arthur Miller's *All My Sons*. Trying to keep up with the house manager, who was flying through the hallway like a cannonball, Seth caught a fleeting glimpse inside a dressing room where performers in various stages of undress were applying lipstick and rouge. At last, with a wave of her hand, the house manager released Seth into a dark place with a wooden floor.

"Enjoy the show," she said before disappearing.

This is odd, Seth thought. The purpose of being led into the theater this way was to avoid the pitfalls of entering a darkened seating area. Yet here he stood in the almost pitch-black.

As his eyes slowly adjusted, Seth began to discern that he was actually in a corner of the backstage. He gleaned this from the wash of light he now could see ringing a group of actors performing in front of him. Beyond the haloed actors, Seth could see the faces of an audience, and he understood that from his current position, he was mercifully protected by shadow. His task, however, was to find a way from his current backstage location into that audience. From what he could see, that could only be accomplished by tiptoeing across the perimeter of the lighted stage. Such a crossing would announce to the world that Seth had arrived late. Worse, interrupting the action would create the very spectacle that is every drama critic's worst nightmare: Actors seek the light. Critics prefer the dark.

Tentatively, Seth pressed forward, to the edge of the light. There he saw to his profound relief a passageway in the dark that led not exactly into the audience but up a stairwell to a landing directly to the side of the audience and high above it. He crept as stealthily as he could toward that passage, and eased his way up, step by step, higher and higher until, at the top of the landing, an even more comforting sight revealed itself — a circular wooden table and chair positioned in the direction of the stage.

With blood pressure now returning to normal, Seth marveled at the ability to observe the action from his private perch while enjoying the benefit of a table to place the folder and program, and to make notes. Normally, he took notes on the back of a press release held in his lap, and later struggled to decipher those chicken scratches. Here, having a personal desk was a luxury. He tapped his fingers on a banister directly to his left. The banister capped the crude plywood siding that separated him from the audience below — a capacity audience of over a hundred people, Seth noted.

The actors were playing out the ballroom scene in *Romeo and Julio,* a contemporary adaptation of Shakespeare's play in which the Bard's text had thankfully been left mostly intact. The play's director, the locally renowned Sergei van Gough, had cast the star-crossed lovers as two men, one of them Latino — to underscore lingering homophobia *and* ethnic divides — even in contemporary, enlightened Los Angeles. Or so Seth read in the director's program notes that he could barely discern in the ever-so-thin beams spilling out from lighting instruments directly over his head.

That's when Seth noticed *Romeo and Julio*'s other striking features. The Capulet family were all hearing-impaired, contrasted against the Montagues, who were not. Meanwhile, the Capulets' signed dialogue was being recited by other actors on the stage. The purpose of all this was to underscore the under-recognized bigotry against the hearing-impaired — even in contemporary, enlightened Los Angeles, Seth read in Mr. van Gough's program notes. Furthermore, Seth observed in the performance that Benvolio was wheelchair-bound, having been maimed serving in the U.S. Army in Afghanistan.

"That's laying it on a bit thick," Seth thought.

When Seth noted a strikingly bullish quality to Julio's ancient Nurse, he began to sharpen an imagined pencil for a scathing review about reducing Shakespeare's tragedy to a manifesto on oppressed minorities. He couldn't deny some impressive performances — particularly by those who were hearing-impaired and displayed wrenching emotion in their body language and facial expressions. He jotted this down on the backside of the press release. And he wasn't going to back off from telling the whole truth, which is for any drama critic the profession's highest calling — next to showing up on time.

At the precise moment when these thoughts were tumbling around in Seth's mind, he noticed that his program was suddenly easy to read, alarmingly easy, because every lighting instrument aimed in his direction was now illuminated to its full capacity. The entire audience could see Seth's hang-jawed expression and his perplexed sky-bound gaze.

With growing dread, he then saw Julio climbing up the same

steps that Seth had used earlier. Julio was coming toward him. The actor vaguely resembled the tranny hooker Seth had spotted on the corner of Santa Monica and Seward. Those stiletto heels were now mere inches from his table. Mortified, Seth realized that the table and chair where he now sat were smack in the middle of the balcony scene — an ancillary stage.

"But soft, what light through yonder window breaks?" he heard from below, while completely blinded by the onslaught of hot, white wattage.

There is only one viable option for a drama critic under such circumstances. Fortunately, Seth, a seasoned professional, had read about this in the *Theatre Critics' Handbook*, an extremely helpful guide to ethics and standards published by the American Theatre Critics Association.

First, he blinked, though that part was an involuntary reaction to the light, and was not part of the instructions in the *Handbook*. He then followed the *Handbook*'s advice for exactly this situation on Page 211, in Chapter 17 ("Duck and Cover"). He plunged behind the plywood partition so that every millimeter of his body was hidden.

And there he crouched, cowering. Unfortunately, in his haste he failed to grab the press release — the one that lay on the table, face down, exposing to Julio the blank side and all the notes that Seth had lodged there, including Seth's latest entry written in large bold script, "This is crap!"

Seth's eyes were now clenched tight, as though that would make any difference, when he heard Romeo's line from below.

"With love's light wings did I o'er-perch these walls;
For stony limits cannot hold love out,
And what love can do that dares love attempt;
Therefore thy kinsmen are no let to me."

With each mention of the word *love*, Seth felt a stabbing pain in the region of his ribcage. Jolting up and opening his eyes, he realized that Julio had him trapped under the sharp spike of one of his/her stiletto heels.

The final jab came after Julio's line, "I would not for the world they saw thee here."

By the end of the balcony scene, Seth had received at least a dozen punctures. Victor Cruz, the actor playing Julio, sent him an apologetic email that night, insisting it was not deliberate. "Sometimes actors in the throes of passion are not entirely in command of their actions," Cruz explained.

Seth's *Observer* review included the following description, later jacked by *Romeo and Julio*'s producers and used in ads that appeared in *Variety* and the *Los Angeles Times*:

"A memorably brave and inventive Shakespearean adaptation, buttressed by director Sergei van Gough's keen sensitivity to the plight of the oppressed," and "Victor Cruz's Julio is a standout."

What struck Seth most when he read other reviews of the show was no mention by any other critic that Julio was a transvestite — had Seth alone observed this conspicuous detail, or was it merely his interpretation?

No complaint against Seth was lodged by the theater, and somehow the few snarky mentions of his unwitting appearance in the balcony scene that cropped up on Twitter and Facebook were either disregarded or blissfully unnoticed by his editors.

On Friday afternoon, the day after his review appeared, Seth was summoned to the publisher's office on the top floor of the *Observer*. The office featured a wall-size window, providing majestic views of the usually gridlocked Hollywood Freeway. Seth imagined that if he had such a grand portal to the city, he'd never accomplish anything.

Hypnotized by the traffic patterns, he'd just stare out the window all day. Then there were the gentle nuances of the ever-changing landscape as shadows and sunlight performed a slow-motion dance in counterpoint.

When Seth entered the office, the publisher, Candace, was sitting behind her desk and dabbing her eyes with a Kleenex. Her maroon blouse nearly matched the color of blotches on her clearly troubled face. Seated in the corner was Olivia, the chic editor-in-chief, dressed in designer jeans, Italian boots and a Bohemian-style green top. Olivia smiled sweetly then stared at the floor. Something was amiss. Seth knew his co-workers well. Their shared history included exchanging holiday gifts and birthday cards.

As Seth gingerly sat down in a chair near Olivia, Candace sniffled three times and blew her nose.

"I'm sorry," she said.

Meanwhile, Olivia sat somber, gazing at her boots.

"Well," Candace mumbled, staring at her new French manicure. "I don't know how to begin."

"They're eliminating the position of Theater Editor," Olivia blurted out. "It's coming from Tampa."

The L.A. Observer was part of a newspaper chain headquartered in Tampa, which had been throwing its senior arts critics overboard across its corporate network — part of a larger national trend of declining revenues in print newspapers. Even though he knew vulnerability hung in the air, Seth had until now preferred not to dwell on worst-case scenarios.

"It's entirely a financial decision," Candace continued. "It has nothing to do with your performance."

"No complaints?" Seth asked, on the alert for furtive glances between them, perhaps over some Tweet on the incident of Saturday night. His right hand unconsciously leapt to his ribcage, the very place he had been punctured by Julio's stiletto. He had felt no discomfort for days, but now a phantom pain revealed itself. Was it a cosmic reminder that he had brought his unraveling upon himself?

"No, they love your work," Candace assured him.

Olivia's eyebrow arched a millimeter, and Seth calmly tried to assess and even rate the authenticity of Candace's words.

Olivia said that both of them wanted Seth to continue doing exactly what he was doing. He could keep his office, his telephone, his company email. The hitch? Instead of collecting a salary, he now would be paid for writing and editing by the piece.

Seth did some quick calculations and figured he was looking down the barrel of a 30 percent pay cut and the elimination of his health benefits.

Candace dabbed her eyes and blew her nose a second time.

"It's okay," Seth said, perplexed and even annoyed that he was the one offering comfort. "It's just the state of journalism. It's just the state of the arts. At least I still have a platform to encourage the best work. I still have a purpose."

"More than that, you still have an office phone," Candace sniffed.

"We fought this for months," Olivia added. "We don't want to lose you."

"It could be worse," Candace said, brightening. "Imagine being a proctologist, having to look up other people's buttholes all day. *You* still get paid to spend every night at the theater."

"Sometimes the similarities are striking," Seth remarked, prompting a small laugh from Candace and a hint of a smile from Olivia.

They each embraced Seth, who then stepped into the stairwell, alone. There was no buoyancy in his stride. Seth wasn't prone to melancholy, but their removal of a large part of his pay and benefits reflected in his step, and in the hollowness of his gaze. Two floors below, Seth entered the break room. He considered pouring a cup of hot chocolate, but the act of stirring boiling water into powder seemed more trouble than it was worth. Instead, he plodded toward his office and rolled his bicycle out. The effort of pedaling in the Santa Ana heat and winds toward Bronson Canyon felt Herculean.

HOME.

At 3 a.m., Seth couldn't sleep, feeling now an intractable sense of erosion all around him, from his job situation to the priorities of a culture, which just seemed to be shifting away from everything that mattered to him. The angst Seth felt actually had started months ago when he spoke in a class at UCLA and asked how many had heard of Arthur Miller. Three hands out of fifty went up. They'd all heard of Marilyn Monroe, but not her spouse. Even an American playwright as seminal as Arthur Miller was disappearing into the static of pop culture.

In Russia, they name train stations after their playwrights and novelists, Seth reflected. In Russia, they're preserved in marble.
But still, who wants to live in Russia?

Oh, to have a television to numb the mind right now, he thought. Or, more succinctly, to have television service. The rate hike six months ago from $50 to $70 a month for satellite "service" in the reception-challenged Hollywood Hills was more than Seth could countenance. So in a gesture that filled Seth with an Off-the-Grid Nobility at the time, but now seemed largely irrelevant, he had cancelled his cable TV service.

And this is why, in a stained T-shirt and underwear, dabbing hydrogen peroxide on what was left of his puncture wounds, at 3:04 a.m., Seth found himself sitting on the couch in the living room of his one-bedroom apartment, flipping through *The Atlantic*, and attempting to read a long article on atrocities in Pakistan in order to get clearer distinction between authentic misery and his own comparatively petty misfortunes.

At 3:10 a.m., after re-reading the same paragraph for the fifth time, Seth figured that it just wasn't helpful to be reading about the Taliban just then, even with the article's artistically rendered photographs of corpses lying in ditches. As though staring into the abyss of the world's most profound horrors would provide some comforting counterpoint to his sense of creeping professional irrelevance. It didn't. Instead, the photographs contained some maudlin fascination that yielded to the onset of listlessness.

At 3:13 a.m., Seth set down *The Atlantic*, crossed through the thin light of his art deco floor lamp and with a sharp tug, released the hollow wooden front door, now slightly swollen into its frame from the summer heat. A cool breeze brushed through his hair. Seth stepped outside onto the magnesite-coated walkway connecting his apartment to the five others on the second floor. In the dim yellow glow of the light bulb screwed into the awning overhead, Seth admired the now-fruiting tomatoes and beans that he'd planted in tubs outside his door. The vines snaked up, tied to the iron railing on the outer edge. The thin streak of a waning moon was sinking toward the northwest foothills, while raccoons clambered through the avocado tree in the next-door neighbor's yard.

HOME.
MOSCOW, RUSSIA. 1 P.M.

Katerina Pavlova, a 48-year-old woman, lived by herself in a two-bedroom apartment in the Ismailovsky Park district, northeast of the city center. She owned her two-bedroom apartment in a *Py-*

29

atetazhe, as they call these five-story, Khrushchev-era apartment blocks. Katerina's mother, now approaching eighty, lived two floors down and alone: Her husband died five years ago of a mysterious blood disorder. That husband was and is the father of Katerina Pavlova, their only child. It was he who bought her the apartment where she now lives. That was on the occasion of her first marriage, thirty years earlier, to an actor named Vanya, whom she met when they were both acting students at the Moscow Art Theatre Institute. They were both employed by a local repertory theater company for about three years. They're divorced now.

On the living room wall in Katerina's apartment hung photographs of Katerina, a baby-faced cherub with shoulder-length hair bleached blonde, embracing a chimpanzee — a scene from one of her movies. There was a photograph of her parents, a photograph of herself in a play she performed in Los Angeles, a photograph of a girl — her daughter, Irena, from her first marriage.

Katerina was now working in the human resources department of a Moscow investment firm that paid her sporadically a fraction of what her contract called for. Katerina said there's nothing she could do about that, since the company had been routinely bribing the judges of the local court. She was looking for another job but was no longer young in Russia's ageist employment culture.

Katerina grabbed a leash from a bucket in the hallway by the front door, and clipped it onto her Chow Chow. She and the dog walked down five flights of stairs to the street landing. Pressing a button on the heavy front door, she released a lock. The Chow Chow bounded excitedly through the open door out onto the slippery sidewalk, nearly causing Katerina to fall. A light rain had just stopped.

As she was turning the corner of *Ulitza Fortunatovskaya,* the street on which she lived, an off-leash Doberman charged at the

Chow Chow, sinking fangs into tissue. As the Chow Chow yelped in fear and pain, Katerina dove onto the dog heap, trying to pry the animals apart. Muscovites now trickled out of nearby apartments, perplexed by the pile of woman and dogs. A young girl screamed. The Doberman's owner stood nearby, a man with a shaved head, a leather jacket and muddy boots. He was drunk and laughing. A leash dangled from one of his hands.

"Sasha! Khvatee!" ("Cut it out!") he finally bellowed. The Doberman let go. The owner leashed the dog, cursing, and the pair scurried away. Katerina remained on the brambly garden next to the sidewalk as the rain resumed. She lay heaped on top of her dog, trembling, covered in mud and blood. Two passers-by helped her up.

At 1:45 p.m., Katerina caught a whiff of stale urine as she staggered up three flights of stairs to her mother's apartment with the wounded dog. They nursed the injured animal with a bucket of water, some rags and hydrogen peroxide, all slopping over the bucket onto the laminate floor of her mother's hallway.

At 3:15 p.m., Katerina, now back in her own apartment, picked up her phone and dialed.

It was, at this moment, 4:15 a.m. in Los Angeles. Seth stood on the walkway outside his front door. Through a fog of exhaustion, he observed a pre-dawn dew coating the tiny green tomatoes, and the moon sliding ever closer to the canyon. He heard his phone ring from inside. He knew from the hour that it was his wife, Katerina Pavlova, calling in distress from Russia. The same wife he so missed, the wife he wished would return. And, because she wouldn't or couldn't return, the same wife he was thinking of asking for a divorce.

They'd tested the travails of their long-distance marriage to its breaking point. Katerina had traveled back and forth between Moscow and L.A., but lately she spent far more time in Russia. When living with Seth in Bronson Canyon, she worked a number of jobs, from stage roles in Moscow's largest theaters to L.A.'s tiniest, to an off-Broadway play for which her performance was lauded in *The New York Times*. On both coasts, Katerina was a darling of the critics. She displayed a comic goofiness and raw vulnerability that charmed and dazzled. She was preternaturally gifted in this way. Between roles, she worked any number of jobs as research for her art. She was a security guard at the County Art Museum and a journalist for a Russian-language newspaper. But she never learned to drive and developed severe pains shooting through her back until she was walking with a cane and taking Vicodin. Eventually, she became clinically depressed in Los Angeles, by Los Angeles. She missed home, she said. After her father died in Moscow while she was in Los Angeles, it was more than she could bear. She and Seth attended his funeral in Moscow, after which she returned to L.A. to see Seth for visits of only a week or so, once or twice a year. This congenial estrangement had now lasted five years.

She was sobbing into the phone that her beloved Chow Chow may be dying.

"I'm so sorry," Seth kept repeating, then, after a pause, "Are you ever coming back? What kind of life is that? They don't pay you. Last month you were mugged!"

"I can't live there," she answered. "My mum is sick. Moscow is my city. It's *home*."

"But this marriage . . . It isn't a marriage anymore. I really don't want to continue like this," he said. "Did you find somebody else?"

"No," she replied calmly. "Did *you?*"

"I asked a colleague at the paper to join me for a play — a friend I've known for years. 'Aren't you *married?*' she said. 'Where's your *wife?*'"

"Is she single?" Katerina asked.

"I don't know, I guess . . ."

"She wants to date you."

"Oh, really?"

"You're such a child . . . Just wait . . . I know how these things work."

"Is that so?" Seth replied. ". . . So what's going on with you?"

"I'm ill. It's not your problem. I need to recover at home," she said. "Why can't you live *here*?"

"What can I do there? You can barely survive there yourself, and you're Russian! You can do anything you want here."

"I'll be there in November," she said. "We'll figure it out then."

After they hung up, Seth felt as if he were suspended from a string attached to the ceiling. Despite the early hour of a new day and lack of sleep, Seth knew exactly what he needed to do.

From a kitchen closet, he pulled out an unopened bag of potting soil that he bought a month ago at Home Depot. He hauled it out onto the landing and dumped it into the last empty plastic tub.

The first light of dawn was starting to break across the city as Seth plunged his bare hands into the soil. He felt it roll between his fingers. It was an oddly comforting feeling. It felt like home.

"Something must grow from this decay," he muttered softly. "Something enchanted from this disenchantment, something from the earth and the ashes . . ."

At 4:30 a.m., with remnants of the dirt comfortably resting beneath his nails, Seth flipped through an old book of quotations: Volume 2 of *Dumbest Things Ever Said*. He found a quote from former Secretary of Defense Donald Rumsfeld.

"There are known knowns. There are things we know that we know. There are known unknowns. That is to say, there are things that we know we don't know. But there are also unknown un-knowns. There are things we don't know we don't know."

The book intended to mock Rumsfeld's words, but at 4:45 a.m., they struck Seth as germane.

Seth was undergoing some profound change but had no idea what it was, other than it stemming from some generalized low-level anxiety that time was slipping away and he wasn't using it well. The dawn was breaking, and this was a moment of resurrection. Seth Jacobson stood at the edge of lunacy, and that didn't trouble him one bit. He stood on the verge of a new life, with no sense at all of what that life would entail.

"There are things we don't know we don't know."

ACT I:
ELYSIAN
FIELDS

ACT I, SCENE 1: THE HATCHING OF MEMORY

963. A baking hot August. A reedish boy sails under the Golden Gate Bridge after a sixteen-day ocean crossing from Southampton, England on a massive ocean liner named S.S. *Oriana*.

It was a dazzling arrival to the United States for Seth, his parents, an older brother and an infant sister. Two weeks and two days earlier they left home forever, home in the concrete and brick suburbs of Worthing, a small, pleasant town on a lip of the English Channel. It was in Worthing that Oscar Wilde wrote *The Importance of Being Earnest*.

And it was in Worthing that the die was cast, when Seth's family was visited by relatives from California. Distant cousin Joe was a ruddy-complexioned Russian émigré, an impish Lothario then in his early sixties. Joe listened to the tales of woe told by Seth's parents. The sagging British economy, the stream of dreary, lousy-paying jobs, the spiraling property taxes in an England that seemed to offer scant opportunity even for survival, let alone advancement.

"California is golden," Joe said through his thick Russian accent. "We sponsor you. You live in the empty house on our chicken farm. You pay whatever rent you can afford."

Joe Rapoport and his wife Sheba were part of a Sonoma County enclave of Yiddish-speaking "radicals" on an FBI watch list. Agents checked in with them once a year at their home until their deaths. A quarter-century of annual scrutiny, it was.

As a teenager, Joe had enlisted in the Red Army of the fledgling Soviet Union — one very sore point for the FBI, even if he enlisted because the Red Army defended Jews from the anti-Semitic purges raging across Ukraine and Moldova at the time.

After a particularly vicious Ukrainian pogrom in 1919, Joe and Sheba (who hadn't yet met) left their respective villages, or *stetls* as they were called, crossed the Dnieper River separating Ukraine and Moldova, and waited in the Moldovan city of Kishinev (where they met) in a synagogue for help from the Jewish underground to emigrate to the United States.

Once in New York City, Joe and Sheba worked in the garment factories and helped unionize the workers — an activity that also didn't score them any points with the FBI. After being hounded west by Senator Joseph McCarthy, who equated union organizing with communism, all that was left professionally to Joe and his compatriots was chicken farming, which he despised. Meanwhile, Sheba worked as an executive secretary in San Francisco.

Sheba was a politically impassioned, quick-to-laugh woman. They both abhorred violence and bigotry and the use of it for political purposes, because growing up in Ukraine they themselves had been the victims of violence and bigotry.

A patronizing Saint of Lost Causes, Sheba didn't help matters with her persistent lectures on the beauty of the Soviet Idea. Her loud and oft-stated admiration for Joseph Stalin remained almost intractable until her death at the age of eighty-nine, though her tone softened somewhat with more and more evidence of how Stalin willfully tortured and starved an entire generation of Ukrainians.

A year before her death, Sheba was a widow when a federal employee, a woman, visited her for the last time. The sun blazed down as the FBI agent, dressed in civilian trousers and shirt, sauntered up to the front door of Sheba's picket-fenced bungalow in Petaluma. The agent held a clipboard and pen. Despite her eighty-eight years, Sheba could replay the exchange verbatim.

"Mrs. Rapoport, how are you this afternoon?"

"Raging gracefully, thank you. Yourself?"

"Oh, I'm okay, I guess."

"Well, that's good."

"So, is there anywhere you've traveled this year?"

"Yes, I just got back from London."

Sheba knew this was utter nonsense. The agent scratched notes onto the pad resting on her clipboard.

"And what did you do there?"

"I had tea with the queen."

The agent stopped writing and looked at Sheba for a moment, who squinted.

"Tea and crumpets," Sheba continued.

"Is there anything else we should know?"

"Currant jam. It's hard to find here."

With that, the agent wandered back to her shiny Chevy sedan and rolled down the hills toward the Old Redwood Highway.

SETH'S FAMILY EVENTUALLY ADJUSTED to their new life under the watchful eyes of Joe and Sheba. Early in the morning, before bicycling down the hill to Cotati Elementary School in rustic Sonoma County, Seth would walk up the path from the green bungalow where his family lived at the base of the ranch, to meet Joe in Chicken House Number 1. Seth always followed Joe on his rounds feeding the chickens, sometimes picking up dead birds that had been crushed into the floor, or killing the sick, dangling them by their feet and slamming their heads against a post. Just like Joe did.

SOMETIMES, IN A SMALL WOODEN SHED, Seth watched Joe feeding chicken carcasses to a clowder of cats, or opening a can of evaporated milk and chopping up stale bread for them with a hatchet.

The ranch housed some 15,000 Rhode Island Red meat chickens, and Seth grew to recognize many of them personally by appearance and personality — the arc of a black-green iridescent tail, the stunning shiny slope of orange-red hackle feathers, the cockiness of one, the docility of another, a rust-brown pullet who bore herself with quiet dignity and seemed uncharacteristically wise among the mob.

In the flock, Seth observed the poultry equivalent of racism — the oddity of a white bird or black bird, ostracized by the red majority, pushed away from food, picked on, pecked at.

Seth's attachment to the flock was perverse, since every fourteen weeks large flatbed trucks carrying stacked wire cages rolled onto the property with a trio of rubber-booted men who seized yelping birds with leather gloves, three chickens at a time, holding them by their feet upside down, and stuffing them into the cages on the trucks. Hysteria yielded to complacency: The birds were calm as the convoy rolled away — beaks and combs craning into the breeze. Chickens are like that, Seth discovered: They live and die in the moment.

Every day, Seth walked up the hill to visit Joe and Sheba in their white cottage. On their black-and-white GE television, he watched the Beatles capture the hearts of America, the aftermath of JFK's assassination, and reruns of The Beverly Hillbillies. It was through Joe's halting Russian accent and Sheba's brisk stridency that he absorbed the heroic rhetoric of Cesar Chavez and his United Farm Workers, of Martin Luther King Jr., and the fledgling Civil Rights movement, as well as his cousins' rabid opposition to the quickly escalating war in Vietnam. Seth helped Joe and Sheba make picket signs, and he accompanied them to San Francisco to march in street protests against the war.

In those years, Seth had no idea that Joe was chasing Seth's young mother around the kitchen when the children were in school and their father, a traveling salesman, was on the road.

Nor did it occur to Seth at this time that many people in Sonoma County actually supported the war in Vietnam. Seth had been a popular and exotic fourth-grade entry at Cotati Elementary School until he started criticizing American foreign policy, aping what he'd heard in the white cottage on the hill. That's when his popularity plummeted. On one occasion, he felt a wave of nausea and dizziness after a fifth-grade patriot smacked his head down onto the hard wood of a lunch table. "If you don't like it here, why don't you go back to where you came from?"

For solace and refuge, Seth sat with the chickens, sometimes in an old chair that he'd brought for the occasion, sometimes for an hour or two frozen like a statue.

Seth trained himself to sit in the chair moving nothing but his eyes, and the chickens would approach, torn between apprehension and curiosity. One would peck at his shoelace, then another would imitate, until the first would take the brave jump to his knee, realize what it had done and run away. Then all would flee, stepping on each other, squawking in a farce staged by instinct until, following some leader, they would re-approach. They really couldn't help themselves, being so inquisitive: one on his knee, then two, one on his shoulder. At the end of an hour, the boy was covered in chickens, absolutely enchanted.

5:02 A.M. BRONSON CANYON. ANXIETY and blind faith tumbled in Seth's mind. His hands tapped the thin, top layer of moist potting soil that now covered the newly sprinkled marigold seeds. In the cool June dawn on the walkway of his Hollywood apartment, the faint yet distinctive odor of chicken manure mixed into this particular bag of potting soil aroused in Seth the singular passion to hatch and own a flock of chickens.

He didn't care if he lived smack in the middle of the second largest city in the United States. He didn't care about the building's rules and regulations. He didn't care that he might be voted off the Board of his Homeowners Association. He didn't care if he was crazy, or if anybody thought him so. He was resolved to engage in the harmless pursuit of hatching and owning a flock of chickens, which now seemed more poetical, meaningful and urgent than anything in his life. He knew nothing about hatching chickens, but that was another matter entirely. For now, he was guided by a blast of idiosyncratic memories that somehow connected him to earth and to hearth, memories that warmed him:

Memories of a thousand baby chicks, chirping and huddled on fresh sawdust under a heat lamp; cascades of golden acacia billowing along Sonoma County roads; ditches lined with blackberries and thistles; eucalyptus windbreaks; riding on the back of a steer; and, to the heart of the matter, the pungent musk of corn feed and tattered feathers ground into the sawdust, and caked chicken shit carpeting the floors of the old wooden sheds where Seth had spent so much time when he was a child.

They're gone now. Those long poultry barns, with their dust-coated windows and spiderwebs and piles of manure stacked against the outer walls. The sheds were starting to sag, even then.

After spending two-and-a-half frenzied hours of research on the Internet, Seth Jacobson understood that the key to this project of hatching a flock of chickens in the heart of Hollywood was acquiring fertile eggs.

He read how the vast majority of eggs sold in grocery stores and supermarkets, whether or not from free-range chickens, are infertile because there are no roosters present among the flock of hens. This male absence has no bearing on the ability of the hens to lay. It means that such unfertilized eggs will simply rot when placed under the warm breast of a brooding hen.

But if roosters are present in the flock, and if the males are sufficiently vigorous to mount the hens, there are good odds that the fledging embryo will have subdivided into a few hundred cells, which can survive in a suspended state for up to a week after the egg is first laid. "It's something like a seed waiting for water to sprout," Seth read on the 4-H website. "But rather than water, the embryo needs the heat of a mother hen to resume its growth."

Seth learned that a hen sitting on a clutch of fertile eggs provides optimal conditions for the hatching of chicks, and that with care, this process can be replicated without her.

The first requirement is a stable temperature of 100 degrees Fahrenheit, maintained for an incubation period of twenty-one days. Variations on that temperature by more than two degrees in either direction for even a few hours can have dire effects on the embryo's development and the chick's health. Also, the eggs must be turned at least twice a day in order to prevent the growing embryos from sticking to the shells — a plight no embryo can survive. The hen does this with her beak, constantly and ever so gently rolling the eggs beneath her.

The final requirement is humidity of about 50% through the first eighteen days of incubation, increasing to 75% from the eighteenth day. In those final three days, as the chick is preparing for the arduous task of breaking through the shell, the increased humidity helps soften the shell and ease the baby chick's burden. In nature, the hen plucks out her own breast and stomach feathers, allowing for direct contact between the eggs and her own humid flesh.

During this time, Seth read, the eggs must no longer be turned, since this is the time when the chicks are positioning themselves for hatching.

At 9 a.m., Seth stood in the dairy section of Gelson's Market, an upscale food store about three-and-a-half blocks from his apartment. He opened the misted glass door of the eggs compartment, looking past three or four standard "organic" and "range-free" varieties that he knew wouldn't hatch. He found at last just what he was looking for: one remaining tan cardboard carton holding six brown ovals labeled "fertile eggs."

He gingerly carried the carton home, balancing the precious cargo with a large cardboard box from the store manager who had wished him luck with Project Hatch. Diligently following the instructions from wikihow.com ("build your own incubator"), he placed a micro-lamp inside the box, along with a small thermometer suspended from and taped to the lid by a piece of string. On the box's floor, he placed a saucer containing a wet sponge for humidity. The first goal, in this carefully contained swamp, was to sustain a humid hatching temperature of 100 degrees.

After an hour Seth saw that the temperature had climbed to a lethal 160 degrees and was still climbing. He let the 60-watt bulb cool for half an hour before replacing it with a 40-watt version. An hour later, the temperature had climbed to 130 degrees and was still climbing. He raced back to Gelson's to buy an array of 30-, 25- and 15-watt bulbs. The store manager showed Seth a kindly interest in his project.

"It's a work in progress," he explained, somewhat dismissively. Eager to return home with the new bulbs, he bounded out the door and headed up Bronson Canyon walking briskly, sometimes jogging until he ran out of breath.

The first bulb sent the temperature right back to 130 degrees, the second to 120, and the third wouldn't heat the incubator to higher than 80 degrees. Getting this right was now becoming Seth's obsession. The ache previously tethered to those gargantuan shifts in his work world had tempered, somewhat.

Putting off writing a theater review due the next morning of yet another production of *Proof,* Seth spent the entire day and night, groggy and fever-brained, trying to regulate the temperature in what was now a series of boxes he'd obtained of various sizes, with light bulbs of various strengths.

Seth was vaguely comforted by a shoebox/15-watt bulb effort that generated a life-supporting temperature wavering between 99 and 101 degrees. Seth marked each egg with an X on one side, an O on the other in order to identify placement when the eggs needed to be rotated. At 11:17 p.m., having placed the incubator on a desk in his living room, Seth carefully set six brown eggs, "X"s facing up, onto the dishcloth that now lined the shoebox floor. The temperature had been hovering at 100.5 degrees for at least three hours. With some peace of mind, Seth collapsed into his bed, which he hadn't seen in a day and a half, and felt the dark corners of exhaustion close in around him.

At 9 a.m. the following morning, the sounds of children splashing in the pool next door jolted Seth from an apocalyptic dream he was having about being rounded up by gun-toting guerrillas, a lingering effect of *The Atlantic* article on Pakistan. He staggered into the living room to discover the temperature in the incubator now at 125 degrees. The embryos, or what were the embryos, had been cooked.

"THE FIRE EXIT IS THE SAME DOOR you came in. Please turn off all cell phones at this time," said a woman, a theater producer, in a slightly ingratiating tone from the front of the tiny stage at Theatre Asylum in Hollywood. It was 8:05 p.m. In the full-house audience of sixty people, to Seth's left sat a large, bearded man in a thin blue pullover sweater. Likely a mistake to wear that, Seth surmised, observing a thin coating of perspiration across the man's face. To Seth's right sat two young women holding hands. With her free hand, the woman to the far right perused the program for the production that was just about to begin. Good idea, Seth thought, plucking his own program from the press folder on his lap, reading the names of actors in the leading roles whom he'd seen in other local theaters. Scanning the audience, Seth noted three other people with press folders just like his — critics from other newspapers and stage blogs.

"The cast has been working really hard on this project, and we're just so excited," the producer continued. "We know you're going to love this, so sit back and enjoy this masterpiece of world theater from the heart of Russia at the dawn of the twentieth century, Anton Chekhov's *The Cherry Orchard*."

The house lights dimmed. Stage lights accented the branches of flowering cherry-tree sprigs dangling over the set, which was decorated to resemble a child's nursery in 1904 provincial Russia. The haunting sound of a train whistle blared over the sound system.

A thin man in a true-to-period white waistcoat and yellow shoes sat leaning back on an ornate floral divan with polished, curvy oak legs. "The train's arrived, thank God. What's the time?" he said to the parlor maid, who stood nearby and replied: "It will soon be 2." She blew out a candle. "It is light already."

They must be very far north for it to get light at 2 a.m., Seth reflected: Even in midsummer, it doesn't get light here until 5. He'd seen *The Cherry Orchard* in various incarnations, at least two dozen times in four languages. Seth strained to concentrate, watching the character in the suit, named Yermolai Lopakhin, still reclining on the divan. An open book lay next to him on that sofa.

"How much was the train late? Two hours at least." The actor yawned and stretched. "I came here on purpose to meet them at the station, and then overslept myself . . . It's a pity. I wish you'd wakened me."

The maid, Dunyasha, played by a buxom actress with a squeaky voice, stopped and stood for a moment, staring into space.

"I think I hear them coming!" she said.

The actor sat up straight and listened. "No," he replied. "They've got to collect their luggage and so on . . . "

Seth loved this play, which is why it was so difficult for him to find a production of it that still moved him. His attention drifted from this intimate theater on Santa Monica Boulevard to Bronson Canyon and the challenges of hatching chickens. He checked his watch and was startled to discover it was only six minutes into the production. Maybe things would pick up. But deep in his heart, Seth knew they wouldn't.

The quality and tone of a theater production reveal themselves in the first few minutes. Yet things might liven up when some other characters appeared. Though drama critics live in dread, they also live in hope.

An awkward clerk, Seymon Epikhodov, entered with a bouquet of flowers, which he gave to the maid, thrusting them clumsily into her face — a nice comic moment. He had thinning hair and black frock coat. He was obviously smitten with the maid. His shoes squeaked when he walked. He made mention of his squeaking shoes, a plight written into the play, trying to endear himself to the maid, who looked back at him with a twisted smile — something between amusement and contempt.

This is better, Seth thought to himself.

Seth diverted his eyes to the large man on his left, now mopping sweat from his face with both hands. The women to his right no longer held hands. The one directly next to him stared at her knees. Seth imagined she might be asleep, or dead. Her partner gazed at the stage with a nondescript expression. She laughed when the clerk's shoes squeaked. This awakened her partner, and the pair resumed holding hands.

Whatever happened next was lost on Seth. Appearing before him were actors in costumes that a designer had carefully, even lovingly, assembled. Appearing before him was an array of highly trained, professional actors who were each receiving a mere $15 per performance, after having rehearsed gratis for two months. This was — this is — a labor of love, Seth told himself. Love of Anton Chekhov and his play. Love of the theater in general. Love of a centuries-old theater tradition that still flourishes in cities like New York and London and Moscow and Paris and Athens, but here still struggles to rise above being a stepchild in this cradle of the movie industry. Chekhov on Santa Monica Boulevard: a snowman in the desert.

Seth ached for this production to be good. But a good production was not appearing before him. The artifice was too strained and staid, the articulation too clumsy, the translation too British for these American actors to wrap themselves in. When magic struck in the L.A. theater, Seth was capable of being transfixed. And this happened often enough, even in turn-of-the-century plays written by the likes of Anton Chekhov, to keep Seth coming back for more. But that simply wasn't going to happen tonight.

And this is why, at 8:47 p.m., during one of Lopakhin's many, futile attempts to persuade Madame Lyubov Ranevskaya and her brother, Leonid Gaev, to chop down their beloved cherry orchard, build summer cottages on the land and lease them out — in order to pay the mortgage on their now bankrupt estate — Seth's mind was on cardboard boxes and thermometers and fertile eggs.

The production's stooping, senile eighty-seven-year-old footman named Firs, representing a mid-nineteenth-century era too ancient to matter even to the other characters, now stood center stage.

"You've gotten so old," Madame Ranevskaya told him.

"Pardon?" he called out. (Firs is deaf .)

Lopakhin came to the rescue: "She says you've grown old."

Firs nodded: "That's because I've lived for a long time."

Seth noticed a small wistful smile on the face of the woman directly to his right. That line should elicit a much bigger laugh, Seth noted. He recalled a production of the play at the Sovremmenik Theatre in Moscow — that very scene.

Firs' line in Russian is *zhivoo dolga* — four syllables, compared to the nine syllables in "That's because I've lived for a long time."

In Moscow, the audience roared with laughter, as though they were hearing the line for the first time. Obviously they weren't. The joke was in the staccato rhythm of four syllables rather than nine — the punch line from an old vaudevillian, a Russian answer to Groucho Marx.

These cultural, tonal and now linguistic divides were insurmountable. They weren't performing a play but a fantasy of a play.

An hour later, the strains of a "Jewish" orchestra playing a waltz for Madame Ranevskaya's guests during a party she could ill afford wafted over the tinny sound system.

But all that Seth could hear, the very coinage of his brain, was the sound of baby chicks peeping from inside their eggs. He imagined them hatching, a memory from the Museum of Science and

Industry, where dozens of nestlings cracked through their shells at eye level behind glass in a large rotund incubator. Scores of museum guests, children and their parents gathered around the glass to see life emerging. It was a sight from years ago that Seth found hypnotic. And now he could see and think of little else.

His focus returned to the stage on seeing the estate's clerk, Epikhodov, crashing the party, entering the room holding — *what?* — a bright red, contemporary fire extinguisher, with hose and nozzle attached.

The actor hadn't even noticed the problem until the moment when he was supposed to pour Madame Ranevskaya a glass of cognac.

The shell-shocked expressions extended from the cast to the audience. He'd obviously picked up the contemporary fire extinguisher by mistake in the too-dim backstage. Seth presumed he was supposed to have been bringing on some chiseled glass decanter filled with cognac, an item the props mistress might have bought for $15 in a garage sale. So how was Epikhodov going to get out of this one?

At first he mimed pouring liquid from the lurid, safety-sealed fire extinguisher, but that transparent absurdity drew expressions of disbelief and contempt from his fellow thespians. The actor then improvised a stupid line about "firewater," and how it was so dark in the anteroom, "one can't tell a dog from a bear." He then waddled backstage, shoes squeaking with each step. He swiftly returned holding the correct prop, and poured Madame Ranevskaya her cognac. The actors all continued resolutely, as though the debacle of a few moments ago had never occurred.

At the curtain call, slightly more than half the audience rose to its feet while applauding the production: friends and relatives, Seth surmised. It was opening night, after all. Seth couldn't be so dishonest as to stand for the ovation, when the production hadn't really stirred him. He knew he was being watched. He liked to keep his opinions close to his chest, but now the situation was conspiring against him to declare his convictions. He remained seated while he applauded, along with a minority of other patrons who felt similarly, even defiantly, unmoved to join the standing ovation. For cover, Seth leaned down to retrieve the bicycle helmet he'd stowed under his seat. When the applause subsided, he rose and fled the theater to his bicycle, which was chained to a parking meter in front of the theater. Seth rode away into the dark blanket of warm night air.

Later that night, Seth was writing a preliminary draft of what would be a mixed review of *The Cherry Orchard*. Seth found it odd that none of the other critics present that night even mentioned the fire extinguisher debacle.

Every production that he'd seen of the play emphasized a different aspect of its themes and purpose. Perhaps because of where he was in his life at this particular moment, the production's emphasis on one way of life yielding to another resonated with him. And it was partly for this reason that even while typing these ideas down on a Neo Office document, he kept jumping online to poultry sites. On one site he found a link that led him to Chick-Bator, the kind of incubator used by teachers in schools.

THE YELLOW CONTRAPTION LOOKED like a mini spaceship, plastic and dome-shaped with a diameter of about two feet. It came with a saucer to hold up to three eggs, some metal grating and tin foil, indentations to hold water for the humidity, a 7-watt light bulb with a small socket and power cord, and a tiny thermometer. The reviews said the incubator was wobbly but reliable, though hatching rate depends on the quality of the eggs. This had to be easier than trying to manipulate the wavering environment inside a cardboard box, and it cost only $25.

Seth ordered two.

"And what are you going to do with them after they hatch?" asked Katerina Pavlova, perplexed during a late-night phone call from Moscow. "What about the furniture?"

These were foolish, trivial questions to ask anyone who, like any of the characters in *The Cherry Orchard*, was passing through one era into the next.

ACT I, SCENE 2:
THE HATCHING OF MEMORY, PART 2

Waiting for the mailman day after day became a kind of anguish. Nine days after Seth had placed his order, there were still no packages in or by his mailbox. On the afternoon of the tenth day, after hauling his bicycle up the rear stairwell toward his apartment, Seth noticed a small cardboard box next to his metal front door screen.

In his kitchen, with the excitement of a child opening a holiday present, Seth sliced open the box with a kitchen knife and removed the two incubators, tucked into each other and secured in bubble wrap.

Seth used a small screwdriver in order to attach mini light sockets to the inside of each incubator. He rotated the bulbs into the sockets, plugged in the cords and beheld a small glow of light and heat create a ghostly flicker on the yellow plastic. He wrapped the thin metal grating with thin strips of aluminum foil in order for it to reflect and sustain the heat. The grating was bent, creating a horizontal floor and a vertical wall for the eggs to sit on, and to lean against. He then used an eyedropper to fill one of the three small indentations in the plastic frame with water, for the right humidity. Seth then placed white "dummy" infertile eggs inside both incubators while the temperature rose — a measurement registered on the tiny mercury thermometer glued and stapled to a small strip of embossed paper that Seth gingerly set on top of two eggs, one corner of the paper poking slightly against the metal grating and balancing the thermometer. Seth covered both incubators snugly with their clear plastic domes. The domes contained a small hole in their tops, allowing the incubators to "breathe."

The temperature climbed to the optimal 100 degrees and hung there through the evening. A blissful feeling washed over Seth. With growing confidence, he returned to Gelson's for the next batch of fertile eggs.

Back in his kitchen, and using a No. 2 pencil, Seth carefully drew "O"s on one side of each egg, and "X"s on the other. He swapped out the white "dummy" eggs and ever so carefully replaced them with the brown, fertile eggs — the "O"s facing up, so that they fit snugly inside the dome.

After the third day of incubation, Seth engaged in a daily rite, standing on the carpeted floor of his claustrophobic pitch-black walk-in closet. He held the LED light of his bicycle lamp behind each egg, placed lightly in the vise formed by his forefinger and thumb. He gazed wistfully for any sign of life: a shadow or, better, the red streak of a blood vessel. After a week of this, of sucking breath through his teeth in anticipation, Seth saw no evidence of any change, any development within each egg's fragile ecosystem. He obsessively studied online photographs of what a "candled" embryo should look like after three days: a streak of red attached to a black dot. There was no such view when he poured light through the translucent eggshells. Seth replaced them with a new batch of eggs.

One week later, despite what appeared to be perfect hatching conditions inside the incubators, the second batch still showed no sign of life. Seth tried a third, but with a growing sense of futility. He began to wonder if the problem lay with the eggs themselves. This realization led him to the Hollywood Farmers Market the following Saturday.

Amid the stalls for organic vegetables and puppy adoption and flower bouquets, Seth noticed a gentle, bearded fellow, his pot belly held in by an apron, wiping his forehead with the back of his hand in the afternoon heat. He operated two stalls, one for knife sharpening, and the other for eggs. One bin was marked "fertile eggs." Seth told him of his ambitions and of his dilemma.

The vendor introduced himself as Mike and explained to Seth that even the fertile eggs in his own bin won't hatch.

"They're bumped around too much on the truck gittin' out here."

Mike then rolled two eggs into each other so that they tapped, ever so lightly.

"See that," Mike explained. "If there's an embryo in there, it's all over. Also, them eggs you bought in the market, they may say 'fertile,' but they're lying. It's bullshit."

Mike handed Seth his business card.

"You want hatching eggs, come up to my farm."

The next day Seth drove the half-hour to Mike's farm in semi-rural Valley Village. The address led to a one-story stucco house. The property was bordered by a chest-high front brick wall and by a padlocked chain-link fence blocking access to the driveway. The front yard was a kind of dust bowl, with dogs playing in a mound of dirt. There was no way in but to hop the wall, thereby confronting an unchained Doberman, among the menagerie of loose canines already barking at Seth.

Hearing the dogs, Mike emerged through a fence separating the far end of the driveway from the carport next to the house.

Puffing from the walk up his driveway, Mike unlocked the padlock bolting the front fence while waving his one free arm and yelling at the dogs, "Back! Back in the house! Git! Git attah here!"

The dogs disappeared in the swirl of a dust tornado. From the ensuing calm, Seth heard the faint sound of roosters crowing from the back, to and fro verses of song, in pitches from soprano to gruff.

All the locks and security, Mike explained, were to protect him from "the government," a word and a concept he spat out contemptuously. As the pair ambled down the driveway, toward the carport and the back yard, Seth was now trying to figure out if Mike, too, received visits from the FBI.

IN THE BACK YARD, THAT FAMILIAR whiff of the chicken farm emanated from three large gated pens containing an array of free-range chickens and roosters. Another pen housed goats, turkeys and a large white goose that honked at the sight of the two men. On the near side of the poultry was an organic vegetable farm, tended and fertilized with the compost from the animals. Mike ranted about industrial farming and genetic engineering, and how Monsanto was trying to shut down the rights of small farmers and the rights of people to eat healthily. The government-corporate alliance, Mike fumed, is "violating our civil rights."

An ostrich emerged from a shed, poking out a long neck at Mike, who plucked a guava from a nearby tree and handed it to the huge bird. The ostrich crushed the fruit in its powerful beak before gulping it down.

"Ever tasted an ostrich egg?" Mike asked, without waiting for an answer.

"Fuckers," Mike continued. "The trick is to know the law, or they'll just keep violating your civil rights."

Mike told of a visit from the city's Department of Animal Services, an inspector who rang his doorbell:

"Yes?" Mike said through the screen door, staring out at what he described as an imperious woman in uniform. After confirming that Mike was the property owner, the officer said that she was there to inspect his farm because of a neighbor complaint.

"You have a search warrant?" Mike chirped back pleasantly, standing barefoot in T-shirt and boxer shorts.

She stared at him, fuming.

"If you don't have a search warrant, you're going to have to make an appointment," Mike oozed.

"I don't need no appointment," the inspector shot back.

"Oh, but you *do*, and I think you know that," Mike said. "Right now I'm on my way to a fundraiser for the mayor." Mike chuckled with self-satisfaction after telling Seth that line.

Mike closed his door. The doorbell rang again. Mike opened it.

"Yes?" he repeated.

Quietly seething, the inspector asked when Mike might be available for her to take a look around his farm.

"Gosh, let me check my schedule," Mike replied with sugary courtesy.

He left her waiting by his front door for ten minutes before he returned with a large wall calendar. "Looks like I'm fully booked for the next year and half. Can you check back with me then?"

Mike said he left the city inspector staring at a door closed once again in her face.

The consequences of Mike's rudeness arrived three months later with the street entirely blocked. Mike cowered in his own living room as an LAPD helicopter buzzed directly overhead his farm, and inspectors from the departments of Building and Safety, Animal Services, the Health Department, and an LAPD SWAT team stormed the property with no notice, smashing through his back door, rifling through his desk drawers, hacking their way into his sheds, knocking down fences and eviscerating his garden.

Mike screamed at the men in his house, demanding to see a search warrant. They ignored him. It was a terrible scene. The first thing Mike did after they left was go online and read how to file a lawsuit against the city for civil harassment. The second thing he did was barricade his property.

"They haven't bothered me in two years," Mike boasted, crediting his victory with the power of his personality and of the lawsuit. But Seth wondered if they'd simply failed to find anything illegal to pin on him.

Inside one of the chicken pens, Mike plucked half a dozen eggs from a nesting box and placed them tenderly in a carton. "Six bucks," Mike said. Seth paid him.

"What breed are they?" Seth asked.

"No idea," he said. "Mutts. Anything could come out of these."

That very afternoon, Seth squirted distilled water into the two tiny plastic caverns and placed six more "dummy" eggs in the incubators, to set their temperature to 100 degrees. While they were heating, Seth again ever so gently drew the "X"s and the "O"s on this, his fifth clutch of "fertile" brown eggs since he started trying to hatch chickens months earlier. While the incubators were heating, he studied each of the fertile eggs through a blast of LED light in his walk-in closet, and observed that through their eggshells, the interiors of these eggs appeared more orange than yellow, compared to those he tried before. Maybe that's a good sign, that subtle difference. He'd been disappointed so many times before.

Later that night, he placed three eggs in each incubator, with the "X"s facing up. The following morning, he lifted each lid, delicately removed each egg and turned it so that the "O" faced up. Through the days, Seth made subtle adjustments to the tin foil tucked onto the clear plastic domes, in order to sustain the perfect temperature. These were the rituals that consumed him for the next four days.

On the fourth day of incubation, when every website that knows anything about hatching chickens says that if the embryos are alive, their hearts have been beating for about two days and that blood vessels should now be reaching across the yolks, Seth looked at the door of his walk-in closet and wondered whether or not he should even examine the eggs.

If he couldn't detect an embryo, that wouldn't necessarily prove it wasn't there, he thought. The shell might be too thick to reveal what's inside. If he just waited for another week, if at that time there was no black shadow permeating any egg's interior, it would mean with certainty that there was nothing there. What's the point of the anxiety now?

And yet . . . And yet . . . What was the harm in looking?

Inside the closet, he held the first egg behind a flashlight's beam. Floating on a very clear yolk, there it was — at last — what he saw online, one to one: a clear red-black dot, the size of a pinhead, with two hairlike follicles extending from it, curling and pink. Life and blood, unmistakable, miraculous, yet so common. The heart was beating. The second egg showed the same. And the third.

Of the three eggs in the second incubator, two showed similar signs of life. Counting his chickens before they hatched, Seth had a flock of five.

On day five, a network of ruby arteries now reached through all of the yolks. At day nine, the five chicks started to disappear behind black veils of their own skins.

Ten days later, just past midnight, Seth heard from inside the first egg's shell three shrill chirps, and then silence. Seth felt a flush of joy. He whistled back through his teeth. The chick answered with three more chirps, and then silence. Man and bird went on like that, call and response, until 2 a.m. By that time, Seth, as fatigued as his unborn friends, went to bed.

At 8 a.m., staggering to the incubator to check the chicks' progress, Seth observed a small triangular crack at the top of the first egg. By 10 a.m., the outer shell had dislodged around the crack, revealing an inner membrane, like thin white paper, or cellophane. This, too, had a tear in it. Through the tear, a little black beak emerged, chirped, pushed at the paper membrane, then withdrew. And that was the sum of activity for the next nine hours: chirping, beak emerging, poking the membrane, withdrawing. Meanwhile, three of the other chicks had started peeping.

The first chick had been trying to hatch all day with little progress. Also, the cheeping was now starting to sound frustrated, like he may be caught in a wedge. It was now 9 p.m.

He scoured the Internet. Backyardchickens.com led Seth to a woman named Marcia in Ohio. On the other end of a phone line, Marcia talked over the squeals of children.

"Okay, let me get this right. You're in the middle of Hollywood, hatching a flock of chickens."

"That's correct, yes."

"Okay . . . And where are they going to live?"

"Back yard . . . I think."

"You think?

"I need permission from my neighbors."

"You have a brooder?"

"A cardboard box with a lamp to keep them warm. A bed of alfalfa."

"Chick starter?"

"You mean chick food?"

"Yes."

"From the feed store."

"Put rocks or marbles in their water or they could drown."

"Yep. That's what I read. It's all prepared."

"Sounds like you've thought this through."

"Yes, I have."

"So the little guy won't hatch."

"Ten hours since he broke the shell."

"Okay . . . you know, it's tough for him to punch through the shell. Sometimes they just recover for hours. If he doesn't break out by morning, call me back."

Seth hung up.

The chick's chirping suddenly turned to chattering. Pieces of shell were bouncing all over the incubator, large cracks now streaked across the shell as the chick drilled in a circle, like a jackhammer.

Within seconds, the egg was smashed open, being kicked by a sopping wet bird, all beak and claws and blood spots, shrink-wrapped and hissing out squeaks. A large piece of shell remained stuck to his back, until he thrust with such power, he knocked the lid from the incubator. A massive, purple, clawed leg poked through. This was a scene out of *Frankenstein*.

Seth stuffed the leg back inside the rickety incubator and held the lid down as the chick kicked and twisted, trying to punch through the cellophane-membrane smashing his head and body into the likeness of a tiny brontosaurus. In seconds, he peeled away the membrane, ripping it from his head, so that two eyelids, sealed shut, could pry themselves open — a pair of dark pools on either side of a narrow black beak. The chick now just lay supine like a dying cockroach, panting, staring at Seth, accusingly: "Are you the one who's responsible for this?"

Seth gently picked him up to remove the piece of shell still stuck to his soggy back. The chick was too exhausted to argue. That's when Seth noticed that something had gone terribly wrong.

Two grey, fleshy tubes attached to the belly led to a larger tube attached to a grotesque, dangling sac. The hatchling lay on his stomach gasping, trying to stand, but he couldn't because of this sac.

The chick yelped out his frustration.

Seth called Marcia back.

"I think it's his liver or something," Seth explained. "He's dragging it around behind him."

Marcia replied in a silky tone. "I don't think any animal can live dragging around a vital internal organ. Sometimes, if they hatch early . . . Did he hatch early?"

"Yes. He's due tomorrow."

"When that happens, sometimes there's yolk left over that hasn't been absorbed. Sounds like he's dragging around some leftover yolk. Keep the chick in the incubator until he's completely fluffed out. Don't let him eat or drink until then."

Sunday morning, Seth saw in that same incubator that Egg 2 had smashed against a mesh barricade and was oozing out the sticky, liquid evidence that the chick would die, or had died already.

To honor a surviving warrior, Seth named the first hatchling Agamemnon, who now stood proudly, chirping, head bumping the top of the incubator's plastic dome, almost knocking it away. The appendage appeared like a piece of lint attached to two brittle twigs. Seth picked him up and snipped the twigs away with a pair of scissors. No protest. No writhing. After setting him back inside, he tied down the incubator's roof with string and waited for Agamemnon to dry. By Sunday evening, Agamemnon looked magnificent — a black and gold cotton puff.

That day, Seth, who had already stopped eating beef and pork, stopped eating chicken.

The next day, Agamemnon was joined by his nestlings, Clytemnestra, Cassandra and Helen. Though there was no way for Seth to determine their sex accurately, he guessed it from Agamemnon's hefty girth, from the tiny comb smashed to one side atop his head. The others were comparatively small and delicate, even in their behavior, so they must be female. Seth understood that this was a wild and probably foolish guess.

And yet his diagnosis turned out to be accurate.

Hatching a flock of chickens, without having resolved a plan for where or how they would live, was not typical for the otherwise organized and forethoughtful Seth. It was an impulse, tempered by his firm belief that if he would nurture them with all his devotion, everything else could be worked out over time.

He had to make it work. Seth felt unwaveringly, personally responsible for their welfare. After all it was he, and he alone, who had brought them into the world. Furthermore, there was nowhere else he could go, or take them. He had bought his one-bedroom apartment in one of Hollywood's higher rent districts years ago when it was bank-owned. His current mortgage, including property taxes, was a fraction of what renters in the buildings on either side of him were currently paying. And now his own paycheck had just been cut 30 percent.

A couple of his neighbors called him crazy for hatching the chickens. When they told him this to his face, their words made Seth all the more determined to secure the well-being of his hatchlings.

These chicks were now his family. His capacity to make this project work, through the power of his bond intermingled with some kind of creative mediation with his community of neighbors, was now something he firmly believed in — as some people believe in the possibility of world peace.

ACT I, SCENE 3: HOME

Seth's apartment perched on the upper level of a two-story motel-like building, built in 1963, and situated in the "Franklin Hills" district at the base of the foothills in Bronson Canyon.

The building with its twelve apartments was wedged between two structures. One was a larger two-story apartment building with a pool to the east. Seth could view it by looking out from his kitchen window, which also offered a distant vista of L.A.'s downtown skyline. On the west side stood a decrepit single-story Craftsman home with a lush and well-maintained garden.

A week ago, last Saturday afternoon, Seth had gazed out his kitchen window to see a familiar sight: Melvin Channing, now approaching sixty, with a lined face, a shock of bleached blond hair and a torso that remained impressively lean. Melvin wore taut swimming trunks and frolicked in the pool with two bikini-clad women, maybe in their twenties. One was a redhead Latina clutching a bottle of dark beer; her friend, a pale-skinned brunette with a vine tattoo that cascaded from her neck to the small of her back, puffed on a cigarette. Waist-high in the pool's shallow end and squinting in the sun, Melvin held a would-be starlet on each arm and waved at Seth, who waved back. They'd known each other for years.

Seth once visited Melvin's place, a tomb-like corner apartment with an overstuffed couch, a glass table and mismatching chairs, a bar and three Formica-top cocktail tables. What Seth observed was the conspicuous absence of books, or even magazines, except for copious stacks of *The Hollywood Reporter* and *Variety*. The shelves, however, were stacked with DVDs, mostly of the movies Melvin had directed over the years. He'd invited Seth to watch his latest effort, a spoof-western videotaped on a single hand-held camera on a hiking trail near Mount Lee.

Seth had declined Melvin's offer to share a joint as they watched, on Melvin's HD widescreen with surround sound, a tubby actor in ill-fitting cowboy attire bark out some lingo about payment for "the whiskey." Melvin snickered at this. "I know the guy sucks," he said.

The corpulent actor's wafer-thin scene partner gave the unconvincing appearance of panic as the larger actor pulled out a toy pistol and fired a blank. The slim guy staggered backwards and fell into the dust of the hiking trail, to the sound of a police helicopter overhead. It was a comedy, Melvin explained, asking Seth if he could write a review of this latest project for the *L.A. Observer.* Seth had told him that he mostly reviewed theater, but he'd mention it to the film editor. Melvin said he planned on using the scene as an audition tape for the weightier actor, who'd paid him $300 for that privilege. And this is how Melvin paid his rent these days.

Seth watched the tattooed beauty climb out of the water, step by step, flinging her wet hair as she wrapped herself in a red towel before disappearing inside Melvin's apartment. Such were the comings and goings in this enclave of Bronson Canyon, a source of perpetual and slightly entertaining distractions.

Sometimes, Seth gazed over the brick wall along the western perimeter of his building to watch the blue jays and squirrels bolting across the expansive lawn and into the pepper and avocado trees next door. Two actors in their thirties rented the Craftsman house situated in the front of that garden. They were a Tom Cruise lookalike named Chuck Peterson, and his Uzbek-beauty girlfriend, Svetlana Grigoryevna.

Mid-mornings, Svetlana used to spread her yoga mat on the lawn of the back garden. As Buster, their black Labrador Retriever, stood guard, Svetlana navigated her poses in the tightest of shorts and the slenderest of tops. Seth wasn't the only resident who enjoyed her outdoor practice, which was also pleasingly observed by many a neighbor in the upper-story apartments that flanked her house.

About eight months ago, Svetlana gave birth to their daughter, Anna. That's when Svetlana's mother, Olga, moved in with them. That's also when Svetlana brought her titillating outdoor yoga practice indoors, drawing a show-closing curtain on her garden burlesque.

After months of seeing Olga hanging laundry from a clothesline suspended from a pole on one side and the pepper tree on the other, or dipping baby Anna — "Anya" — in a plastic children's wading pool, Seth asked Chuck how long his mother-in-law was staying. "Forever," Chuck sighed.

The 1910 house and its large expanse of garden were actually owned by a ninety-three-year-old spinster named Florence Baker, who inherited it from her father, Horace Baker, in 1953.

Horace had bought it in 1924, for himself and his bride, Agnes. This was the same year that Marcus Loew purchased Louis B. Mayer Pictures and installed Mayer as head of the studio's California operations. Horace Baker was under contract to the studio as an associate producer at the time, which was remarkable for a Presbyterian in the mostly Jewish studio. Yet the religious divide might also explain why Horace remained an associate, an underling, until the day he retired. A related reason for Horace's professional stagnation might have been his decision to buy into Bronson Canyon, which was then off-limits to non-Christians and non-Caucasians by restrictive covenants and deeds. Not surprisingly, this created resentment among the Jewish movers and shakers at the movie studios. They answered by creating and claiming Beverly Hills as their own, and by keeping guys like Horace Baker at a slight remove from the reins of control. Just enough to make the Bakers and their ilk grow a little batty as the years trickled by.

None of this entered young Florence's mind as she walked down Gower Street between her mother and her father every Sunday morning in 1931 to worship at the First Presbyterian Church of Hollywood, or so she once told Chuck, who shared the story with Seth.

Florence never married. There were rumors that she was a lesbian, and she did nothing either to dispel or confirm the gossip. Though she traveled to Istanbul and Serbia and did missionary work in the Congo, that little Craftsman in Bronson Canyon was the only place she ever called home. Even after the death of both her parents, she continued to live there. It was Florence who planted the avocado and pepper trees. She tended the lawn. She hosted the monthly meetings of the Hollywood Homeowners Association, and the emergency meetings when yet another corpse was discovered under the Hollywood sign.

Ten years ago, Florence determined that the upkeep on the house and land was all too much for her in her declining physical condition. She couldn't bear to sell the house, so she leased it to two industrious actors, Svetlana and Chuck.

The young couple had hoped to buy it one day, to build yet another high-rise condo on the garden land behind the house, but Florence dashed that idea early on, refusing to sell what she regarded as her life and her legacy. Ten years ago, Florence relocated three blocks away, to a ground-floor condominium on Tamarind Avenue.

Chuck came to L.A. eight years ago after graduating from Iowa State. His chiseled physique had been sculpted by hours at the gym, and he always greeted the world with a buoyant boisterousness and a temper that flared quickly, then receded just as quickly. His goal was to work in TV; he had an agent who landed him some work in commercials.

Chuck was always a handy guy. He could build a new transmission in just about any truck or car that crossed his path. And there had been quite a few parked in that long driveway, sometimes for weeks at a time, over the past eight years that Chuck and Svetlana had been living next door. Chuck was also a whiz at home repairs. He could install a roof on a house. He and his friends had repaired some structural flaws in the house, replacing large beams from the ravages of termites, all for a break on the rent, but the house remained decrepit nonetheless.

Chuck met Svetlana during an audition for a TV horror movie being produced by Paramount Pictures. Neither of them got roles, but they got each other. Svetlana first worked as a fashion model in L.A., a career that waned when she entered her thirties, though she continued to make good money playing Amazon women and Angelina Jolie-like athletes in horror movies.

One week, Seth could have sworn he saw tiny age-lines forming around her eyes, but the next week they were gone. One day she was a redhead, the next day a tinted blonde. One day she had piercing brown eyes. The next day they were blue. While she fell prey to the city's obsession with looks, she possessed a depth that belied the façade fixation.

For in the care of the garden, it seemed that Svetlana had absorbed the historical energy left behind by Florence Baker. Svetlana dragged hoses to and from various corners throughout the day: the side yard, the front, the back. To the sound of hisses and spits, water danced in circles and in arcs, as it had on that same ground since 1910. And that alone made the ground hallowed. Svetlana left dog kibble out at night for the raccoons and coyotes, and she took in a homeless cat. Every night her voice echoed up and down the canyon, calling in the cat to protect it from the nocturnal predators:

"Brewster . . . Breeeeeewster . . ." Svetlana honored the Bakers' legacy of turning their garden into an Elysian Field, a paradisiacal sanctuary for the blessed and the virtuous.

The property that Chuck and Svetlana leased was the last remaining echo on the block of a single-family residential district of yore, where children might have romped in gardens. Despite the home's sagging roof and the crumbling garage, Seth associated it with an early twentieth-century visage of home, in stark contrast to the unadorned and functional boxes of his building and most of the buildings on the block, occupied mainly by single people with singular ambitions. Some were owners who had lived in their boxes for years: an accountant, a graphic designer, an architect, a real estate agent. Then there were the renters: the actors, writers, and directors who, with the possible exceptions of guys like Melvin, came and went with the winds of fortune.

Seth bought his apartment years ago in a fire sale, in the real estate crash before the crash of '08.

The building wasn't exactly a condominium, but a rare, hybrid cross between a condo and a co-op called an "Own Your Own," in which owners such as Seth didn't own their apartments per se, but a 1/12 percentage of the building and the exclusive right to occupy the apartment designated in their grant deed.

Seth noticed how cracked the magnesite had become, and how chipped the blue paint of the railings, all the way down the length of the building.

This pained him because Seth was the president of the building's Homeowners Association, having beaten out Eddie Angelis and his mother "JoJo" in the election last year. Those who admired Seth said that the building had in residence a "published author." Those who didn't described his newspaper as "a rag that pays him from ads for prostitution and plastic surgery."

As president, he had in the last twelve months overseen the painting of the exterior, the installation of a new water heater and the repair of three leaks in the roof. But the state of the magnesite and the railing troubled him — something he might bring up at the next Board meeting.

In retrospect, Seth should have been wary of the enthusiasm by the otherwise surly Angelis mother-and-son duo when he presented his proposal to the Board for a chicken pen in the narrow strip of a back garden. That "garden" consisted of a cement walkway next to the building that ran along a long, narrow plot of half-dead ivy. It all rested in the shade of a giant elephant ear tree planted in the spacious garden of the house to the north. That tree's canopy cascaded over the brick wall dividing the properties.

JOCASTA AND EDDIE ANGELIS owned and lived in separate apartments in the building. They were almost all that remained of a once-large Greek clan that fled Athens to join family in California during the Greek military coup of 1967.

Now in his late twenties, Eddie sported bleached-blond hair and matching goatee. Eddie liked to wear green: green T-shirts, green jeans, green sneakers. Pudgy and rugged-looking, he lived upstairs, worked as a manager at the nearby Pep Boys and collected artifacts and books about tyrants throughout history. Though on his wall, amidst portraits of Che Guevara, Fidel Castro, Hugo Chavez, and even Joseph Stalin, there hung a respectful photo of his mother, JoJo, who lived downstairs.

Eddie was always anxious and frequently angry, so much so that his hands trembled.

When Seth first bought his apartment, Eddie served as HOA

president, where he earned his reputation for rashness. Once, President Eddie took a crowbar and slammed it through the ceiling of the laundry room in order to access a pipe he presumed was leaking. Not only was it not leaking, it wasn't even there. The source of water dribbling out the laundry room door was actually behind the washing machine, which any plumber could have told him. But Eddie wasn't big on professional diagnosis when there was a crowbar within reach. It cost the HOA $570 to repair the laundry room, which nobody complained about, because nobody really cared.

One day, Eddie started dating Jolene, a regular customer at Pep Boys. Jolene was a wealthy thirty-six-year-old *divorcée* with a squeaky voice. When she first moved in, Eddie's next-door neighbor, Winston Pendleton, his wife Suki, and many occupants of the building to the east were kept up all night by Jolene's squeals of sexual ecstasy, which Winston insisted were accompanied by all manner of room-shaking quakes from a system of pulleys and ropes installed by Eddie inside his apartment in flagrant violation of the rules and regulations. Eddie smirked that Jolene wasn't so loud, and laughed off the complaints as envy.

Melvin Channing next door, along with the morally offended Iranian and Guatemalan families, still insist that the noises were put on, like a parody of a porno flick. Winston complained that the squealing and quaking escalated when he pounded his fist on the wall dividing his bedroom and Eddie's, proving that the behavior was just spite. Still, nobody would sign Winston's petition of complaint against Eddie and Jolene, because everybody understood Eddie was rash enough to use a crowbar with no consideration of the consequences.

That all changed after Chuck brought home a macaw parrot with French aristocratic gold wings folded over a coat of blue. Displaying a rare lack of imagination, Chuck and Svetlana named him "McCaw."

During the day, Chuck brought out McCaw's birdcage, lined with lettuce and pumpkin seeds, into the back garden by the garage, beneath a thick rope that Chuck had strung for the bird. The cage was left open so that McCaw could crawl up and onto the rope and sashay along it for about two or three feet before working his way back, bobbing its head, puffing up his neck, screeching and offering a monologue that parroted the voices of prior owners going back decades.

The bird's routine was a morning and evening repertoire of lunacy that became familiar to the residents of Bronson Canyon: A gruff "oy-oy-oy-oy-oy-oy-oy," before the bird would mutter complete sentences in Yiddish, then a *screech!*, followed by the "Queen of the Night" aria from *The Magic Flute*, then "helloooo, hellooo, pretty boy, pretty boy, pretty boy." McCaw would bob his head to anybody he spotted, screeching, "Helloooo." "Oy-oy-oy-oy-oy-oy." *Screech.* More Yiddish. More Mozart. "Brewster . . . Breeeeewster." The final intonation was a perfect match with Svetlana's nightly ritual of calling in her cat.

It probably was inevitable that McCaw would start to imitate Jolene's squeals of sexual ecstasy that Eddie insisted "weren't that loud." Early one morning, Seth was leaning up against his walkway railing when he heard McCaw screeching out the rising cadence of one of Jolene's extended orgasms. Svetlana came tearing out of the house in curlers and a pink bathrobe. Her face was flushed pink with fury as she grabbed the bird and dragged him back into the house. Seth advised Winston, who was at that time formulating his noise complaint against Eddie and Jolene, "You want to clinch your case? Drag that bird into court as a witness."

Finally, during one particularly lengthy episode of Jolene's squealing at 3 a.m., Winston finally called the police, telling them he suspected a child was being molested next door. LAPD showed up in six minutes and pounded on Eddie's door. Then all went quiet for about half an hour. The residents on the entire block speculated on the meaning of the siren and the flashing red lights. Winston could hear an amicable discussion through the thin walls. He and Suki lay in bed holding hands with a kind of fearful satisfaction. That ended the late-night sexual noises, at least for a while, but it also inflamed the malice between Eddie and Winston.

The event also cost Eddie the presidency — a fall from grace he never quite recovered from. In an unspoken gesture of consolation, the owners elected his mother, Jocasta, to serve as secretary-treasurer. In that same election, Seth was voted in as president by a margin of two votes.

JOCASTA ANGELIS WAS FIFTY-EIGHT years old and lived downstairs. She was a lanky, athletic cropped-haired brunette who considered herself the rational half of the duo. This self-image might have had credence if not for "JoJo's" repeated mentions of the double-gauge shotgun she claimed to keep in her closet for self-defense. JoJo insisted that public knowledge of her shotgun kept the building crime-free.

Cutbacks at her office had her working largely from home as a social worker. Dealing professionally with people who suffered from pathological misery had taken its toll on JoJo's patience and her empathy.

Shortly before the election, a news story had run in the *L.A. Observer* about a social worker who had actually encouraged a patient, a thirty-year-old stockbroker facing prison time on corruption charges, to take some pills to relax. The social worker insisted to the press that she was simply encouraging the man to take his prescription medication. The next day, however, the stockbroker was found at the bottom of his swimming pool in Brentwood, having imbibed a lethal Lunesta-tequila cocktail.

Winston started the rumor that JoJo was the social worker profiled in the *L.A. Observer*. Winston had not read the article, had not even seen it. He had simply heard about it from Seth's next-door neighbor, Sam, who had heard about it from Melvin, who had seen the story on Channel 5 local news. Winston then leapt to the conclusions that because the story first ran in the *L.A. Observer*, it must have been written by Seth, which it wasn't. And that because it was written by Seth, the article must have been about JoJo, which it wasn't.

In response, Seth took a proactive stand, insisting at the homeowners' meeting before the election that his neighbor JoJo Angelis had nothing to do with the tragic suicide of the stockbroker whose name he couldn't recall, and that JoJo had been wronged. At the meeting, Winston apologized to JoJo and to all of the homeowners for spreading the rumor, before withdrawing himself as a candidate for office.

Winston's wife, Suki, dabbed a tear from her left eye, not because she was so moved by her husband's noble gesture but from sheer relief that he'd have nothing to do with the HOA for another year. Meanwhile, Eddie muttered under his breath that Winston was an idiot, while JoJo listened to Winston's apology with the stoic dignity of the persecuted.

Being wronged was among JoJo's primary virtues, and she did it well.

When Svetlana, next door, placed peanuts on the garden wall for the squirrels, JoJo was almost tearful describing the plight of having to sweep up the shells that tumbled into the ivy to the east after the marauding critters had taken their fill. She trembled with indignation that everybody in the HOA had been wronged by Svetlana and her reckless disregard, but certainly nobody was more wronged than JoJo.

The prior year, an Armenian child from the house to the north built and launched a homemade pipe rocket fueled with sulfur. It was airborne for about five hundred feet before crashing down, scalding, onto JoJo's patio. It didn't do any damage, but it might have, had it landed on anything flammable, or had it contained enough fuel to propel it through a window; but it didn't. Still, the injured party, who hadn't been injured at all but might have had she been on her patio at the time, stormed over to her Armenian neighbors and stammered out her indignation to the boy's stunned parents that she had been wronged. Sophia and Stepan Avakian concurred. They summoned their twelve-year-old son, Gary, to the door, so that the child could apologize in person to JoJo for firing off rockets like a terrorist.

JoJo repeated this story to the owners of the HOA as part of her campaign for office. Winston's withdrawal as a candidate, combined with JoJo's crusades for law and order, probably helped JoJo win the post of secretary-treasurer. And Seth's part in it, as a defender of JoJo's maligned professional reputation, helped explain why the otherwise surly Angelis duo congratulated him on winning the presidency and, even a year later, why they supported his carefully crafted proposal for a chicken pen in the rear of the building.

AT 2 P.M. ON A WARM AFTERNOON early in July, Seth lay on his stomach on his living room floor, holding a handful of millet in one clenched fist. The quartet of week-old chicks had left their desk-lamp-heated cardboard box that constituted their makeshift home. Still a month or so away from being able to live outdoors, they more or less followed each other around the living room on such adventures, one giving the next courage, chirping out generalized chatter and specific warnings. The flight of a sparrow directly outside the kitchen window prompted an alarm squeal from Agamemnon, the sentry and commander. Now about one-third larger than the others, he held himself semi-upright like a penguin, his back sloping up at about 45 degrees. Black pinfeathers sprouted from his wings and tail poking through black-and-gold down. The comb on his head had already straightened, thickened and turned from the color of ash to a light pink — matching two small wattles dangling from either side of his beak. After he let out his shrill alarm with his still soprano voice, the quartet stood frozen in a tableau that lasted about five seconds.

Sisters Clytemnestra and Cassandra were small balls of gold and brown fluff, peeping as they crept along the hardwood floor onto Seth's back. His sports shirt gave them a better grip to move. Clytemnestra nestled onto the flesh of Seth's neck and trilled contentedly from the warm flesh. Seth pretended to sleep.

From their golden down coats, stubby rust and brown feathers sprouted on their tiny wings and on the stumps of their tails. Seth lay absolutely still as the two chicks crept up his shoulder blades to the base of his neck. Seth could only see the laminate-wood floor in front of him and the roll of paper towels placed there to wipe up small deposits. These arrived every five minutes or so from each chick. He felt light scratching from Clytemnestra's tiny toenails on his neck, and the heat from her delicate feet, while Cassandra hovered at the threshold between his shirt collar and the skin of his neck.

Of the sisters, Clytemnestra was friendlier with people — fearless. Seth wondered if her amiability was in her best interests. When Seth scooped his hand into their cardboard home to lift them outside, Clytemnestra didn't flee. Rather, she stood frozen, not because she was terrified or playing 'possum, but because she seemed to enjoy the rite of having a human hand slide beneath her tiny belly, fingers on either sides of her legs. For Clytemnestra, Seth was clearly one of them, which explained her comfort level around him. This was unusual for a chicken hatched in a flock. Sometimes she trilled in satisfaction when hoisted into the air, landing on Seth's shoulder and being rewarded with a handful of millet. Clytemnestra rode contentedly on his shoulder for up to half an hour, sometimes pressing her face into his neck. The others would tolerate the ride for up to several minutes before becoming agitated, heads bobbing, eyeing their nestlings below, eager to return to them. But not Clytemnestra.

Her sister, Cassandra, had a similarly trusting disposition though was more guarded. Cassandra, too, responded to human contact cheerfully but she was slightly less attached, less trusting, as though Cassandra had considered the possibility that Seth might be one of them, but she wasn't quite sure. Cassandra hedged her bets. She was affectionate until it dawned on her that she's a chicken, and this giant, on whose shoulder she rode, isn't. After ten minutes or so, Cassandra would start yelping until returned to the comfort of her siblings.

Helen had now moved into Seth's sightline on the floor, not far from the clenched fist at the end of his arm that's extended forward. She was mostly gold but with a large black spot on her head. Her wings and tail were peppered with the stubs of white feathers. Helen was more alert and ambivalent than the sisters about her trust of this giant who brought food and changed their water. She knew there was millet packed into Seth's clenched fist, which was why she stayed close. She also felt an impulse to follow the sisters onto Seth's back, but she chose not to — possibly from fear, probably from defiance.

Even in chickens, there is often the trait of free will, the quiet dignity of standing apart from the flock, or from the bully. Such traits emerge early in their lives, and become the essences of their personalities.

Seth opened his fist and Helen plunged in for the seeds. Within two seconds, the sisters leapt off Seth's neck to join her, the three of them chattering as their bobbing heads dove for their reward.

From a distance, Agamemnon, the penguin, saw all this and crept into the periphery of Seth's vision. Even at one week old, Agamemnon showed early signs of authority. Whenever a shadow crossed the room, or a dog barked outside, it was Agamemnon who sounded the alarm. When Seth dangled a marigold blossom in front of them, twisting it irresistibly, the females didn't hesitate to lunge for it. Agamemnon, however, would stare at it for a moment or two before taking a meager, apprehensive peck. He was nobody's fool.

Only as a last resort would he jump onto Seth's neck or back. Even now, as Helen and the sisters were in the middle of a feeding frenzy from Seth's now open palm, Agamemnon approached tentatively, just in case there was a problem. He stood on one foot, staring at them with head tilted to one side, his most common tableau. They saw the world head-on. Agamemnon saw everything from an angle. Watchful. Leery. At the age of one week, Agamemnon already understood just how dangerous the world is.

SHORTLY AFTER 3 P.M., SETH KNOCKED on the door of his next-door neighbor in Apartment #2F. Sam Rowland is an aging rocker, and underground crooner who recorded albums in the studio with a new generation of rising rock stars who found Sam to be exotic. The boom-boom bass from Sam's subwoofer speakers rattled the walls between them. His gruff voice crooned Tom Waits-like:

"You can have my heart, but my liver is mine,
You can have my heart, but my liver is mine,
You can have my heart, but my liver is mine,
Gotta save my bile, for a heartless time."

Acoustic guitar riffs accompanied Sam's ballad. Seth knew the song well.

Sam invited him over a couple of months ago, made him a cup of coffee. Seth sat in a stuffed chair while Sam parked himself on his couch, guitar in hand. His craggy face clenched up when he started strumming. When Sam started singing, it was like an old rooster's crow, gruff and urgent. Seth respected that.

"My piles is sore, my heart's grown hard,

My poor reputation, it be somewhat scarred,

FBI's got me on their list, something to do with that sheep I once kissed,

I told 'em, I told 'em, I ain't done no crime.

'Book him,' they said. 'You doin' time.'

'Clem ain't no pervert,' said Flossie that night,

'We was just talkin', he was polite.'

Next thing I know I'm back out on the street,

Sometimes in my dreams I still hear Flossie bleat.

My piles is sore, my heart has grown hard,

My poor reputation, it be somewhat scarred."

Seth liked Sam a lot. Sam told sophomoric, scatological jokes. He'd watch Seth's face for tell-tale signs of shock. Sam recited a new lyric:

"I been to London, I been to Rome,

There's only one place that I call home.

And that's Hemet."

Sam was now wheezing with laughter.

He played in local clubs late at night and boasted of the groupies still begging to come home with him. But his thirty-year-old son, Timothy, lived with him, so that wasn't possible, he said. And he didn't want to betray his wife, Tim's mom, who lived in Palm Desert and visited on weekends. No, he couldn't live with himself doing that. Sam was about the kindest man Seth knew, yet he wrote songs that were either violently funny, or just plain violent. The man was almost seventy and lived to create music, as he'd done since he was fifteen. Sam could keep a secret. Sam was benign until he got mad. When Sam got mad, you really didn't want to mess with him. Sam was just a big kid.

After Sam hadn't shown up half an hour into last year's meeting, Seth knocked on his door to see if he was coming.

"Oh, crap," Sam complained. "Nah, I don't want to listen to those cocksuckers. They never do anything they say. Then they never discuss what they finally do."

"So hold their feet to the fire," Seth answered. "You need to be there, or they'll do what they want without you."

Seth ushered the reluctant Sam into JoJo's apartment for the meeting.

"Hey, Sam, glad you could make it!" Eddie greeted him.

"Oh, heavens," Sam chimed back, all enthusiastic. "I wouldn't miss this for the *world*!"

When they started discussing new landscaping for the front of the building, Sam proposed pulling out the pine trees, cementing over the ivy and putting up two concrete statues. One should be something like Michelangelo's David pissing into a pond below that would recycle the water. The other statue, he said he didn't care what it looked like. It should just be on the other side of the cement, for balance. The effect would be enhanced, Sam said, if all the windows on the building's front were installed with security bars. He said all this entirely straight-faced.

A friend of JoJo's translated all this into Spanish for Sergio and Rosita, who lived in the front. As the translation rolled in, Rosita burst out laughing and Sergio turned red with fury.

"He's mocking us," Sergio complained.

But with Sam, one could never know for sure.

Sam was the ninth neighbor Seth had approached this week on his issue of concern.

"So I've got these baby chicks," Seth explained. Sam stared back expressionless.

"When they get bigger, I'd like to build them a small pen in the back and keep them. This is what I'd propose to the Board: no smell, except for maybe straw, no noise. I'll take full responsibility for maintaining them. Technically, they'll belong to everybody, since nobody can make a claim on any of the common areas. They'll be a community flock. If there's noise or smell that starts to bother you, give me a week to fix it, that's all I ask. If I can't fix it, then the birds go away. Before I take this to the Board, I wanted to see if this is okay with you, or if there's anything else I can do or say that would make this okay with you."

After an entire minute of silent contemplation, Sam replied, "If it doesn't work out, do we get to eat them?"

"No," Seth answered. "You do not get to eat them."

Sam smiled. "Can I trust you?" he asked.

"How long have you known me? You're the only one who can answer that."

"What does everyone else say?"

"Almost everyone's willing to give it a try."

"Almost?"

"Vera says she left poverty in Romania. She didn't come all the way here to live on a farm."

"Well, fuck her," Sam replied. "What about the Angelis duo?"

"They're okay with it."

"The *Angelis duo?* Really? Holy crap!" Sam said, shaking his head incredulously and wiping his hand through his electro-shock of silver hair.

"Okay," Sam concluded after a moment's thought. "Have your chickens."

A WEEK LATER, IN JOJO'S APARTMENT, Seth called a special meeting of the three-member Board: Seth, JoJo and vice president Vera Pentcheva, a bleached blonde in her forties who lived a mile away and rented out her apartment. Vera was so slight that when she smiled, her face receded behind the wall of her teeth. Yet when she smiled, she could also cheer up a room. When she laughed, it was infectious.

For this occasion, she wore jeans so tight they swallowed what little waist she had. Seth presented a written proposal for a chicken pen on the common ground of the back yard. Though the pen would be community property, Seth would pay all costs, bear full responsibility and liability, keeping the pen quiet and odor-free. If any neighbor had a complaint about noise or odor, and if the Board determined the complaint was valid, Seth would have seven days to remedy the source of the complaint to the Board's satisfaction. Failing that, the Board reserved the right to demand immediate removal of the chickens and of the pen.

"Is this legal?" Vera piped, melodious.

"What do you mean, is this legal?" Seth asked.

"I mean, having chickens in the city. Is it legal?"

"Of course it's legal!" Seth fired back, knowing that Vera was the only owner to go on record opposing his proposal. He showed the Board a petition of support signed by ten of the twelve homeowners.

(Absentee landlord John Malholtra, owner of Apartment #2C,

emailed Seth that he would abstain.)

"Haven't you seen Eloise's chickens over on Chula Vista Way?" Seth continued. "Eloise told me that Animal Services is over there every couple of months, they're fully aware of her three hens and haven't said a thing!"

What Seth was saying was true, but not entirely truthful. It was true that chickens are legal in the city of Los Angeles. However, there were restrictions as to how close those chickens may live to human dwellings. And Seth was fully aware that there's no place on the property allowing for the required thirty-five-foot barrier between chickens and the outer condo wall. However, it was also true that Eloise's chicken pen smacked right up against the wall of her bungalow, that city inspectors knew this and had said nothing for the five years she'd had her flock. Their main concern was that the flock was clean and properly cared for. What triggered enforcement, Seth learned through an anonymous call to the Department of Animal Services, was a neighbor's complaint.

So long as nobody complained, Seth reasoned, his four chickens would be as good as legal. Besides, if somebody complained, his own contract with the Board stipulated that he remedy the complaint or lose the chickens. So what's the difference? What, exactly, was Vera's point?

These were the thoughts tumbling around in Seth's head from the moment Vera asked the inflammatory question "Is this legal?"

"I know this . . . this *project* has the support of the owners," Vera continued. "But is it really for everybody's benefit, or just for Seth's? He's very charming," she added, avoiding eye contact with Seth by addressing her remarks to JoJo. "Seth can persuade people because they like him. But is this just another of his crazy projects? Like the vegetables on the walkway? When I lived there, I could barely get my groceries in the door, those tubs took up so much space . . ."

"Why didn't you *say* something?" Seth chimed in.

"You were my next-door neighbor! You liked your garden. Why would I . . . ?"

Vera stopped mid-sentence and stared blankly at the screen door. After a pause, she sighed, "But chickens?" Pause. *"Chickens? This isn't why I bought a property in the middle of the city!"*

Seth quietly removed from a manila folder a series of magazine articles about the urban farming movement, and laid them on the table where the three sat. "Just because you don't like it doesn't make it crazy," Seth said, a bit too piously even for his own liking. "And if that's your best argument, you're a long way from respecting what the people in this building have said they want."

"They didn't say they *wanted* it," Vera snapped. "They said they'd *put up* with it!"

She's right, Seth thought, and finally said so: "That's quite true . . . But it does mean that most of our neighbors are willing to give it a chance. Everybody understands there's a means to have the chickens removed if they cause problems. All I'm asking for is a chance to make this work."

JoJo suddenly turned chirpy, sitting up straight in a stuffed chair. She clearly enjoyed the role of mediator. JoJo offered a proposal, a motion, that because of the support of the owners, Seth's project be allowed "on a trial basis," to be reviewed and reconsidered after three months. Now brightening, Seth seconded the motion. It passed on a vote with two in favor, one opposed.

ON THE SECOND SATURDAY OF AUGUST, an unprecedented camaraderie united Eddie, Sam, Sam's son Timothy, and Seth. Into the back garden, they hauled lumber, a level, steel angle plates, a sledgehammer, a battery-powered drill, chicken wire, wood screws, staples, and a hammer and nails. Seth and Eddie shoveled and pulled out the half-dead ivy, while Sam and Timothy laid out the pen's perimeter with a tape measure. By sundown, an enclosed wooden box standing on cinder blocks constituted the coop. Its lid was attached with hinges. One side had a ramp for the chickens to strut outside to the ground, to the straw-carpeted area enclosed by green chicken wire.

Three dowel rods, attached to posts at various heights, created a trio of perches. Beer and pizza, ordered by the grateful Seth, marked the start of a new era of community and common purpose for the Bronson Canyon Homeowners Association.

In late September, storm clouds rolled over the city, announcing a prelude to the coming winter. They blew away as quickly as they'd arrived without delivering a drop of rain, but daytime temperatures had dropped to the comfortable mid-70s, from the blistering 90s the week prior.

In a planter on the railing outside Seth's front door, the marigolds he'd planted on the morning of his resurrection now sent out globe-blooms of yellow and orange. Deep red tomatoes hung on nearby vines. The beans had already been harvested, leaving green-brown vines struggling for a reason to continue living.

In the back garden lived a flock of four chickens in a wire-fenced pen that Seth had built with the help of his three neighbors. They walked on timothy hay that Seth had purchased from a feed store in Burbank. It emitted a pungent aroma of alfalfa, and every three or four days, Seth swapped it out for fresh straw.

The chickens were still quite young, personable and aroma-free, which is largely what made their existence possible on a community-owned property in the middle of the city.

Agamemnon had feathered out into a burly fellow, a mostly black Barred Plymouth Rock but with white stripes through his feathers so that he resembled a prison convict. He was starting to strut with his large black feet. He bore an imposing comb and bright red flesh around his eyes.

Sisters Clytemnestra and Cassandra had evolved into rust-colored pullets, like the Rhode Island Reds Seth had grown up with.

And Helen was white with spots of black, perhaps a Mottled Java. She, like Agamemnon, showed occasional flare-ups of temper, pecking at the others, while the red sisters were entirely sweet-natured.

The chickens became the talk of the neighborhood. The building's iron gating was never locked, so neighbors wandered into the back, just to see if the rumors were true.

"It reminds me of home," the Iranian woman living next door remarked. Sergio and his wife Rosita, a Mexican couple who lived in the front of the building said the same. Sergio's heart opened when he first saw the flock: "It's just like home."

One day, Gabriella, a single mom from Ecuador living in the building to the east, brought over her seven-year-old son Martin to see the flock. Martin had never seen live chickens before and stared at them, transfixed. Seth was inside the pen at the time, and he invited the boy to join him while Gabriella watched from the perimeter. Seth told Martin to stand slightly bent with his hands on his knees and to stay still. Then he told the boy to open one palm, and Seth poured wild birdseed into it. As Martin remained in that position still as a statue, Cassandra jumped up onto his back, and then Clytemnestra. Martin beamed. Seth did too.

In this moment, Seth was reliving his own childhood, vicariously, through the eyes of another immigrant child.

As the two red pullets traversed Martin's shoulders, reaching for the millet in his palm, the child's radiant smile revealed a missing front tooth. Finally, Helen joined the sisters and Martin started laughing as the trio scratched his back. When Agamemnon launched himself up to the others, Cassandra took one more jump, landing directly on top of Martin's head. The boy was covered in chickens, absolutely enchanted.

ACT I, SCENE 4: HOMER

Two days later, from across the garden wall, Svetlana asked Seth to come over. Almost furtively, she and Chuck led him into a work shed next to their garage. Chuck pulled a string so that a single bulb threw a dim, wavering light onto a large but slender red chicken with a white tail, housed in a cardboard box. The bird clucked at the light. Seth stared at the chicken, and his silence posed the obvious question.

"We found her this morning on Wilshire Boulevard," Svetlana explained. "She was in the middle of the street."

"Probably escaped a Santeria church sacrifice," Seth remarked. "They drink the blood of farm animals — goats, sheep, chickens. I once saw severed chicken legs in the street right here, with the feathers still on. Looks like you rescued one that got away."

"How do we take care of her?" Chuck asked.

Seth continued staring at the chicken, whose head jerked to and fro — a gesture revealing the bird's innate curiosity. "I'm not so sure she's a she," Seth remarked. Svetlana slightly bristled. She had been certain the bird was a hen.

"See those hackle feathers?" said Seth, pointing to the chicken authoritatively. He knew the difference between a rooster and a pullet from his childhood on the ranch. "See the tail feathers starting to arc down? I think you just saved a young rooster."

Svetlana squinted, skeptical. "But he's never crowed."

"Just wait," Seth answered. The bird started to pant, fleshy, dangling wattles rising and falling beneath a dark yellow open beak. A lizard-like tongue appeared and retracted in conformity with his heaving throat.

"He needs water," Seth said with the self-importance of a veter-inarian unveiling the mysteries of the bird kingdom, though even he understood he was just stating the obvious.

Svetlana slid out of the garage while Seth picked up the chicken, lifting him from the cardboard box with one hand under each wing. The bird's yellow feet dangled at odd angles below the rust-feathered torso, until Seth cradled him in one arm, resting the chicken against his chest, while Seth's free hand rubbed the warm flesh under the chicken's beak.

The chicken let out a series of gentle, satisfied clucks, between intervals of panting.

Svetlana returned with a red plastic bowl filled with water and held it in front of the bird's head. Seth wiggled a finger from his free hand into the water, showing the ripples to the bird who, even while being held by Seth, instantly plunged his beak into the liquid. The chicken slurped up what he could before raising his beak to the roof, as though in a prayer of thanks. He was actually allowing the water to slide down his throat. For a good five minutes, the young rooster kept bobbing his head into the water then raising it to the sky. After a dozen or so doses, the bird sneezed, shook his head — spraying droplets onto both Svetlana and Seth — and took one final drink before preening the feathers under his right wing.

"I wonder if he's hungry," Svetlana whispered. "What do we feed him?"

"I'll bring you some chicken food," Seth replied, handing the bird over to Svetlana, who now cradled the rooster, rocking him back and forth, as she did so often with her baby Anna.

Meanwhile, Seth sprinted across the garden and jumped over the garden wall that divided the house from his apartment com-plex. From the shed's open door, Chuck and Svetlana watched Seth bounding up the rear stairwell toward his own apartment. He returned shortly with a brown paper bag filled with corn mash. Svetlana set the chicken down while Seth poured the corn from the bag onto the ground. The chicken ate voraciously, gulping wads of mash, almost choking, stopping only to catch his breath, heaving asthmatically, before re-gorging. Svetlana, Chuck and Seth watched this with rapt attention, until Seth warned them about the obvious —— the bird needed to be protected from raccoons and coyotes.

The next day, after begrudgingly acknowledging his gender, Svetlana named him Homer, and he soon began to own the garden. McCaw dive-bombed him in screeching attacks. After being swiftly hoisted back into the house several times, the jealous McCaw eventually caught on that his aggression was getting him no rewards.

Homer grew fat and crowed a bit, but not often enough to annoy most neighbors. Except for Eddie, who swiftly called the city to lodge a complaint. Even so, Homer didn't actually bother him. Eddie was instead using the rooster's presence to exact revenge on Chuck and Svetlana for McCaw's repeated imitations of Jolene's sexual noises. Eddie's strategy didn't work: A city inspector determined that Homer was legal. Chuck knew this because he was present when the inspector came out to measure the distance between the house and the shed that Chuck told them was Homer's residence. It could have been an anonymous complaint had Eddie not screamed belligerently from the second-floor landing that he was the one who'd called the Department of Animal Services.

Knowing Eddie's disdain for McCaw, Chuck's response to Eddie's move against Homer was to transfer McCaw's birdcage from one side of the garden to the other, as close to Eddie's apartment as he could. Naturally, McCaw made a point of integrating his impersonation of Jolene's sexual screams with increasing frequency into his repertoire, and he did so now almost directly outside Eddie's door.

Meanwhile Homer's routine was to strut in the home's back door, cross the hardwood floor of the living room, and cluck a few times before slowly working his way out the front door. He soon became a member of the family, at peace with their dog Buster, with their cat Brewster, and, finally, even with McCaw.

Seth cautioned them about leaving Homer alone with the baby. There was no predicting how a rooster might behave around a human infant. Through a fog of memory, Seth remembered how one rooster on the chicken ranch of his childhood was free to wander the grasses, and one day attacked his toddler sister. He remembered the child, three years old, screaming and jumping in panic while the large bird kept lunging at her repeatedly, drawing blood on his sister's tiny arms and legs, until Seth — then only ten years old himself — rushed over to grab the rooster and rescue his sister.

And so Chuck and Svetlana made sure that Anna was enclosed in her playpen whenever Homer was loose, even though Homer showed no evidence of aggression toward anybody or anything.

Svetlana's mother, Olga, was supposed to have been watching Anna the following Sunday afternoon, when Svetlana was at her fencing class and Chuck was out on an audition. Instead, exhausted from a night of fitful sleep, Olga was napping on the living room couch when Anna, dressed only in a diaper, slipped out of her playpen and crawled on hands and knees into the back garden, where Homer was digging for slugs in the shade of a lilac bush.

Anna was drawn almost irresistibly to the shine in Homer's dark red wings, and so she crawled toward him. And yet, en route, feeling the warmth of a sunny spot, she stopped and crash-landed on her bottom, folding her chubby legs under her. She gurgled happily.

Hearing the baby chatter, Homer emerged from the shade of

the lilac bush and watched the baby pensively. Because of Seth's warnings, he wasn't allowed near her, but at this moment, on a sunny Sunday afternoon, there was nothing, nobody, to stop him. And so he strutted, slowly, in Anna's direction, which delighted the baby, who now squealed with excitement.

When Homer was a mere foot away from Anna, he arched up on his toes and flapped his wings, sending a gust of breeze in her direction that left her shrieking with laughter. Homer then clucked a few times in a deep voice and stepped yet closer toward Anna who, unable to resist temptation, reached out toward Homer and pulled at his tail feathers.

Homer spun away, slightly annoyed, and stood at a slight remove from the baby, who then crawled in Homer's direction. She reached out one more time and tried reaching for Homer's tail, but this time he swerved so she couldn't reach it, which made her laugh all the more.

For Anna, this was now a game. She kept lunging for Homer's tail, who kept swerving it out of her reach. He tried pecking at the ground near her, as though inviting her to eat some blades of grass he'd just discovered, but all she wanted was to pull at his tail.

At about this moment, Svetlana pulled her ten-year-old Mercedes-Benz sedan into the driveway. Upon entering the living room, Svetlana instantly saw Olga sleeping on the couch and Anna's empty playpen. Feverishly searching for Anna, Svetlana checked all the rooms of the house and, finally, the back garden. What she saw there didn't assuage her concern for her baby's safety, but the picture remains to this day enshrined in her memory.

Anna lay on her back, in the grass, almost asleep. Homer sat next to her, his chest pressed against one of her chubby arms while, with his beak, he ever so gently preened her hair. Svetlana found this to be an amazing spectacle. It didn't stop her from rushing over and sweeping up her child, away from the docile rooster and whatever danger Seth had warned them of. But it also deepened her respect and her affection for Homer. Or so she told Seth that night.

Homer eventually slept on the upper shelf in the laundry room near the back of the house. The shelf was about eight feet high, which Homer reached by launching himself from the top of the clothes dryer. Homer's home was exposed to the outside because the room had no curtains, and every night from behind the garden wall Seth would see Homer sleeping on the top shelf, nestled amidst white sheets and pillowcases. Seth found the sight inexplicably beautiful.

It surprised nobody that JoJo, knowing that her son's complaints had gained no traction with the city, took over the campaign of harassment by snapping photographs of Homer's repose in the laundry room before calling the city once more to complain, citing photographic evidence proving that the shed by the garage was *not* the rooster's home, as Chuck had falsely claimed, and that Homer was therefore in violation of the city's distance requirements. The inspector on the phone told JoJo that if Homer was sleeping inside, then he was a pet, so there was nothing more the city could do.

In the meantime, Seth noticed a marked change in the behavior of his own flock, as though they intuited Seth's fascination with the rooster in the garden next door, and they grew increasingly cranky. As a flock, they could see Seth staring over the garden wall and calling out to Homer, speaking to him in affectionate clucks, which they fully comprehended. And they didn't like it, or so Seth imagined. Or perhaps Seth's theory was nonsense. Perhaps they were growing increasingly cranky because that's what chickens do, like people, with the passing of time.

Both Agamemnon and Helen grew slightly more distant, not with Seth but with Cassandra and Clytemnestra, on whom they acted out their own frustrations with their poultry lives. On one occasion, Seth noticed Helen shrieking at Clytemnestra for no offense at all. On another, Agamemnon took a gratuitous peck at Cassandra's neck, leaving her cowering in a corner of their pen. After a month or so of tending his own flock, he came to understand, or at least theorize on, what was transpiring in his own garden.

This was because Seth visited his neighbors more often than he did before Homer joined the clan. The care and mutual affection for chickens could provide endless hours of conversation. During one visit Seth was struck by the sight of Homer on the hardwood living room floor, looking slightly lost. Svetlana leaned in to him, her hands on her knees, asking him face-to-face what was troubling him. Homer cackled his reply, whatever it was. That sight and sound moved Seth beyond words.

However, as political intrigues go, Seth's fondness of Homer, and his alliance with Svetlana and Chuck regarding Homer, did not bode well for the future of his own birds, and for the delicate agreement he'd forged with the Angelis duo to secure his flock's safety. As Seth's own flock might have taken offense with his allegiance to Homer — an anthropomorphic theory that was probably nonsense, Seth later concluded — the Angelis duo decidedly took offense with his allegiance to Chuck and Svetlana, whom they considered the latest affront to their quality of life.

Svetlana, meanwhile, determined that Homer was unhappy because he needed the company of other chickens. When a movie producer friend of theirs was visiting from out of state, he too fell under Homer's captivating spell and offered to take Homer back to the countryside in Idaho, where Homer could join his flock. The producer even paid Homer's airfare for a seat next to him, business class, Svetlana told Seth.

"*I* don't even fly business class," Svetlana pointed out.

And so, one day, Homer was gone.

ACT I, SCENE 5: AGAMEMNON

t probably comes as no great surprise that eventually Agamemnon started to crow. The first occurrence was between 6:30 and 7 a.m. on the second Friday in October — at least according to Eddie.

Agamemnon was by now a massive, imposing bird, resembling a small turkey. His size meant that his crowing was not a piercing soprano, that rural, aural backdrop heard in movies and on TV. No — Agamemnon's first crows were throaty and toneless. Agamemnon's first few shouts elicited a concerned text message from Winston Pendleton, who feared that Agamemnon might be dying. The first time he crowed, Seth rationalized it as a petty annoyance. But after two or three weeks, Agamemnon found his voice. His bellowing picked up speed, volume and frequency. It still sounded like a deep and painful moan.

"Is he ever going to get any good at that? Or at least better?" Melvin asked Seth, as they stood on opposite sides of the wall dividing their two buildings.

"Probably not," Seth replied candidly. And he was right.

For the first week of Agamemnon's bellowing, always at the cusp of dawn, Seth tried to convince himself that the bird's noise wasn't really so loud. There was, after all, the birdsong from the local sparrows and larks and doves that could be heard at about this same time, and which was very much part of nature; Seth tried to convince himself that Agamemnon's crowing was just another voice in this avian chorus.

He did, however, also observe a thundering silence, an averting of eye contact, from almost all of his neighbors. And this caused him some distress and anxiety, though nobody confronted him directly with a complaint about Agamemnon. Seth simply imagined the complaints to be unspoken. Or maybe they weren't complaints at all? Maybe people sliding by each other in a ritual of mutual evasion was simply the nature of co-existence in a crowded city? Perhaps his neighbors simply weren't particularly *friendly*. Perhaps they'd *never* been friendly and he'd just never before noticed. Perhaps he was inventing the entire crisis?

Still, he felt he had to do *something* about it — not only because it was the right thing to do, but because it would show that he cared. What is the difference between actually caring, and making gestures of caring? It was on the sixth day of Agamemnon's crowing that Seth reflected on that distinction, arriving at no particular conclusion. Whether or not he actually cared, or needed to *show* that he cared, action was imperative. And this is why on the seventh day of Agamemnon's crowing, Seth purchased a twenty-foot tube of six-inch-thick soundproof foam from Rampage Hardware Supplies on Western Avenue. He cut the foam into strips and spent the better part of two hours gluing and stapling the foam onto the walls of the coop, hoping that, with Agamemnon bolted inside until 10 a.m., his crowing would be so muffled as to be inaudible.

On the morning of the eighth day of Agamemnon's crowing, Seth was awakened, pre-dawn, by the sound of his rooster's muffled bellowing. The tone was quite different from when the coop was not insulated with foam, but the insulation made almost no difference to the decibel level. Or, if it did, Agamemnon was getting so much louder that his vocal prowess mocked Seth's attempted to mute it.

This was why, later that day, Seth purchased a large dog carrier, lined it with straw and placed it in his apartment hallway. The intent was to keep Agamemnon indoors overnight, in a darkened hallway where, presumably, he would sleep through the dawn, thereby allowing his neighbors to sleep as well. Agamemnon would then be placed in the garden at the more reasonable hour of 10 a.m.

That very evening, around 10 p.m., in the light of a first quarter moon, Agamemnon was fast asleep on one of the outdoor dowel perches in their pen. He sat, clutching the dowel with his feet, his head drooping in repose into his chest. There had been no need to secure him inside the insulated coop, since this was to be his first night indoors since his youth.

Seth lifted the large, groggy bird, one hand under each wing, and cradled the large bundle of hot flesh and feathers next to his chest as he carried him up the stairwell. Agamemnon let out a deep, satisfied cackle as Seth ran an index finger under his beak. Once inside, Seth placed him next to the dog cage's open door. Agamemnon stood outside, perplexed. Seth got down on his hands and knees, twirling pieces of straw from inside the cage with his fingers, trying to induce Agamemnon inside. The bird just stared at him as though he was insane.

Seth then tried to nudge him toward the open door, guiding him from behind with a hand on each wing. Agamemnon refused to budge. Seth pushed harder, until Agamemnon jumped up onto the cage's roof, shook all of his feathers creating a small whirlwind, and started preening his wings. Not quite knowing whether to leave him on the roof for the night or to close him inside, Seth finally determined that leaving him on the roof was a formula for chaos in the morning. As docile and contented as Agamemnon appeared in that particular moment, Seth nonetheless scooped him up and swiftly deposited him inside the cage, before he had any opportunity to realize what was happening or to react against it. Seth snapped the door shut.

Agememnon stretched inside the cage, wings and legs, until he bumped his head on the roof. After Seth clicked off the hallway light, Agamemnon settled down into a nesting position and closed his eyes. After about ten minutes, his head was bobbing against his chest, bobbing almost to the straw-covered floor.

Agamemnon slept in the dark hallway of Seth's apartment until 10 a.m., behind sealed windows. This resolved the issue of Agamemnon waking the neighbors.

It also established a bond between Agamemnon and Seth, a daily rite understood by both man and prodigal chicken. Seth cradled the huge bird in his arms during this walk up and down the stairwell every evening and morning. Seth spoke gently to Agamemnon during these journeys, and Agamemnon cackled his reply in a *basso profundo*. Seth rubbed his fingers across Agamemnon's fleshy comb, under his throat, and through the feathers on his head. Agamemnon muttered deeply in reply, so that Seth felt the bird's speech rumbling and resonating all the way through the hot skin of his now thickly feathered chest.

Before bringing Agamemnon downstairs each morning, Seth slid open the doors of the coop and the pen, so the hens had access to the entire garden area. There was a reason for this, having to do with Agamemnon's now-surging hormones and virility. Upon being set on the ground, Agamemnon chased the hens, waddling as fast as he could, his nails clicking on the cement steps as he jumped up, step by step, or down, click, click, click. Of course they ran from him. Clytemnestra was the first to figure out she could leap from the ground to the safety of Seth's shoulder. Cassandra followed, landing on his other shoulder.

One morning, while Helen hid behind a cactus on the far side of the garden, Agamemnon circled, wheezing, looking up at Seth and the sisters, cackling with growing annoyance. He had grown too fat to jump up and join the hens. There was now also a glint of anger in his eyes at Seth's betrayal of their friendship.

On the evening of November 11, as Seth was preparing for bed, he lay down on the floor of the hallway to say goodnight to Agamemnon through the mesh of the dog carrier door. From inside his crate, Agamemnon puffed up his feathers and let out a disturbing scream of frustration and anger. Seth opened the door. Agamemnon ambled out, shook off his feathers emitting a small cloud of dust, and began chattering in his deep voice. He strutted over to a nearby bowl and took a few pecks of chicken scratch. Then he just stood there on one leg, yellow chicken scratch smeared on his beak, looking at Seth askance. Man and bird watched each other in this tableau for about five minutes. Finally, Agamemnon placed the leg that was tucked under his stomach back down on the ground, joining the other. He continued to stand like a weathervane for another few minutes before Seth ushered him toward the dog carrier. Agamemnon blurted out his annoyance. Crouching behind Agamemnon, Seth placed his hands on both wings and nudged him inside. Agamemnon twisted his head backwards toward Seth, letting out a deep, annoyed trill.

On the morning of November 12, as Seth was carrying Agamemnon down toward the garden, Agamemnon committed an unprecedented breach. He took a sharp peck at Seth's bare arm, biting into the flesh and twisting. Seth bonked him on the head with a finger, further inflaming Agamemnon, who answered with a second sharp peck.

There is no reasoning with an angry chicken.

In order to protect himself, Seth held Agamemnon by his thick legs so that the bird dangled upside down. Agamemnon flapped his heavy wings briskly, sending out gusts of air, while craning his neck upward and shrieking, reaching in vain for more flesh to bite. When he landed on the garden ground, Agamemnon shook himself off and stared at Seth indignantly. This time he didn't chase the hens, who watched perplexed.

Seth searched for a rational cause of Agamemnon's growing anger. Perhaps Agamemnon imagined he was being punished for something every night, being placed in solitary confinement for a reason he couldn't make sense of, knowing that his girlfriends were free to roam in the pen below?

Agamemnon had formed the closest attachment with Helen, now a beautiful white creature with black spots mottled into her coat. It was for her benefit that the rooster chattered excitedly when finding a worm or a twig of particular interest. Helen paid attention to his discoveries, she valued them and gave him purpose, while the red sisters largely ignored him. Helen and Agamemnon parked next to each other during the day, sometimes for hours, while the red sisters were off somewhere occupying themselves. For this reason, on the night of November 12, Seth carried both Agamemnon and Helen upstairs, so they could sleep snugly together in the dog carrier. That night, the couple nestled in, side by side, heads bobbing. For a brief and fleeting moment, Agamemnon looked content. When Seth carried both of them downstairs in the morning, together in his arms, there was no sign of aggression from Agamemnon.

Unfortunately, Agamemnon then started to crow in the afternoon. This drew the attention of JoJo, whose windows were directly next to the pen. Sometimes JoJo threw vegetables and fruit at him to distract him. But after Agamemnon gobbled them down, he would just crow more.

"So I'm on the phone trying to talk this guy out of slitting his wrists, but I can't hear what he's saying because your rooster's crowing," JoJo complained. "I look out my window and I can see straight down his gullet. It's like he's doing it out of spite!"

Her son Eddie had also started weighing in, claiming that neighbors were complaining. Seth did his own research, talking to people in the building and beyond it. He found Eddie's report to be unfounded.

"Well, they're not going to tell you the truth," Eddie sneered.

Curiously, Winston, who filed the noise complaint against Eddie and Jolene, found the rooster's crowing charming, or so he said. Seth mentioned this to Eddie, thereby hinting at Eddie's hypocrisy when it came to consideration for noise and his neighbors.

"City noises," Eddie barked back defensively. "Ours are just normal city noises, like a siren or a car alarm. Nobody in the city expects to hear roosters."

ON NOVEMBER 20, KATERINA PAVLOVA arrived from Moscow for her semi-annual one-week stay, as she had promised Seth in that summer phone call. As always, she brought her now-adult daughter from her first marriage, Irena, as yet another barrier, Seth surmised. Seth loved Irena, and the pair got along well. He had met her in Moscow when she was eight; it was his first of ten annual sojourns there.

As a playwright-in-residence at Katerina's theater, Seth was assigned to live in her home. He fell in love with her and with her Russia. It was all a vibrant dream, starting with the dank smell of Sheremetyevo Airport, of muddy tires on the streets and drifts of snow piled into ditches, of fur-capped merchants in kiosks quietly selling contraband, imported cigarettes, of a cab ride anywhere in the city for an American dollar, of KGB agents slinking around corners, of secret, thrilling gatherings of poets and musicians, singing their defiance of the authoritarian Soviet government, whose policies were determined to keep its people isolated from the world beyond its domain, and in rigid conformity with its doctrines.

These were the early 1990s, when President Mikhail Gorbachev tried to ease Russia into the West, but the legacy of oppression he'd inherited lit a fire under a movement headed by his challenger, Boris Yeltsin, who emulated the West, its economics, its values.

Seth saw local pop singers using autographed headshots as bribes for butter that was too scarce to be stocked. Loudspeakers in municipal parks blasted out Cyndi Lauper, Elton John and Mick Jagger. In those years, just being from the West rendered Seth a celebrity in Moscow. The new McDonald's in the city's center tried an unheard-of policy of having a hostess stationed by the front door greeting every patron with a cheerful "hello" when they finally reached the restaurant's entrance after waiting in line for half an hour: *"Zdtrastvoytye." "Zdtrastvoytye." "Zdtrastvoytye."*

Seth stood in that line with Katerina and Irena, and they heard the hostess greeting one local customer after another, in Russian, as they crossed the threshold.

When Seth got to the front of the line, though he'd said nothing to identify himself as American, the same hostess looked at him and said in English: "Hi. Welcome."

Russians could tell that Seth was not one of them, merely from the shape of his face and his complexion. His eyes lacked the deep pockets of Russian sadness, Katerina explained.

The year Seth first arrived in Russia, the nation was making a bloodless exit from the same Soviet Union that Joe and Sheba Rapoport saw born with such bloodshed. Seth was in Red Square when crowds were chanting "Yelt-sin! Yelt-sin! Yelt-sin!" The Army watched alongside a barricade. Seth saw their faces. Some looked fifteen years old.

Gorbachev looked so weary on television. He saw his nation evaporating, losing itself to this blind infatuation with the West. Gorbachev was a reasonable man, and this was not a reasonable time.

There is almost never a reasonable time.

Seth fell in love with the children's parks behind the apartment blocks, and with the woods. He visited Irena's class then, her English lesson. "We are very fond of tea," he remembers thirty Russian eight-year-olds reciting in unison. He visited a youth orchestra playing Vivaldi, perfectly. The oboe soloist was a twelve-year-old boy. It was a young nation. Yet over the coming decade, Seth would watch it slide back into its old authoritarian ways. From Ivan the Terrible to Stalin to Putin.

The year after they met, Katerina visited Seth in L.A. The year after that, they were married in Beverly Hills.

Having been weaned on British reserve, Seth was beguiled by their Russian exuberance. In amazement he watched Irena and Katerina swoon during the Main Street Parade at Disneyland. Cartoons and cuddly toys were irresistible to both of them. At the age of twelve, Irena broke down in tears when Winnie the Pooh waved at her from his parade float. The twinkling lights, the music, and the parade of Disney characters were all too overwhelming for the child. Her mother stood by her side, also jaw-dropped at the spectacle. Disney toys decorated both their beds, along with Russian kittens and puppies with oversized eyes, and soft, stuffed raccoons and lions and frogs.

IRENA WAS NOW IN HER LATE TWENTIES, a slim brunette with a fashion-model face, and Katerina clung to her as though to life itself. Irena's long-term boyfriend was a threat to Katerina's possessive view of their maternal bond. Seth knew this from Katerina's constant expressions of concern over how the young man treated Irena, or "Ira," over his selfishness, his haughtiness, and his almost sadistic disregard of both his girlfriend and her mother.

"She's just a toy to him," Katerina complained. "Five years together and no hint of a marriage proposal — only his lectures on Ira's character flaws, and how she needs to improve them."

Seth's new vegetarianism was mystifying to the carnivorous Russians. Seth showed them the literature on brutal factory farms. He hoped this would appeal to their intrinsic love of beasts. After all, Katerina risked her life to protect her Chow Chow. Katerina respected the arguments, but the divide between cuddly pets and farm animals wasn't one she was willing or able to cross. And so at night, in the living room, Katerina and Irena sucked pork ribs while Seth poked at a Chinese tofu salad.

"You've become obsessed," Katerina told him, "and I like that. To a point. I think you're still looking for home. You've been here all your life so you call it home. But Los Angeles isn't home. It's a place people pass through. You've been passing through for twenty years, and that's why you've become so obsessed."

"Obsessed?" Seth asked. Helen clucked from the hallway, having just laid an egg.

Katerina and Seth both understood that when she returned to Moscow, Katerina may never come back. They understood this from the overnight visits of Agamemnon and Helen to the hallway. They understood it from the straw and mash strewn onto the floor in the mornings. They understood it from one brief conversation on November 22 between Seth and Katerina concerning the chickens.

"Do they *have* to spend *every* night inside?" Katerina asked.

"They're my children."

"I can see that."

"This is their *home* ... If they could be outside, they'd be outside ..."

"This is also *our* home," Katerina said. "I painted these walls. I chose this furniture."

"But you don't really want to live here anymore . . . right?" Pause. "Did I get that right?"

Katerina took a long, hard drag on a cigarette while looking around the living room. The wedding portrait. The Russian décor. The framed photos on the shelves of their two dogs and a cat, all dead now.

"I need a real home," she said.

The next day, after a one-hour ocean crossing on a tour boat from Long Beach to Catalina Island, Katerina, Irena and Seth stood at a ticket booth near the city of Avalon, preparing to board two kayaks in order to row around the Avalon bay. Seth bought three tickets from a sunbaked woman behind the booth, who stowed their coats and jeans in a locker, so they could board the kayaks in shorts, sandals and swimwear. Even in late November, the sun was baking the island to 85 degrees. The ticket-seller handed Seth three sets of lifesavers and pointed them to the siding of a wooden dock, where they were met by a barefoot teenage boy wearing sunglasses and swimming trunks.

"These won't hold three," he said, referring to the kayaks. "You can have one double and one single. Who's together?"

Seth pointed to Katerina and himself, and the boy prepared them the larger kayak.

"I can't go without Ira," Katerina protested.

"She's twenty-eight years old," Seth interjected, but Katerina started to panic: "She can't be out there *alone*!"

"Ma — it's okay!" Irena said.

"No, it's not okay!" Katerina fired back. They then argued in Russian.

And so mother and daughter climbed into the wobbly kayak for two, Katerina behind Irena. The boy used his foot to shove the boat away from the dock as Seth climbed into his own vessel. He watched the women float in a lunatic circle as they struggled to manipulate the paddles, while the boy yelled instructions to them from the dock — reiterating what he told them earlier about how to turn, how to gain speed, how to brake. After about five minutes, they got the hang of it, and Seth followed their almost majestic trajectory parallel to the shore. He followed them up and down the island's coast for about half an hour. On two occasions, they waved and smiled, though Katerina had a muted expression of terror. It occurred to him that Irena was the parent, and probably had been for some time. He had thought perhaps Katerina was just afraid of *him*, but he settled into the idea that she was simply afraid: an actress who put on a brave face, or faces; a mistress of the grand gesture, her passion was operatic.

Katerina could talk with discrimination about her love for Goya's sketches and Tchaikovsky's concertos, but it was Michael Jackson who sent her into ecstasies — Jackson, and the Broadway tour of *The Phantom of the Opera*. Because Katerina refused to learn to drive, Seth was compelled, to the limits of his patience, to listen to both Jackson and *Phantom* for extended hours on the car radio during drives through L.A.'s rush-hour traffic, between grocery and discount clothing stores. And he reflected that perhaps this aesthetic divide, however exotic, was the reason they now floated in different kayaks in the Avalon bay — close, but not quite together.

Irena and Seth both heard Katerina's hacking cough and her announcements that her red blood count was becoming dangerously low. Seth once made the mistake of suggesting to Katerina that if she was so concerned about her lungs and her red blood cells, perhaps she should stop smoking. This is not what you tell a Russian for whom smoking is on par with breathing. Katerina snarled back at him that people who quit smoking are subject to gaining weight, and that's out of the question for an actress.

From across a fathom of water, Seth shouted out that he wanted to row further out, that he'd find them or meet them at the dock. Katerina's face revealed a momentary panic that he might just float out to sea and never come back, but Irena nodded cheerfully and waved him off.

The thin bow bounced up and down, a dance choreographed by waves generated by speedboats, until, beyond the boats, all he could hear was the soft rhythmic splashing of the paddle sliding in and out of the turquoise current. Seth surged past a cruise ship, docked at a safe distance, where the water was deep. And on. And on. Until the town of Avalon shrank into a blur, and all Seth could see from almost every angle were expanses of the mighty Pacific, ocean swells, sprinkles of white foam, all-engulfing, a cradle and a tomb.

These are the moments in life that should be shared and not just spoken of, Seth thought to himself, remembering the hours of reports over transcontinental phone lines that had constituted his marriage for the five years Katerina had been gone: the music of her voice, her gushing support of all his projects, her wisdom at odds with her flaring temper. The drama she manufactured. The drama. And now, the distance. They never actually discussed her return to Moscow to live and work. She simply did it, with vague promises of a return, promises like sea foam dissipating.

Katerina and Irena had been waiting and smoking on the dock for about twenty minutes when Seth paddled in. Earlier they enjoyed some ice cream cones and led him to the shop where they'd bought them, so he could have one, too. The three walked side by side, Irena in the middle. Katerina held Irena's hand while they walked.

THAT NIGHT, SETH FOUND HIMSELF solo once again, at the theater.

"California law requires us to tell you that, in the unlikely event of a fire, there's one exit through the stage and another through the walkway you came in," chirped the tall, bearded fellow in a shiny suit from the tiny stage of Hollywood's Lex Theatre, before he bounced offstage and slinked away. The houselights went dark on the seventy-three patrons who filled the bleachers. Stage lights crept up onto a night view painted-on-canvas vista of a decrepit farm, where an actor portraying the alcoholic Farmer Jones staggered across the terrain, muttering incoherently, drinking from a flask, and rudely shining a bright flashlight onto a flock of chickens.

The birds were also played by actors, wearing vivid masks, and they squawked and clucked in annoyance when disturbed by the flashlight's beam.

Seth had left Katerina and Irena at the apartment, where they could relax after a day in the blazing sun. Seth, too, felt the dull yet satisfying ache of exhaustion weighing down his limbs and clouding his eyes. And yet he remained alert, perhaps because the production he was viewing held a combination of interests for him. It was Peter Hall's stage adaptation of George Orwell's 1945 novel *Animal Farm*, presented by a company called Son of Semele Ensemble. Seth was mesmerized, not only by the depiction of farm animals drawing on a torrent of experiences from his youth, but also by Orwell's view of how yearnings for power and control can turn so toxic.

Farmer Jones next pointed his flashlight onto a herd of swine — actors with equally evocative masks — who snorted and tucked their snouts under their front legs.

Unlikely they're doing these roles to get on TV, Seth thought. That was a common assumption about the existence of theater in Los Angeles.

Seth had seen many terrible stage productions over the years in Los Angeles, but seldom were they terrible because their motives of creation were corrupted by Hollywood: They were terrible because they were incompetent, which is an entirely different matter, and a circumstance common to theater in every city Seth had ever visited.

This is why, when viewing a production like this *Animal Farm* that was not terrible, a production with passion and intelligence, Seth felt a fire of advocacy light in his heart. These artists knew what they were doing, and why they were doing it.

After Farmer Jones returned to his home, a crusty boar named Old Major convened a secret late-night meeting of all the farm animals. Old Major spoke in a deep voice, languorously, from the wisdom of his years. Human beings, he said, reaped the benefit of the farm animals' efforts and existence, for the most part returning to the beasts a miserable life and a cruel death. This would continue unless the animals stood up for themselves. There it was: the Russian Revolution in allegory and with songs.

Orwell's story was of insurrection, of the pigs' takeover of the farm, of a leader named Napoleon who bore a striking similarity to Joseph Stalin. The pigs rose over the other species; dogs guarded the pigs' newly consolidated power. The pigs spoke about equality, while their actions demonstrated the opposite.

Curiously, no other review mentioned Old Major's speech. causing Seth to wonder if he hadn't just imagined it on the stage, having read it in the book.

Returning home at around 11 p.m., Seth opened his front door to find Katerina and Irena both standing on the living room couch — held hostage by Agamemnon and Helen. Seth was immediately drawn to the scratches and cuts on both of the women's legs. The birds strutted around and over two suitcases, pulling out socks and panties, and clucking contentedly.

"We've been trapped here for almost an hour," Katerina said calmly.

"I'm so, so sorry . . . Why did you let them out of the cage?" Seth asked.

"He was screaming!" Irena said.

"He sounded very unhappy," added Katerina. "Then he attacked me."

"She kept biting my legs," said Irena.

After Seth ushered both birds back into the cage, his wife and stepdaughter stepped back down to the floor. Seth located a bottle of hydrogen peroxide and cotton balls in the bathroom, and gingerly offered it to them.

What appeared to be a kind of armistice was, in fact, merely a lull between battles.

Six days later, on a Sunday morning around 11 a.m., Seth was rifling through boxes in his garage storage space, just around the corner from the chicken pen, when he heard JoJo calling out, plaintively, "Seth . . . *SETH!*"

Seth bolted out of the garage and around the corner to discover JoJo backed up against the west garden wall. Agamemnon was facing down JoJo. The bird's head bobbed and his neck feathers flared out, threatening a full frontal attack. Seth raced along the cement, up the two small landings and dove for Agamemnon's feet, snaring him in mid-air, just as the bird was lunging for JoJo. Again, Seth dangled Agamemnon upside down by his feet. Again, Agamemnon shrieked out in protest, flapping violently, and sending out a small whirl of dust. The rooster craned his neck upwards and tried to bite Seth, who dumped him unceremoniously into the pen and closed the gate, which Agamemnon had somehow pushed open prior to attacking JoJo.

"I just don't understand how a bird that was hatched and raised on nothing but affection and kindness can turn out like this," Seth said, dusting off his hands.

"He's a rooster," JoJo remarked dryly. "It's no mystery. That's what roosters do. That's who roosters are. It's their nature."

"Testosterone," Seth replied. "He's got too much testosterone . . . And yet we all have to live with each other," he added.

"No, we don't," replied JoJo. "Are you going to do something about this, or not?"

Seth understood that Agamemnon's behavior was untenable, that he was obligated to provide some remedy. These were the terms that he himself had offered.

IT WAS A DAY OF FAREWELLS.

In the morning, Seth drove Katerina and Irena back to LAX and watched them slip away, waving, up the stairwell toward the security check-in. And that was that. They both felt it. A month later, Seth asked Katerina for a divorce. They both reeled after those words were spoken.

A week later, Katerina called back, seething, with a proposal for a financial settlement, the return of family photos, and the threat of hiring a Russian lawyer who would impoverish him if he didn't co-operate. Seth told her that he didn't recognize her, she now sounded like the Russian Mafia. She replied that she, too, didn't know who he was anymore. A week later, her tone and strategy both softened.

She said that the advice of some of her Russian friends probably hadn't been the best approach.

"Then I was talking about this with my mum," she said. "You

never did anything bad to me. After twenty years of marriage, I don't want our good memories to be poisoned."

After they agreed to terms, Katerina told him, "I could tell you weren't happy. More than anything, I want you to be happy. You deserve to be happy."

Seth wasn't entirely sure at first if her sentiment was generous, tactical or some combination of both, because it filled him with a guilt so profound, he felt he'd been poisoned.

"Love alters not with its brief hours and weeks, But bears it out even to the edge of doom."

Seth had written these lines from Shakespeare's Sonnet 116 in a years-ago Valentine's Day card to Katerina. And now she read it back to him, with the commentary, "You see how wrong you were."

His inclination was to give her the benefit of the doubt, that her motive was magnanimous, not spiteful, despite her roller-coaster changes of mood.

With the consultation of a family law attorney, Seth FedExed her a copy of the divorce terms on U.S. court documents, which, living up to her words, she signed and had notarized at the U.S. Embassy in Moscow.

Still, after a review that took three months, the L.A. Superior Court refused to recognize the contract because, the clerk's office noted, Katerina hadn't been served per the Hague Convention, signed by both the Russian Federation and the U.S., which mandates that court documents delivered from the United States to citizens of Russia on Russian soil cannot be sent via mail or courier. Instead, they must first have the permission of a Russian court to be delivered, then they must be delivered by a central Russian government authority via a Russian consulate in the United States — a process that can take months.

Seth's attorney mailed a "letter of objection" to the supervising judge of the Family Law division of the L.A. Superior Court. The attorney wrote that in fifteen years of practice, during which he'd studied how to file paperwork from the head clerk of the Court in question, his law firm had "never seen paperwork rejected for the reasons cited herein." He wrote that Katerina had left Russian soil of her own volition in order to sign and notarize their contract at the U.S. Embassy, i.e. on U.S. soil, where the Hague Convention does not apply.

After another three months, the court finally replied by returning the documents with "REJECTED" stamped across the top in red ink, and "See Hague Convention" hand-scribbled, as though his attorney's argument had been written in Martian.

A month after that, Seth finally got through by telephone to the head clerk in the Family Law division. Seth explained the conundrum. The clerk found the case file on her computer and told Seth that there was the possibility that Seth's argument had legal merit, and that if court staff had erred, she would look into it. She asked him to resubmit the entire case file, which he did. Seth noted on the Court website that his re-filed case had been duly received (for the third time), but that because of staff cutbacks, family law cases were now taking up to four months to review.

Six months later, the paperwork came back once more with "REJECTED" stamped in red across the top, and "See Hague Convention" hand-written.

Seth called the head clerk once more. A week later, she dutifully returned his call and explained that the case would need to go before a judge for a hearing. Unfortunately, because of staff cutbacks, the earliest hearing date was another six months away, some eighteen months after Seth first filed the paperwork.

MEANWHILE, THE SAME AFTERNOON after taking Katerina and Irena to the airport, Seth drove to Valley Village. Agamemnon sat clucking in the dog carrier, in the back seat of Seth's Honda Civic. Seth felt he didn't understand this bird at all. He didn't understand so many of life's entanglements.

Mike had said that the front gate would be unlocked. That if he wasn't home, to just leave Agamemnon in the carport in his cage. This was because Mike first needed to vaccinate Agamemnon for his own protection before introducing him into one of Mike's own flocks. And that's how Seth left him: in a cage in a carport in Valley Village on a brisk afternoon in late November.

Seth finally reached Mike by phone that night.

"Oh yeah!" Mike chuckled. "What a bastard! He beat the shit out of four other roosters trying to mess with him. He's back in the pen where his egg came from. He's gonna be fine. He's home."

A week later, Mike said he'd seen him out his kitchen window and that Agamemnon seemed to be looking good, that he was in with maybe seventy other chickens. Mike wasn't absolutely sure it was Agamemnon. But Mike figured that Agamemnon was doing okay.

The following week, Seth asked Mike if he could visit. Together, they searched the pen looking for Agamemnon. Mike confessed he hadn't seen him in a few days.

Searching through the pen's field, with dozens and dozens of chickens, Seth focused on trying to find the familiar feather pattern of white bars across a coat of black. He saw miniature black Bantams, large cream and black Araucanas, huge Rhode Island Reds, grey and white Polish with beards and feathered feet, a couple of White Leghorn hens, but no sign of Agamemnon. Finally, in a dry ditch, Seth found a nondescript bird lying caked in dust, panting. The comb was grey, pressed over sharply to one side and coated in blood. And yet, on the hip, on the hackle feathers, Seth recognized the telltale white-bar pattern. The feathers weren't shiny, like Agamemnon's had been, but they were the only evidence Seth had seen of his breed. The feet were just like Agamemnon's. The body was decimated.

"Aggie?" he said to the bird.

The bird raised his head half an inch, all he could, then set it down. Seth noticed that the chicken was missing an eye.

"That's him," Seth told Mike. Seth picked up the bird and cradled him. From the movement in his ribs, Seth could tell that Agamemnon was trying to cluck, but hadn't the strength.

"Looks like they got him back," Mike said. "I'm sorry."

"I need to take him home," Seth replied.

"Sure . . . Look, I can't vouch he'll live through the night."

When they got home, Seth held Agamemnon on his lap, sitting at his desk, dabbing his bloodied comb with hydrogen peroxide, smearing gashes with antibiotic cream. Mostly though, he spoke gently to the bird, and the bird listened and tried to speak back. He placed millet seed in a dish on the desk, but Agamemnon wouldn't eat. He poured fresh water into a dish on the desk, but Agamemnon wouldn't drink. Finally, late in the night, when Seth held the seeds in front of him, Agamemnon ate, tentatively. When Seth held water in front of him and asked him to drink, pleaded with him to drink, Agamemnon began to drink. And that's when Seth understood that Agamemnon was going to live through the night. And he did.

Agamemnon spent the next month mostly sleeping in Seth's living room, in the large dog cage Agamemnon knew from before, carpeted with straw. Day by day, the red flush returned to his face, and the shine to his feathers. He started to chatter, at first with a thin reedy voice, mostly air. But over the weeks, the familiar bass cackling returned. His girth also returned, and he started to look like his former self, except for the missing eye. Agamemnon was now a pirate.

Early one morning, in the fourth week of Agamemnon's recovery, Seth was awakened by the primitive sound of Agamemnon crowing. He should have dreaded what neighbors would say. After all, he had assured them that Agamemnon had left the property, which was true at the time. But Seth was glad, because crowing is the rooster's call that he's alive and believes that he's in charge. It would have been more convenient if Agamemnon had never crowed again, but Seth loved this bird too much to hope for that.

The next day, on Seth's lap, Agamemnon took a sharp peck at Seth's arm: not as vicious as before, more like a challenge. Agamemnon stared at Seth through his one eye. Seth glared back. Agamemnon chattered something or other, and the moment passed without further incident.

Agamemnon crowed again only one more time that week. And not in a stream of shouts, but just once, and he was satisfied for another several days. And so on: One crow, once or twice a week from inside Seth's living room. Agamemnon was like a reformed felon still being blamed for crimes of long ago.

That blame came from JoJo. At 10 a.m., on the morning of that first infraction, Seth received an indignant phone call from his aggrieved neighbor, who had heard and confirmed reports of a rooster's crow coming from Seth's apartment. Seth listened to JoJo's lecture on how she had been deceived, on how the Board and all the owners in the building had been wronged by Seth. The rooster had to leave the property, as Seth had promised weeks ago. Seth said he understood.

But he didn't. JoJo's demands seemed harsh and unreasonable. After all, Agamemnon was doing no harm. He was making less noise than the car alarms that would wake the dead two or three times a week with their shrieking. Far less noise than the police and ambulance sirens blaring at all times of day and night.

One crow, twice a week. That was all.

No, JoJo and the HOA had not been wronged. And Seth decided to grant Agamemnon asylum from those trying to prosecute him for the crimes of his past. It's true, the bird did not have an easy character. He wasn't cute or cuddly, especially now. He wasn't even particularly loyal. But as the man who had incubated his egg and literally eased him out of his shell, Seth felt a paternal responsibility to protect the bird from further harm. It was the least he could do.

ACT I, SCENE 6: ELYSIAN FIELDS

Despite JoJo's lecture and mandate, Seth kept Agamemnon inside the apartment. Agamemnon continued to crow once or twice a week with a single shout, generally between 8 and 9 in the morning.

For the first week, this aroused in Seth a sense of dread. He dragged himself out of bed, groggy, and in a state of semi-consciousness hissed "Shhhhhhh!" at Agamemnon, who looked at him quizzically through his single eye. Agamemnon had no idea what could possibly be the problem. Man and bird stared at each other for a few more minutes — Seth stooping with a hand on each knee — and after Seth was confident that no more crowing was welling up in his rooster, he staggered back to bed.

Sometimes in his dreams, he heard Agamemnon emit a single crow, but he convinced himself that the noise in his head was a product of memory and dread rather than of Agamemnon himself, and perhaps he was right. He was having an increasing difficulty distinguishing between what was real and what was imagined.

By the third week, Seth was starting to relax somewhat. Agamemnon's crowing had not escalated in volume or frequency, and he started to regard the brief shouting as an eccentricity rather than a nuisance, since — aside from the Angelis duo — none of the neighbors mentioned it. A delicate victory is how Seth regarded the entire situation.

There finally seemed to be a tolerable balance and a rhythm to Agamemnon's crowing, and when Seth relaxed his guard just a little, JoJo initiated a recall campaign to remove him from the presidency of the Bronson Canyon Homeowners Association. The tactic was to knock Seth out of contention for the upcoming election, to reinstall

Eddie as an officer, and to give the Angelises two out of the three seats on the Board.

JoJo composed an impassioned email that she would send to every owner, followed up by snail mail:

"Dear Fellow Homeowners, I am calling for an emergency meeting at my apartment on January 5 at 7:30 p.m. I invite all owners to discuss the impeachment of Seth Jacobson as president. I believe he has recklessly placed the HOA in jeopardy by advocating for his personal chicken pen in a common area, when he knew full well the pen violates city law. I recently discovered that the municipal code requires a distance of at least 35 feet between the outer walls of the pen and our building. Please find attached a copy of that code. I measured the distance and found it to be nine feet and three inches at its closest point. Our rules and regulations say that no owner is permitted to engage in any activity that violates city, state or federal law. I find it unacceptable that such behavior should be coming from our own president. Yours sincerely, Jocasta Angelis."

Seth really didn't know to what extent the tide of public opinion truly had turned against him. Sam saw him on the walkway and gave him a sympathetic smile. Vera averted her eyes. Sergio told him that he found JoJo's email annoying and that he just wanted peace in the building. But it was Winston Pendleton, the same Winston Pendleton whom Eddie Angelis had accused in public of being a spineless gossip and an idiot, who stepped forward at the last minute, placing his own version of a scalding pipe rocket on JoJo's doorstep. Winston sent his own email, and posted a hard copy over the community mailboxes:

"Dear Homeowners, According to Section 5, Item 3 of our CC&Rs, any call for the impeachment of an elected officer must be accompanied by a petition signed by 2/3 of the homeowners. I have attached a copy of Section 5. I have seen no such petition, and my neighbors say the same. So any impeachment vote taken at tonight's meeting will be non-binding. Sincerely, Winston Pendleton."

About an hour after Winston pressed the "send" button, the sound of JoJo's and Eddie's front doors slamming could be heard throughout the building. Both Winston and Seth saw the mother and son scurrying back and forth between their respective apartments. In what Winston dubbed "their typical failure of due diligence," the Angelis duo had scrutinized the municipal code, but had neglected to read their own building's rules for impeaching an officer. That night, other than JoJo and Eddie, only Ruby Malholtra, John Malholtra's estranged wife who now rented his apartment, attended the impeachment meeting. According to Winston, who heard the story from JoJo, Ruby sipped half a glass of wine while they all waited for more people to show up. Forty-five minutes after she arrived, Ruby went home.

The next morning at 8:47 a.m., Agamemnon emitted a single crow from inside Seth's apartment. This was recorded in a log JoJo was now keeping. JoJo duly reported the offense to her son Eddie, who made a phone call to the Department of Animal Services. Two days later, a city inspector, a male in his mid-thirties, paced back and forth outside Seth's door, rang the doorbell several times and knocked, but nobody replied because Seth wasn't home. Seth learned all this from Winston, who had been peering through his screen door. Winston dutifully told Seth that he also saw the inspector go into the back garden but lost sight of him after the inspector turned the corner behind the building.

On January 14, exactly one week later, Seth received a notice from the city — a boilerplate form from Animal Services that said nothing about the rooster, likely because that inspector had seen no rooster behind the curtained windows, or so Seth conjectured. It did, however, cite Municipal Code 53.59 for distance requirements for chickens. It ordered Seth, as the owner of the hens, to comply with the distance requirements immediately. And while the notice didn't actually say the chickens had to go, the laws of geometry pointed in that direction.

Winston started the rumor that Eddie had called the city and filed an anonymous complaint, prompting the inspector's visit. When asked about this by Sam, Eddie gloated that it was true.

At the annual meeting before the election in February, four months overdue, Seth explained to the assembled owners that he had done nothing to jeopardize the HOA, that both his contract with the Board and city policy provide remedies for infractions. He added that he simply couldn't understand the reasons for the Angelis duo's prosecutorial actions and attitudes. Seth maintained that the mother and son shared responsibility for the acrimony in the building, which had no genuine cause, served no purpose and had no place in a community of only twelve owners. Because of that acrimony, Seth said in conclusion, he no longer wished to serve on the Board. He threw his support behind Winston Pendleton.

When the votes were counted, Winston emerged as president. When the result was announced, Winston's wife, Suki, bore an expression of dread. Vera and JoJo continued on, respectively, as vice president and secretary-treasurer.

Seth's primary concern at the time was the unanswered question of what to do with the flock of four chickens that he had hatched, and to which he had grown so attached.

The next day, after gazing out over the garden behind Chuck and Svetlana's Craftsman home to the west, Seth paid another visit to the young couple.

"My flock has no home. They've turned on me, the Angelis duo. You have this beautiful garden . . ."

Seth's appeal fell on sympathetic ears. Svetlana hadn't forgotten JoJo's complaints about her feeding the squirrels, or Eddie's complaints to the city against Homer.

"Do they run that place?" Svetlana asked.

Seth reflected on her question: "I guess in a way they do."

Budding crape myrtles announced the coming of spring, along with the narcissus sprays — in the gardens of the few people in Bronson Canyon who care about such things.

AGAMEMNON, HELEN, CLYTEMNESTRA and Cassandra now strutted in the garden behind the Craftsman house. Chuck had strung a couple of fences to protect Svetlana's herbs and bulbs from the chickens. Agamemnon still crowed only once or twice a week, early in the morning, but now from the confines of the shed adjoining the garage, where all of them slept inside a new, massive, straw-lined plastic dog carrier.

Each morning, around 10 a.m., Seth hopped the garden wall, crossed the yard and opened the shed with the key Chuck had given him. He hauled the carrier outside and flung open the gate. The four chickens bolted around the garden while Seth cleaned out and refreshed their water bowl and set them down fresh corn mash. Cassandra, however, was far more interested to see if there was any remaining kibble in the bowl Svetlana had left out last night for the raccoons. Following Cassandra's lead, all of them raced for the bowl and bobbed their heads inside, picking up some dust from the now crushed dry dog food.

At dusk, Seth returned for the ritual of returning them to the carrier.

At first, he used to try to catch them one by one. He would chase one, then another, but because chickens are instinctively wired for the chase, they loved darting away from his grip. Then Seth tried stalking them, one by one, trying to hide his motive of ensnaring them. Slowly, he'd creep up on them as though he were interested in something completely different, like picking an avocado. But they weren't so stupid as to not know when they were being stalked: They let him get within inches, then tormented him by slipping out of his reach at the last second. It took hours to get them inside. Finally, Seth figured out the technique which he came to use every night.

First he set out the carrier with the door open, placing pieces of bread inside and around the door. He then sat in a folding chair by the garage, sometimes with his laptop on his knees, and wrote one of his theater reviews, or checked the latest headlines, or simply waited for time to pass.

With the ever diminishing light, the birds got more agitated, caw-cawwing, bobbing their heads. This is when, every night, Cassandra approached him and jumped onto his knee, and then his shoulder. Clytemnestra followed. Every night it was the same. Meanwhile, Agamemnon poked his head inside the carrier, took a step inside, and then outside. He saw Helen scavenging for worms on the far side of the garden wall. He cackled at her, bossy, ordering her inside. She listened, thought about it for a moment, then continued her foraging. Agamemnon now barked at her. She responded by approaching the carrier and nibbled on some of the bread by the door, while Agamemnon stood one-eyed, heroic, behind her.

Agamemnon used to bark out his commands to the sisters, now perched on Seth's shoulders. He stopped that long ago, when they figured out they could ignore him and suffer no consequences.

Helen was the first to settle inside the carrier, then Agamemnon, and the couple snuggled beside each other, trilling happily. Seeing this, Cassandra dove from Seth's shoulder to the cage door, standing there outside, looking a bit troubled. She eyed Clytemnestra, still on Seth's other shoulder. Clytemnestra caught the look, and made the same dive. Together, the sisters squeezed into the door, and there the quartet resided for the night. All Seth needed to do was close the door, and return the carrier to the shed.

There are several ways to get what you want in life, Seth reflected. One is to hunt what you want through fear and duplicity. Another is to employ patience, tenacity and encouragement. On some occasions, though not often, your goal might simply come to you.

Seth needed help putting the chickens to bed when he was out reviewing a play, so he visited Gabriella, the single mom from Ecuador living in the apartment building to the east. Her son, Martin, had often visited the chickens, ever since they first perched on his head and shoulders months ago, when they were all a bit younger. Seth asked Gabriella if Martin wanted a job, or if she wanted him to have a job.

For two nights in succession, Gabriella and Martin watched how Seth got the chickens to safety at night. Seth offered Martin $20 to do the same, just as he showed him, on those nights when Seth's job called him away at sunset. Martin did a test run supervised by Gabriella. He performed it without problems. And so the flock became a community project, engaging people in three buildings, side by side.

Seth regarded as enchanted the moments at sunset every evening when he sat on the rusty folding chair and observed four chickens retire for the night.

Svetlana and Olga found large brown eggs daily throughout the property. Their garden was an Elysian Field.

THE FOLLOWING WEDNESDAY, AT 11:15 a.m., Seth was on the way to do his laundry in the machines behind the building. He saw that his vacant chicken coop had been torn down, violently. Smashed lumber and chicken wire were strewn on the ground and stuffed into the trash dumpsters against the building's east walls. The yard was now all open and dusty, like in the aftermath of a bomb. Seth called Winston, who told him that the Angelis duo did this in a fit of rage.

"It's tyranny," Winston complained. "What's the point of being HOA president if owners just do things like that to other people's property?"

"I don't know what the point is," Seth replied.

"They think your flock being next door is a personal insult against them," Winston added. "After all the help they say they gave you."

"What does my flock have to do with *them*? It's off the property!"

"They have to look at it, they say. And the city won't do anything about it."

"That's because it's legal."

"It's war. You know that, right? And her noises have started up again. And the pounding at 3 a.m. Suki is talking about leaving me if we don't move. It's personal now. It's war."

ON THE THIRD SUNDAY IN MAY, AT around 3:30 p.m., a black Buick sedan pulled into the driveway of the Craftsman house to the west. The car was driven by Rosalinda Juarez, the caregiver for 93-year-old Florence Baker, who sat in the passenger seat dressed in black cotton trousers and a cream blouse. Her thin hair was dyed brown. Her skin was alabaster. In a mauve polyester suit, Rosalinda opened the rear right door and removed a folded-up walker. She unfolded it, and stood it next to the front passenger door. Rosalinda helped ease Florence up so the latter could grip the walker. And together they ambled, and pushed, and rolled along the driveway toward the front door.

Buster barked and then fled after Chuck ordered him away.

Any number of sensations percolated in the mind and heart of Florence Baker during that walk toward the house she still called home. A swirl of memories from old Hollywood: Greta Garbo, Charlie Chaplin, Buster Keaton, Clark Gable, Joan Crawford, Mary Pickford, Hattie McDaniel, F. Scott Fitzgerald, Thomas Mann, Bertolt Brecht, people who, across a span of decades, had eaten dinner prepared by a chef and served by a staff of four in the dining room she was about to re-enter.

Chuck had built a swing for Anya that hung from the elephant ear tree in the front. It reminded Florence of a swing her own father, Horace, had built there for her. She suddenly recalled the view from the front window of her father making this same walk along this same driveway when he returned home from MGM Studios some eighty years earlier. Florence remembered swinging open that same front door, then shiny and hardy, and now so decayed with gashes, cracks and chipped paint. She remembered the cook, Marianne from Avignon, pulling boiled potatoes from a pot, sprinkling them with rosemary, and placing mint leaves around slices of lamb. Florence could still smell that dinner. Eighty years. Where does it go? Eighty years of friends and family, now all gone, of impressions and voices locked inside an eroding cerebral vault.

Florence spotted three chickens and a rooster poking around from behind the back garden, and she smiled. She liked that. She liked their colors. She liked their comedy.

Svetlana opened the front door and invited them into the dining room, where Chuck already was waiting. Rosalita helped ease Florence into one of the dining room chairs. Rosalita and Florence sat on one side of the table faced by Chuck and Svetlana who, looking deferential, sat on the other. Olga poured ice water for all of them before returning to a side room with Anya, whose cheerful babbling could be heard through the hallway.

"I received a phone call from a nervous man named Edward Angelis," Florence began. "Do you know this Edward Angelis? He says he's a neighbor of yours."

Chuck and Svetlana exchanged a quick glance.

"That man," Chuck began, "along with his mother, they spend their whole lives complaining about their neighbors. I don't understand how anybody has so much time to file complaints. They've complained to the city so much, the city has stopped responding to them. 'Malicious complainants': that's the term the city uses for them. One of their inspectors told me that himself."

There was a long pause as Florence considered Chuck's words.

"He said there are chickens here," Florence continued. "And that chickens are illegal in the city of Los Angeles."

"That's just not true," Svetlana interjected. "Chickens are legal in the city, they're legal here."

"The city told him just that," added Chuck. "That's why he's so upset."

"Yes, he is upset," Florence said. "He's threatening to sue me. But can we first establish some points of fact. Are you keeping chickens in the garden?"

Florence had seen them herself. She was testing them.

"We're . . . um . . . hosting them," Chuck replied.

"Hosting?"

"They're not ours. They belong to a neighbor," said Svetlana.

". . . who takes care of them," added Chuck.

"How many?" asked Florence.

"Four," said Svetlana.

"Four," Florence repeated. "And for how long do you plan on *hosting* them?"

She stressed the word *hosting* with pointed condescension.

"It's uhm, I dunno, people like them. The baby likes them. Many people like them. They're not doing any *harm!*" Chuck said, his temper starting to flare.

"Edward Angelis doesn't like them. He made that abundantly clear," Florence said dryly.

There was another long pause, as Florence considered the situation.

"I'm ninety-three years old," Florence continued. "I have no desire to defend a lawsuit over four chickens, no matter whom they belong to, or how little harm they're doing."

"He has no lawsuit. There's nothing illegal about them!" Chuck exclaimed a bit too sharply.

"Regardless of all that," Florence intoned, "I haven't the time or the will. One day you may understand what time actually means, what it means to use it productively, and what it means when it's almost extinguished. We have to choose what's worth the effort, and what isn't. There used to be chickens all over this neighborhood," she added. "It was commonplace then. It's exotic now. I understand. As the saying goes, I wasn't born yesterday. No matter. I like chickens, even living ones, but I must ask you to remove them."

"We're allowed to have pets. It's in our lease," Svetlana interjected.

"You're allowed two animals," Florence shot back wearily. "I already saw the dog. I already saw the cat. The four chickens would be just about four chickens over the limit. That's not even counting the parrot.

"But I do want to thank you for paying your rent more or less on time. And I do appreciate your upkeep of the house and the garden. You are good people. Hard-working people. I like you. Rosalita, we need to go."

Rosalita shot up from the table and helped ease Florence within grasp of the walker. They ambled out at much the same pace as they'd ambled in.

Chuck stood at the end of the driveway, watching the black Buick sedan back out toward Bronson Avenue, then down and out of the canyon.

Six days later, Seth was still scurrying to find a new home for his flock. He posted S.O.S. notices on Facebook, Twitter and even Craigslist.

Nothing.

In the afternoon, Clytemnestra was missing. He called out her name desperately. He scoured all corners of the property. Olga said she'd seen her mid-morning, sleeping. No squawking. No blood. Not a feather strewn. No evidence of a natural predator.

Early next morning, Seth saw flies buzzing around Clytemnestra's decapitated head lying in the tub of marigolds by his door.

ACT II:
THE FURIES

ACT II, SCENE 1: THE FURIES

Word of Clytemnestra's capture and slaughter spread swiftly through the block.

A white rage surged through Seth and wouldn't let go. He was so angry, he felt that his entire existence had become reduced to a long, hot tunnel of rage. Their act of ripping down the chicken coop was a mostly petty show of vigilante justice, compared to this "murder," this "gesture" that was just so needless, and needlessly cruel.

Seth also felt the need to do something quickly, but he also knew, from a long tradition of Greek and Shakespearean tragedies, that the biggest mistakes were always made in the heat of anger. He kept repeating that tired mantra: "Don't get mad, get even." But he couldn't begin to imagine how. Not yet.

His first act of defiance was to leave Clytemnestra's decapitated head in the marigold tub, at least for the time being, for maybe one day, a kind of open coffin for the morbid curiosity and strategic upset of neighbors.

That same morning, Seth proposed an emergency meeting of the Board. Though he no longer served on the Board, any Board member could have called a gathering on his behalf to get the matter aired.

JoJo was out of the question, since she and her son were the most likely suspects.

Vera told Seth that what happened was truly upsetting, but that it obviously was a personal matter and that she wasn't interested in dragging the Board into it.

This left Winston, who argued that because the crime was committed off the property, it wasn't really an HOA issue. Seth's annoyance with such bureaucratic fine points bubbled to the surface:

"Her head was found *on* the property!" Seth shot back. "This is a hate crime!"

Winston went online to look up the legal definition of *hate crime*, found little support for Seth's interpretation, and told him so. "I think *vendetta* is the word you were looking for."

What vexed Seth most was that all the initial expressions of shock, disgust and dismay by every neighbor with whom he spoke withered so quickly — by the end of the day — into their weary desire for all the acrimony to just go away. The easiest road to peace, they each finally suggested in their own ways, was simply to appease the Angelis duo by removing the chickens.

That wasn't going to happen. For Seth, the emotions were reaching beyond grief over the loss of a pet. They were tapping into a primal, ideological and impulsive defiance of bullies. They were tapping into a long-ago memory from a time when some sixth-grader slammed Seth's head onto a lunch table, telling him, "If you don't like it here, why don't you go back to where you come from." And this, for Seth's crime of voicing an opinion. Seth's words as a child, mimicking his elders by opposing the War in Vietnam, may not have been politic or polite, but they were legal. His flock in the garden next door had been declared by city authorities to be legal. And no amount of expedience for the sake of weary neighbors was going to make him stand down from what was not just an idiosyncratic, personal pleasure but also a legal entitlement. He recalled the words of Martin Luther King: "The arc of the moral universe is long, but it bends toward justice." And yet at the bottom of all this, at the heart of all this, was grief.

Seth brought up the Angelis duo's long history of harassing neighbors, of their pathological need for control. Seth cited British Prime Minister Neville Chamberlain trying to appease the Nazis. He dragged out the Soviets. But those arguments went nowhere. Seth finally concluded that everybody simply was scared of them.

"Both sides are very, very angry," Winston explained. "Both sides believe they've been wronged. The larger problem is that we don't know what really happened. Maybe Clytemnestra died, and they just found her. I know she can be difficult, but JoJo does belong to the Humane Society. She keeps talking about how much she loves animals. We don't really know what happened, or how the head found its way to your front door!" Winston's eyes welled with moisture as he spoke.

With this same surge of emotion, Winston proposed bringing Clytemnestra's head immediately into the LAPD's Hollywood Division for a forensics investigation. Winston said he'd even go with Seth.

"What we need is hard *evidence*," Winston kept saying.

Even in his state of apoplectic rage, Seth knew that this was a stupid idea. Both men leaned over the walkway railing outside Seth's front door. They gazed out onto Chuck and Svetlana's garden.

"The cops are going to be interested in solving a *crime*," Seth reasoned. "Do you honestly believe that they're going to see the death of a chicken, even if she was murdered, do you honestly believe they're going to see that as a *crime*? On any given day, there are about seven million chicken carcasses in frozen food bins across the country."

"Well, I don't know," Winston retorted. "This is completely different. She was your pet. She was your friend."

The setting sun now engulfed the two neighbors as they looked down on Agamemnon showing Helen a berry he'd unearthed, while Cassandra foraged on the other side of the garden. Buster lay on a dog bed on the lawn, watching the chickens with only vague interest.

"Besides, isn't forensics about evidence found at a crime scene?" Seth added.

Winston nodded sagely at this, and credited Seth for taking the larger view. Still, as HOA president, Winston felt compelled to do *something* for his tormented and aggrieved neighbor. It was Seth, after all, who had endorsed Winston for office.

"You know what we should do?" Winston said finally. "We should just ask them. We should just ask them if they did it. They'll either tell us the truth, or they won't."

Winston's posture suddenly straightened, and his face clenched into an expression of stoic determination, as though he were a Churchill instead of a Pendleton.

"Follow me," he commanded.

Together, Winston and Seth walked the seventeen steps to Apartment #2B, and rang the bell by Eddie Angelis' door. After a minute or so, Eddie opened the door, but not the screen. The men watched Jolene, in a purple bathrobe, scamper out of sight. Eddie squinted from behind the still-closed front screen.

"What?" Eddie snapped.

"Do you know anything about the chicken head found this morning in Seth's tub of marigolds?" Winston asked, swaggering.

"It's a crying shame," Eddie replied severely. "Pisses me off."

"You have any idea who might have done it?"

"I'll ask around," said Eddie. "Whoever it was, was probably trying to send a message." That's when he glared at Seth. "If you really care about your pets, move 'em to a safer place. Maybe inside your apartment," he sneered. Then, back to Winston: "Anything else?"

"No. As you were!" Winston said briskly, like an officer in some nineteenth-century British Army regiment, feeling slightly ridiculous as the words left his mouth.

Eddie's door slammed shut. The two men strode back toward Seth's apartment and said nothing. Seth now felt an unrelenting depression doing battle in his bloodstream with defiance.

At sundown, Santa Ana wind gusts rattled windows and sent palm fronds crashing to the streets below. Seth made photocopies of a cell phone snapshot of Clytemnestra's gory conclusion, as part of twenty-five posters he was planning to post on telephone poles and community mailboxes. Beneath the image of the severed chicken head came the words:

"$$$ reward for information leading to the conviction of our local pet killer."

Seth really wanted to get the word "murder" in there somehow, but he could find no precedent for the "M"-bomb applying to barnyard fowl.

He welcomed nightfall after such a harrowing day. Between 3 and 4 a.m., Suki slept in Winston's arms. Sam was out in Palm Desert visiting his wife, where they slept together on a king-size bed in a large stucco house nestled into the sandy bedrock. Sam's son Timothy was sleeping alone in their Bronson Canyon apartment next door to Seth's. Vera's tenant, Julia, also alone in her bedroom, snored softly in her cotton negligee. On the other side of Julia's bedroom wall lay Ruby Malholtra, who hadn't bothered to undress after arriving home drunk. Still in her blouse and miniskirt, Ruby was sleeping off a hangover next to a guy named Bill, a guy she'd just met. He'd bought her too many whiskey sours that night at a club called the Music Box on Hollywood Boulevard. JoJo had fallen asleep on her couch watching a Netflix copy of *Casablanca*. Even Eddie and Jolene were sleeping soundly, as were most of the residents of Bronson Canyon. But not Seth.

In the pale moonlight, Seth knelt at the base of the garden wall separating his apartment building from the Elysian Field next door. Seth knelt on his own side of the wall, gouging out a small trench in the soil with a garden trowel, beneath the ivy. Into that trench, about one foot deep, he placed a cardboard Diamond match box, the kind that slid open and shut. It was a box that once held wooden striking matches, but now contained the remains of Clytemnestra that somebody had placed in his tub of marigolds.

As he covered the box with earth, he whispered a line from a play familiar to him.

"There is special providence in the fall of a sparrow. If it be now, 'tis not to come; if it be not to come, it will be now; if it be not now, yet it will come — the readiness is all."

He gently placed two marigold blooms atop the ivy-shrouded grave, one yellow, one orange.

Kneeling by that tiny grave in the pre-dawn hours, and having whispered those lines — the first and only lines that popped into his head, because he hadn't actually prepared a funeral service — Seth wondered what the character who first spoke those lines would have done. What would Hamlet have done? And Seth recalled Hamlet's plight, his seething over the murder of his father, and his own relatives who had so offended him by their capacity to mask that crime in the interlocking arms of secrecy and authority. And suddenly, tears streamed down Seth's face, trickling onto the ivy and onto the marigold blooms that he'd placed there so carefully. At the same time, through this surge of emotion, Seth understood he was weeping not for Clytemnestra, and not even for himself: He was weeping for Hamlet.

The weeping and the comparison to a character in a play struck him as entirely nutty, even as he wept. After all, what's Hamlet to him, or he to Hamlet that he should weep for him? What would he do, had he the motive and the cue for passion that Seth had? "He would drown the stage with tears. And cleave the general ear with horrid speech. Make mad the guilty and appall the free. Confound the ignorant and amaze indeed the very faculty of ears and eyes," Seth recited to himself.

That's when Seth recalled so vividly the picture of Eddie through his screen door, sneering at him:

"If you really care about your pets, move 'em to a safer place. Maybe inside your apartment."

There was something Seth remembered about the way Eddie's lips twisted in sarcastic contempt when he said this, and Seth suddenly understood exactly what he needed to do.

He jumped the wall, opened the shed next door, and removed the sleeping Agamemnon, Helen and Cassandra to a secure cardboard box. They were so groggy, they could barely tell what was happening. Seth hoisted their large, now empty wire cage across the garden, back over the wall, and up the flight of stairs into his own apartment, lining it with fresh straw. He then retrieved the trio of birds and carried them all upstairs in his arms, a massive warm, groggy ball of feathers and beaks and claws, before re-depositing them inside the cage, inside his apartment, which was to be their new refuge.

Seth knew that this was neither a convenient nor sensible solution. The cage was so large that it consumed much of the living room. He would refer back to this period in his life as "The Occupation." Seth barely had room to move around. And yet the birds had space to stretch and walk and jump onto one low-lying perch within the cage, if they wanted. It was not ideal, but it was at least humane, Seth reasoned. But it also was an act of spite. Because when Eddie would complain to his Board-member mother JoJo, as he was bound to, that Seth was housing three large chickens in the tiny living room of an already small one-bedroom apartment, Seth was prepared to reply that he was merely following Eddie's advice. He would express his gratitude to Eddie for his suggestion. That would be his revenge. And he did. And it was.

"But I was joking!" Eddie roared back in fury the next morning, when Seth and Eddie stood next to the building's mailboxes.

Rather than canvassing the neighborhood for what, in a clearer state of mind, Seth determined was probably a local rather than a regional crime, Seth resolved to post only a single copy of his "pet killer" poster over the mailbox in his own building, and leave it at that. By day's end it had been torn down. The next day he taped up another copy, which was also ripped down that afternoon. And so it went for twenty-five days, until Seth had exhausted his supply of flyers, and the entire building was fed up with the controversy over Clytemnestra's demise.

Meanwhile, events unfolded largely as Seth predicted. The Board went into executive session following an emergency meeting called by JoJo. Seth had asked that the meeting be held on a Thursday. JoJo said that was inconvenient and pressed ahead for the next day, Friday, when Seth told them he was committed to be at the theater for his job.

And so time passed, as it does, with little regard for all the creatures in its snare.

"THE OCCUPATION" COMMENCED near the end of June, and the small, local theaters were mostly extending their spring hits, or suspending operations altogether during the summer's heat. Meanwhile, the mid-size and larger theaters were concentrating their efforts on the upcoming fall season. The most active theaters were taking their shows outside.

Theatricum Botanicum, for example, was an amphitheater founded by actor Will Geer —— the crusty, world-wise "Grandpa" on the popular, homey TV series *The Waltons*, based on a Virginia family during the Great Depression and World War II. The series ran on CBS from 1972 to 1981. Geer named it "Botanicum" because of his design that the property should have a sample of every plant mentioned in Shakespeare's plays.

The Geer family was a tribe of Lefties. Along with the likes of Pete Seeger and Paul Robeson, Will Geer had been called before the House Un-American Activities Committee for his "communist sympathies." Geer had himself played Mr. Mister, the villainous capitalist-overseer of "Steeltown" in New York's W.P.A. Theater Project production of Marc Blitzstein's 1938 opera, *The Cradle Will Rock*.

After Geer died, Theatricum Botanicum was run by his daughter, Ellen. The rustic, platform stage was carved into a thickly wooded hillside situated on a southern upslope of the Santa Monica Mountains. Within that bucolic setting, the theater staged Shakespeare, along with any number of plays and musicals that glorified Will Geer's pro-worker, pro-union legacy, while the rest of the world spun politically in precisely the opposite direction.

On the last Friday in June, a few days after "The Occupation," Seth sat on a soft cushion on bleachers next to his twelve-year-old niece Sarah, his sister's daughter, who was visiting from Houston. Moths buzzed around the stage lights, themselves dimly lit by a first-quarter moon. Seth had brought Sarah so she could see Theatricum Botanicum's own staging of *The Cradle Will Rock*, not because he believed the opera was particularly good, but because in its own way, it reincarnated the views of Will Geer and, more to the point, the views shared by Joe and Sheba Rapoport, relatives whom Seth thought Sarah should know about.

Seth had never actually seen the musical, and he was struck by its raw indignation at social injustice, its reductive determination to glorify the struggling workers and to demonize their oppressive bosses.

Spirited and robust, with fine acting, Theatricum Botanicum's *Cradle* wasn't a bad production, even if the opera was a simple-minded affair, Seth thought, checking on the lanky, shy Sarah sitting next to him during intermission.

Over the years, Seth had established a bond with her based on absurdist humor: In her presence, Seth transformed into a trinity of "uncles," each with his own distinct voice and dialect. They sort of emerged from him: "GET DOWN ... NOW," Uncle Cyrus barked at her in a gruff voice when she was sitting on the couch. At first Sarah was chastened by this, but after a few times she squealed with laughter and ignored him. Then there was Uncle Sid, a horrible character who, for her birthday, gave her a box of chewing gum from Starbucks and cautioned her to "make it last the whole year, it's expensive gum!" Worse, he'd call her periodically throughout the year, with an inquisition as to how many pieces of gum she'd chewed, and how many remained. Finally, Uncle Tex was a mild-mannered fellow from her hometown, Houston, who mediated disputes between Uncle Cyrus and Uncle Sid, and counseled Sarah in his gentle drawl to ignore both of her other uncles, "because they're crazy."

Seth and Sarah continued to sit side by side on the bleachers, as the audience milled around in the open air.

"Are you okay?"

She shrugged.

"Do you understand what this is about?"

She shrugged.

"Do you like the songs?"

She shrugged.

"Do you want some hot chocolate?"

She nodded.

Together, they ambled toward the concession stand. A few minutes later, Seth and Sarah stood a few steps away, near a picnic bench at which neither wanted to sit. They each clutched a cup of steaming chocolate and sipped, against the sounds of the orchestra warming up for Act II. Sarah set her chocolate on the table. Seth watched her fiddle with her cell phone for a few moments.

Perhaps one does need to be mugged before being able to take a stand against mugging, Seth pondered, still mulling over the pro-union musical that now seemed so naïve.

Seth then wondered what his Homeowners Association was plotting.

JOJO HAD PRESSED AHEAD WITH THE "emergency meeting" of neighbors, concerning Seth's behavior, on the one night, this night, that Seth told them he had a professional obligation. JoJo nonetheless refused to reschedule. There were five people present: JoJo, Eddie, Vera, Winston and Sam. According to Winston, the mother-son duo presented a litany of stories demonizing Seth as a rabble-rouser and threat to property values. Winston and Sam both said that Seth should really be present to defend himself before any vote was taken, since he was the subject of the dispute. They were both ignored, however, and the Board retired into executive session. With Winston dissenting, they passed a resolution on a vote of two to one banning all chickens from the property. This was the result of "popular consent," JoJo announced. Besides, she added, the outrage in the building was so intense, nothing Seth might have said could have altered the outcome.

Predictably, the vote, and JoJo's defense of it, further stoked Seth's rage. For any HOA to deny an accused member the right to defend themselves against "popular consent" was an argument against argumentation itself, against the power to persuade, against free speech, and against the English traditions of jurisprudence that the United States had embraced in its own Constitution. Seth also understood that JoJo's kangaroo court violated the State's *Davis-Stirling Act* governing voting procedures by HOAs, as well as the building's own Bylaws; both mandated that accused homeowners had the right to defend themselves in person.

Furthermore, this was now devolving into a civil liberties issue: It was one thing when his flock was in a common space shared by neighbors, it was quite another for the HOA to dictate what was and wasn't allowed within the privacy of his own home. Seth looked up the CC&Rs, and found the following assertion: "The Board is entirely disinterested in the private lives and activities of the owners."

Pets had been allowed inside the building for decades. Seth wasn't convinced that the Board could retroactively decide which pets were permitted and which weren't, unless there was some issue of public health or safety, which there wasn't.

Finally, Seth figured their resolution was unenforceable. Even with "popular consent," the Board had no keys and no right to enter any apartment without the owner's permission, meaning that nobody could prove the presence of chickens on any given day, nor could anyone therefore do anything about it.

So Seth kept his living room curtains drawn and established a policy of changing the birds' straw daily, neither denying nor confirming the existence of chickens inside his apartment whenever anybody asked, which wasn't often.

It was a ludicrous way to live. As the summer wore on, the

heat bore down so that his single wall-unit air conditioner only feebly kept the heat at bay. Before The Occupation, Seth would have swung open his front door to cool the place down with the night air, but for obvious reasons, this now wasn't possible. The chickens felt it, too. Agamemnon and Helen, working as a team, started to bully and peck sweet Cassandra. Seth found Cassandra spending hours cowering in one corner of the cage. Sometimes he would let Cassandra walk freely through the apartment. This set off temper tantrums by Agamemnon and Helen from within their cage. On the third Wednesday in August, Svetlana gave Seth the phone number of a veterinary technician named Susan Epps. Svetlana had met Susan at a local pet clinic when she took Buster in for a checkup. Svetlana had told Susan all about Seth's flock, and Susan said that she could house them. But Seth would need to bring some chicken food.

ACT II, SCENE 2: SUSAN

Susan lived in Fontana, some fifty miles east of Hollywood, where sharp gusts cut through eucalyptus windbreaks.

Fontana is one in a chain of dozens of small cities that extended through the San Bernardino Valley.

It was known for a while as the meth manufacturing capital of the world, before local laws tightened up, and that honor went south to Mexico.

Joan Didion once referred to these lowlands as "an alien place . . . not the soft Westerlies of the Pacific, but a harsher California, haunted by the Mojave just beyond the mountains . . ."

On clear days, the looming rocky peaks of those San Gabriel Mountains could be seen to the north — one of the region's three constants. The second was small earthquakes.

The third constant was the hot, dry Santa Ana winds blowing west, fast and furious from the desert. They knocked diesel trucks off the freeways. They toppled freight trains winding between L.A. and Chicago as they passed through the city.

The wind "comes down through the passes at 100 miles an hour and works on the nerves," wrote Didion.

For a thousand years, the indigenous Tongva Indian tribe bathed in saunas and fished from the San Gabriel River that poured out of those passes and snaked to the Pacific Ocean. They traded trout and beads with the Chumash and Serrano peoples, part of a network of tribes in a thousand-year civilization.

The nineteenth century brought Spanish rancheros and cattle and smallpox and syphilis and the demise of the natives. By the middle of the twentieth century, the Gringos' vineyards and orange groves blanketed the Valley.

At the height of its economic power, decades ago, the region's largest employer and economic engine was the Kaiser Steel plant. This was built during World War II to aid the war effort. The factory used to belch puffs of black smoke from its chimneys, even before the brown-grey smog now hovering over the region started to blow in from the west. The orange orchards were the first crop to yield to the post-World War II tracts of suburbs; next to go were the vineyards.

A common sight in Fontana in the 1990s was rows of tractors standing in a brittle, parched vineyard. They were parked near a brick wall — the outer barricade of the latest housing subdivision.

Fontana was and remains a commuter base for Los Angeles, a patchwork of aging mid-century suburbs, single-story wood-frame homes with small lawns in the front and pools in the back. Later came the gated, planned communities with names like Pacific Estates, Shady Oasis. These consisted of stucco, rust-toned Spanish-style manses, the echo of so many rancheros, but crammed together and patrolled by private security companies.

Piles of slag — gravel-like material that's the residue of the steel production — are still visible from Interstate 10, otherwise known as the Christopher Columbus Transcontinental Highway, that 2,460-mile stretch of asphalt that runs from the Pacific Ocean in Santa Monica to Florida. It cuts straight through Fontana, whose economy is now fueled by auto dealerships, cement works, junkyards, chain restaurants, the Kaiser hospital and, primarily, real estate — a boom-bust industry that has been driving the region's economy for some time now. Real estate is what unites family, and turns them against each other.

HOME.

Seth drove his Honda Civic slowly along Bishop Pine Way, a narrow, potholed road off Foothill Boulevard. North of the Carl's Jr. on the corner, grassy fields extended up the road. The fields were bordered by wire fences and eucalyptus windbreaks. Seth was looking for "479 North." There was an unprepossessing house sitting alone to the right. The "410 BPW" painted on a mailbox perched atop a leaning stake didn't match the address Seth was looking for. As he passed the house slowly, a lone pit bull chained to a pole in the front yard snapped at him. Seth rolled up his window to stop the rattle from the harsh wind whistling through in gusts. It was now silent in the car. Agamemnon and Helen slept in a dog carrier resting on the back seat.

Given their bullying of Cassandra, Seth left Clytemnestra's surviving sister at Bronson Canyon.

After crawling past another seven hundred yards of open fields on both sides of the road, "479" came into focus through blowing dust: numbers painted by the city of Fontana onto the left-side curb.

A chain-link fence blocked access to the long driveway, so Seth parked on the other side of the street, facing north. Looking ahead, to the end of the road, he saw in the distance the cement blocks of some kind of warehouse — or maybe a car dealership. Across the street, behind a slatted wooden fence, he noticed a large yard in the front of what must be Susan's property. The yard was a patchwork of short, thick grass and dirt. Susan's ramshackle, single-story wood-frame house stood precariously on the land. The roof sagged. Linen sheets and wool blankets blocked every window. Flies swarmed around a large black plastic trash bucket on the side of the house. The driveway was strewn with cat carriers, dozens of them, piled on top of each other. There was another house off one side of her property;

on the other side lay fields of stubby dried grass and gopher mounds. Gusts of hot wind sent up sprays of dust.

Susan was working in the shade of a towering eucalyptus tree. She was building a chicken-wire enclosure attached to stakes that she'd pounded into the hard dirt with a sledgehammer. She worked in sneakers, and jeans stained with the spillage of who-knows-what. Perspiration soaked the back of her yellow T-shirt, which boldly proclaimed in green on the front, "I [heart] Cats." Susan was slender with blonde-silver hair cropped at her shoulders. From her craggy face, Seth estimated that she was around sixty years old.

Noticing Seth approaching with the carrier, Susan stopped her work and opened the driveway fence.

"Almost done," she said, scraping the gate open with one hand, and wiping sweat off her lined forehead with the other. Seth still held the dog carrier containing the chickens.

"You built that all by yourself?"

"Uh huh. I'm used to it."

"You don't have your own chickens?"

"Oh, no. They got chickens down the street. They told me what to do."

"Listen, let me pay for the wood and the wire, at least."

"Okay."

Seth set down the carrier and opened the squeaking plastic door. Seth and Susan stared down. They waited. Slowly, Agamemnon emerged, shook himself off, looked around, cackled, and pecked at the dirt by his feet. Helen followed. Both birds appeared tentative, at times surprised. They'd never felt such gusts of wind before. Agamemnon arched up on his toes and flapped his wings hard, then shook more dust out of his feathers. He wandered over to a grassy knoll, discovering tender shoots growing where Susan had been hosing.

He clucked out his excitement to Helen, who raced over to join him. Two heads bobbed in and out of the grass, clucking.

"Oh, they're beauties!" Susan exclaimed.

Seth felt glad, and pained, and angry, and relieved — a mix of dissonant emotions deriving from so many circumstances beyond his control, circumstances that compelled him to farm out his new family. Though he was doing his best, he felt that his best would never be good enough. He went back to the car to haul out a fifty-pound bag of corn feed from the trunk. Beyond the upper end of the driveway stood a small walk-in metal shed, which Susan bought years ago, pre-constructed, from Home Depot. Susan opened the padlock and asked Seth to dump the sack on top of the sacks of goat food. She showed him behind the house to a large field where she keeps goats and sheep. On seeing them, the bleating animals raced over to her. She opened a fistful of carrots she'd taken from the shed and hand-fed an eager ewe. Snorting faces butted her arms as she fed them all, beaming with pride like a child, and exposing the gap where an upper right molar should have been.

SUSAN RETRIEVED A LARGE TIN BUCKET from the side of the house and placed it inside the almost-completed enclosure in the front. She dragged over a hose connected to the front of the house and filled the bucket with water. Seth placed the empty carrier inside the enclosure, under the shade of the eucalyptus, and helped Susan hang a gate onto hinges and string wire across the top of the pen, to protect the chickens from hawks and raccoons.

After another forty-five minutes, the pen was completed, with Agamemnon and Helen strutting around within, all under the shade of the eucalyptus tree. Their new coop would be their carrier and Susan pledged to bolt them safely inside the small but safe space at night.

Susan went into the house and re-emerged with two glasses of iced tea. The pair stood watching the chickens while Susan talked nonstop about the stream of woes that comprised her life. Seth noticed some striking similarities between Susan and JoJo. A driving impetus to both of their attitudes toward themselves and those around them was how they'd been wronged. Yet from the time Seth spent with Susan, he found no indication that she had any of JoJo's malice.

Nonetheless, Susan hadn't a kind word to say about any of her immediate relatives who, from her words, had dismissed her as a loon. Agamemnon looked at Seth with his familiar perplexed expression, while Susan rattled on about her father, who died twenty years ago.

Meanwhile the birds were confused. "What are we doing here?" Agamemnon seemed to plead with his one eye. "What have we done to deserve this?" Seth wanted to grab both birds and return them to Bronson Canyon, but thought better of it, listening instead to Susan's epic saga of her family, of her mother who lived in nearby Rialto and visited two or three times a year. She never went inside the house, Susan said. Even when it was raining, they'd stand under the protection of this same eucalyptus tree, drinking coffee or iced tea, while Susan's mother gave her daughter a stream of irritating, unsolicited advice.

Of Susan's six siblings, only one may or may not still live in California: "Melissa," who lives in her car — a 2003 Buick sedan. Two years prior, Melissa parked said car in Susan's driveway for twenty-three weeks and refused to leave. She ate Susan's food, used her bathroom, filed the location as her legal mailing address and otherwise sat and slept in her Buick, during the day reading newspapers and magazines she'd stolen from nearby Starbucks and motel lobbies. According to Susan, Melissa reported back to their mother and their brother, Dwayne, about Susan's "appalling living conditions," including a toilet that had stopped flushing.

According to Susan, Melissa had gloated when telling Susan that part. Susan, meanwhile, called the San Bernardino sheriff, who showed up within the hour, and told Melissa that if she wasn't gone by sundown, he'd cite her for trespassing. Looking out her living room window that evening, Susan watched Melissa back out of the driveway in her dust-coated sedan, overstuffed with sleeping bags and pots and pans, and roll away down potholed Bishop Pine Way into the sunset. And that was the last time Susan had seen or heard from Melissa.

Agamemnon and Helen were standing in a mud patch, dozing. Seth wished he could doze as well.

ANOTHER OF SUSAN'S SISTERS, IRIS, HAD a family law practice in Portland, Oregon, having just divorced her third husband. Susan also had siblings in Amarillo, Texas and Deming, New Mexico, doing something or other. Susan didn't specify. The only significant detail, and reason they emerged in conversation, was that Susan pleaded to each of them for help when she was in dire financial straits.

None had responded. This was another in a stream of illustrations of how Susan had been either abused or abandoned throughout her life.

In her early twenties, Susan served in the Navy as a medical technician, which is where she received her training to be a non-licensed veterinary technician.

"I rescue animals. I've always loved critters," she explained.

Seth walked inside the pen, waking Agamemnon and Helen from their slumber. He squatted and clucked to them, and they each clucked back.

Meanwhile, standing outside the wire mesh perimeter, Susan just kept talking: While in the Navy, she was raped by her immediate superior officer. When she filed a complaint, she received an honorable discharge, giving her access to VA hospitals. Yet when she went into hospital years later after a traffic accident had cracked a couple of her vertebrae, the hospital screwed up the procedure, leaving her upper torso painfully twisted.

This was not something Seth had noticed to this point, but now that she mentioned it, he did see that Susan walked oddly.

She was able to purchase the house six years ago through a special VA financing program. The feds handled the down payment and Susan was responsible only for the mortgage, which remained less than most of the current leases in Fontana for housing with similar square footage and acreage.

But now, she lamented, her brother Dwayne was trying to take the house from her.

"He's trying to make me homeless, like Melissa. I think they're working on this together," Susan sighed.

Seth pulled out two crisp $20 bills from his wallet and handed them to Susan. She took them and stared at them for a moment before tucking them in her front jeans pocket.

"Come out and visit anytime you want," Susan said.

Leaving the property, Seth felt like Lot's wife from the Bible, ordered by God not to look back or she might turn to stone. Agamemnon and Helen watched their foster parent leave with an air of determination and confidence. They figured he'd return soon. And he would, but not as soon as they imagined, if chickens imagine such things. They tried to follow him, but were prevented by the wire mesh. Their heads bobbed around and through the small openings in the mesh. Seth couldn't bear looking back. He rendered the appearance of knowing exactly what he was doing, and why. Neither were true.

The following week, around mid-afternoon on the first Saturday in September, Seth sat at his desk, reading the comments on his review of the Broadway spectacle, *War Horse*, on tour at the Ahmanson Theatre. Cassandra perched on his shoulder like a parrot, clucking, as he read.

"*War Horse* is the story of an English farm boy with a cruel, alcoholic father. The boy loves his horse. Yet for cash on demand, the father enlists said horse in the British Army to fight the Germans in World War I. Though underage, the boy sneaks his way into the Army to seek out his horse on the battlefields of France. There are many horses in the story, all portrayed as spectacular life-size puppets. Boy searches high and low for his horse. At last, the boy finds his horse, wounded and dying. They embrace. The puppets are terrific. The story is predictable, sentimental drivel."

It was the only negative review of *War Horse* nationwide.

"You are a bitter man," Seth now read in the comments section.

"Cynical," wrote another.

Cassandra perched on his shoulder, clucking while pecking lightly at his hair.

"Do *you* think I'm cynical and bitter?" he asked, rubbing the underside of her beak.

Seth heard a light tapping on his front door. He crossed over, looked through the peephole, and there stood Susan. He greeted her apprehensively, asking how she located him. He gave her his phone number but was certain he never gave her his home address.

"I got it from Svetlana. I just got off work at the clinic," she replied, standing on the outside of the door, now cracked open slightly.

"What's wrong? What are you doing here? Are the chickens okay?"

"Oh, they're fine."

Seth invited her in. Susan watched Cassandra, now strutting across the hardwood floor back into her cage. She jumped onto a perch and settled in for a nap.

Susan stood in the middle of the living room.

"You had me worried," Seth said.

"No, the birds are fine. They're both fine. This is the one you left behind? What's her name?"

"Cassandra. She's a bit lonesome. They're fine in the heat out there?"

"They're in the shade. They're fine."

"So I don't quite understand . . . Are the neighbors complaining? Is he crowing too loud? Too much?"

"No, no. They don't care. They got roosters down the street. I rescue animals. They know I rescue animals. You know I rescue animals?"

"I know, you told me. Well, thank you for taking them."

"You're welcome."

"I just don't quite understand. Is it food? You need money for chicken food?"

"No, no, I'm fine. Well, maybe. If you got any to spare."

Seth handed her a $20 bill. They both stood, awkwardly.

"Is that why you came?"

"Not really."

"Susan, what's going on?"

"Can I sit down?"

"Sure. Can I get you anything?"

Susan parked herself on the living room couch, staring at the closed curtains at every window.

"You got any ice water?"

"Sure, just a second."

"From the tap is fine."

"Sure."

Seth crossed into the kitchen as Susan looked around from the couch. He returned with a glass of ice water, which Susan drank with the fury of a parched Sahara wanderer. Seth sat in a wooden chair opposite the couch. They sat for about a minute in silence. Awkward silence.

Finally, Susan spoke softly, conspiratorially. "I think I'm being watched."

"You mean, like, watched by your brother?"

"Maybe. No. More like the government."

"What gives you that idea?"

"Cars parked out front all the time. Never there before. Went out and checked the plates, and they had that diamond on 'em. Doesn't that mean some kind of government?"

"Has anyone approached you?" Seth asked.

"No. They're just watching."

Another minute passed as they both sat in silence.

"Look," Seth finally said. "It's easy to get paranoid." He didn't know what else to say. Was she being watched? Who knows?

"It's like I can't even talk without being afraid that someone else is listening," she said. "Recording. I don't use the phone anymore. Email's out of the question, even texting. I mean, not to talk about nothin' personal."

Seth mulled this over for a few seconds.

"Susan, I think this all stems from your brother. I looked your place up on the public record. You really need to talk to a lawyer. Do you have a lawyer?"

"I talk to him all the time."

"You talk to your lawyer all the time? Does he know your name isn't on the grant deed?"

"Yes, that's 'cause my brother tried to buy it out from under me."

"He didn't just *try*, Susan. The property's in his name. He had it transferred to his name less than a month after you bought it. 'Intra-family transaction.'"

"I know that. But it was bullshit. I never signed nothing. He forged my name. And I'm the one who's paying the mortgage. And then you know what he did? He says he's the owner, right, so does he fix the toilet? No, he calls the Health Department to file a complaint against *me*, so it looks like I can't take care of things and I'm crazy."

"You have to fix that toilet, Susan."

"I know that. That's what my lawyer said."

"What does he say about your brother owning your property?"

"He says it's fraud. Totally illegal. He called in my brother to fix up all the paperwork, but my brother's in Las Vegas, after the bankruptcy, see, living with his girlfriend. I think she's a meth addict too."

"So now your brother's in Vegas?"

"I think so, yes. He's a very smooth operator."

"So let me get this straight. Your brother, who's the owner of record, stole your property out from under you, he goes bankrupt, leaves town, and you're left paying all the bills for a property you don't legally own?"

"And dealing with the Health Department."

"And what exactly has your lawyer done?"

"Nothing. I think we have a court date in eight months or something. I don't remember."

"You need a better lawyer."

"I can't afford to fix my toilet, you think I can afford a new lawyer?"

"Your brother wants your property, Susan."

"Not anymore. He already sold it. He's trying to make me homeless, like my sister, Melissa. He's working with the government. They're totally supporting him. They all want me out of here. I got a notice to be out by the end of the month."

"Your own brother served you with an eviction notice?"

"Before he left, he sold it to some real estate agent in San Gabriel. Nieves, something, I can't remember his name."

"Your brother is the owner of record."

"It probably wasn't recorded yet. That's what my lawyer told me. My brother sold it last week. It's not even his to sell, and the government approved the documents."

"Susan, that'll get overturned. This is total garbage!"

"Welcome to the neighborhood. Police on every block and no security. All I really care about is the animals."

"It'll get straightened out. As soon as all the evidence comes in. Sometimes it takes a while, but the gears of justice eventually . . ."

In the middle of that sentence, all three in the room — that would include Cassandra — turned their attention to the front door, where they heard a light knocking.

Cassandra let out a soft clucking alarm call, reflecting everyone's apprehension. Seth rose to look through the peephole. Through the distorted glass, he saw what looked like a rotund woman in her mid-fifties. Seth opened the door a crack.

"My sister here?" the woman asked. "Susan here?"

"Who are you?" Seth inquired.

"My name's Melissa. My sister here? Susan here?"

The woman who called herself Melissa then started wheezing and coughing in a fit that lasted about two minutes.

"That's my sister," Susan said. "You can let her in."

Seth opened the door and the large woman, dressed in black polyester slacks and a peasant blouse that bore no aesthetic relation to the trousers, crossed to the center of the room and stared at Susan. Seth fetched her a glass of ice water, which she gulped, much like Susan had earlier.

Susan looked up at her, defiant. "Why are you following me? You think I'm going to be intimidated by that? You think I'm gonna be running scared of someone who don't even have a roof over her head?!"

Melissa turned to Seth.

"You were in the middle of saying something about the gears of justice. The gears of justice, what? Grind us all down to a pulp?"

"Actually, I was about to say just the opposite."

"That bird must be awful lonesome," Melissa said, looking at Cassandra.

"What are you doing here?" Seth replied, bearing down on Melissa.

"Agamemnon!" Susan piped in enthusiastically before Melissa could answer Seth. "That big guy. He's like my guard rooster. She came back into my yard last week, and he *attacked* her!"

"He attacks *everyone*," Seth said, dryly.

"He don't attack *me*!" Susan shot back. "Used to walk around him with a big stick. Don't need it no more. He don't attack *me*!

"Then you're special," Seth said.

"Yes, I am." Susan replied.

All went quiet for a moment.

"The gears of justice," Melissa continued. "So I interrupted something hopeful?"

"Susan's having legal issues," Seth said.

"And you're offering her some assurance?" Melissa smirked.

"*Reassurance*," Seth replied.

"That's *twice* as good," Melissa quipped, "coming from a guy who says the sky is falling."

"I never said the sky is falling."

"Yes you did. In a review of *Death of a Salesman.* 'Even then, just like now, the sky was falling.' That's what you wrote. Or something like that."

"The sky *is* falling," Seth shot back, seriously pissed off at being quoted back to himself. "But that doesn't mean the gears of justice don't occasionally work the way they should."

"That's a sweet thing to say," Melissa cooed.

"It's what I believe," Seth replied with a twist of self-righteousness.

"That makes it even sweeter," Melissa replied, before turning to Susan. "You believe him?"

"He's kind," Susan said. "He loves his animals. It's not what people say, it's what they do."

"Do you believe people who love animals as much as he does, or you do — do you believe such people can also love people? Or do they love animals as a replacement?"

"I don't love people at all," Susan said, glaring back. "I don't even *like* 'em. I love my critters."

"You mean, like your cats. How many you got now?"

"About a dozen, why?"

"That's a lot!" Melissa said.

"I rescue them," Susan replied. "They come to me."

"That's very kind," Melissa said in a honeyed tone, which Seth took as sarcasm. Melissa then turned to Seth. "You seen her cats?" Melissa asked.

"No," Seth said.

"Her critters, that she loves so much?" Melissa added.

"No," Seth repeated.

"Why not?" Melissa asked. "You *should*. See for yourself how much she loves them critters."

"I didn't let him in," Susan answers. "My place is messy. If that's what you're driving at."

"Her toilet is broken," Melissa added. "So sometimes she pees in the field next to her house, or she goes to the Carl's Jr. on the corner to use their bathroom and sink."

"I think you need to leave," Susan said.

"Thanks for the water," Melissa told Seth, before adding, "Did you give her the money?"

"What money?" Seth asked.

"For the chicken food, or her groceries, or whatever it was she came here for?"

"You really *do* need to leave," Seth reiterated.

Had she been sitting, Melissa would have relished taking the time to heave herself up from the couch. But she'd been standing the entire time. So for dramatic effect, she initiated another spasm of wheezing and coughing, holding out her empty glass, which Seth took and refilled with water. She gulped down the water, returned the glass to Seth, and with as much dignity as she could muster, waddled toward the front door and waited. Seth opened it for her.

"I've been thrown out of better places than this," Melissa said, and walked out.

Seth closed the door behind her. All that could be heard for the next minute was the sound of Melissa clumping down the magnesite-coated stairwell, hacking her way out to the street.

Every second weekend, Seth drove out to Fontana to visit Agamemnon and Helen, and to bring more chicken food. Usually Susan was there, though sometimes she was working at the pet clinic, and

Susan said it was fine if he hopped the front wall to access the garden. Seth soon realized that the house next door to Susan wasn't exactly a house. More like a halfway house, or a mental clinic. Because when he was out with the birds, a man who seemed to have mild Down syndrome came to the garden wall and stared. On seeing him, Helen and Agamemnon strutted through the now open pen toward the wall, and stared back. This excited the man, who clutched the wall, rocking back and forth on the balls of his feet, and laughed in high-pitched, nasal squeals at the birds who, responding to his laughter, first emitted their alarm call, then calmed into clucking, and then into foraging in the dirt.

There were others, too, across the wall, men and women playing dominoes or checkers, or sitting in garden chairs with their upper bodies rocking to and fro. Sometimes they waved. Sometimes not.

The guy staring over the wall was named Dave, who told Susan what was going on. Dave told her when Seth jumped the wall to visit. Dave told her about the cars parked in front of her house. Dave told her when the drivers of those cars used a telescopic lens to photograph her barricaded windows.

On the third Saturday in October, Susan pulled into the driveway in her Chevy pickup truck while Seth was already there. He'd been bending down, talking to Helen, when Agamemnon blindsided him, attacking from behind and cutting his arm.

"What a booger!" Susan said, referring to Agamemnon. As angry as she often got, Susan never cursed. Seth waited on the front porch while Susan went inside for some antibiotic cream. When she re-emerged, in the brief time while the front door was open, Seth was overcome by the smell of cats. This was how he came to understand why her windows might be shuttered with sheets and blankets. Susan was a gentle nurse, dabbing Seth's cuts with antibiotic ointment.

The following Wednesday at 5 a.m., Susan was awakened by the faint sound of a helicopter circling somewhere. Agamemnon and Helen cowered in their pen, terrified. Susan jumped when she heard a pounding on her front door. She peeked through her front window to see four sheriff's squad cars, two trucks from the San Bernardino Department of Animal Control, a white car marked "Health Department," and a truck labeled "Building and Safety" all parked on the street by her front yard.

"Susan Epps!" a female sheriff shouted while pounding on the door. "Susan, this is the sheriff. We have a search warrant. You need to open your door *now!*"

Susan could see through the window eight people in tan-green uniforms waiting on her porch.

She could now hear the helicopter blades slicing the air directly overhead in a terrifying drumbeat.

Paralyzed by fear, Susan lay still in her nightgown, staring at the ceiling in silent dread. When she heard the front door crash open, she leaped up to throw on her jeans and shoes.

All she remembered, when she told Seth the story, was that she screamed and cursed as men and women poured into her home with cages and cameras, snapping flash photos and seizing every cat she had rescued, stuffing them in cages before hauling them out to the waiting trucks in a procession. They took her litter boxes and dumped them on the floor, she said, then they photographed the spilled sand and feces. Seventy-nine cats were seized from all the rooms in the house, squirming cats plucked from and under couches and stuffed chairs, cats that had been dumped in her yard, she said, cats recovering from ringworm and lice, cats lost in the recent fires, cats recovering from lung infections. She obtained the medicines from the clinic. She saved their lives. She found them homes, she said.

"I rescued them!" she screamed at one sneering sheriff who handcuffed and arrested her for "obstruction" and "endangering an officer of the law."

They took them all. Every last cat. But not the chickens or the goats or the sheep. Just the cats. Susan didn't see the trucks roll away with all the creatures that gave her life meaning, because she herself was taken in the back of a squad car to the holding pen of Fontana City Jail, where she was held for twenty-four hours.

In those same twenty-four hours, Agamemnon and Helen remained cooped in their carrier without food or water. They were perturbed that nobody fed them in the morning. They noticed and were annoyed, but they didn't dwell on it. Nobody fed the goats or the sheep, either.

The cats were all taken to the county animal shelter in a town called Devore, outside San Bernardino. After six months, three kittens had been adopted. All the others were euthanized or had died.

Susan tried to visit the cats but was forbidden: standard policy for animal hoarders.

The charge filed against Susan was administrative, not criminal. The clerk at Devore told her that she was not being charged with felony animal cruelty, which carries a possible three-year jail sentence and $20,000 fine. The charge was a far lesser misdemeanor, "failure to provide proper care for an animal," which carries no prison sentence, but instead the monitoring of her pets for the next five years.

This was not news to Susan. She'd read it in a notice sent to her a week after the raid, ordering her to attend a hearing three months later at the Fontana Superior Court.

Animal hoarding is a psychological condition that requires counseling, the hearing officer explained.

Susan was indignant. If the animals looked awful, as they did in those photographs presented as evidence, it was because they'd shown up at her house sick. Worse, they'd been wetted down by Animal Control so that they resembled drowning rats, she insisted. Susan was their healer.

The hearing officer explained that there wasn't sufficient space or food found on her premises to maintain that many cats in healthful conditions. And Susan was not a licensed veterinarian authorized to administer the kind of care she claimed they needed. Furthermore, the cats hadn't been separated by sex. There was even a litter of feral kittens found under the floorboards of a back room.

"So it's more humane to kill them than to save them?" Susan answered with petulant anguish.

After the case was closed, Susan remained convinced that she had been wronged, that she'd been spied on by Melissa and reported by her brother, Dwayne, who was trying to rack up legal points against her in order to hasten her eviction and his cash flow from her property.

Susan told Seth that she'd been called in for a deposition by her brother Dwayne's attorney. Seth looked up the case number. He discovered that Dwayne's attempted sale of 479 North Bishop Pine Way had been blocked by court order, and that a dispute over rightful ownership of the property was on the record in San Bernardino Superior Court as *Epps v. Epps,* scheduled for a non-jury trial on May 12.

In the meantime, Agamemnon and Helen intuited that something had changed — Agamemnon in particular, who took pride in being her protector. Susan spent less time with him, less time talking to him with her being constantly diverted by legal issues, so that a new wave of agitation started to grow within him. Chickens are nothing if not sensitive.

ACT II, SCENE 3: HELEN

t was the first Sunday in December when Susan had just about recovered from the stress of the raid on her property, if one can ever recover from such traumas. Susan was behind the house feeding her goats and sheep when Seth showed up and hopped the wall. Agamemnon greeted him, running over to the pen's wire fence and cackling excitedly, showing Seth what grubs and seeds lay within the pen. Helen refused to come out of the carrier. Seth stepped inside the pen to check if she might be ill. Helen puffed up her white feathers, mottled with black spots, so that she looked triple her size, huddled, and then she screeched out a warning.

Helen was always an odd bird. As a chick, she was more apprehensive than the trusting red sisters. She was also less affectionate and more jealous. When Seth was doting on one of the sisters, she would display her wrath with piercing cries. She wasn't as violent as Agamemnon, whose obnoxious behavior she emulated and learned from, but she was anything but docile. Where Agamemnon was incorrigible, Helen was feisty.

It occurred to Seth that Helen adored Agamemnon perhaps because he was so aggressive. She never had the inclination to bite people, or the other chickens, until she watched Agamemnon doing it. She studied him. She learned from him. He was a terrible influence on her.

As she grew older, when guests came to the apartment and met her, even in the garden, sometimes she'd peck them on the arm, just to let them know they had no right to be on her turf. If the meeting took place inside the apartment, especially after she started spending the nights there with Agamemnon, her aggression was magnified. Like the startling tag-team attack of Katerina and Irena, once the women had released the chickens from their carrier. Katerina still spoke of that night with a mix of bemusement and resentment.

Seth knelt down and extended his hand toward Helen's breast and she pecked his hand sharply. Still, he lifted her up by about six inches, while she complained, to see that she was sitting on a clutch of three eggs.

"I see," Seth told her, while Agamemnon watched, leery, from behind the carrier. "Do you not realize it's December?" he told her. "What's the matter with you? *Spring* is the season for hatching baby chicks. What do you think you're doing?"

Helen glared at him for a few seconds before clucking, and turning one of the eggs with her beak.

Susan and Seth then draped a clear plastic tarp over the top of the pen near the carrier, to protect both birds from an impending storm.

The oddities of Helen's excursion into motherhood didn't stop there. Normally, brooding hens leave their clutch of eggs for a few minutes to eat and drink, and then return before the eggs can cool. Both Susan and Seth witnessed behavior they didn't imagine possible: When Helen got up to eat, Agamemnon crawled inside the carrier and, ever so gently, settled down on top of the eggs. He sat there for hours, giving Helen a respite from the drudgery of incubating their clutch. This was a kind of teamwork completely uncharacteristic of chickens. Then again, Agamemnon was no sultan with an array of concubines at his disposal. He had little else to do.

On the drive back to Hollywood that day, a warm feeling of satisfaction radiated through Seth — that after all the contrivance of artificial incubation, a more natural cycle of nature was finally emerging. A hen, herself born in an incubator, possessed the instinct to hatch her own eggs, as nature intended. Her would-be chicks couldn't be in better, safer circumstances to arrive into this world in about three weeks, as nature intended.

When sitting in the theater watching a Eugene O'Neill play, or an experimental project in which he and the audience traveled from room to room in a former warehouse, watching actors perform within the ever-shifting enclosure of patrons, Seth was filled with the diverting comfort of having seen Helen, her feathers puffed pillow-like, turning an egg with her beak, and clucking with indescribable satisfaction.

Three weeks later in Bronson Canyon, Seth received a phone call from Susan, who told him that one large black chick with gold spots had just hatched. Helen was protecting her baby ferociously, Susan reported, while Agamemnon was guarding them both, either by standing beside the carrier or snuggling within, next to Helen, while a hard rain poured down around them.

Seth drove out there the following Saturday to watch the parents dote on the one chick, the only chick that hatched. Seth noted its long black beak, resembling that of Agamemnon when Seth eased him from his shell. The newborn had similar markings as his father once had, and large feet for an infant, just as Agamemnon had. Seth determined that the hatchling was male and he wanted to name it A.J., as in Agamemnon Junior. Then it occurred to him that if Agamemnon had been named after a Greek warrior, why not do the same for A.J.? And so A.J. became Ajax.

True, Ajax of Greek mythology competed for the affections of Helen of Troy with other warriors. This might impose an Oedipal curse on the flock. Seth explained this to Susan, who said matter-of-factly that she felt that the chickens could rise above that. Though she worded it differently: "I don't think they'll care much, and nor do I."

Susan had filled their water bucket with stones, so there was no point deep enough to allow the chick to drown. Susan told Seth she'd seen Helen teaching the baby how to drink, which Ajax doubtless would have eventually figured out on his own. Still, formal education speeds things along.

As Ajax sprouted black feathers, he learned from his parents how to forage for insects and sprouts. Both parents would cackle excitedly upon discovering any item of interest, and Ajax would race over to see what the fuss was all about.

Two weeks later, Ajax was now half feathered out and spent ever more time outside, away from the warmth of his mother. Seth felt like a bit of a weekend father, visiting the fostered flock and learning not much more about Susan. She didn't talk about Melissa, which seemed odd, given Melissa's random appearance at his apartment. Susan really did love animals, and he was thankful she took his birds under her eccentric but capable wing. It was an odd arrangement, but it was working, and Seth watched contentedly as Susan let the gang of three out of their pen to wander in the open field next to her house. Seth changed the water, making it a point to be active in their care during his visits.

During one such visit, he heard a screech in the sky and didn't think much about it. Agamemnon, however, let out an alarm call — "b-CAW-buk-buk-buk" — in a panic. Seth looked up and saw Helen bolt, half-running, half-flying into the field. That's when Seth saw a hawk diving for Ajax, who was unprotected in the field. Helen was racing to protect her small chick from being scooped up and away. Seth felt his stomach drop when he realized that this was a suicide mission. Helen was putting herself directly in the line of a hawk attack. Agamemnon followed, shouting out his warnings throughout his plodding gait. She was much quicker than he. Beating the hawk to Ajax by mere seconds, Helen dove on top of her chick, puffed herself to three times her normal size, and screeched as menacingly as she could. The hawk plunged on top of Helen, and all Seth could see in the grasses was a flurry of feathers through the battle of screeching. By now, Susan, drawn outside by the bird-sirens, raced from her front porch toward the battle scene, while Seth did the same.

From their respective distances, Seth and Susan each watched the hawk slowly take flight, screeching. Meanwhile, Agamemnon stood in the field, still shouting.

Seth was the first to catch up with Helen, who sat bleeding and trembling, still puffed out. Seth talked to her as gently as he could. He stroked her feathers and checked beneath her, where Ajax lay frozen. By now Susan had joined them. Seth picked up Helen while Susan took Ajax back to the house, where she administered anti-biotic cream to cuts on Helen's shoulders and back. Ajax had no wounds.

It took about a week for Helen's cuts to heal, during which Seth pleaded with Susan not to let either of them out in the field without monitoring. Susan, too, was rattled by the incident, assuring Seth that she'd no longer allow them outside of their pen unless she was watching them. Seth took her at her word but still suffered from anxiety about the safety of his flock.

And several weeks passed, without further incident, until, in poultry terms, Ajax came of age.

IN FEBRUARY, WHEN AJAX WAS TWO months old, he was fully feathered out, yet still trying to snuggle under the warmth of his mother. Helen pushed him away, which shocked him. Ajax tried again to crawl under her wing and she pecked him sharply. Ajax couldn't understand or believe what was happening. He went to Agamemnon, who let him stay close. When Agamemnon sat, Ajax settled directly next to him. They pecked at the same patches of mud, side by side.

Helen was through with motherhood. Her decision arrived one day, quite suddenly, and was irreversible. Slowly, Agamemnon figured this out. He watched her scold Ajax and peck at him. Ajax simply annoyed her. In their youth, Agamemnon had taught Helen about aggression. Now, in parenthood, the lesson was reversed. After a week or so, just like Helen, Agamemnon pecked Ajax out of his way, screeched at him, telling him to keep his distance.

Eventually, neither would allow him inside the carrier. Young Ajax was banished from the house, forced to sleep outside. That they had once almost lost him to a hawk had no bearing on the natural evolution of forcing a chick to step outside the family nest and make his own path. Where weeks earlier Helen would have died for Ajax, now she all but ignored him.

THIS RITE OF PASSAGE STRUCK SETH as brutal, and dangerous for the banished chick. Seth bought Ajax his own small carrier to protect him from nocturnal predators. Ajax now slept alone. He was no longer of the flock. In Greek mythology, the severest punishment, worse than death, is exile.

Susan allowed Ajax to wander outside the pen, within the confines of the front yard, and Ajax seemed to enjoy this, having turf of his own where he wouldn't be bullied or harassed for the crime of being.

By May, it became clearer that Seth had misdiagnosed Ajax's sex. Though the bird had picked up Agamemnon's genes for growing so large, there were no hackle feathers, no arching tail, and a shape more rotund than statuesque. Seth's suspicion was verified on the third Tuesday in June, when Susan discovered a small brown egg tucked onto a patch of dry grass in the front yard where Ajax had been wandering, and Helen hadn't. Ajax, it seems, was an uncharacteristically large black hen — even larger than she might have been had she not shown an obsessive interest in a large Styrofoam ice chest at the top of the driveway.

Neither Susan nor Seth were concerned by Ajax's interest in the ice chest, even though Ajax would frequently strut over to it and relish the soft texture, pecking at it voraciously. Eventually Susan noticed that Ajax had stopped laying eggs and was markedly thinner and lethargic. Neither she nor Seth understood why. After a week of Ajax not eating, Susan saw her vomit clear grey liquid and then lose consciousness. It was a Friday afternoon when Susan rushed Ajax to Dr. Varac, a veterinarian bird specialist she knew of in Santa Monica. Seth joined them there.

Dr. Varac said that her crop — the sac directly under her throat that stores food before it passes into the stomach — was blocked with Styrofoam; she had been starving for some time. Ajax was being given oxygen in the hospital area when Dr. Varac was explaining all this to them in a private examination room. A vet tech rushed in to say that Ajax was having seizures. The doctor ran into the back, returning within ten minutes to say that Ajax was gone.

Seth stood at the cashier's desk, numb, tapping his hands on the vinyl barrier between him and the cashier in white, who rifled through paperwork looking dour. She then told Seth there would be no charge. Seth nodded, and thanked her in a blank tone, though he felt almost nothing in that moment, and during the long drive home.

Yet another drama unfolded within two weeks of Ajax's death, though Seth had to rely on Susan's word that it was true. Susan's lawsuit against her brother resulted in a May court decision to block her brother's attempted sale of the property until ownership issues were sorted out. This unleashed what Susan described as her brother Dwayne's "spiteful streak."

A pickup truck rolled into a driveway up the street. Somebody had released a trio of Rottweilers into the vacant field directly beside Susan's property — the same field where Helen had performed her heroic rescue of young Ajax. The dogs easily scaled the fence enclosing Susan's sheep and goat herds. They killed and ate two goat kids and broke the back of a ram, leaving the beast bloodied and splayed behind the house. Seth could never get a clear answer from Susan whether or not Dwayne was actually driving the pickup truck, or whether the driver was hired for this seeming task of intimidation. Susan was certain that the act was a warning of more to come, unless she dropped the lawsuit about saving her home.

At this point, Seth started wondering if Agamemnon and Helen might be better off someplace else. It wasn't Susan's fault that Ajax had eaten lethal doses of Styrofoam; then again, Seth also saw Ajax gorging on the icebox, and it never occurred to either of them that the Styrofoam was so dangerous. So if Susan was guilty of negligence, so was he. If this was negligence, it certainly wasn't willful.

Still, Susan's domicile did seem to be cursed. Seth sent out a few inquiry emails to people who might be willing to provide sanctuary to a half-blind, violent rooster and his mate. The results were not encouraging.

Meanwhile, relations between Agamemnon and Helen grew increasingly and inexplicably abusive. Agamemnon started to peck at Helen. At first, Seth figured that Agamemnon blamed Helen for shunning Ajax, and for Ajax's consequent death, but then Seth concluded that such anthropomorphism was ridiculous. Still, Helen initially seemed to accept the punishment, as though she realized she was guilty of something. The pecking became so severe that, according to

Susan (the vet tech and self-professed authority on animal medicine), it caused some nerve damage on Helen's left side, so that Helen started to walk with a limp and sagging wing. After removing the lethal Styrofoam ice chest, Susan allowed Helen the recovery and refuge of the shed and the front yard, separated from Agamemnon by the pen's wire.

Though the birds were separated for Helen's protection, they would spend entire afternoons napping, snuggled up to each other on opposite sides of the chicken wire, like an abused wife visiting her husband in jail.

Seth worried about Helen being alone in the garden and with access to the adjoining field, and of all its dangers. He told Susan this, and together they rigged a wire mesh across the fence separating the garden from the field, creating a barrier.

On the first Saturday in June, Seth showed up to deliver food for Agamemnon and Helen and was startled to see three massive Rottweilers in the field, just as Susan had described earlier. Worse, Helen must have been able to fly over the "barrier" because there she was, in the field's distant tall, dry grasses. In a panic, Seth shouted for Susan but she was nowhere to be found. Agamemnon was shrieking an alarm call from within his locked pen. Seth ran as fast as he could through that field, chasing one of the dogs who was bolting after Helen with a furious pace in the very field where she'd saved Ajax. This time, the life she was desperate to save was her own. Though he'd never run faster, Seth still was no match for the dog's bounding ferocity. A sharp wind sliced into him as he saw nothing but the black bullet of the Rottweiler's torso rising and falling through the grasses. The dog stopped, huddled for about a minute while the others joined him. When Seth finally reached them, shouting angrily and waving his arms aggressively, they scattered —— not in response to Seth's invectives, but in answer to the call of a bullish man in striped overalls, shouting at them from a pickup truck in the driveway. Seth desperately searched the scene of the assault to find nothing but a small pile of black and white feathers swirling in gusts of wind. Not a bone, not a remnant. As though Helen had never existed.

The truck with three dogs drove down Bishop Pine Way toward Foothill Boulevard.

Seth stood there for a moment, stunned by the abruptness and the violence of Helen's demise. He glanced over to Agamemnon, who was locked inside his pen and shrieked out all the anguish that Seth was silently thinking and feeling. Man and bird now shared their closest empathetic bond. Agamemnon arched up onto his toes, flapped his wings, and crowed and crowed and crowed out cries of agony barely discernible through the wind. Seth cautiously met him inside the pen, but Agamemnon wouldn't stop crowing. His voice grew reedier, but he just kept crowing. After half an hour, there was no sound at all, just the sight of the one-eyed warrior reaching up to the sky on the tips of his toes, screaming the silent despair of all he'd done and seen in his life.

ACT II, SCENE 4: CASSANDRA

Cassandra perched contentedly on the wall of a child's playpen. The playpen replaced the large wire dog carrier that used to house the three birds during "The Occupation" — largely because Seth found the straw so much easier to swap out in a roofless pen.

The four-by-six-feet playpen folded out to an area of twenty-four square feet. Its walls were made of soft-coated mesh and nylon, rising to a height just shy of four feet. The playpen had no roof *per se*, though when he needed to ensure confinement Seth placed a wire mesh screen across the top. But this hadn't been necessary for some time, as Cassandra spent most of her time perched on the top of any of the walls. Seth situated the pen near his work desk and chair so that Cassandra could leap, as she wished, from the pen to Seth's shoulder and back again. Upon returning from obligations away from the apartment for any length of time, Seth found no evidence that Cassandra had strayed from her pen, even without the roof to keep her contained. When he was home, she wandered more, but Seth didn't mind since he was there to quickly clean up whatever messes she might leave on the hardwood floor.

Unlike Agamemnon and Helen, Cassandra was a model pet: inquisitive, personable, and talkative without being noisy. Her most agreeable trait, however, was an affection uncorrupted by any trace of aggression. She trilled softly at night as an expression of her happiness. She balanced herself like a parrot on Seth's shoulders when he walked around the apartment. Sometimes, while he sat working, she would fall asleep on his shoulder and he could feel the heat of her drooping head pressing into his cheek.

After Seth evacuated Agamemnon and Helen to Fontana, he resolved that continuing to live in a state of siege because of a single, docile hen like Cassandra was foolish, and probably unnecessary. Seth began opening his living room curtains once more during the day, letting in the afternoon sunlight. Sometimes he kept his main front door open, allowing the air through the screen door to cool the apartment during the evenings. And Seth chose to no longer hide Cassandra in a back room. In fact, he chose not to hide her at all, because he determined that she was a harmless pet with the same rights of habitation as any of the dogs or cats who dwelled in neighboring apartments.

Cassandra, for instance, ran to greet any human who entered the apartment, and she wouldn't stop clucking until she was properly acknowledged by being fed a grape or a leaf of spinach. She particularly relished treats of blueberries and spinach leaves, as a supplement to her staple of corn mash. In fact, Cassandra learned to leap for blueberries, sometimes to heights of four feet, launching herself from the hardwood floor. A fistful of spinach thrown onto the straw of her pen would keep her entertained with foraging for about fifteen minutes at a time. Her constant delivery of four to five fresh brown eggs per week was shared with neighbors.

Seth's prevailing thought during this period was that, having committed no crime, he would not live in a tomb. He remembered Hamlet once again, this time taunting Rosencrantz and Guildenstern about the qualities of life as a prison.

"Denmark's a prison," Hamlet says.

"Then is the world one," Rosencrantz replies.

"A goodly one," says Hamlet, "in which there are many confines, wards, and dungeons, Denmark being one o' th' worst."

Answers Rosencrantz, "We think not so, my lord."

"Why then 'tis none to you," retorts Hamlet, "for there is nothing either good or bad, but thinking makes it so. To me it is a prison."

Nothing good or bad, but thinking makes it so. In short, Seth effectively brought Cassandra out of the closet, knowing that his decision likely would have consequences. This was among the reasons he eventually took Cassandra to Dr. Varac for a checkup. The chicken underwent a full physical examination, squawking with apprehension at being prodded and poked in her nether regions, and having a man with rubber gloves stare down her gullet with a penlight. An X-ray revealed a very small metal object lodged in her intestine, probably a key of some kind, Dr. Varac said. Still, she was in perfect health.

Seth told the doctor about the neighbor dispute in the building, and requested some written confirmation from the licensed veterinarian that Cassandra was harmless. Dr. Varac wrote the following letter on animal hospital stationery:

> "Dear Sir or Madam:
> I have inspected the chicken (Cassandra) and she appears to be clean and healthy. There is no evidence that maintaining a chicken inside an apartment, if maintained with the kind of sanitation that would be appropriate for a domestic cat, poses a health threat to the owner or the neighbors in adjoining apartments.
> Sincerely,
> Earl J. Varac DMV, ABVP"

One day, at the request of his colleagues, Seth brought Cassandra to the offices of the *L.A. Observer.*

Seth observed as Cassandra led a posse of seven adults, creeping stealthily behind her, down the carpeted hall of the paper's art department. The art director, a burly black man with a serious, imperious demeanor, was in his office, on the phone and clearly annoyed by a conversation he was having with a photographer. Intently, and to avoid distraction, his focus was away from the door of his office toward a wall, so initially he didn't see Cassandra standing on the threshold of his office. He did, however, hear a clucking that he couldn't make sense of. Finally he saw Cassandra, who was now strutting across his office toward his desk. And that's when he realized there were seven people partially hidden behind his door, trying to silence their snortling amusement at the prospect of a chicken wandering into his office. He tried to maintain his tone of annoyance at the photographer on the other end of his phone line, but on seeing Cassandra, his body started to convulse with silent laughter.

"I'm sorry, I'm sorry," he said into his phone. "I didn't hear the last thing you said. A chicken just walked into my office. No, really. A chicken. A large brown chicken. She's staring at me now. She's pecking at my shoes."

Stardom is largely propelled by being in the right place at the right time, and Cassandra's debut was not very different. On observing first-hand Cassandra's personable disposition, the art director thought she might be the perfect model to accompany a story that Seth was writing for the newspaper.

The article was on Australian performer Burt Coolridge, now living in L.A., who hosted his own weekly Internet pet show called *Bein' With Burt*. For the story, Cassandra posed with Coolridge for a photographer. Cassandra spent all day in and around Coolridge's Mid-Wilshire apartment for the shoot. She posed on his desk, she posed on his shoulder. By day's end, Cassandra perched precariously but calmly on Coolridge's head, atop a cap he was wearing. All of the photos appeared both in the newspaper and on the Web.

In April, Cassandra had a cameo at the annual L.A. Observer Theater Awards, which Seth produced as part of his job at the paper. All day, during rehearsals for the evening event at the swank Avalon Nightclub on Vine Street, Cassandra mostly perched backstage on a wall of her playpen. Occasionally she leapt out, crossing the stage during a dance rehearsal and creating some amusement and distraction.

Seth wrote to the artistic director of Center Theatre Group, the organization that oversees the city's three most established and prestigious theaters: the Mark Taper Forum, the Ahmanson and the Kirk Douglas theaters. Seth asked him to present a speech during the theater awards on the state of the arts in America. The only condition, Seth explained, would be the presence of a medium-sized Rhode Island Red hen perched on his shoulder during the address. The key, Seth explained, was that the speech must be serious, and must make no reference to the chicken. It was to be a twenty-first-century Dada moment.

The artistic director was a good sport. He showed up meticulously clad in a Bottega suit. Shortly before the director's address, Seth found him backstage rehearsing his speech. The theater maven was an urbanite who'd never been around a chicken before. Because he wasn't wearing glasses that night, Seth thought it would be safer to park Cassandra on the director's wrist rather than his shoulder, in order to keep her beak as far away as possible from the director's face. (Cassandra sometimes found the sight of gleaming white teeth irresistible.) While the artistic director held his arm extended, Seth gently placed Cassandra near his hand, where she settled in comfortably.

It came to pass that a hush fell over the slightly inebriated crowd of eight hundred, when the artistic director of Center Theatre Group made his appearance on the stage, at a podium, with a rust-colored chicken perched on his left wrist. While he spoke, Cassandra appeared calm. She bobbed her head occasionally, responding to flashing cameras. For a while she watched as her host spoke, as though she was as deeply concerned over the plight of the arts in America as he, and everybody else in the room, which included the director of the city's Department of Cultural Affairs, the president of the City Council, and the chairman of the county Board of Supervisors. About three minutes into the speech, Cassandra folded her head into her neck, closed her eyes and took a small nap.

STARDOM IS BOTH FLEETING AND irrelevant to any star's detractors. The following week, Winston Pendleton approached Seth with news that the Angelis duo were continuing to complain about Cassandra and the health threat she posed to the building. Seth showed Winston Dr. Varac's letter, which Winston said he would file, but there also was their complaint about the potted plants outside Seth's front door.

Seth explained that the plants had been there for seven years, that he had modified the tubs to a smaller size, addressing and satisfying next-door owner Vera's concerns, hitherto the only concerns he'd heard from anyone in seven years. So why was this now an issue? Seth wondered.

Winston showed Seth the following letter, sent to Winston in his capacity as HOA president:

"Bloomberry and Hendricks LLP, Attorneys at Law, 524 South Figueroa Street, Nineteenth Floor, Los Angeles, CA 90071, Re: Eddie Angelis Maintenance of HOA Rules, Our File No.: 384686.

"Dear Mr. Pendleton:

"This letter is notice that Mr. Edward Angelis has consulted with this law firm regarding the housing of a chicken within a unit of the Bronson Canyon Homeowners Association ("Association"). This unit is owned by a Mr. Jacobson. Mr. Angelis is also concerned about Mr. Jacobson obstructing the common area walkways.

"With respect to the housing of birds, Mr. Jacobson was originally granted permission, by vote of the Association membership, to construct an aviary in the common area. This license was later revoked due to violations by Mr. Jacobson of the conditions for maintaining the aviary. When the aviary was removed, Mr. Jacobson subsequently housed a chicken in his condominium unit. The Bronson Canyon Homeowners Association has been informed of this situation and a demand for the Association to insist on removal of said chicken has been forwarded. However to date, no action has been taken to rectify this problem.

"The Bronson Canyon Homeowners Association is advised that the housing of the chicken in question is in violation of the governing documents of the Association. Specifically, housing a chicken in a condominium unit is a violation of the city code of the Department of Animal Services and is thus an affront to the Association's mandates. These mandates prohibit the violation of city codes. Further, this situation is conduct that materially affects the quiet enjoyment of Mr. Angelis' property.

"With respect to the blockage of the common area walkways, this behavior on the part of Mr. Jacobson is clearly a potential increase to the Association's liability for possible bodily injury and could result in a higher insurance premium. Such actions are specifically prohibited by the Association's Rules and Regulations.

"In light of the above circumstances, Mr. Angelis is insisting that the Association honor its fiduciary duty to him under the *Davis-Stirling Act* to enforce the governing provisions of the Association to avoid the necessity of litigation.

"Mr. Angelis has been advised of his legal rights and remedies if this matter cannot be resolved in a non-litigious manner.

"Your written response to this demand, directed to Mr. Angelis, is expected within seven (7) days of receipt of this correspondence.

"Yours very truly,

"Bloomberry & Hendricks LLP,

"By Isaac B. Shettleford."

Seth read the letter standing on the walkway in the noonday sun. He then smiled.

"So you're not supposed to respond to the lawyer, but directly to Angelis?" Seth noted.

"Yeah. That's what it says," Winston replied, before adding, "Can we step inside?"

Winston was right. The building's acoustics were unusual. Out on the walkway, for instance, sound was amplified and the quietest of conversations echoed through the building.

The two men stepped into Seth's apartment, into the comparative cool and dark. Winston sat down on the couch. Cassandra leapt off the playpen wall to greet him, while Seth found some grapes in the refrigerator. He lobbed them across the living room to Winston, who tossed them, one by one, onto the hardwood floor. With maniacal interest, Cassandra hunted down the grapes and gobbled them up.

"So their lawyer doesn't actually want to deal with this crap himself, not if he's telling you to respond directly to Angelis," Seth said.

"That's what it looks like," Winston replied.

"There's been nothing from the city ordering me to remove Cassandra," Seth continued. "And you know they've reported her. If she were violating city code, wouldn't the city have said something?"

Winston just shrugged. "I checked with the insurance company. JoJo filed a claim that she had tripped and fallen on the pavement downstairs because she said it was wet and slippery after you watered your plants."

"I never heard anything about that," Seth replied.

"Probably because it didn't actually happen. The insurance company wanted a medical report and nobody could provide one, so their claim was denied. The insurance company knows all about your planters. They've known about them for years. Our broker says there's no liability issue from their point of view, and they don't want to get involved in a neighbor dispute."

"Okay . . . So what are you going to do?"

"So here's what I'm proposing," Winston said gravely. "In the larger interest of peace in the building . . ."

"That'll never happen," Seth interjected.

"You need to let me finish," Winston continued. "You need to take this seriously. You need to take me seriously."

With these words, and with Winston's uncharacteristically firm tone, Seth didn't quite know what to expect. He sat on the wooden chair by his work desk. Cassandra, now sated by half a dozen grapes, leapt up to a wall of her playpen, relieved herself on the straw below and then launched herself onto Seth's shoulder, where she settled in for a nap.

"I'd like to propose a negotiated truce," Winston intoned. "If each side gives up *something*, then nobody is left feeling defeated. If nobody feels defeated, we have a chance of restoring relations to what they were before . . ."

"Before what? . . . Before the chickens?"

"Just before."

"The chickens aren't to blame."

After a silence, Cassandra pecked Seth lightly on the ear. He reactively brushed her off his shoulder. She floated down to the floor, looking up at Seth perturbed. She then leapt from the floor up to the nearest wall of the playpen, sending up a light breeze.

"It would be helpful," Winston continued, "if you could simply move your plants downstairs to the garden wall, clear the walkway, and in return, they'll stop harassing you and me about Cassandra. They'll leave you, me and her alone."

"They said that?"

"They promised me," Winston said.

"The same people who threaten the owner next door, Florence, an old woman, the same people who threaten her with a lawsuit over what they know is perfectly legal? The same people who file false claims with our insurance company?"

"We don't know it was false. We only know they couldn't prove it was true."

"You believe them?!"

"I believe this might work!"

"And what exactly are they giving up?" Seth asked. "You said that each side needs to give up something. What are they giving up? I'm giving up my porch tub garden. They have no claim on my garden. They have no case for liability. But if I agree to give up my garden, which I've enjoyed for years, they agree to stop bullying me to give up my pet, which the city has raised no objection to. And what exactly am I getting out of this marvelous deal?"

Seth's voice and fury were now rising. "Winston, it's like me saying that if you give up your living room sofa, which is yours free and clear but it annoys people, then you can then keep your dining table, which is also yours free and clear! So what exactly are they giving up?"

Winston sighed deeply.

"They give up their bullying," he said. "They see bullying as their entitlement, something they've owned for years, the same way you see your garden. So you say no, they're not *entitled* to bully, and they say, but we've been bullying for years! Of course it's our right! Then they say your garden is on a commonly used walkway, you don't *own* that walkway, it's not an *entitlement* for you to put your garden there, it never was. It's a *permission*. And you say, no, my garden has been there for years! So if you give up your garden, or at least move it downstairs, and they give up their bullying, all for the sake of the building, *both* sides are making sacrifices."

Seth thought this over for a moment. Even Winston was impressed with the precision of his own logic.

"They'll never give up their bullying," Seth answered. "It's not something they own, it's who they are."

Thoughts of Neville Chamberlain appeasing the Nazis returned to Seth's mind, but he knew better than to drag Hitler into this again. Thoughts of Stalin and of the Cambodian killing fields also returned to Seth's mind. But he chose, probably wisely, to steer clear of comparing the petty bullying in Bronson Canyon to the horrors of genocide. Finally, Seth came up with an argument he thought Winston might hear: "You know in *Hamlet* . . ."

"Don't bring *Hamlet* into this right now!" Winston squealed. "I'm not interested in *Hamlet!*"

Seth had never heard Winston actually shout like that. Seth rose, stepped into the kitchen, grabbed a fistful of spinach and threw it onto the floor of the playpen. Cassandra instantly dove onto and into the greens.

"You and the Angelis family, you used to be best friends," Winston said softly.

"We were never best friends."

"JoJo supported the coop. Eddie helped you build it. He worked in the hot sun, side by side with you."

Cassandra hopped back up to the top of the playpen wall. She saw that Seth was agitated and started to "caw" repeatedly and plaintively. Seth crossed over, picked her up, and placed her on his wrist, where she perched.

"I don't trust them," Seth said.

"I know," Winston replied. "But I don't know what else to do to end this acrimony. I'll help you move the plants."

"What's the assurance they'll leave Cassandra alone?"

"Their word. They gave me their word. Both of them. Eddie *and* JoJo. They swore it on their Bible," Winston said slowly.

Seth smirked. "They're as Christian as the Crusades," he said.

"Yeah, yeah," Winston remarked.

"I name my pets after violent people. It's truer to their form. It's truer, in general."

"Well, good for you and your truth," Winston said.

They shook hands. Winston rose, opened the front door, and checked up and down the walkway to see if anyone was watching before he slipped out into the afternoon sun.

ON THE SECOND WEDNESDAY IN APRIL, late afternoon, performing a painfully difficult task, Seth unclipped half a dozen plastic containers from the railing near his front door. Still saturated from the morning's watering, their weight took their toll on his back and his thighs as he carried them down the two semi-flights of the walkway's stairwell. Six rectangular containers with young tomato plants, eggplants, some marigolds, green beans, basil and cilantro. After half an hour or so, they were sitting below, on top of the west garden wall.

Seth was now standing on the fourth step of a small steel ladder he placed on the walkway to snip down the plastic netting that was to be the climbing space for the bean plants. With a bleach solution, he scrubbed off the stains from soil and hard water that had dripped for years into the magnesite floor. After an hour of labor, the walkway was clean and clear, sterile. The new vista wasn't to Seth's taste at all. The foliage had been a comfort to him. What was left in its absence was an agitation borne of this new sterility.

Exactly nine days later, on the third Saturday in April, at around the same time Ajax, banished by Agamemnon and Helen in Fontana, was starting to gulp down wads of Styrofoam that would be her undoing, Seth descended his stairwell to water his garden, now situated on top of the west garden wall. He saw to his dismay that his garden was gone. Every tub, every plant, disappeared. He checked the dumpsters by the east wall. Inside one dumpster, there sat crushed, vanquished plants and his rectangular plastic containers amidst coffee grounds and old newspapers, and white plastic garbage bags tied shut. This was the reward of Winston's negotiated truce? For Seth, that all too familiar, loathsome sensation returned, of falling into a tunnel of white, hot rage. All he could do to quench the anger was clean his apartment. He scrubbed every surface, bleaching it out, dusting, sanitizing every corner, laundering every sheet and pillowcase, while Cassandra followed him from room to room, pecking at his toes while he scrubbed. Still, fury surged through him. That night, in order to find some rest, he popped two Sominex.

The following morning, on the third Sunday in April, at 8:30 a.m., Seth was awakened by a pounding on his door. Still groggy from the sleeping pills, he staggered from his bedroom to peek out the front-door peephole. There he spied a woman with a clipboard, a badge and the khaki top of a city inspector. Still in his underwear, he withdrew back into his bedroom without opening the door.

"It's Sunday morning!" he muttered to himself.

Still, after half an hour of reflection, he threw on his jeans, a shirt and some boots, and headed downstairs to the street, where he found a truck from the city's Department of Animal Services. The inspector sat in the driver's seat. The driver's door was closed but the window open. Standing outside that window, Jocasta Angelis gesticulated wildly while the inspector stared forward into her front windshield.

Seth approached the truck. Seeing him, JoJo turned her wrath on Seth: "You get out of here! It's my turn now. You'll get your turn!"

But the inspector was having none of it. She leaned out the window.

"Are you Seth Jacobson?" she called.

Seth nodded. As he approached the truck, he heard her ask JoJo politely to back away from the truck and return to her apartment. "I need to speak with Mr. Jacobson," she said.

Seth approached the truck, and JoJo withdrew. JoJo glared at Seth as they crossed paths. Seth now stood by the truck's open window.

"My name is Inspector Lopez," she said, looking at Seth, who just nodded. "There's been a complaint." Seth nodded again, without saying anything. Lopez took a deep breath. "You have chickens in your apartment?" she asked wearily.

Seth didn't know what to say, or not to say, but he sensed that this was no time to dissemble.

"May I see your driver's license," Inspector Lopez asked. Seth handed it to her. She recorded his license number and official address before returning his license to him.

"I have a pet," Seth finally said. "A single pet, a single, quiet harmless hen. This has nothing to do with my pet. The issue here is a neighbor dispute, and she's trying to use the city to harass me."

Lopez fiddled with the string on her clipboard. "Would you mind if I take a look at her?"

Seth sighed and said nothing.

"You don't have to let me in," she added. "But the complaint is serious."

"Serious?"

"Animal cruelty."

Seth had no words. He stared at Lopez, aghast.

"This isn't just going to go away." She continued: " . . . until we can close this case officially. And we can't do that until we determine what's going on."

"Animal cruelty?"

"That's what she said?"

A number of thoughts jumbled around in Seth's head. First was the rank betrayal of the "truce" negotiated by Winston. Notwithstanding the vandalism to the potted garden that Seth had moved in exchange for leaving Cassandra alone, now the Angelis duo were spitting on that very promise. Amidst these betrayals, Seth began to understand their strategy, which was an extension of the tactic they'd used when complaining about the "disgusting odor" coming from Seth's apartment. That complaint obviously hadn't gotten the city inside his unit — though Winston had told Seth that inspectors did pass by the outside of his apartment and told him there had been nothing wrong that they could find. So now the Angelis duo were raising the stakes to animal cruelty, which the Department was not allowed to ignore and could only confirm or disavow by gaining access to the apartment. Once inside, the city could no longer argue that the distance requirements were not enforceable for lack of access or proof. Or so Seth feared.

Mike's story of the raid on his farm popped into Seth's head, and he weighed the potentially dire consequences of needlessly provoking the city.

By now, Winston had staggered downstairs in a bathrobe and flip-flops to join Seth. Winston introduced himself to Inspector Lopez as president of the HOA and asked if there was anything he could do to assist. Winston was, of course, as furious as Seth that his "truce" was now in flames. Winston corroborated Seth's explanation that this was all part of a neighbor war, that he had visited Seth's apartment multiple times and that the complaint of animal cruelty was groundless.

Lopez nodded, sighed, then asked Seth what he wanted to do.

To cooperate, or not? Would this woman seize Cassandra, a harmless pet?

Seth and Winston stepped away from the truck. Seth didn't ask him what to do, because he no longer trusted Winston's judgment, nor did Winston offer his opinion. Yet these recent events had been such an affront to Winston's authority as to propel Winston from an impartial diplomat into Seth's camp, and Seth knew that.

Seth then remembered how he'd scrubbed the apartment yesterday as therapy for his rage and outrage. If the city had to inspect, there couldn't be a better day. The place had never been cleaner. There was a certain providence in that. Mostly, though, Seth followed an intuition that this inspector was kind.

Seth returned to the truck and leaned in the window. "Come on up," he told Lopez.

The three trudged up the stairwell toward Seth's front door. Heads were now poking out behind every curtain and screen where people were home in the building. Seth opened his front door and the three stepped inside, greeted by the lavender aroma of nontoxic cleanser. Lopez looked around, at the ceilings, the floors, the couch, and the playpen where Cassandra clucked from her perch atop one of the playpen walls.

Based on JoJo's testimony, Lopez was expecting to see chicken feces lining the floor and dripping from the ceiling. "My God!" She whispered, "This place is spotless."

At the sight of Cassandra, something happened to Lopez, observed by both Seth and Winston. The stern expression on her face started to melt a little into a slight smile as she knelt in toward the hen.

Seth placed his wrist under Cassandra's breast. The chicken jumped aboard and clucked as he hoisted her sky-bound. Winston went to the refrigerator, withdrew a piece of spinach, crossed back into the living room and hand-fed Cassandra as she perched on Seth's arm.

"I have a parrot," Inspector Lopez said. "Had her for years. This is all very familiar. They're quite close, the species. From the same jungles, I think. The same tropics."

Seth handed Lopez a copy of Dr. Varac's letter, which Lopez said she'd file with her report.

Seth extended his chicken-laden arm to Lopez, who held out her own arm. Cassandra jumped from Seth's arm to Lopez's, crawling up to her shoulder before sitting there.

"I hatched her," Seth said. "She's been around me her whole life."

"Here's what I'm going to do," Lopez said, with Cassandra now perched on her shoulder. "They've been told over and over that the distance requirements don't apply to pets, and this is clearly a pet. If you don't mind, I'd like to take some photographs for the file. We don't normally do this, but next week, you can pick up a copy of the full report from the shelter on Lacy Street. You may need it for court. I'm going to leave packets for all of you on neighbor dispute resolution through the city attorney's office. I'm also going to advise the department not to respond to any more complaints concerning this chicken."

With that, Lopez picked up a camera that had been dangling around her neck and snapped photos of Cassandra, now back inside the playpen.

VERA PENTCHEVA SAID SHE WAS stunned that the city didn't seize the chicken. However, nobody was more stunned than JoJo and Eddie Angelis, who refused to accept the neighbor dispute resolution packets from Inspector Lopez. Instead, together, they followed her out to her truck, pleading their case. Lopez listened to them for about half an hour before telling them there was nothing more she could do. She drove down Bronson Canyon to the Hollywood Freeway, sailing toward downtown, and then north- east, to the Department of Animal Services on Lacy Street, where she filed her report. The following Friday, Seth retrieved the full report from the Department. This is what it contained:

"August 15: Request for Service. 1637 Hrs. Remarks: Distance Ltr Sent. No smell coming from door. There is no violation if fowl are in apartment. File til further. Enriquez, #038.

"April 23: Cruelty Investigation Checklist, 1212 hours. 597 Penal Code. Received by Bartell. Requestor: Jocasta Angelis. Type of Violation: Unsanitary Conditions, Medical Conditions. Description of Complaint: Suspect is keeping chickens in his apartments as pets. The chickens are sick and dying from unknown diseases. Suspect is also breeding them. Conditions visible from requestor's property."

"April 24: Request for Service. 1110 hours. Remarks: I arrived at above address, knocked at door, no answer. No sign of any fowl on outside of apt. No smell detected through door. Posted 84A to contact Department. Rec: Possible weekend DFU for Contact/Inspection. Billings, #503.

"April 26: Request for Service. 0830 hours. Remarks: Arrived at location. Attempted contact. Initially no response. Contact was made with woman at Apt. #2D. Inquired if any chickens/fowl lived in Apt. #2E, which common wall was shared with. Her response was that she doesn't think Apt. #2E has any, and wasn't sure; and that she never heard or saw any. Neighbor did confirm that Seth Jacobson resides in Apt. #2E. Contact was attempted at Apt. #1F to obtain more info; initially no response. While filling out 84A to post, "JoJo Angelis" made contact in public street, claimed to be complainant, and informed me that she is upset of chicken(s) creating unsanitary living conditions for everyone in complex; and that fowl owner has had chicken/fowl problems in the past; and refuses to get rid of the chicken(s). She continued on about violations of municipal codes and health codes that chicken owner was violating. "Seth Jacobson" then made contact, and JoJo Angelis stated repeatedly that she will not talk to Seth Jacobson and wishes to continue in private. Angelis was then advised of need to conduct immediate investigation with fowl owner and to let officer handle the rest. Seth Jacobson granted immediate inspection upon request. One Rhode Island chicken was observed in a makeshift pen approximately 4 feet wide by 6 feet long, alfalfa hay being used as bedding. Food/water available. Inside of apartment, dwelling was clean. No sign of unsanitary conditions anywhere; and no smell of chicken droppings as alleged by neighbor inside of Apt. #1F. Chicken was very clean and healthy in appearance and was tame. Owner stated chicken is his pet since a hatchling. Owner provided veterinarian's health certificate of examination of chicken "Cassandra" done on April 18. Winston Pendleton president of homeowners association of location also made contact, stated resident in Apt. #1F has always been making false complaints and that there is no problem of "Cassandra" being kept inside owner's location as a pet. Upon leaving, complainants made contact again. They were advised more than once that 53.59 is not enforceable for fowl/birds when kept inside dwellings. Dispute resolution packet issued to all upset parties involved. Note: ongoing civil dispute. Lopez, #223."

ON THE LAST WEDNESDAY IN APRIL, at approximately 5 a.m., the single blast of a double-gauge shotgun was heard through Bronson Canyon at a sufficient volume to set the coyotes howling for ten minutes. The source of the blast was JoJo Angelis, in Apartment #1F. A single bullet ripped through two divides: the ceiling of Apartment #1F thereby entering Apartment #2F directly above, whizzing inches by the sleeping Timothy Rowland — Sam's thirty-year-old son — dinging the chandelier over his bed and ricocheting at a 94-degree angle through the bedroom wall into the unit next door, Apartment #2E, where Seth Jacobson slept. With its inertia now exhausted, the single bullet came to rest in the water-capture tray of an indoor begonia that Seth had planted the prior week, and that he kept on his bedside table.

The gun blast had startled Seth awake, and he actually saw the bullet rip through his bedroom wall and fall into the begonia, a mere foot from his head, before tumbling down into the watering tray. He waited with some trepidation for a second blast, but it never came. He was, however, unable to return to sleep that morning.

ACT II, SCENE 5: LOVE THY NEIGHBOR, PART 1

Seth used plastic gloves to retrieve the stray bullet and place it in an empty Diamond matchbox, keeping it as evidence. This ultimately proved to be unnecessary, since JoJo Angelis admitted without hesitation that the pre-dawn blast was from her double-gauge shotgun that she was cleaning at the moment it discharged.

At least that was her story, as told to Sam Rowland, who had rushed downstairs at 5:12 a.m. and pounded on JoJo's door upon seeing a bullet hole in the bedroom floor where Timothy had been sleeping. There was no question in Sam's mind that the origin of the new cavity had come from JoJo's apartment.

To her credit, and with excruciating reluctance, JoJo was nonetheless the first to tell Winston about the accident, since in his capacity as HOA president, Winston was obligated to manage repairs of any structural damages inflicted upon the building, and to collect the cost for said damages from the party responsible.

JoJo never denied that she was the party responsible. Nor did she apologize to anybody. Her attitude toward the incident was nonchalant, and through all discussions of it, her face remained dour and unemotional. It was a simple matter to JoJo: She was cleaning her gun, and it went off by accident.

For Seth, however, this was not sufficient. It came too close on the heels of JoJo's false reports to the insurance company and to the city's Department of Animal Services. For Seth, the incident was far more insidious. He had, after all, seen a bullet tear through his bedroom wall and settle onto a planter mere inches from where he slept, and the city now had on record that there was a neighbor dispute between him and the woman who fired the "shot heard around the block" — as it was eventually dubbed by the neighbors of Bronson Canyon.

This was, in fact, the biggest story to float around the canyon since 1999, when Johnny Prescott, drunk on JB, staggered onto the roof of the building next door and howled at the moon before propelling himself in an ostentatious dive to the swimming pool below. Tragically, Johnny missed the pool by a foot and a half, fatally cracking open his head on the cement surrounding the pool.

Seth attempted to float the theory that if JoJo's "accident" wasn't just a warning, it was attempted homicide. Ever the diplomat, Winston pointed out the strain of simple logic in JoJo attempting to kill somebody in an apartment both upstairs *and* next door from hers by firing a single bullet into her own ceiling. The bullet's final resting place, Winston said, "had to be the result of chance, not planning."

The following morning, over coffee in Winston's apartment, after Winston had seen Suki off to work, Seth told Winston he intended to file a police report. The larger issue, he insisted, was gun-wielding zealots in the building.

"This is a battle for civilization itself," Seth intoned.

Winston thought over this hyperbole for a moment before remarking that the battle was not for civilization, but for the more modest cause of just getting along.

"You know," Winston said, "The same Bill of Rights that allows you to keep Cassandra is the same Bill of Rights that allows them to keep guns."

Seth blanched. Winston continued. "It was an accident. They have the Constitutional right to be idiots."

"I just don't like it," Seth said. "I don't feel safe in my own home. They say a chicken is a threat to their —— what was the expression in their lawyer's letter . . .?"

"Peaceful enjoyment of their . . ."

"Yeah, yeah. I'd say a double-gauge shotgun in that whack-job's possession is a bigger threat to the peaceful enjoyment of our homes than a chicken."

"So file your police report," Winston said.

"*They* would," Seth replied. "You want to come with?"

"No. I think they've driven you batty."

"Okay," Seth said. He set down his mug of coffee on Winston's kitchen table. Seth thanked Winston for the coffee and stepped outside.

At about 10 a.m., Seth was cycling down Wilcox Avenue, approaching the Hollywood Division of the Los Angeles Police Department. He locked his bike to a tree, retrieved from his backpack the Diamond matchbox containing the bullet, and stepped inside the lobby. Standing at the counter, a frumpy, distraught woman of about fifty was reciting the litany of possessions she'd just lost from a car that had been broken into three hours prior. The desk officer calmly wrote his report by hand: "one costume jewelry bracelet, one carton of milk, one unopened box of Lucky Strikes, one car radio and CD player, a toothbrush, two lottery tickets, a hair dryer, four blouses, one coat, three pairs of high-heel shoes, one pair of boots . . ."

The woman said she'd been living in her car. The officer wrote down each item, asking her to assess its value. After fifteen minutes of listening to this, and realizing the list was going to include all the woman's worldly possessions, and that she'd only just gotten started, the absurdity of Seth's "magic bullet theory" finally penetrated his wall of rage, and Seth stepped back out onto Wilcox Avenue, unlocked his bike, and rode home.

On re-entering the building's property, Seth saw Winston, JoJo and Sam standing on the front sidewalk speaking with the building's handyman, Enriqo. Out of breath from the uphill bike ride, Seth joined them to learn that they were, as Seth imagined, negotiating terms for the building's repair of JoJo's gunfire damage. This included replacing a floorboard in Sam's apartment, and repairing the heating elements wired into JoJo's ceiling. And then there was the wall between Sam's apartment and Seth's, through which the bullet had ricocheted. To repair this wall would require minor patching and painting on both sides. From the way JoJo glared at Seth when he joined the assembly, Seth decided to catch up on the details later and check his mail instead, which he'd neglected for almost two weeks.

Seth was standing by the bank of mailboxes when he reached into the front left pocket of his cargo pants, only to discover that his mailbox key was missing. It had been attached to a key ring that contained keys to his Honda Civic, his front door and his bicycle lock, but the mailbox key was no longer part of that ensemble. Seth scoured all his pockets to see if the mailbox key might somehow have become detached from the key ring and fallen into another pocket. A combination of panic and dread washed over Seth, realizing that a small key had been identified in Cassandra's intestine on an X-ray the prior week. Being his small and shiny mailbox key, Cassandra had surely swallowed it, and he had no duplicate.

Before accepting this theory as fact, Seth thought it prudent to search his apartment for the key. He hoisted his bicycle over his right shoulder and scaled the rear stairwell.

"Don't scrape the tires on the walls!" he heard JoJo shout from below. Seth checked the building's off-white walls, and found one smudge mark from a bicycle tire that he'd inadvertently scraped against the wall months ago, during the hundreds of times he'd carried his bike up those same stairs over the years.

Seth thought of a response such as "Or what? You'll shoot to kill?!" but he thought it wiser to say nothing.

Cassandra nipped at Seth's socks as, in a frenzy, he searched all the surfaces of his apartment for his mailbox key. He rifled through stacks of bills and envelopes, he scoured through a jar of coins, he flipped through a box containing business cards going back decades. He rummaged through old paper clips that were dusted with a light coating of chicken-mash residue.

When Seth finally returned to the mailboxes half an hour later, Winston, JoJo, and Enriqo were gone. The mailboxes, which had been there for a quarter-century, consisted of two banks each of six small vaults, one bank above the other. Each vault had its own keyhole. Seth's mailbox was second from the right on the top bank. Seth peered through the cracks of his own mailbox to see that it was stuffed with papers and envelopes.

Directly above the top metal bank was a large round keyhole used by the mail deliverer. Of particular relevance to Seth was a slight gap between the panel that the mail deliverer would open with his or her key, and the metal rim behind it, intended to seal that panel shut. There should be no gap, Seth thought, imagining the main lock might be broken. If so, this was something that should be reported.

To test it, Seth stuck his finger in the large keyhole at the top of the bank, curled his finger around the rim, and gave a light tug forward. With this tug and a slight squeak, the entire top bank of six vaults easily slid forward from its vertical position to an angle of about 30 degrees, thereby exposing the contents of all six vaults — the same space through which the mail deliverer deposited letters and sheaths of newspaper containing slick-coated coupons.

With this discovery, and with some relief, Seth was able to retrieve his mail. He reported the situation to Winston, requesting a replacement key and proposing that the building install new mail-boxes, since, Seth explained, he had just discovered that the security of everyone's mail was compromised, or at least those who collected their mail from the top bank of vaults. This might also be a good opportunity to discuss the Angelis family's renegade destruction of Seth's garden, not to mention the vacant chicken pen in the back garden, Seth suggested.

Winston, however, believed that neither issue was worth the acrimony that discussion of it would inevitably provoke. And when Winston brought the matter of the mailboxes to the Board, JoJo insisted that Seth had broken the mailboxes and was therefore responsible for the cost of replacing them. All of them.

Naturally, Seth countered that he had not broken anything, that the breakage was "pre-existing," and that his ability to flick open the bank of mailboxes with one finger merely *exposed* the damage rather than *created* it.

JoJo, however, argued that the building had again been wronged by Seth, that his rogue act of retrieving mail without a key constituted vandalism, and that if Seth did not agree to the reasonable request to pay $700 plus labor for the replacement of all the mailboxes as an apology for the damage he had caused, JoJo would file federal charges against him of "mailbox tampering."

All of this was brought up at an "emergency meeting" the following Saturday morning, held in the back yard, amidst the remaining detritus of the former chicken pen that the Angelis duo had decimated. Of the building's twelve residents, the only attendees were the Board members (Winston, JoJo and Vera), along with Seth, and Sam, who was bleary-eyed and barefoot in a stained T-shirt and pajama bottoms after a night of heavy partying at the Roxy. Seth thought Sam might be there as his defender, but Seth soon caught on that Sam mostly just didn't want to be in his own apartment while Enriqo fixed the floorboard blasted through the prior week by JoJo's double-gauge shotgun.

JoJo said that she was setting an example by so willingly paying for her foolishness — that everyone in the building should pay for his or her own foolishness. With these words, JoJo looked in Seth's direction. When Vera stoically nodded, Seth understood that things were not going well for him.

"The hole in my wall and in Sam's floor wasn't a pre-existing condition!" Seth snapped.

"Can you prove that you didn't damage the mailboxes?" Vera asked.

"Can you prove that I *did*?"

At this moment, Sam, who had said nothing, ambled into a corner between the northern brick wall and a large cactus. With his back facing the meeting's attendees, Sam quietly vomited into the cactus, and stood there for half a minute, stooped over, clutching his knees.

There was a long silence before Vera finally spoke: "Somebody's going to have to clean that up."

Slowly, Sam stood and walked across the yard, a strand of spittle containing minuscule pebbles of semi-digested toast dangling from one corner of his mouth.

"Three babes wanted to come home with me last night," Sam said, before disappearing around the corner. Even though he was wearing slippers, everybody heard the series of thuds as he ascended each step to return to his apartment. And that was the entirety of Sam's contribution to the meeting, which concluded, like most of their meetings, with no conclusion at all.

Winston gave Seth permission to continue retrieving his mail by jimmying open the bank until new mailboxes were installed. But that installation didn't happen, because there was no consensus on the Board as to whether it was worth taking legal action to compel Seth to pay for it. Winston argued that the HOA should simply pay for new mailboxes that had so obviously outlived their usefulness. Vera and JoJo both believed Seth was responsible, or so they said, but Vera was squeamish about bringing the matter to court. And so, nothing happened.

Seth asked Winston to put in writing the latter's permission for Seth to jimmy open the mailboxes, which Winston did, in an email. In the meantime, Seth mostly waited for the sound of the mail deliverer's jangling keys, and ran downstairs to collect his mail directly from him or her. If, however, more than ten days passed without this happening — because Seth wasn't home at the time, or the postal worker's keys weren't loud enough — Seth snuck out under cover of darkness and stealthily jimmied open the upper bank to retrieve his mail.

Had Seth been more sensible, he would have rented a post office box until the matter was resolved. And though he was no fool, this simply never occurred to him. Or even if it did, there was some subliminal, even perverse, desire to goad JoJo to continue her campaign of harassment. Had Seth possessed a nobler disposition, he would have sought a way to extricate himself from yet another ludicrous dispute with the Angelis duo. He would have forgiven his enemies, in the manner of Christ, or Gandhi, or Martin Luther King, all of whom he revered.

Seth was always moved by the scene in *The Tempest* where Prospero forgives, or appears to forgive, the enemies who betrayed him. Seth recalled how when he watched that scene the prior summer at the classical repertory company in Pasadena called A Noise Within, tears had welled in his eyes. For some reason, though (which may well be the fallacy of literature's humanizing influence), when it came to his own life, Seth spurned the lesson of Prospero that so stirred him as an observer. Seth rejected the kind of forgiveness in his own life that so moved him in a play — the retraction of spite that might curtail endless cycles of vengeance, leading to what might be called transcendence. Instead, like his prodigal rooster Agamemnon, Seth favored the lesser impulse of warfare. Barely realizing it himself, Seth actually relished the conflict with JoJo. It might even be said that it gave both of their lives purpose. It's true that this particular purpose was as pointless as most wars, as pointless as a cockfight — but it was a purpose nonetheless.

And it's always easier to live with a purpose than without one.

Two days after the initial incident, Winston told JoJo that he'd provided Seth a letter of permission on behalf of the HOA, allowing Seth to pry open the mailboxes until new mailbox vaults were installed. That didn't stop JoJo from making good on her threat to file a federal complaint with the Post Office, charging Seth with vandalism. Approximately one month later, after hearing Seth prying open the mailboxes in the middle of the night, JoJo posted a notice on the mailboxes that read: "Mailbox tampering is a federal crime per Title 17, Section 1705. Please report anybody seen attempting to open our mailboxes without a key to any member of the Board, and to LAPD."

The notice provided the phone number for the police.

On seeing it, Seth tore down the notice. The next day it was re-posted. And so the pattern recurred for about a week, until somebody told JoJo to stop re-posting the notice.

In the meantime, Winston was able to reach the Postmaster of the Hollywood office, Eric Lee, at first by email and later by phone. This is how Winston obtained written evidence that the Post Office had no intention of prosecuting Seth, or even responding to JoJo's charges.

"We have inspected the mailboxes on your property," Lee wrote. "They are of a model that generally wears out after 15 years. From their current condition, it's clear that they exceeded their ability to provide secure service at least 10 years ago. We recommend that you replace them promptly."

But even this authoritative support of Seth's position wasn't sufficient to budge JoJo and Vera from their now intractable stance that Seth was to blame for vandalism. Seth's and Winston's position, meanwhile, was equally intractable: that in order for the accusation to stand, there needed to be proof that the mailboxes were lock-solid until Seth managed to open them with one finger. And so, amidst the swirl of accusations and devoid of such evidence, nothing was repaired, replaced or resolved.

ACT II, SCENE 6: LOVE THY NEIGHBOR, PART 2

Vera Pentcheva had been renting her apartment next door to Seth for over three years to a woman named Julia Morgan. For the first year and a half, Julia and Vera had gotten on swimmingly. This might have been because Julia was Vera's first tenant, after purchasing the condo herself some six years prior.

When Vera lived next door to Seth, before he hatched his flock, Vera grew contentious over his potted plants, which were situated on the common walkway near his own front door, but Seth didn't realize the plants were a source of tension because she never said anything about it. Instead, Vera engaged in passive-aggressive behavior, such as returning home with shopping bags, and when passing in front of Seth's apartment, slamming the bags into his tomato and bean plants with the kind of cavalier consistency that eventually caught Seth's attention. Fearful of confrontation, Vera would pretend that these petty assaults were accidents of circumstance — that the pathway was too narrow for her to pass without damaging his planter garden, and that her bags were too large and heavy. At the time, the plants were mature and fruiting, and so Seth couldn't have replanted them into smaller planters without destroying them. Instead, he knocked on Vera's door, explained his side of things, and offered that for the next planting in a few months he would purchase smaller, or even "upside down" planters that would hang from hooks and therefore use up no walkway space at all. Vera gushed with a toothy smile and in a squealing voice that this really wasn't necessary, or a problem.

Nonetheless, in the next planting season, Vera complained to the Board that Seth's tomato plants were unsightly. She added that he should either grow prettier plants, or none at all. To complement this complaint, she created what would become a recurring expression: "I didn't come here all the way from Romania to live on a farm."

Shortly after, because Vera moved out of the building and rented her unit to Julia, and because Julia had no complaint with the tubs or the plantings they contained, the entire matter was dropped, and Seth continued growing his balcony garden as before.

All of this occurred before Seth was petitioning the Board to use the empty garden space behind the building for an "aviary" — a euphemism for "chicken coop" that got by nobody. The Board meeting concerning the chicken coop occurred when the chicks were one week old. Vera was now living a mile away in a condo with her boyfriend, Reginald McCallister, and her mother, Bronislava. Meanwhile, Julia was renting Apartment #2D, next door to Seth. Julia's rent checks paid for Vera's new mortgage.

The April report filed by Inspector Lopez for the Department of Animal Services, investigating JoJo's "animal cruelty" complaint against Seth, came about six months after Seth had filed for divorce, a case which, at that time, remained in bureaucratic purgatory. Inspector Lopez's report included the following paragraph: "Contact was made with woman at Apt. #2D. Inquired if any chickens/fowl lived in Apt. #2E, which common wall was shared with. Her response was that she doesn't think Apt. #2E has any, and wasn't sure; and that she never heard or saw any. Neighbor did confirm that Seth Jacobson resides in Apt. #2E."

That neighbor was Julia Morgan, who was fully aware at the time that Cassandra the chicken lived next door. Furthermore, on several occasions Julia had heard Cassandra clucking quite loudly for about a minute after laying an egg. Julia had mentioned this to Seth, inquiring if the bird was okay. In reporting her ignorance to the city, Julia was simply trying to protect Seth, or at least to distance herself from taking a stand in the dispute over Cassandra. When Seth read this in the report, his heart warmed toward Julia.

Julia was a fit, shapely woman in her early forties who lived by herself, though she was frequently visited by a rough-hewn Hollywood cowboy, whom she described as a business partner. By avocation, Julia was an accomplished singer who re-interpreted ballads from the 1940s. She and her partner, Edward, were working together on creating a vintage-themed album. His 1969 Bronco pickup truck could be spotted in her parking space behind the building many evenings of the week, though he always would leave by midnight. Julia owned no car of her own. Often, in the mornings, Edward would appear in his Bronco by the building's front curb to drive Julia to Capitol Records, where she worked as an associate producer.

Julia rarely wore makeup — at most, a dab of lipstick. She often wore her cascading red hair pulled back behind her head in a clip, which only accentuated the more severe aspects of her chiseled, aristocratic face. In a husky voice, Julia spoke in tones of gushing warmth, or, depending on her mood, in lilting cadences of what might be called East Coast haughtiness. Though she had grown up in New Hampshire, Julia, had Turkish parents; Seth and Julia shared a style that sometimes appeared aloof from and even condescending toward the world around them. It wasn't that they actually felt that way, it's what others perceived.

"You're cold," native Angelenos would say to Seth, and he had no idea what they were talking about, given how his passions actually bordered on lunacy. The same might be said of Julia.

Her laughter was often heard echoing across the driveway below and out through the courtyard of the apartment building to the east. Julia likely was not aware of how loud her conversations were, or even that the way she routinely greeted her fuzzy black and grey cat, Pretense, could be heard from the street below. These were usually cuddly, sung greetings of "Ooooh, preety Preeetense, how beauoooootiful you are today," answered with high-pitched meows at a similar decibel level. Pretense was almost fourteen years old, and Julia boiled up stews of rice, free-range chicken and organic carrots for her. This diet, Julia insisted, accounted for Pretense's longevity. Sometimes, however, after Pretense had thrown up on Julia's bed or scratched through a denim pillow, Julia's tone turned into an aggrieved and exasperated lecture, punctuated with curses.

Julia's apartment was sparsely decorated. Even from his apartment, through their shared living room wall, Seth heard when Julia walked across the hardwood of her living room, because her steps echoed from the absence of furniture: There was a single stuffed reading chair and a coffee table. Books remained unpacked in cardboard boxes that lined the living room wall, years after Julia had moved in. Her kitchen adjoined the walkway. She often sat crouched over a laptop computer on her kitchen table, visible to passers-by. Julia chose to leave her living room and kitchen exposed by the absence of curtains or blinds.

Julia held her head high and walked with a slightly imperious gait. Even when carrying a bag of laundry along the walkway and down the northern flight of steps to the washer below, Julia strode with a singularity of purpose, often accompanied by an intimidating, furrowed brow, and lips pinched into a declarative expression of someone with a goal in mind who was not to be deterred.

On a Tuesday night in May, when Seth knocked on her door to thank her for her protection of Cassandra, he found Julia by herself. Their interactions to this point had been restricted to fleeting, friendly greetings —— never so much as a conversation that lasted for more than thirty seconds.

After she opened the door, Seth detected a hint of wine on her breath. She jocularly remarked how strange it was that next-door neighbors in L.A. could be so isolated from one another. Standing outside her screen door, Seth awkwardly shifted his weight from leg to leg. She then proposed matter-of-factly that he come over at some point in the future for a glass of wine.

Two weeks later, at 7 p.m. on Friday evening —— confirmed via text message — he did just that. He brought over a bottle of pinot noir that he'd bought at Gelson's. They consumed that bottle in less than half an hour. The next three bottles were hers. By night's end, with Pretense rubbing herself against his leg, Seth sat on the single, stuffed chair in Julia's living room embracing Julia, who cuddled on his lap. With two brief interludes when Julia slipped away onto the back porch for a cigarette, they spent the evening drinking, talking and kissing, while she played a collection of Ella Fitzgerald, Joe Cocker, and Yo-Yo Ma that she broadcast from her computer's iTunes program to a pair of woofer speakers.

The music was so loud that Winston Pendleton kept crossing to and fro along the walkway outside her door, and Seth privately wondered if Winston could see in. The only light in Julia's apartment was coming from the thin glow of a candle still flickering on her kitchen table, very close to the window. But in the recess of the living room, where Seth and Julia sat kissing, they were engulfed in shadow. Still, Seth wondered what could be seen and what couldn't, and he felt the thrill of being so exposed and yet so clandestine. At about 2 a.m., with shadows forming below her eyes, and after a lingering kiss by her front door, Julia escorted Seth out into the night air, and closed the door behind him.

At 9 a.m. the following morning, Seth hoisted his bicycle down the northern stairwell for a ride to an editorial meeting at the *L.A.*

Observer. On the lower landing, he saw Julia elegantly dressed for work in dark purple trousers with thin white stripes, and a matching jacket draped over a white cotton top and pearl necklace and earrings. She smiled at him fleetingly and then bolted, embarrassed, clippety-clopping in high heels toward Edward, sitting in his Bronco that was parked in front of the building. Seth watched them squeal away. He texted her during the day asking if everything was okay. He received no reply.

That same evening, Edward was back. Seth heard the pair talking and laughing and then eating a dinner Seth had seen her prepare. Later, from his own bedroom, Seth heard them talking in hushed tones on the rear balcony, where she stood smoking. Shortly before midnight, Seth heard Edward drive away. Meanwhile, Julia avoided all contact with Seth. Two phone messages went unreturned. When she saw him on the property, she bustled swiftly by him, avoiding eye contact. Seth concluded that the wisest policy under this circumstance was to leave her alone, which he did. And when he did, because he did, she initiated her re-approach. And though Seth found this cat-and-mouse game to be juvenile and undignified for people their age, he decided to play one more round anyway.

Seth had noticed through Julia's window a new bicycle parked in her living room. They were standing together on the walkway when she explained that she didn't want to rely on Edward for rides. Seth never understood why Julia had no car. The bicycle she had just bought would give her independent access to the Capitol Records building, a quarter of a mile away, where she worked. There was a "superwoman" at work named Marcia who inspired her, Julia said, who rode to work on a bike, and encouraged her to do the same. At the time Julia explained this to Seth, she said he had also inspired her purchase, by the way he rolled up to the curb on his bike and skidded so gracefully to a quick stop in front of the building. She told him he looked like a dancer, dismounting from the bike with a single sweep of his leg. She then asked if he might be interested in going for a Sunday morning bicycle ride together, three days later.

The next morning, just after Seth had chowed down a bowl of cold cereal and milk, Seth opened his front door to let fresh air in through the metal screen door grating. Cassandra cackled by the door, and tried to sunbathe in the beams of light pouring in. She rolled on her side, puffed up her feathers and kicked her uppermost leg back and forth, while scraping the toes of that same leg on the floor. This caused her to gyrate in a semicircle. Seeing this, Seth opened the screen door. Cassandra instantly dove outside onto the now bare walkway that once contained Seth's planter garden. Within a few minutes, he could hear Pretense meowing loudly at Cassandra from Julia's kitchen window. When Seth finally crossed the threshold to retrieve Cassandra, there stood Julia, hands on knees, speaking to Cassandra face to beak: "Aren't you a pretty lady . . . Choook, choook, chook."

Julia wore sweatpants, sneakers and a sleeveless white cotton top. Upon seeing Seth, she straightened up, crossed her arms over her chest and grinned a toothy grin. When Cassandra leapt up onto Seth's arm, Julia slid inside her own apartment and reappeared holding a cell phone to snap photos of Cassandra. The chicken was now parked on Seth's shoulder. Seth created a perch with his arm and guided Cassandra onto that perch. Meanwhile, Julia held out her own arm, also like a perch, so that it touched Seth's. Nudging the bird's feet with the fingers of his free arm, Seth urged Cassandra to cross over from his arm onto Julia's. It took about fifteen seconds for Cassandra to make the hop and clamber up Julia's arm to her shoulder. Using Julia's camera, Seth now took a photo, which Julia promptly emailed to her mother in New Hampshire. Julia spoke with effusive affection about her mother, and Seth often heard Julia through the open windows speaking with her mother on the phone.

On Sunday morning, Winston and Sam saw Julia and Seth standing next to each other by the mailboxes, each holding a bicycle as they donned helmets, and, a few minutes later, pedaling down the canyon road. Inevitably this started a barrage of gossip in the building about Seth and Julia, and Edward's role in Julia's life.

A crisp springtime nip in the air flushed their faces as Seth rode behind Julia, single file in the bike lane along the heavily trafficked streets, lined with apartment buildings and condominiums with ostentatious names painted in cursive: "Cabana Apartments," "Pelican Arms." These buildings were either deteriorating off-white or off-salmon stucco, multi-family dwellings set back behind the sidewalk, with plantings of low-lying palms and myrtle trees. Some of these apartment blocks were half a century old, some newly constructed. The design of the old and the new buildings bore scant resemblance to each other, other than a certain blockiness and the unifying tawdry effect of having been built quickly and cheaply — the very effect that contributes to the city's overwhelming architectural tackiness.

Once they cut away into the wide and quiet tree-lined streets of Hancock Park, Seth pulled alongside Julia, and they rode side by side. There, they passed single-family homes set back behind spacious lawns, circular driveways and wrought iron gates — mansions, really — pristinely landscaped with hedges and the last tulips of the spring, occupied by the inheritors of old money, by Korean families, and by university students living communally.

On the ride home, Seth and Julia each wore a light coat of perspiration. They locked their bikes in front of a cheese-and-wine shop near Franklin Avenue, and sipped lattes for half an hour.

Some of Julia's phrases snagged onto Seth's consciousness like barbs: "politicians —— always men —— who oppose women's rights. I'm talking about in India and Iran, women persecuted for seeking an education, or even after being raped!"

They both nodded in agreement and indignation. For Seth, these were horror stories he'd heard on National Public Radio, and they contained a too-obvious rectitude for any meaningful discussion. So he just nodded. Julia, however, was on a tear.

"America may once have been a cradle for social mobility and economic opportunity, but that cradle is now crashing down."

Seth could not, would not argue with Julia's insistence that "The greed and hegemony of global corporations, and their influence over domestic politics, media and the courts, is responsible for this crisis."

They discussed that to live in this sliver of American history was to live in a nation paralyzed and backsliding on labor issues, on workers' entitlements, on privacy and so on; and yet it was also exciting to live in a nation racing forward so rapidly, technically, so that the place might be unrecognizable in fifty years.

"How can change be so stubbornly regressive and yet so swift and possibly hopeful at the same time?" Julia remarked with a firm grasp of paradox.

They nodded in quiet contemplation and sipped foam off the top of their drinks. The immovable boulders of certainty and agreement had them both pinned to this café table. A young bearded fellow in a yellow and purple tie-dyed cotton shirt sneezed loudly behind them as he ordered his organic soy milk Frappuccino. Annie Lennox crooned "Why?" over the sound system. And though Julia spoke about matters of national and global importance, the long-ago recording of Annie Lennox's plaintive voice threw Seth into a reverie that summoned Katerina Pavlova to the center of his thoughts:

"This is the book I never read

These are the words I never said

This is the path I'll never tread

These are the dreams I'll dream instead

This is the joy that's seldom spread

These are the tears . . .

The tears we shed

This is the fear

This is the dread

These are the contents of my head

And these are the years that we have spent

And this is what they represent

And this is how I feel

Do you know how I feel?

'Cause I don't think you know how I feel

I don't think you know what I feel . . ."

Julia spoke about how men had destroyed the planet, and how much better things might be if women ruled the world.

Seth thought about that for a moment, and finally felt sufficiently moved to say something.

"And so Queen Elizabeth I, Golda Meir, Maggie Thatcher, Condoleezza Rice, and Hillary Clinton," he cited. "These women in positions of global power haven't perpetuated the very barbarities you find so objectionable?"

Julia stared into her latte pensively. "Well . . ." she started to object.

"Perhaps the crux of the matter," Seth added, "isn't so much the attachment of wisdom and compassion to gender, but the nature of power itself."

Julia just smiled, unprovoked, and Seth admired that. They both sat quietly while Annie Lennox still crooned from a loudspeaker. Seth tried to fathom whether Julia's self-assurance, which he found so enticing, was really self-assurance or a mask to cover some lurking secret.

Once back on the building's property, Seth and Julia walked their bicycles side by side. Out of windows, neighbors peeked. Seth shrugged them off. Julia held her head high as though the neighbors didn't exist. The couple hoisted their bikes up the northern stairwell and retreated, sans conversation, into their respective abodes.

The following Friday night, Seth took Julia to dinner at La Poubelle Bistro on Franklin Avenue, a thriving French family-owned eatery now catering to television executives, casting directors and actors living nearby. It had opened in 1969, at that time as a creperie. In a dark, candlelit booth in the back, Seth and Julia shared a bottle of Sonoma County Chablis over a pre-dinner salad of organic spinach, cucumber, orange slices, walnuts and apple. Julia loosened up sufficiently to unleash the mysteries of Edward. They had been lovers, Julia explained, but that had ended over a decade ago after she determined that he had no intention of keeping his promise to divorce his wife — a promise declared to Julia on several occasions with defiant resolve, she maintained.

"The fact is," Julia expounded, "his wife supports him financially, and he feels he really can't afford to leave her, but he doesn't have the honor or the honesty to tell that truth to her or to me."

A busboy whisked away their now empty salad plates. A recording of Jacques Brel singing "Ne me quitte pas" played in the background, behind the clatter of cutlery and patrons' voices exploding with laughter.

"Does she know about you?" Seth asked, meaning Edward's wife.

"Oh yes. She invites me to her Christmas party every year. She knows everything. She doesn't care. She knows he's weak and that he'll never leave her. The point is, he's very jealous. Vindictive. He has a wife he goes home to every night, but he doesn't want me seeing anybody else. That's when he gets nasty."

"Hmmm . . . If it were a play, I'd give it a bad review," Seth replied.

Julia emitted a laugh heard throughout the restaurant, and probably beyond. Seth was enchanted by Julia's capacity to laugh like that.

She returned her ravioli dinner three times because it didn't have a consistency that satisfied her, and she did so in an imperious manner that struck Seth as odd, given her egalitarian politics.

He learned that her sister was an award-winning cellist, and Julia spoke of her in awe. Then she told Seth a story from years ago, of her affair with another journalist, a Scotsman, who had been desperate to marry and have a child with her.

"Of course this was impossible," Julia explained to Seth. "We both were children ourselves. So he went back to Scotland. So you must understand how I've come to have such a low opinion of men."

Seth watched her from across the table and fiddled with his napkin.

"Maybe he loved you."

Julia's lips twisted in contempt. "It was crazy. Too young. And now I'm too old."

After dinner, Julia and Seth, having consumed too much wine for their own good, lay on their backs, side by side on the hardwood floor of Julia's living room, holding hands and listening to Schubert's *Mass No. 6 in E flat major.* Seth had brought the music and knew it well. He pointed out how, in the Third Movement's "Credo: Et incarnatus est," the waltz melody was passed like a baton between and among two tenors and a soprano, and how Schubert interwove the motif among the three voices that floated around and across each other like silk scarves.

Julia kept replaying the Credo, melting into a reverie at the waltz. On one replaying, she held Seth and they listened together in an embrace. Later, Seth watched her dance by herself, with herself, gingerly turning in place, her arms held out and floating like wings, like feathers, caught on breezes of the music.

Two hours later, they both lay on their stomachs, on that same hardwood floor. Seth rolled to one side. Julia sat up sharply upon hearing the clicking sound of a ring he was wearing on his left hand as it struck the floor. Seth saw that she was now softly crying. He asked her what was wrong.

"The ring," she said. "I didn't understand you were married."

"I filed for divorce some time ago. My wife moved out years ago. The case has been snagged in the courts for a while."

Julia wiped her eyes with her wrists and said nothing.

"I don't quite understand," Seth continued. "I've been wearing it this whole time. How can you not have noticed?"

Julia sniffed and stared at the floor.

"It's not like I was trying to deceive you," Seth added.

"No, no, you've been *lovely*," Julia said.

She hoisted herself up to her feet, wobbling, holding onto the wall for support.

"I think I need to go to sleep," she said. Seth nodded. Julia held out her arm. Seth wrapped his own arm in hers as she escorted him to her front door. Before she opened it, they stood there, silent, for about five minutes, watching each other's faces, as the Schubert *Mass* played itself out. Julia took one hand and gently rubbed the side of Seth's face. He kissed her on the forehead. She opened the door at last, and Seth reluctantly stepped across the threshold onto the walkway and then to his own front door, neither looking back toward Julia nor into her apartment as he crossed in front of it.

The following day, Seth received an angry email from Julia: "You could have told me you were married."

He wrote back: "I hid nothing. Ring was on my finger the whole time. You said as much yesterday." Seth received no reply. The day after that, he tried calling her and his call went to voicemail, so he left a message asking to clear the air since they were next-door neighbors. Seth received no return call.

Exactly one week later, around midnight, Seth heard the booming chorus and orchestra of Schubert's *Mass No. 6* coming from Julia's apartment. Edward was with her, and they were dancing to the Credo, or so Seth later learned from Winston, who had seen them when he was crossing the walkway. Seth heard their voices when Julia went out to smoke on her rear balcony. She was telling Edward how Schubert had constructed the trio in the Credo as a single motif shared by two tenors and a soprano, aping Seth's explanation as though it were her own.

The following morning, Seth emailed Julia that he considered it tasteless of her to recycle their intimacy with somebody else. Julia wrote back, saying she was perplexed by Seth's annoyance. She also asked if Winston's complaint about the volume of her music at midnight, when she was with Edward, had anything to do with him. Seth replied that it didn't, though her music had been loud enough to wake the dead in Oxnard. Julia wrote back that she was, again, perplexed by Seth's prickly tone, since the object of her question was not really him, but Winston's snooping and peeping into her apartment, and violating her privacy. Seth's reply was even more prickly: "If you had had the remotest interest in privacy, you might consider installing blinds or curtains in your kitchen and living room windows, like everyone else, since the windows adjoin a public walkway and can be viewed by the entire apartment block to the west of Chuck and Svetlana's house, and many points beyond."

The very next day, Edward helped Julia install blinds on her kitchen and living room windows.

Two more weeks passed, with no further communications between Seth and Julia.

The next Saturday morning, Julia texted Seth, asking if she might come over. He texted back that he needed an hour. Julia had never visited his apartment and he wanted to feed Cassandra and tidy up a bit.

In his living room, Julia stood in sweatshirt, sweatpants and flip-flops, staring at Katerina Pavlova's very Russian decorations, which Seth had left untouched, despite Katerina's years-long absence and their agreement to divorce. Seth offered and then made Julia some green tea, which she sipped from a floral China cup while sitting on the couch.

"It's very dark in here," Julia remarked. "Like a cave."

"I like to think of it as private," Seth answered.

As Julia sipped her tea, Cassandra descended from her playpen perch, and lightly began pecking Julia's red toenails, an act Julia found mildly amusing. After giggling and cooing at Cassandra, Julia looked up at Seth.

"They've discovered a lump on my lower spine," she said matter-of-factly. "They don't believe it's malignant, but they think it's better to remove it. So I'm going in for surgery next week. I'll be in hospital for a few days. Wondering if you can take care of Pretense."

Seth couldn't quite fathom what was going on. Julia must have understood this from his gormless expression.

"I want to give you a key to my apartment," Julia continued. "You're the only person here I can trust," she added. "I certainly wouldn't give my key to Edward."

Seth stared at Cassandra for a long time before returning his focus to Julia.

"Why not?

"Why not, what?

"Why wouldn't you give your key to Edward?"

"He always disappears in moments of crisis," she explained. "He's a coward."

"I see."

"He said you were sixty years old," Julia remarked.

"I'm not even fifty!"

"He said you showed him your driver's license, and that you're sixty years old, and that you're lying to me about your age."

"Do I need to show you my driver's license?"

"Of course not."

"I never showed him my driver's license. Why would I show him my driver's license?"

Even Seth was surprised by how indignant he felt by this petty slander.

Julia continued: "He said you crossed paths on the walkway, that you were looking for a business card and he saw your driver's license."

"I have no memory of any of this," Seth said.

"Because he made it up. It's typical for him."

"Are you serious?"

"He's 55, and he's trying to build a false case that you're too old for me."

"He's older than I am."

"He's trying to prove that you're deceiving me. That you're not trustworthy."

"And what if I were sixty? So what?"

"That's not the point."

"One day we'll all be sixty, if we're lucky."

"Not necessarily."

"Or even if we're not so lucky."

"Not necessarily."

"This thing you have . . . "

"It's called a spinal tumor."

"Is it life-threatening?"

"Life is life-threatening."

"Why would he *say* a thing like that?"

"He's pathological. *That's* why I don't trust him."

"How long have you known him?"

"Almost twenty years."

"Was he always like this?"

"Worse with age . . . but yes."

"For twenty years, he's been telling you he's going to divorce his wife?"

"Yes. Pretty much."

"And you believed him?"

"Not after five years. I'm not a total idiot."

"You didn't answer the question."

"What question?"

"Is it life-threatening?"

"If it continues to grow, it could impact my balance and my ability to walk."

"Okay."

"Okay, what?"

"I'll feed the cat. You don't have to worry about that."

"Thank you."

Julia rose from the couch, setting her teacup down on a side table.

"I can't tell you what this means to me," she continued. "I'll leave clear instructions."

"How are you getting to the hospital?"

"Marcia from the studios."

"Ah . . . Wonder Woman."

"Exactly."

After Julia left, Seth couldn't fathom if any of what had just been said was true. Whether Edward had really said anything to her about Seth's age. Whether Julia really had a tumor. Maybe she was just planning to spend a couple of days with Edward in some ocean-view B&B in La Jolla, while Seth would be feeding her cat.

And yet, less than a week later, Seth saw a woman in a business suit escort Julia down the northern stairwell. Julia carried a small suitcase. The appointed time for surgery came and went. Seth spent a couple of hours a day with Pretense every day of Julia's absence. Pretense meowed when he arrived and the sound echoed through and beyond Julia's apartment. Pretense rubbed against his leg after she ate kibble and fresh tuna. (Julia had been sensitive enough not to have Seth prepare Pretense's standard boiled chicken diet.) Every evening, he cleaned her cat box. One day he even cleaned up cat barf from a kitchen corner.

Seth was at Gelson's when Julia called, groggy, asking how Pretense was faring. From the tone of her voice, Seth could tell she was sedated. And yet under the influence of morphine, or whatever they were giving her, she had never sounded so kind, so warm, so grateful. If the drugs revealed her true character, it was a dear character, child-like, far dearer and gentler than she dared reveal without opiates. He asked if she needed a visit, and she said she'd prefer not, that she'd be home tomorrow. They were giving her two weeks off work. There would be enough time to visit then.

Seth swept and mopped her apartment for her return, placing a bouquet of lilies and chrysanthemums on her kitchen table. She called him when she got home, thanking him for the care of Pretense, and for the flowers. She asked him to visit in the morning, that she didn't want to sleep too late. That if she wasn't up by 9, to come right in, into her bedroom, and wake her.

At about midnight, Seth was in bed, slipping from a quasi-conscious repose into a deeper sleep, when his phone rang. He picked up, groggy. On the other end he heard a female voice with a faint Turkish dialect.

"Hello? Is this Seth?"

"Yes, who is this?"

"My name is Constance Morgan. I'm Julia's mother. I'm terribly, terribly sorry to disturb you at this time of night. I'm calling from New Hampshire. It's 3 in the morning here, and I truly wouldn't call you at such an hour if I weren't so concerned."

"No, no, it's okay. What is it?"

"She promised to call me when she got home from the hospital, and I haven't heard from her, so I'm in a bit of a panic . . ."

"There's no need, she's fine . . ."

"She got home safely then?"

"Yes, I mean I haven't seen her, but she called about three hours ago. She sounded sedated, but fine . . . I'm sure she just collapsed into bed."

"I can't thank you enough. I wanted to come out there, but my husband is very ill. Thank you for the way you've cared for her . . ."

"Oh, it's nothing . . ."

"No, it's something. It's really something rare. I do hope one day we can meet."

"I would enjoy that. Julia speaks very admiringly of you," Seth said. And it was true.

"And she's very fond of you," Constance replied. "I wish she'd break free of that Edward. He's really not good for her."

"I'm sure it's all quite complicated," Seth replied.

"I assure you it's not. It's transparent."

"Well, yes, that's also true."

"I really shouldn't be talking this way. Blame it on the late hour," said Constance.

"That's not important. If you have any concerns, call anytime."

"That's very good of you. It's a comfort knowing you're there, next door. It's a great relief."

At about ten minutes after 9 the following morning, Seth called into Julia's open living room window from the walkway and heard no reply. He felt very strange slipping a key into her front door lock, knowing she was home. Partly because his temperament was paranoid, partly because of their earlier cat-and-mouse game, and partly because of the series of groundless charges lodged against him by the Angelis duo, Seth imagined any number of accusations Julia could make, of breaking and entering — or worse — which he could counter only with feeble excuses that there had been some terrible misunderstanding. After all, there was no written evidence of her invitation to enter her apartment. That invite was made in a phone call.

Seth crept on tiptoe across her living room floor, if padding across a hardwood floor in Italian boots can be called creeping. Pretense ran out of the bedroom and greeted him with a series of meows, and rubbed her tail against his legs. He called from the living room toward the bedroom: "Julia? . . . Julia?"

He heard a soft moan from the room beyond the hallway, which he had never actually seen.

"It's 9:15," he called in as gently as he could.

"Thanks," he heard back in her husky voice. "Thanks so much. Think I'll keep sleeping. I'll call you."

"Okay."

And with that, he crept back across the living room, though he was struck by the absurdity of trying to make his exit so stealthy after he'd woken her up.

In the days that followed, Julia received a stream of visitors: friends from her work bearing gifts and flowers and cards. When Seth was home, Julia called him with an invitation to meet her colleagues, to whom she introduced Seth as "my very dear friend and neighbor."

At just about the time when Julia was strong enough to return to work, on a Friday afternoon, a cab pulled up in front of the building. Out stepped Katerina Pavlova and her daughter Irena, hauling four suitcases up the northern stairwell. Their arrival was neither anticipated nor seen by Seth, since he was at the *L.A. Observer* at the time, but it was noted by Winston, who from his balcony could see everybody who entered the property; and by Sam, who heard the suitcases thud on the landing and the jangling of keys in Seth's front door lock. After the two women slipped inside the apartment, they were warmly greeted by Cassandra. Shortly after this welcome, both Sam and Winston heard a series of low-pitched moans and plates smashing against a wall. It was a fever of destruction that raged for almost fifteen minutes. Without corroborating with each other, or with any of the neighbors in the apartment building to the east, who also heard the fracas, Sam and Winston independently determined that these sounds came from Julia's apartment.

What they heard from Seth's apartment was the sound of Irena and Katerina cooing in Russian to Cassandra, who clucked excitedly in return. Julia must have heard the same — greetings between family and fowl — which is probably what incited her to hurl her entire supply of Buffalo China dinnerware at the kitchen wall. Though the Russians' curiosity was piqued by the sound next door of smashing dishware, they'd seen and heard far worse in Moscow, and so they shrugged it off.

When Seth returned home early that evening the only thing untoward that he observed, when hauling his bicycle up the northern stairwell, was the sight of several neighbors peeking at him from out of windows and from behind curtains. He took note of their overcurious attentions, particularly since he was this time arriving by himself and not with Julia. Seth imagined that the curiosity attached to his arrival was prompted by voices heard coming from Julia's apartment: Julia and Edward loudly singing *a capella* and off-key Hal David and Burt Bacharach's "What the World Needs Now Is Love Sweet Love" in giddy and maniacal tones.

"It's the only thing that there's just too little of . . ."

Seth understood that both had been drinking, and likely were in for a long night more. This already had Seth on edge when, after three attempts, he was unable to unlock his own front door. Finally, to his shock, the main door opened from the inside, and Seth saw Katerina and Irena standing in the living room and beaming at him.

"Hi!" Katerina squealed.

Both women saw the tension that swept across Seth's jaw-dropped face.

Even Cassandra stopped foraging for seeds on the straw-lined floor of her playpen, and froze.

"I told you this was a mistake," Irena said quietly to her mother, in Russian.

"You might have let me know you were coming," Seth said.

"We wanted to surprise you!" Katerina replied.

"Well, it worked," Seth retorted, with faux cheerfulness.

Seth rolled his bike across the living room and parked it in the hallway.

"We missed you," Irena called out.

Over dinner with Katerina and Irena at the Cheesecake Factory in Beverly Hills, Seth shot off a text message to Julia, explaining he had no idea that his Russian family would be showing up, and that they would be around for less than a week, because Irena needed to return to her job. Late that night, after Edward had left, Julia texted back: "This cruel awakening probably best. Hurt and upset. Taking xtra wk off. Going to mtn cabin w friends. Marcia taking care of Pretense."

And that was the entirety of their contact for the following week.

Meanwhile, Seth dropped off Katerina and Irena at Ross Dress for Less, on Hollywood Boulevard and Western Avenue, just east of Vine Street and the Boulevard's much-ballyhooed Walk of Fame. There, the women spent hours hoovering up gifts to take back to Moscow: clothes, and the kinds of gift baskets they sold all year — soaps and lotions and talcum powders, shrink-wrapped in cellophane — the kind of packaging and pricing that was non-existent in Russia. When Seth picked up the women three hours later, they asked him if he could take them seven miles northeast, to the expansive Glendale Galleria mall, so they could continue their gift-mining expedition. In rush-hour traffic, it took over an hour to get there. Another hour later, Seth worked on his laptop computer in the food court while the women shopped.

In the early evening, wedged between a Panda Express and a Surf City Squeeze, Seth sat with Katerina at a stained, white plastic table. Michael Jackson's child-voice crooned "I'll Be There," behind the echoes of other diners and the whizzing of blenders: the churning of milk and fruit and ice. Irena had slipped away to a Victoria's Secret to buy sexy lingerie that she could wear for her boyfriend, whose paternalistic, patronizing treatment of her still caused Katerina no end of distress, or so Katerina told him as they both sipped scalding coffee from plastic cups.

"I can see we're not exactly welcome here," Katerina added. "We can go back earlier if you want."

"That's not true. That's not necessary. You took me by surprise. We are in the middle of divorce proceedings."

"That's a reason to be enemies?"

"Of course not."

"I guess I had some secret hope we still could be together."

Katerina gazed into the latte she was drinking and continued speaking, eyes down: "I miss you." Then she looked directly into Seth's eyes: "Are you listening? . . . I miss you." A rim of moisture welled in her eyes. Seth could tell she meant it.

"I miss you too," Seth countered. And he meant it too. "But I didn't marry you to live by myself. Didn't you just start a knitwear business in Moscow?"

"I would need to be here, for supplies, for yarn."

"How often?"

"Two, three times a year."

"For a week?"

"Yes."

"That's not a marriage, that's a business arrangement. I don't want to spend my life betraying you."

"You found somebody? . . . Tell me the truth."

Seth stared into his coffee cup.

"Okay," Katerina continued. "I see what's going on."

"Katya, you left me."

"Remember when you told me you didn't need anybody else. 'Love is not love which alters when it alteration finds . . .'"

"We didn't separate because of war," Seth countered. "We didn't separate because one of us got thrown into prison. We didn't separate because hostile governments were keeping us apart. Nor illness. None of the reasons you find in Russian novels . . ."

". . . And Hollywood movies," Katerina interjected.

Seth continued: "We grew apart because you wanted to leave, you needed to leave, and so you left!"

"I was lost. I couldn't find my place. I couldn't find myself. I still can't . . . You could have followed."

"How?"

"You still can!"

"How? For me, the prospect of life under Putin isn't exactly a fairy tale!"

"And I didn't leave *you*," Katerina snapped. "I left this *place*, speaking of fairy tales."

Seth pushed back his chair, stood and stretched, before dumping his coffee cup in a nearby garbage can. He returned, sat in the same chair and leaned backwards, so that the chair arched on its back two legs.

"Don't do that, you'll fall," Katerina said.

Seth re-settled his chair onto all four legs.

"I don't blame you for leaving," Seth continued, soothingly. "I don't blame you for wanting your life, your home. Please don't blame me for wanting mine."

"I don't blame you," Katerina conceded. "I want you to have what you need."

"Thank you," Seth replied. "That's exactly what I want for you."

Irena returned, holding a large Victoria's Secret bag.

"Ready?" Katerina chirped. Irena nodded.

It was now dark outside, and raining. They drove back to Hollywood listening to a CD of Lady Gaga, and the squeaking of windshield wipers. Nobody said much.

After Seth returned from taking them back to the airport three days later, he discovered a photograph of himself that Katerina always had held in her wallet. It was a photo of himself, considerably younger, from maybe a year or two after they were married. It lay on his desk, torn in half.

It didn't surprise Seth to find Julia aloof when she returned from the mountain cabin. There were no emails and no texting between them, just superficial niceties on the rare occasions they crossed paths to or from their apartments, or by the laundry room.

In the meantime, in Moscow, Katerina, now in her late forties, was finding it increasingly difficult to find employment, even in her native land. She said she needed at least part-time work to help support her knitwear design company she had opened, licensed, and for which she had created a marketing team and website.

Katerina landed one job as an administrator, another as a shopkeeper. Within two weeks of being hired, she lost each job when some pretty eighteen-year-old came looking for work. One human resources director, a woman no less, told Katerina how, given her age, Katerina should have been more successful by now, and would better use her time seeking out a plot in a cemetery — or so Katerina told Seth.

When Katerina got a job keeping the books for a floral company, the company simply neglected to pay her at all. After she mentioned that she had been passed over for three pay periods, they apologized and said that the company was having financial difficulties, and that Katerina's salary would be caught up within two weeks. At the end of the two weeks, Katerina said she received a check for one-quarter of what she was owed.

A month later, Katerina was thrilled to have landed a job near her apartment, keeping the books for a hair salon, three days a week for $1,000/month. After an unpaid trial period of one week, she discovered that they actually expected her to be in the shop fourteen hours a day, seven days a week, for the same meager pay, leaving her exhausted, and with no time to develop her knitwear business.

Seth found Katya's plight particularly exasperating, given that a similar business she had launched in Los Angeles while living with Seth had started to take off. She had built a client base, which demonstrated that her creations were not only artistic, but commercially viable.

Furthermore, in Moscow, she had recently signed a contract with a reputable investor, willing to display a collection of her knitwear, with her own label, in one of Moscow's high-end department stores. She wasn't some *babushka* with knitting needles, pipe-dreaming. Her talent for design, like that for her acting, was a preternatural gift. She needed undistracted time and backing to bring her ambitions to fruition.

"What can I do to help?" Seth asked her in a phone conversation, after she'd told him of her experience in the hair salon.

Katerina sobbed that life had humiliated her, that she had no right to accept his help, that she was not a "Russian gold digger."

Seth told her to stop with the melodrama, that her best chance for rising from her perceived humiliation resided in her running her own company.

"Okay," she said, after she stopped crying. "I would need about $2,500 to get things started."

Seth wired it to her the next day.

Meanwhile, a man named Frank moved in with Julia next door. At least, he was staying overnight three to four nights a week, Seth observed.

THE CONFLUENCE OF THESE EVENTS — his estrangement from Julia and his own languishing divorce case — sent Seth into the kind of depression in which one questions the wisdom of one's actions and the purpose of one's life. He lost his appetite and suffered from stomach cramps. Before bed, he'd treat himself to a shot or two of tequila in order to induce sleep, which was becoming increasingly light and disturbed.

It's hard to determine whether his state of mind or the cheap tequila were responsible for the visions that began to appear to him — usually during the day, but sometimes in the middle of the night. One time, at about 3 a.m., Seth sprang out of bed absolutely convinced that three bats were circling in his bedroom. He flicked on the light and searched every corner, but found nothing.

A few days later, while in the offices of the *L.A. Observer,* the face of his late father appeared in his computer screen. The cheeks of the phantom were scarlet with rage, and the vision propelled itself from the screen toward him. His colleagues observed him abruptly lurching backwards such that Seth almost fell out of his chair.

Meanwhile, Seth's relations with Julia took one more unexpected turn.

That turn was related to the latest scandal to engulf the Bronson Canyon Homeowners Association, concerning a large, decrepit sliding glass door that Vera Pentcheva had been storing in the building's garage. This all started in mid-July, and played itself out through November.

The Angelis duo had insisted that Vera remove the door, since the garage was a "common area" and was not intended as a storage site for refuse. After weeks of rebuffed requests that Vera remove the door, and their offers of help to do so, their campaign culminated in an official letter, approved by President Winston and signed by the HOA's attorney, Bradley Fujimara, ordering her to remove it from the property within two weeks, or allow the HOA to remove it after that deadline. Vera's belligerent response was, instead, to install it inside her apartment — between the living room and the balcony that extended over the building's driveway — under the bogus description of home improvement. In fact, there was no improvement involved at all, since the sliding glass door already installed in the apartment was in far better condition than the battered and chipped door intended as its replacement. Furthermore, the disputed sliding glass door didn't even fit the frame it was intended to fill — and altering the building's structure to accommodate the crappy new door required the written approval of the Board, which simply wasn't going to happen.

For his part, Seth understood why Vera was being so difficult. She had grown up in communist Romania, where most of the population devised creative ways to work around the authorities' patronizing intrusions on citizens' activities. For Vera, the HOA was behaving much like the communist government she'd grown to despise. There was no way she was going to submit willingly to their pressure, even if their requests were fundamentally reasonable.

Seth also understood that the HOA requests *were* reasonable, as were Julia's arguments, which aligned with those of the HOA. At the same time, Seth felt reluctant to involve himself as Julia's advocate, given their brief, tempestuous romantic history. Seth just wanted to wash his hands of the entire controversy.

"The sliding door that's there is just fine!" Seth heard Julia yell over the phone to Vera. What Julia was mainly trying to avoid was the intrusion of Reginald McCallister, Vera's boyfriend and handyman.

Slightly more than a year ago, Reginald tried to repair a malfunctioning oven range. The result was six-foot flames cascading from the entire unit, until the fire department arrived to extinguish it. It took two weeks for Vera to replace the charred oven and range. Three months later, Reginald tried repairing a leak under the kitchen sink, resulting in an open pipe dangling uselessly for three weeks, and rendering Julia's kitchen unusable — until, for health code reasons, the HOA summarily brought in its own licensed plumber to complete the work. (Only after a small claims court judge ruled against her did Vera reimburse the HOA for the plumbing bill.)

So the history of relations between Vera and the HOA was peppered with acrimony. The Angelis duo described Vera as a "renegade owner," but then again, they said that of more than half the people in the building, including Seth. As president, Winston was caught in the middle, since Vera was close friends with his wife Suki, and they attended "church" services every Sunday for a cult that believed our destiny is in the hands of extraterrestrials who circle the planet in UFOs. Vera and Suki's wine-induced squealing laughter was often heard coming from Winston's apartment. This annoyed the Angelis duo deeply. Then again, almost everything annoyed the Angelis duo deeply.

On a Sunday afternoon, Reginald knocked at the metal screen door of Apartment #2D. His tools were stuffed into a canvas bag slung over his shoulder. Julia warily opened her main front door, leaving the screen door shut, as Frank, a slender intellectual-looking fellow, peered anxiously from within.

"I'm here to replace the sliding glass door," Reginald announced chirpily.

Julia merely glared through the screen door before hissing

through the barrier, "State law requires landlords to give twenty-four hours notice for inspections or repairs. These repairs can only be performed Mondays through Fridays during business hours."

Reginald's body stiffened and his face glowed with rage.

"Bitch," he muttered, before stalking away.

ON MONDAY AFTERNOON, UPON returning home from work, Julia found a Notice of Inspection/Repairs, signed by Vera, taped to her screen door. It had been posted at 1 p.m., and announced the intention of her "agent" (Reginald) to appear on Tuesday, 10 a.m. for "improvements/repairs."

Julia sent an email addressed first to Vera, then copied to the Board, and blind

copied to Seth.

"The time differential between the 1 p.m. posting of the notice on Monday and the announced 10 a.m. arrival on Tuesday does not constitute 24 hours, as required by law," Seth read. "The notice is not valid, and I will not be granting Reginald access to my unit on Tuesday."

Seth was now particularly grateful that he no longer served on the Board.

On Tuesday, Julia forwarded to Seth a cease-and-desist email from the HOA attorney, Bradley Fujimara, addressed to Vera: "Should you or your agent alter the building's structure without the Board's written consent, the Board will assert its right to restore the building to its original condition, and charge you for the expense."

The letter had no effect. On Wednesday evening, Julia discovered another Notice of Inspection/Repairs taped to her screen door, announcing Reginald's intended arrival on Friday morning at 10 a.m. to replace the sliding glass door.

Julia took that Friday off work. While the Angelis duo lay in wait in their respective units, Julia and Frank hunkered in the apartment waiting for Reginald, who never showed up.

On Friday evening, Julia found another notice, announcing Reginald's arrival at 10 a.m. on Monday.

That same Friday evening, Seth finally intervened. He sent an email to Vera, which read as follows:

"I totally empathize with your aggravation with the Board's Soviet restrictions and style, but Vera, if Reginald shows up, the Angelis duo will call the police, you know they will . . . Personally, I like Reginald," he added. "If he were somebody I cared about, I wouldn't put him in this situation."

On Saturday morning, Seth received a reply from Vera, thanking him for his kindness. Seth, however, had been around the building long enough to understand that her reply bore no connection to her intentions.

On Monday morning, at 10:20, Reginald showed up at Apartment #2D. He knocked several times and called inside. Nobody answered. Meanwhile over at the Capitol Records production department, Julia received a call from JoJo Angelis reporting that she'd seen Reginald entering the unit.

From his rabbit hole in Apartment #2E, Seth heard Julia and her friend from work Marcia clumping up the stairs. He heard two LAPD officers urging Reginald to calm down. He heard Reginald yelling at Julia, "This is MY apartment, and I can come in here whenever I want!" And then: "Fucking bitch, you are SO evicted!"

Later, from his kitchen window, Seth peered down into the driveway, only to see Reginald slumped against a wall in handcuffs, being guarded by one officer. The other officer was speaking to Vera, who was calmly pleading her case: "I'm the building's owner and this is my agent. I provided notice for repairs all in compliance with the law. This . . . tenant . . ." (she actually spat the word *tenant* as she glared at Julia) "has engaged in willful obstruction . . . "

Seth saw the first officer un-handcuff Reginald. He watched as Vera and Reginald walked through the building's security gate and out into the street. He heard the buzz of the police walkie-talkies soften and dissipate as the uniformed pair also walked away.

That night, Seth read an irate email from Vera to the Board. "I hope you're pleased, colluding and conspiring with my tenant! Interfering with the terms of our rental contract! Now your lawyer's going to have something to do. I hope you've got reserves in the account!"

Meanwhile, Vera had posted an eviction notice on Julia's door, claiming that Frank had no contractual right to live there, even though she had no proof that he was actually living there.

The following morning, Vera put the question directly to Seth, asking him what he'd seen going on next door.

Seth had no intention of being Vera's stooge, especially when recalling how Julia had pleaded shrugging ignorance to the city regarding Cassandra. Seth told Vera — and Julia's attorney — that he wasn't aware of any full-time occupants in the unit besides Julia. It's true Frank pissed him off, for obvious reasons. So did Julia, for obvious reasons. Yet Seth tried his best to overcome the kind of petty spite that already permeated the building. In Seth's view, Vera's biggest legal problem was Reginald's threat, which had made its way into the police report: "Fucking bitch, you are SO evicted."

Landlords aren't really supposed to evict tenants for reasons of personal revenge.

In the middle of the eviction case, Julia and Frank found a vacant apartment on the next block of Bronson Canyon. They quietly moved out on the night of March's full moon, and the civil dispute between Vera and Julia simply evaporated.

The entire tawdry, stupid spectacle had so upset the building's occupants, Winston called an emergency meeting for all homeowners to vent. Winston was hoping that perhaps he could inspire some renewed sense of unity among his neighbors.

Seven of the building's twelve owners attended, crowded onto couches and chairs around Winston's living room table. Vera, who had picked up some weight, and looked much the better for it, tried to be calm, but her temper revealed itself in her flushed cheeks. Her long, silver-streaked hair splayed from her scalp, slightly unruly, contributing to her appearance of being utterly exhausted.

The Angelis duo were predictably confrontational and insulting, accusing Vera of being a slumlord and blatantly disregarding the By-laws. Eddie didn't say much. He just trembled with rage and interjected half-sentences in support of his mother, JoJo. Vera, for her part, accused the HOA of being worse than communists.

"My sliding glass door isn't even visible from the street," she chided them, calling into question the purpose and profit of their vindictive interference. "Besides, the Board should be representing the owners, not their tenants," Vera cautioned.

Seth listened to all this wearily. He hadn't slept well the night before, and he remained gripped by his aforementioned depression. He studied Winston, who was listening to the debate and looking abject. Perhaps there might one day be harmony among this crew, but it wasn't going to show its face tonight. Arms and hands gesticulated in anger. People shouted and cursed with self-importance.

And then the most extraordinary thing happened: The furniture shook slightly. Some feared the early tremors of an earthquake. But it wasn't that. The shouting and cursing suddenly stopped and all eyes turned up toward Winston's ceiling, which was now visibly cracking.

The cottage-cheese ceiling started to crumble and wads of dust and dirt came crashing down.

Within one crack, now at a length exceeding two feet and about nine inches wide, they witnessed the sole of a boot descending, and then a leg attached to that boot, wrapped in green army trousers.

Within seconds of the first boot, small chunks of lumber came tumbling to the floor, revealing a second boot and foot and leg, enshrouded in dust, until a figure came into focus, descending from the ceiling, dressed in formal military attire with a jacket flush with dust-coated medals. Seth noticed that the medals were imprinted with foreign words.

The figure, a man, then tumbled onto a narrow strip of carpet that had been cleared by the assembled owners, who stared agog. The man landed on the carpet with a thud. There emerged a small groan from the now-bent mustached figure, who quickly straightened, dusted off his jacket and wiped his medals with a handkerchief. While doing this, he hacked and coughed and spat into the same hankie.

"*Vadah,*" he repeated hoarsely. The owners had no idea what he was saying, except for Seth and Vera, who, knowing Russian, understood that the man was pleading for water.

Seth rushed into the kitchen, filled a glass of water from the tap and handed it to the Russian man, who gulped it down in two swallows and pleaded for a refill.

"*Spaseeba,*" he said to Seth, returning the tumbler. By now almost everyone in the room recognized the man from old photographs and posters and documentary movies.

Their new guest was a living embodiment of Joseph Stalin.

After gaining his composure and licking his lips from a second glass of water, Stalin greeted all seven owners with a handshake and a smile.

"Thank you. Thank you for having me," he said in broken English.

Stalin then approached one of Winston's two couches and politely urged Winston's guests aside. He dusted off the three floral cushions that formed the couch's seat, and he lay down, prone across them, with his boots propped up on the sofa's far arm.

Joseph Stalin then closed his eyes, breathed heavily, and finally started to snore.

With that, Winston called the emergency meeting to a close. Suki showed everyone to the door.

On the walkway outside, the owners stood in amazement discussing the scene that had just transpired. Their conversations lasted for well over an hour. Eventually, everyone dispersed.

Upon entering his apartment Seth lay down directly on the living room floor and stared at the ceiling. Cassandra fluttered over from her perch on the playpen wall and settled onto his chest. Both fell asleep in that position, and the image of Stalin crashing through Winston's ceiling recurred in Seth's dreams.

For their part, Winston and Suki lay together on their backs with open eyes, holding hands, and listening to the snoring of their enigmatic guest in the front room. They tried in vain to fathom what the morning might bring.

Eddie stayed that night with his mother JoJo. The pair discussed the events of the night well into dawn, until they fell asleep, both in one bed, as they had when Eddie was a child. Sometimes, families from the Mediterranean regions of Europe are closer than those from more northerly and westerly climes, and don't regard that closeness as anything out of the ordinary.

That night, all residents of the Bronson Canyon Homeowners Association, human and fowl, finally enjoyed some repose, but none slept as soundly as their visitor from who-knows-where.

ACT III:
PEACE IN
OUR TIME

ACT III, SCENE 1:
THE BRONSON CANYON TULIP CRISIS

B y the end of February, Enriqo had repaired Winston's ceiling and fortified the roof above it. What Seth found so strange was that as the weeks passed, Joseph Stalin's arrival through the building's roof — this seminal event in the building's history — started to erode from people's memory, like a collective, early onset of Alzheimer's disease. When Seth brought it up, they'd say, "Oh, right!" as though it were snapping back into memory but otherwise might have been forgotten. By the end of June, even Winston and Suki stared at Seth sympathetically when he tried to remind them of the bizarre incident, as though he, alone, had invented the scene, and they had no desire to provoke his lunacy by contradicting his version of events, which was now his alone.

For everybody else's part, this newcomer named "Joe" was simply a "nice enough guy" who had paid an exorbitant half a million dollars in cash for Vera Pentcheva's apartment— exorbitant for a difficult-to-finance co-op that hadn't even been converted to a condo. Joe now resided in Apartment #2D. He was Seth's new next-door neighbor.

Joe was in his mid-thirties, and had shaved his moustache shortly after his arrival. Also, his spoken English quickly improved. What Seth remembered as an unmistakably thick Russian accent receded from his speech, replaced by American tropes, such as "Hey guys," and "Wasssup?" and "Sweet." He was barely five-and-a-half feet tall, with short dark hair and glistening white teeth. How he got his money or made his living were mysteries. He said he was in "securities and exchange," whatever that meant.

On the rare occasion that Seth was able to see through the triple layers of heavy curtains that Joe had installed along every window adjoining the walkway, Seth observed banks of computers inside his apartment. Looking out of his kitchen window onto the balcony next door, Seth could see Joe peering through a telescope that Joe had installed there. Joe would spend hours looking through that lens into all corners of the city, which Seth might have construed as a benign fetish were Joe not tapping out his observations onto the keyboard of a device resembling an Android phone.

The only question that remained for Seth was whether Joe was employed by the NSA, the FBI, the FSB, or all of them.

Nobody else in the building shared Seth's concerns about Joe. Rather, to most of the other owners, Joe was the embodiment of amiability. He went out of his way to engage in conversation anybody he met on the walkway or in the laundry room, never failing to shake their hands and engage in superficial chatter about the charm of the neighborhood, property values and the lurking threat of break-ins by homeless people.

While Seth was waiting for a load of laundry to dry, Joe cornered him and asked him if he could recommend some good plays to check out in the neighborhood. Seth was unsure of whether he was being mocked, or whether Joe really had some genuine interest in L.A. theater — so few did. Seth asked him what kinds of plays interested him.

"Musicals, mysteries, and monologues," Joe said. "I'm open to anything." Joe's alliteration aside, Seth found Joe's professed curiosity about esoteric local culture to be unconvincing. Still, Seth sputtered out the names of three theater productions — not necessarily anything that conformed to Joe's interests, whatever they might be, merely the last three Seth had seen and therefore jumped into his mind. One was a spoof of a horror flick, *Attack of the Rotting Corpses*; the second was a solo show, a portrayal of Mark Twain, written and performed by Val Kilmer; and the third was a small-theater staging of a big musical based on Toni Morrison's novel *The Color Purple*.

Two weeks later, Joe reported back that he'd seen all three, that he'd enjoyed them all, and how grateful he was for Seth's wise counsel. Joe then went into detail describing the qualities of the leading actors and his reservations about some of the directorial and design decisions. His favorite, he said, was *Rotting Corpses* — the gothic-macabre parody about zombies biting the necks of shallow-hearted tenants in a San Fernando Valley condo, thereby spreading the cult of zombie-ism. Joe reported all of this to Seth with unwavering enthusiasm, as though Joe had been hired as a publicist, and his job was to promote local shows. Seth was both enthralled by, yet skeptical of, Joe's buoyancy. After all, Seth was a critic while Joe was an enthusiast, or appeared to be. Mainly though, Seth saw Joe as a player.

During his first month in Bronson Canyon, Joe had already witnessed one mugging and heard of two others. Was everything possible being done to protect the building? he asked everybody he ran into.

This expressed concern for the public welfare in conjunction with Joe's unfettered positive energy led to him being elected as president of the HOA in the next, much postponed vote. Winston served dutifully as his vice president, and JoJo Angelis continued on as secretary-treasurer.

Joe's first call for action was to unify the building physically by having everybody's door painted the same color. At present, some were blue and some were green. "Bad for property values," Joe argued, "bad for curb appeal" — though none of these doors was anywhere near a curb.

Joe never asked what color people would like. He knew that from the interpersonal dynamics as they existed, that would only lead to a more deeply entrenched acrimony. Rather, he pulled aside each owner, one at a time, and showed him or her a color card containing a swath of deep mauve. He then painted his own door deep mauve as an example of what was possible. This itself was a violation of the Bylaws — altering a "common area" without Board approval — but nobody said anything about it in public, not even Seth.

Joe then asked what they thought of the new color, while in the same breath arguing how good it would look on everybody's door. Not wishing to offend Joe, each owner either agreed with him or, like Seth, simply changed the subject. For those who didn't change the subject, Joe had them sign a petition he'd created for this purpose.

Joe then sent around a memo saying that a super-majority of owners had voted for mauve as the color of choice, and that the color change was therefore in compliance with the Bylaws. He then asked everybody when it might be convenient for Enriqo to come by to repaint their front doors. By the end of three months, even with some stragglers like Seth, every door in the building was deep mauve. This had largely to do with the perception that battling Joe over the color of the building's front doors just wasn't worth the trouble. This was democracy in action, under President Joe.

One afternoon in early June, Seth cycled home to discover that the trio of sculpted pine trees and ivy that had formed the building's front landscaping since 1963 was gone, along with the ivy that carpeted them. There stood Joe, shovel in hand, turning over the soil.

"What happened?" Seth shouted as he rolled onto the property. "What have you done?"

"Subterranean termites," Joe chirped. "In all the roots."

"Look," Seth said, trying to contain his rage. He was now holding his bicycle with one hand and gesticulating with the other. "You can't go around cutting down trees like that. The front garden belongs to everybody. Changes like this need to be discussed and voted on!"

"The insurance company ordered me to remove the trees!" Joe pleaded with a tinge of indignation while mopping his brow. "They were *infested*! What's the problem? Haven't you guys been talking for years about changing the landscaping?" he added.

"There needs to be a vote!" Seth yelled.

The next day, Seth called the insurance company. The agent he spoke with implied that Joe was dissembling, that he had indeed called, but only after he'd already cut down the trees, asking if his removing the "infested" trees might qualify the building for a rate decrease. They said no.

Using much the same technique in getting his own color on the doors, Joe had the entire garden replanted on the building's front, back, and sides with low-lying shrubs and cacti, all in conformity with his own taste, and in consultation with Winston. Joe tended the garden as though it were his own, watering it for an hour each afternoon while regularly announcing how much money he had saved the building by planting drought-resistant flora.

What Seth found so grating in all this was the HOA's imperious double standard that Joe's personal garden, created on entirely, yes, false grounds, was in the public interest; whereas Seth's personal garden — what *had been* his personal garden before it got trashed when he wasn't looking — was perceived as some kind of demonstrative self-interest that clashed with the common good. This was more than a double standard, it was hypocrisy, though none of that was Joe's fault because Seth's garden pre-dated Joe's arrival.

For all these reasons, Seth quietly purchased six decorative railing planters and in the middle of a chilly night, he installed them on the railing directly outside his front door, slightly above where his former plastic containers had once sat, and from where he could see his garden, as he used to, from his living room window. Before doing any of this, however, he confirmed with the fire department that railing planters violated no safety code. They didn't, because they didn't block anybody's path along the walkway. Still, Seth anticipated that the Angelis duo would roar once again that Seth was breaking the law for his own idiosyncratic satisfaction. And that's exactly what they did.

The planters were of a design called "horse trough": metal cradles bolted onto the railings. They held a straw-like base mat that folded up the sides. Onto that mat, Seth poured potting soil and planted daffodil, tulip and hyacinth bulbs, and then dusted a seed-coating of white and purple sweet alyssum on the surface.

On a Tuesday afternoon, Seth was gently watering his newly planted garden with a yellow metal watering can that had been a gift from Julia, as thanks for supporting her during Vera's spiteful fit. Winston, who was now vice president, sidled up to Seth and suggested that his plantings were a needless provocation.

"I'm not sure I understand what daffodils, tulips and hyacinths have to do with 'provocation,'" Seth countered.

Winston walked away, shaking his head.

Within a week after the spring planting, Seth received a letter from the HOA attorney, Bradley Fujimara, saying that "The walkways and their adjoining railings are part of the building's 'common area' and that any alteration, hangings or decorations on the common areas must first be approved in writing by the Board. (HOA Bylaw,

Article III, Item 4). Kindly remove the six planters you attached to the railings of the upper common walkway within two weeks of the date of this letter in order to avoid a fine. Failure to do so could result in further legal action, including a lien on your property."

Seth confronted Winston over this letter. He said the Board had discussed it and found the railing planters to be out of keeping with the style of the new plantings below. Much of the discussion, Winston reported, was centered on whether, if there are to be railing planters, they should extend along the entire length of the building rather than being boxed in by Seth's apartment. The issue was stylistic unity. Seth said he had no objection with that.

Of course, being on community property, Winston added, the Board would have to choose what plants they contain, and the Board would then hire an independent contractor to maintain them. That's what their lawyer had advised.

"Then they wouldn't be mine," Seth argued.

"They're not supposed to be yours," Winston countered. "They're on the common area, which means they're supposed to belong to everybody."

As an illustration of Seth's indignation, he consulted a lawyer recommended by an old friend. Putting yet another dent in Seth's bank account, his lawyer drafted the following reply to the HOA attorney:

"Dear Mr. Fujimara,

"I have been retained as counsel for Seth Jacobson, a co-owner in the Bronson Canyon common interest, regarding the HOA of that interest, and its decision to deprive my client of his right to the simple peace and pleasure of gardening outside his own home, i.e. of enjoying flora growing in six decorative railing planters which he located outside his own living room window, and nobody else's.

These planters violate no city, county or state code.

"The HOA is now threatening to enforce its Bylaw (Article III, Item 4) demanding that he remove said planters until receiving written permission from the Board for any 'decorative changes to the common area.'

"This argument might have credence had the current HOA president not in the past three months unilaterally decimated the front garden, also 'common area,' tearing down three pine trees and uprooting ivy and long-extant, thriving plantings on three of the building's sides, before replanting all of those areas with plants of his choosing. I would be happy to receive a copy of the Board's minutes of the meeting in which these actions were approved. Because these minutes don't exist, because there was no such vote, the HOA president stands in violation of exactly the same Bylaw (Article III, Item 4) now being directed against my client.

"If the HOA believes that it's a worthy use of its time and energy to engage in the double standard of enforcing a Bylaw against one co-owner while ignoring that same Bylaw for another co-owner who happens to be the Board president," the letter oozed, "my client will be seeking injunctive and monetary relief against the Bronson Canyon Homeowners Association for abuse of process, discrimination and civil harassment.

"Sincerely yours, Mayank J. Munjabi,

"Christopher, Munjabi and Spelling, LLP, 300 Wilshire Blvd., Ste. 408, Los Angeles, CA 90012."

In the weeks that followed, all went quiet on the issue of what came to be known as the Bronson Canyon Tulip Crisis. With some delight, Seth observed the first of many green spikes emerging from the soil of his planters. These were the daffodils. Then came the hyacinths, which unfolded like soaked wads of tissue paper as they dry. The alyssum was next, at first appearing like tiny, isolated weeds, but soon creating a pale green carpet at the base of what were now spears of green from the daffodils and hyacinths and, last to emerge, the tulips. From planting to bloom, the hyacinths took barely a month to send up sprays of bright red, yellow and dark blue cylinders, swaying at a height between a foot and eighteen inches. They emitted a sweet aroma. Shortly after, the alyssum groundcover cascaded over the metal sides with ever-elongating washes of white and purple. The Prince Albert yellow daffodils were an aristocratic announcement of spring, second only to the royal red tulips, two dozen delicate burgundy teacups in a row soaring above all other bursts of color and swaying in the afternoon breeze.

Seth's creation was a fragrant, English/European/Turkish garden parked above and in one corner of the desert landscape created by Joe and Winston. Seth's garden was a defiant stand of the old world against the new — each created with a singularity of purpose and by skirting the rigors of a democratic process.

From his second tier, Seth tended his bulbs daily, snipping out weeds with his fingers, inhaling their fragrance, watering them gingerly — sometimes with Cassandra perched on his shoulder, each of them squinting into the afternoon sun, renegades in tandem. The railing garden was, for Seth, an evolving sculpture, an homage to the glory and elegance of empires now in tatters.

Meanwhile, at the same time, Seth looked down on Joe taking similar satisfaction from the garden he and Winston had created below. It was indigenous to arid Pacific Rim terrains, from the mighty Mojave Desert all the way to the flatlands of Mexico, to the Gobi desert in China. It was prickly and with thick fleshy leaves that could store water even in the scorching heat. Seth understood full well that Joe and Winston's garden represented the future, a botanical adjustment to global warming. And that the way Joe and Winston had installed it, through their subtle and not so subtle skirting of the rules, was also the future. If meetings were held to discuss the community's garden, Seth wasn't invited. There were certainly no minutes to record whatever public approval and disapproval there might have been for their decisions. Their rule of law consisted of pushing forward their agenda, rolling over legal and ethical impediments, inconveniences of process, and then calling the outcome inevitable. It was as American as Manifest Destiny. It was also as Russian as the Soviet Union, and all that preceded it, and all that followed it.

Seth also understood that his own stubborn defiance was a form of crankiness, even as he raised his protests, even as he tightened the bolts securing his horse trough planters to the railings that technically belonged to everybody in the building. As though such a gesture showed the resolve and dignity of the individual over the tyranny of oligarchs. Seth fully comprehended the absurdity of such symbolism, but he did so enjoy tending his garden and, in the larger scheme of things, it did no harm. This is what Seth was thinking as he used his forefinger and thumb to pluck an invading dandelion weed from his genteel yet unruly sanctuary.

Joe didn't raise any complaint with Seth's garden, at least not to his face, and certainly not after receiving the letter from Seth's lawyer. Nor did Joe or his now good friend Winston ever give it a single compliment. Rather, they tolerated it, as one tolerates a small dent in a new car, or a chip in the windshield.

What transpired next, however, caused Seth some confusion.

He had determined with certainty that Joe, by his actions, was a tyrant. He had watched Joe circumvent the democratic process in the building with a cunning blend of unilateral action and artful persuasion, and he had succeeded in all this because of the general apathy of the other apartment owners toward due process.

So long as the end result was acceptable, who cares how that result came to be?

Such was the pervasive attitude in the building that allowed Joe to gain power and influence so quickly, and Seth found this expedience to be lazy at best, and dangerous at worst. The way the recent changes in the building had come to pass was more translucent than transparent, and this bothered Seth.

He didn't like Joe because he didn't trust him.

It is, however, just as lazy and dangerous to box somebody into a label, such as "tyrant," because the label, and the certainty of it, is a cement that calcifies all possibility of arriving at a larger truth.

Seth arrived at this conclusion on the first day that Joe paid a visit to Seth in his apartment, and confusion set in.

It was Cassandra who caused this confusion. It was Cassandra who compelled Seth to reconsider his fixed, unrelentingly stern view of Joe.

At 11 a.m., just after Seth had emailed his review to the *Observer* of Neil Simon's comedy *The Sunshine Boys* at the Ahmanson Theatre, he heard a quiet tapping on his front door. Through the peephole, he could see Joe standing outside, holding a bouquet of spinach leaves. Seth opened the door.

"I brought these for Cassandra," Joe said, standing outside the door. He was wearing sandals, khaki shorts and a Hawaiian shirt, and he clutched the clump of spinach next to his chest, so that it blended into the pattern on his shirt. The spinach was tied at the stems by a rubber band.

The picture of Joe standing there, like a teenage suitor trying to woo a high school sweetheart through her father, left Seth speechless. That the object of Joe's affection was a chicken only compounded Seth's bewilderment.

"Do you want to come in and give it to her yourself?" Seth said after a moment of awkward silence.

"You sure that's okay?" Joe said with a gentle courtesy so overflowing with trepidation, it almost left puddles on the welcome mat outside the door.

Seth nodded. Joe crossed the living room toward Cassandra, who had been rummaging on her playpen floor. Seeing Joe and the spinach, she sprung to a playpen wall and perched there, waiting impatiently, caw-cawing.

What happened next was a revelation.

Cassandra gobbled down the spinach directly from Joe's hand, while Joe cooed at her, spoke to her in English, in Russian and in Chicken — perfectly imitating her cawing. After she had consumed the entire bouquet in about thirty seconds, Cassandra leapt from the rim of her playpen wall directly onto Joe's shoulder, while he continued to speak to her. She crossed from his left shoulder across his back to his right shoulder, then back again to his left. Then she sat, preened his left sideburn and parked her face directly against his cheek, and held this position for a good twenty seconds, while Joe whispered endearments to her. In short, it was a love scene, and Seth hadn't seen anything like it between Cassandra and anybody else, except for himself.

What struck Seth so powerfully was that Joe wasn't acting; his affection for Cassandra was sincere. Being a drama critic, Seth knew the difference. He could see Joe's love for this bird in the delight that crossed his face when Cassandra returned his conversation, in Joe's spontaneous smile when she pressed her face against his, in the gentleness with which he rubbed the underside of her beak, and caressed the top of her head.

"Nobody's going to take this bird away from you," Joe told Seth. "You have my word."

This wasn't some act. Joe meant it. Seth had presumed that Joe was in the pockets of the Angelis duo and their agenda to derail Seth's every source of domestic tranquility. Here was evidence that Seth's presumption wasn't entirely true. And with that realization, Seth's sanity started to return. The return of his sanity was slow, but it was a return nonetheless. The evidence of Joe's humanity provided Seth with some small comfort, which Seth determined to be a significant improvement on no comfort at all.

That small comfort would, over time, grow larger.

On a Tuesday afternoon in late March —— at about the same time the hyacinth blooms were starting to unfurl, Seth returned on his bicycle to the building from the *L.A. Observer* and attempted to retrieve his mail. Despite the new administration and the determination by President Joe to upgrade the building's appearance, and despite numerous requests by Seth to Joe and to Winston for a new mailbox key, no move had been made to replace the mailboxes, or to provide Seth with a new key to his own box. It was now over a year since Cassandra had swallowed Seth's one mailbox key. That was during the Winston administration. And so, as he sometimes did, Seth jimmied open the upper casing of mailboxes with one finger so that those six adjoining mailboxes slid open, providing access to his own vault, and to the bundle of papers that resided inside it.

Before he could reach inside his own compartment, Seth heard clumping bootsteps fast approaching. In the same moment Seth turned to face the interloper, he felt the thump of Eddie Angelis' open palm smack into his chest, sending him reeling backwards into the mailboxes.

"Why don't you use a key?" he heard Eddie snarl.

Seth's first impulse was to strike back. That impulse was almost too strong to resist, yet he did resist. The tiniest shard of wisdom snagged his impulse for vengeance. This shard was the understanding that Eddie wanted a messy street fight. It had all come to this. And Seth understood that even if he prevailed, a difficult prediction to make, or if he didn't, the outcome would be twisted against him. Seth would be portrayed as the aggressor. He saw the trap. He saw yet another false accusation, this time for assault.

"You just hit me," Seth said.

"I was trying to close the mailboxes," Eddie explained.

Seth's chest was now starting to ache and reveal a bruise. He walked away, though he hadn't even gotten his mail. Trembling from shock and anger, he almost tripped up the southern stairwell on his way to Winston's apartment, 2A. He rang the doorbell. Suki answered and let him in. Winston emerged from the kitchen in a bathrobe and flip-flops, even at 3 in the afternoon.

"So now we're supposed to tolerate neighbors assaulting each other on the property!?" Seth blurted out, before relaying his version of what had just happened.

"Assault is assault," Winston said, nodding sagely. "You want me to call the cops?"

Seth pondered this for a moment. Yes, it really was assault.

"I want this on the record," Seth replied.

Seth heard the blur of Winston speaking by phone with a police operator. During this time, Seth tried to imagine how Eddie could have moved so quickly against him. Eddie was at the mailboxes within seconds of Seth's arrival there. It then occurred to Seth that he must have been seen from JoJo's front door on the ground floor, which was routinely open and barricaded by a metal screen, so that JoJo could see out into the bright daylight, but nobody could see in.

It also occurred to him that the Angelis duo were working together, lying in wait, for just the moment when they could catch Seth in the midst of what they determined was a criminal act.

After half an hour, Winston opened the door to two burly uniformed LAPD officers, whose squad car Seth observed parked by the building's front curb red zone.

One was a woman, Officer Simpson, looming at six and a half feet tall. She resembled the kind of Amazonian Olympic athletes that once comprised the East German female weightlifting team. The male, Officer Crandall, similarly imposing physically, appeared Arabic despite his name. He had a shaved head and wore his sunglasses even in the dark apartment. Their uniforms hugged their bulk, thanks to the bulletproof vests worn beneath their black polyester shirts, which stretched and strained over the contours of the protective undergarments. Simpson took notes on a small, yellow pad as Seth told her what had just taken place.

"Why don't you have a mailbox key?" she asked.

"I lost it over a year ago. I've been asking the HOA for a replacement ever since." He chose not to explain that it was probably swallowed by his pet chicken.

Simpson glared at Winston.

"You're on the HOA?"

"Yes, ma'am," Winston answered deferentially.

"You need to get him a key," Simpson said calmly. "You need to do this tomorrow. You understand?"

"Yes, ma'am," said Winston, nodding.

Simpson then turned to Seth: "So you want us to arrest him?"

Meanwhile, Crandall stood near the couch at a distance of four feet from Simpson, his legs slightly apart, his hands folded over his chest. He glared through his sunglasses.

"Oh," Seth blurted out, dreading the fallout from being responsible for Eddie's arrest.

"No person is allowed to strike another person," Crandall said. "If you want, we'll go next door right now and arrest him, but only if you're willing to press charges. If what you say happened actually happened, this is what we recommend you do, or this will just keep happening."

Seth stood in solemn contemplation, reflecting on the cycles of vengeance that could bring ruin to the House of Bronson.

At this precipitous moment, Joe knocked at the screen door, asking what was going on.

Winston let him in, introduced him to Simpson and Crandall, and updated him. Joe was barefoot, wearing a polo shirt and brown khaki shorts.

When Joe heard that Eddie had thumped Seth on his chest, Joe's cheeks flushed with rage. He actually blew air through his teeth like a boxer while nodding, trying to temper his fury.

"Have him arrested," Joe advised Seth in an intense whisper. "They're right. It's time to send a clear message. We can't have violence on my property. There have to be consequences to violence."

Seth was grateful for Joe's public display of support, even if he found Joe's tone a bit high-handed. The cops also couldn't fathom the meaning of Joe's anger. Seth discerned this from a twitch on Crandall's otherwise impenetrable face.

What struck Seth, however, was Joe's cavalier use of the expression "my property." The incident had not occurred on what was exclusively *his* property, but shared grounds — though Joe clearly regarded the entire building as his, and his alone. The rest, to Joe, all this business about co-ownership and democracy and shared responsibilities, was just a bundle of clumsy and arcane formalities.

Then again, this didn't really bother Seth as much as it had before Joe brought his spinach bouquet to Cassandra. Even if he was a blowhard, Joe had a heart.

"Could you just speak to him?" Seth asked the police. "I mean, without actually arresting him?"

Joe interceded. "No, Seth. Go for the jugular. Send the bastard to jail!"

"He's right," Crandall urged Seth. "The man knows what he's talking about."

Joe and Crandall both nodded while exchanging a fleeting machismo-saturated glance.

Seth thought it over some more. "Look, it was the first time. It was a temper tantrum. He didn't really *hurt* me."

"What about *next* time?" Joe interrupted.

"Once the violence starts . . . " added Crandall. "But it's your choice, of course," he told Seth, who expressed what was now his resolve: "I think it would be best if you just spoke with him."

Seth could see the disappointment, if not disgust, on Joe's and Crandall's faces. Simpson, for her part, remained neutral. Seth also detected palpable relief on the faces of Winston and Suki, who did not find this conflict particularly entertaining.

"Sure," Simpson replied. "Wait here, please."

Winston closed the screen door behind the two officers but kept the front door open. In this way, he could press his face against the metal grid and witness what was about to unfold next door at Eddie's apartment. It also allowed the conversation to be heard by Seth, Suki and Joe, who hovered inside Winston's living room.

They all heard the knock on Eddie's metal screen door, followed by nothing for about thirty seconds. There was another, harder knock at Eddie's door, followed by nothing for about thirty seconds.

The third knock was accompanied by Simpson's shout, "Eddie Angelis. Police! Open up!"

The tension in the next thirty-second silence resonated with everyone. It was followed by the sound of Crandall's nightstick pounding on and scraping up and down the metal of Eddie's screen door. Crandall yelled as though in a scene from any number of cop movies made throughout the ages: "LAPD! OPEN UP! —— NOW!!!"

Within five seconds, everybody heard the squeak of Eddie's front door opening.

Seth had no vantage since Winston was blocking everybody else's view by peering as best he could out the screen door from the threshold of his own living room, but from Seth's position in the middle of the room, he was able to hear snippets of conversation between Eddie and the police, who both remained standing on the walkway outside Eddie's screen door. The sounds of their voices drifted into Winston's apartment intermittently in tones ranging from calm to sarcastic.

"You find this funny?" he heard Crandall say. "You know what's funny? You look like a guy who wants to go to jail. That's what *I* find funny."

This remark obviously secured its purpose, because Seth couldn't hear anything more for a few seconds, until he heard a fragment of Eddie telling Simpson that he hadn't intended to shove Seth, that his intent was simply to close the rack of mailboxes that Seth had illegally pried open, thereby threatening the security of everybody else's mail.

"So you were just trying to close the mailboxes?" Crandall clarified.

"That's right," he heard Eddie answer.

"And Mr. Jacobson just happened to be standing between the mailboxes and your fist," Simpson chimed in, sarcastically.

By this time, JoJo had drifted upstairs to speak with the police, explaining that from her view — she insisted that she'd witnessed the entire altercation through her own screen door — she saw Seth throw the first punch and that her son was merely acting in self-defense.

"But your son just told us that he was trying to close the mailbox, that he punched Mr. Jacobson by accident," Simpson said.

"Can you two get your story straight?" Crandall piped in.

"I know one thing for sure," Simpson continued, bearing down on Eddie: "If we get any more calls that you have even raised a finger to anybody who lives here, you are going directly to jail, do I make myself clear?"

From Winston's living room, Seth heard no response. He did, however, hear Simpson repeat her rhetorical question, "Do I make myself clear?"

"Yes, ma'am," everyone then heard Eddie mutter.

The police returned to Winston's living room, where they politely refused Suki's offer of iced tea, but engaged in an ever so amiable discussion about Eddie and Jolene's sexual noises next door at all hours, noises that frequently forced Winston and Suki out of their own bedroom to sleep on their living room couches. Simpson shook her head: "How much did you pay for this place?" she asked.

They discussed property values and the current real estate market.

"That's the bitch of owning property," Simpson intoned. "You don't get to choose your neighbors."

After everybody had finished nodding in agreement, Seth asked if he might get a copy of the police report.

"Sure," said Crandall, withdrawing a business card. He wrote something on the back of his card with a pen he'd plucked from one of his pockets. He gave the card to Seth. On the clear, unprinted side was the date and time scribbled onto a corner, and the words, "Kept the peace." Then the initials JC. That's rather Biblical, Seth mused.

JC kept the peace. Seth knew that the "C" stood for Crandall, and that the "J" was either John, Jack, Joseph, maybe Jacob, Jamal?

For a reason Seth didn't fully understand, another image from *The Atlantic* crept into his mind and wouldn't let go. It was the image of dead bodies wrapped in white funeral shrouds — some men, some women, some children, all in rows. They had been killed with chemical weapons. The Syrian government was blaming the atrocity on the rebels. The rebels blamed the government. The Americans were considering what action to take against the Syrian government, if any. The Russians were encouraging the Syrian government to pursue a full investigation, or so Seth had read.

"Is there any species on the planet as vile as ours?" Seth pondered, wondering if his energies might be better spent on causes that actually mattered, rather than a dispute over a mailbox in Bronson Canyon — even if the latter was a petty allegory for global conflict.

There was never a police report on the incident between Eddie and Seth. After six months, the assault had officially evaporated.

Meanwhile, JoJo disseminated her own version of the altercation to anyone who would listen: that the police were prepared to arrest Seth for striking Eddie, and only Eddie's benevolence had kept Seth out of jail. Such is the arbitrary nature of history and the legends that evolve from it.

"You should have had him arrested," Joe reminded Seth at least once every two weeks until midsummer. "An opportunity like that comes once in a lifetime."

THE FOLLOWING WEEK, SETH RECEIVED a letter from "Bloomberry and Hendricks LLP, Attorneys at Law, 524 South

Figueroa Street, Nineteenth Floor, Los Angeles, CA 90071, Re: Eddie Angelis, Mailbox Security, Our File No.: 384687.

"Dear Mr. Jacobson,

"This letter is notice that Mr. Edward Angelis has consulted with this law firm regarding vandalism by you to the mailboxes of the community interest of the Bronson Canyon Homeowners Association. There are multiple witnesses to your forcefully prying open these mailboxes with your hands and other implements, thereby jeopardizing the security of everybody's mail. Mr. Angelis' mother, Jocasta Angelis, for example — the owner of a separate unit in the common interest — is now the victim of identity theft. She has been forced to cancel all of her credit cards, change her bank accounts and all User ID and PIN numbers associated with dozens of her electronic transactions. She attributes these burdens directly to the access to community mailboxes made possible entirely by your actions. She even found one of her credit card bills lying on the sidewalk approximately 15 feet from the mailboxes.

"Your actions, and your actions alone, have forced my client to lease a P.O. Box in order to ensure the security of his mail, and he is demanding that you reimburse him the cost of that lease, in the amount of $155, within 14 days of this letter, or my client will pursue this matter further through legal channels.

"Very truly yours,

"Bloomberry & Hendricks LLP,

"By Isaac B. Shettleford."

Given Joe's public display of anguish over Eddie's behavior, Seth chose to show this letter to Joe. Since Joe had once sauntered down the walkway to knock on Seth's door with no appointment or notice, Seth figured it would be okay to do the inverse. And so he knocked on Joe's door.

From the walkway, Seth heard padding footfalls approach the front door from the inside. Seth could tell Joe was peering through the peephole in the front door. All other views were blocked by Joe's triple-layered heavy curtains.

"Hi," he heard Joe call from his sanctum.

"You got a second?" Seth shouted back.

"I'll be right over," Joe replied.

This is a man who values his privacy, Seth reflected. Privacy was a right that Seth treasured, though he did wonder what exactly Joe was hiding behind, or simply hiding.

About fifteen minutes later, Seth was in his own kitchen boiling hot water in an electric kettle for a cup of tea, when he heard Joe knocking on his door.

When Seth opened the door, a most remarkable spectacle unfolded. Without any prompting, and at the sight of Joe merely standing across the living room by the front door, Cassandra leapt from her playpen floor to one of its walls. Then, in a second, spontaneous gesture, she flew in an impressive arc, traversing the entire width of the living room in order to land directly, with gentleness and accuracy, onto Joe's left shoulder.

Keep in mind that Cassandra was not an eagle or a hawk or one of any avian species, even a pigeon, famous for their aeronautics. Rotund chickens like Cassandra generally don't fly at all. Rather, they jump or run while flapping their wings, which is an entirely different category of propulsion when it comes to the grace, or even the dignity, of the action. But in this instance, the first time in Cassandra's life ever observed by Seth, she took flight. It's true that a mountain of papers that Seth had kept in piles all over the room were now strewn and dislodged by the gust of wind that Cassandra had created by her flight. The smattering of papers detracted ever so slightly from the elegance of the flight, and a beautiful flight it was, inspired by Joe, who now stood next to the front door. He stood there with a chicken on his shoulder like a statue of Odysseus on the island of Ithaca — until he broke his pose to offer Cassandra a handful of grapes that he'd brought for their meeting.

Whatever dignity Cassandra may have conjured by her flight she instantly trashed on seeing the grapes. She was so eager, and greedy, for the bounty of fruit, she slid down Joe's front while overreaching for the grapes. She then had to scramble, flapping directly into Joe's face, in order to restore her balance. Joe winced and laughed. In fifteen seconds, all the grapes were gone, and Cassandra perched happily on Joe's shoulder while he sat on Seth's couch. Cassandra didn't just like Joe, she adored him, and he, her. This pleased Seth even more than during Joe's prior visit.

Seth showed Joe the letter from Eddie's attorney. On reading it, Joe's eyebrows crinkled.

"There's no way to prove that JoJo's identity theft has anything to do with 'common access' to the mailboxes," Joe said. "Chuck and Svetlana's mailbox next door is just a bin on a post. Her identity theft could have been from somebody hacking into her computer."

Joe barely noticed Cassandra shifting from his left shoulder to his right.

"Why is only Eddie named as the litigant, and not JoJo — if JoJo has been so wronged?" Seth asked.

"JoJo's on the Board," Joe replied. "I told them I don't want any lawsuits in the building. More than that, I told them I don't want anybody on the Board filing a lawsuit. Let me see what I can do."

The next day, on a hot Friday afternoon, Joe and Winston oversaw the replacement of both banks of mailboxes. A letter was taped over the sparkling new mailboxes that everybody could receive two keys to his/her mailbox by retrieving them directly from Joe, who was holding them for security reasons.

When Seth got home that evening, even before going to his own apartment, he knocked on Joe's door in order to receive his mailbox key. From behind the fortress, Joe asked who it was, and shouted that he'd be right over.

Ten minutes later, Joe stood at Seth's door and handed him two sparkling gold mailbox keys. Never again would he remove it from his car keys ring, he told Joe. The second copy he would keep in a high closet, sealed in a small cardboard jewelry box — safe from Cassandra's reach. That night, Seth slept with a rare peace of mind.

THAT PEACE DIDN'T LAST LONG. The following week, Seth discovered a large dead brown-and-black rat nestled in the still-flowering sweet alyssum on the second railing planter from the southern end. Before removing the rat, Seth made sure that both Winston and Joe witnessed it first-hand. Seth then took several photographs of the rodent.

Joe's reaction was bemused. "I told you," he said. "You should have had him arrested. Now he thinks you're weak. He thinks he can get away with these provocations."

"As unsettling as it is," Winston intoned meditatively, "there's no proof that the rat didn't just wander in and die."

Seth pointed to the forensic evidence: The foliage around the rat was robust. Had the rat "wandered in" and suffered death throes in the planter, wouldn't some of the leaves have been broken and flattened? The visual evidence, including the very position of the rat, strongly suggested that the rat had been placed *post-mortem* in the planter face down, after being suspended by its tail.

After meeting in executive session about the dead rat, the Board resolved what it had resolved so many times on so many different occasions: that there was nothing it could do.

The following day, after Seth had disposed of the rat, Seth purchased a surveillance camera and positioned its gaze from his living room window out onto his railing garden.

This annoyed the Angelis duo, and even Joe. Eddie and JoJo argued that Seth's actions constituted an affront to everybody's privacy, but Seth — doing a 180-degree turn on his entire view of privacy rights — countered that nobody could claim any expectation of privacy in a public space. Joe had to concede that video security-monitoring of one's own private possessions was within everybody's rights. And the fact that the garden was Seth's private property was the basis of the HOA's complaint against him. That the garden was situated on a common, *ergo* public, area further reinforced Seth's claim. Seth never dreamed that he'd one day be an advocate for video surveillance, but there you have it.

On his computer screen, Seth now observed images of everybody who crossed by his living room window. Sometimes it was a neighbor striding by with a laundry bag or groceries. More often, it was JoJo, who crossed in front of his window to peer in. There Seth watched on his computer, while Cassandra nuzzled his neck. There he saw JoJo discovering the video camera and peering into it. He saw JoJo render an obscene finger gesture directly into the camera. After that, almost every day, JoJo walked by frequently, as though to prove she would not be deterred, but without making any faces or gestures into the camera.

All of this pleased Seth immensely.

One week later, Seth received a notice from the Los Angeles Superior Court, Small Claims Division, that he had been named as the Defendant in a lawsuit filed by Edward Angelis for the amount of

$155, to cover the cost of Eddie's P.O. box for one year. That's when Joe sprang into action once again.

That action unfolded in Seth's apartment, with Cassandra planted firmly on Joe's left shoulder, as she was now wont to do, while Joe fed her blueberries by hand and paced the living room. This pacing gave Joe the authority that comes with the ability to reposition oneself in any location of the room, in order to accentuate a point. This authority was only slightly undermined by the picture of the brown hen perched on his shoulder, and only Eddie, who was sitting on the couch, took exception to that sight. Eddie was sitting next to Winston.

"Can you put the chicken back in its . . . pen, or whatever that is?" Eddie snapped.

"And what exactly is bothering you about the chicken?" inquired Joe.

Eddie now suffered the scrutiny of everybody's gaze, and could offer no reply.

"You guys really need to get over this thing you have about the chicken," Joe added. "How are you harmed by Cassandra?"

On hearing her name, Cassandra nuzzled her beak in Joe's ear and started preening him there. Eddie looked away in disgust, before sighing heavily.

In tandem, Joe and Winston both begged Eddie to drop the lawsuit against Seth. Eddie simply stared at the floor and said nothing.

"Look," Joe said, "the Board has discussed this. It was the Board's fault that the mailbox wasn't replaced sooner, so the Board is willing to pay you the $155 directly for you having to lease your P.O. box. "

"I don't want anything from the HOA," Eddie insisted. "I want it from *him*" — referring to Seth.

Seth now stared at the floor.

Joe then laid two $100 bills on the dining room table. "It's not from the Board. It's a private transaction between you and me. Just take it and drop this fucking lawsuit!"

"I don't want anything from you," Eddie said, picking up the two crisp Franklins and returning them to Joe. "I want it from *him.*"

Winston then turned to Seth. "Seth, would you be willing to pay Eddie $155 and put an end to this matter?"

Seth thought about it for a moment, looking at Eddie, then at Winston, before replying, "No, I wouldn't."

Eddie emitted a perverse, snorting laugh.

Added Seth, "I think we all know that this lawsuit is petty revenge for me calling the police on him after he hit me. But calling the police was my right, under the circumstances."

Feeling the tension in the room, Cassandra jumped from Joe's shoulder back to a wall of her playpen.

"I want it directly from *him,*" Eddie repeated, "with a letter of apology to me and all the other owners."

Neither the $155 nor any letter of apology would be forthcoming from Seth. This was a fact known by everybody in the room, in the building, and in the buildings directly to the east and west. The trial was set for July 17 in the Small Claims Division of the Stanley Mosk Courthouse in downtown Los Angeles.

THE FOLLOWING TUESDAY, SETH WAS summoned once again to the executive offices of the *L.A. Observer,* to the editor's office overlooking the Hollywood Freeway, which was just as gridlocked as the last time he was called to this office. The city had transformed itself in variegated ways in the intervening months, but traffic was its one constant.

Olivia the editor had resigned almost a year earlier, while Candace the publisher had resigned after being harassed by the numbers people in Tampa over plummeting advertising revenues. This was not the way she wished to spend her life, she had said at the time.

The meeting with Seth was between the chirpy new editor, Blanche, an attractive redhead who was probably in her early thirties and looked ten years younger. She was joined by Gary, the newly hired arts editor whose age placed him within recent memory of graduate school.

Seth was in fact the oldest person in the building. He knew this because everybody addressed him as "Sir," which he should have taken as a mark of respect, but he merely found it discomfiting. He didn't feel like a "Sir." Upon reflection, he felt his own recent behavior had been quite childish.

For his part, Gary said nothing while Blanche spoke in a matter-of-fact, fast-talking style that nonetheless had an underpinning of compassion.

"As you know," Blanche began, "we've been protecting the theater section for some time now. All the other sections have been sliced down while theater's been untouched."

This was true. The news section, once spread over five pages, was now down to a single page. The classical music page was gone. Event listings had been reduced by 80%. A book or gallery review was an exotic entry these days, when books and art each used to have their own section. Even the rock music department, that staple of populism, had suffered an implosion of ad revenue due to the closings of music stores, and the availability of free product online. The entire L.A. Observer newspaper, once a kind of city beacon at a bulky two hundred pages, wasn't even hitting one hundred anymore. To think that the paper once had "Environment" and "Spirituality" sections. But that was when it was locally owned. That was before it had been sold to a private equity company bent on positioning it for resale at a higher price. Its current editorial focus was local news scandals and sex, but even such glitter and trash weren't drawing ads. Perhaps, Seth theorized, it was actually driving them away. It had certainly driven away an entire generation of readers who now openly ridiculed the paper. The new managers said they didn't care, that the paper was now appealing to the young.

"They've given me a new budget," Blanche continued, "and I have to make it work . . . There's simply nowhere else to cut. The web hits on the theater reviews are not strong, so I just can't justify giving them so much space anymore," she continued. She was referring to the capsule reviews that Seth now assigned to his staff of critics, some of whom he'd worked with for decades. "So we need to go from eight reviews a week to two."

Seth absorbed this news for a moment before expressing, without malice, the essence of his reaction: "What's the point?"

Blanche looked at him askance, not quite understanding his question. Gary simply gazed out the window.

"What's the point of the theater section? Twenty to thirty productions open every week, and we're now covering *two* of them?

"*Around* two," Gary clarified.

"There's some flexibility," Blanche added. "Depending on the week."

"I wouldn't know how to begin assigning two reviews a week," Seth said. "What's the criteria?"

"Gary will be taking care of that," Blanche explained.

"I see," Seth said.

"What I don't want to lose," Blanche continued, "are the longer reviews that you write for us — where you have the space to get into something meaty. That's what I look for in the best magazines in the country. Perspective. Intelligence."

"Thank you," Seth replied apprehensively.

"What I'd like to do is have your column appear every two weeks instead of every week — that allows us to cover dance and music and opera and comedy."

Each of these other disciplines once had their own page, Seth recalled. Given the paper's current anemic condition, her proposal wasn't unreasonable. Still, there went another 50% of Seth's income from the paper.

"And can you write a bit shorter?" Blanche added. "Maybe eight hundred words instead of 1200."

"No problem."

When news got out about the cutbacks to the *Observer*'s theater section, the reaction across the city was one of weariness. That all this was another inexorable step in the diminishment of print journalism in general and the arts and humanities in particular, with their antiquated, reflective temperaments.

A lyric from Joni Mitchell's song "Dog Eat Dog" popped into Seth's mind.

"Land of snap decisions/Land of short attention spans/When nothing's savored long enough to understand/In every culture in decline/The watchful ones among the slaves/Know all that is genuine will be scorned, and conned, and cast away."

Seth quickly got on the phone to community leaders and proposed a professional website of arts coverage, to replace what the *Observer* was cutting, perhaps eventually expanding into architecture and politics, all initially funded by the community.

The first responses were favorable and came with some quick offers of funding. Seth had little sense of what kind of financial model would prevail for such an enterprise. Profit or nonprofit? The thing about a revolution, when the old institutions collapse faster than new ones can be created to replace them, is that even the revolutionaries don't really know what's happening.

Shortly after, Seth drove Joe to Fontana for one of Seth's biweekly visits to Agamemnon. Joe had heard Seth's stories of the infamous one-eyed rooster and told Seth he wanted to meet him.

Together, they drove out along a freeway that snaked through the foothills of the San Gabriel Mountains. The freeway adjoined inland communities punctuated with Home Depots and Lowes. Clusters of the same banks, auto dealerships, insurance companies, fast food and restaurant chains recurred every few miles. Sometimes it seemed that as few as a dozen companies owned the entire region.

As Seth was driving along the Foothill Freeway in the Honda Civic that he still hadn't replaced, despite the increasingly frequent urgings of his mechanic that he do so, he asked Joe how he made his living.

"Investments," Joe replied bluntly. Joe said he had stock in AT&T, in British Petroleum, Chevron, Time Warner, Pfizer, Hyundai Engineering & Construction Company, Wal-Mart, Deutsche Bank, Bank of China, JP Morgan Chase, the Royal Bank of Scotland . . . The list went on. He served on seven Boards of Directors, and so on.

"Stay away from precious metals," Joe cautioned. "They all say go for the gold, but precious metals always flatline when interest rates go up. All that glitters is not gold," he quipped.

They whizzed over the incline approaching Glendora. The sky was silver.

"Do you believe that money is everything?" Seth asked.

"I don't understand the question."

"What is the value of something that doesn't necessarily make money?"

"Like what?" Joe asked.

"Like a poem. A painting."

"I worked for a publishing house," Joe said. "Big New York firm specializing in fiction and poetry. Some guy like you, an artsy type, he worked for the company, he wanted to publish two books by this unknown poet he liked. I forget her name."

"You were the guy who could say yes or no?" Seth asked.

"Exactly," Joe replied. "I told him we need an eight percent return on the investment. That's not much. I told him to fill out a profit-and-loss sheet, based on how many books he figured would sell. He came back with some bullshit figure for potential sales. Over the moon. I knew he was lying, He knew he was lying. I told him we could double our profit if we put that same money into shares of AT&T. But I signed off on it anyway. Does that answer your question?"

"How did the book sell?"

"Terrible. Barely broke even."

"So why did you do it?"

"I liked the guy. He believed in this poet."

"And what would AT&T have done with this money?"

"I have no idea. Invested it in fiber optics, maybe."

"*Somebody* bought those poems. *Somebody* supported the chain of businesses around the bookstores that sold them . . . That investment supported jobs, no?"

Joe shrugged.

They were now at the end of the freeway exit, caught at a red light. "Did *you* believe in this poet?" Seth asked.

"I never read her. I don't read poetry. It makes my teeth itch."

Before Seth could conjure a meaningful response, he was driving up Bishop Pine Way. It was starting to rain. Seth pulled in alongside Susan's front fence. He called her cell phone. After a brief conversation, Susan emerged from her side yard and opened the fence for Seth and Joe.

Agamemnon followed her, the one-eyed guard-rooster, strutting ceremoniously with a fleshy red face, comb and wattles. He shook his head and feathers vigorously, spraying off raindrops.

Joe was impressed by Agamemnon, by his self-respect, by his girth, by his enduring all that he'd suffered in his life. Having emerged from the car, Joe now stood by the fence. He introduced himself to Susan, who explained she was busy tending to an ewe. Meanwhile, Seth crossed from the car's trunk into the yard carting a bag of chicken food. He stowed it in the metal shed at the side of Susan's house before returning to the front yard. Susan closed the fence then slipped away around the side of the house, followed by Agamemnon, leaving Joe and Seth together in the front yard.

The two men now stood aimlessly, side by side in the light rain, more of a mist really. Joe wore a blue Polo shirt and jeans; Seth, a crumpled striped dress shirt and cargo trousers. Neither had jackets yet neither of them wished to return to the car's protection from the moisture. Droplets formed on Seth's glasses.

"There's a poet named Samuel Beckett," Seth said. "He's dead now."

"I've heard of him," Joe replied.

"A poet and a playwright. He wrote a play called *Waiting for Godot*. Samuel Beckett and that play, in tandem, have been the most influential force on world theater in the past fifty years," Seth continued.

"And?"

"When the play opened in London, in 1953, it was a debacle. People stormed out at intermission. One of the actors said he heard audible groans coming from the audience. The first reviews were disastrous."

"So?" Joe remarked.

"Do you know what saved it? *Who* saved it?"

"Who?"

"Critics. Two of them. Harold Hobson in *The Sunday Times,* and Kenneth Tynan, writing in *The Observer.* They wrote such loving reviews, they turned the play from a travesty into a triumph. Because of them, it changed the world."

"Did it? I don't see how any poem or play has changed the world. The world has not changed, from what I've seen."

"That play changed the way we see it."

"Your point?" Joe asked.

"Critics. This could never happen today. The Harold Hobsons and Kenneth Tynans get kicked to the gutter. The largest market share isn't *necessarily* what's most valuable, don't you think?"

Joe thought about this for a second or two.

"What's happened to you?" Joe asked, astutely.

"What's happened to me?" Seth responded.

"What's bringing this on?"

"Something is slipping," Seth replied.

"Somebody told you your job doesn't matter?"

"It's much larger than me," Seth replied. "If we forget why a poem matters, or a person, any person, we turn into Philistines. So that a very few people can grab all the wealth as quickly as possible? Who's left behind? What's left behind? A world where nothing grows — nothing that actually matters, maybe not even food."

"Arise ye prisoners of salvation . . ." Joe quipped. "I've heard that song before."

Agamemnon ran around from the side of the house to greet Seth, a belated greeting. He flapped his wings. He pecked at the ground in front of Seth, clucking and cackling excitedly. Seth cackled back.

Joe laughed, enjoying the comedy.

After a pause, Seth turned to Joe: "My relatives," Seth said, "I guess you'd call them ancestors . . . they adored you."

"Their mistake." Joe's brow crinkled, before he stared at Seth with a look that bore into him. "Who do you think I am?"

"A guy with a shady past," Seth said.

"You got that right," Joe nodded and laughed.

Agamemnon stared at Joe through his one eye.

"Cyclops," Joe remarked. "You should have named him Cyclops." He then reflected for a moment. "That crap you were just spouting — your indignation at the super-rich for destroying the world. Is that something you actually *believe*?"

"It's a theory," Seth said.

"I make money," Joe said, clasping his hands together and then stretching them out to his sides. "I make a lot of money. More in one month than you will see in your lifetime. I study the markets, global perspective, maybe a dash of insider trading, nothing serious. I'm richer than God, and I work very hard at it. My few compatriots and I, we are the workers of the world. And we *did* unite, and we've given a lot back: We've built museums, opera houses, medical centers, concert halls, sports stadiums." Joe reached his hand into his trousers pocket. "And what have *you* done?"

Joe withdrew two cigars from his trousers pockets and offered one to Seth, who declined. Joe slipped the second cigar back into his pocket and somehow lit the other cigar from a damp book of matches he'd been carrying, emitting small rings of smoke through his lips. Agamemnon watched the smoke rings, entranced, as the rain now came down in ever harder streams.

"Once we bomb the Muslims," Joe continued, "once they de-clare war on the West, once the dollar gets kicked out of its place as the standard for world currency, then try to tell me how money isn't everything."

Both men and the rooster remained in the downpour like statues.

ACT III, SCENE 2:
THE BRONSON CANYON ARMS CRISIS

While Seth was pulling into the garage, a question for Joe finally occurred to him. Seth knew this was something he should have asked right after Joe's sanctimonious proclamation about his value to the world that he'd made to Seth —— and possibly to Agamemnon, too —— in the Fontana drizzle. The question now gnawing at Seth only occurred to him as they approached the motel-like apartment building back in Hollywood. Joe was sitting beside Seth in the passenger seat. The rain had passed. The storm had drifted further east, while the pair had driven in the opposite direction, into the setting sun.

Seth brought the car to a lurching halt in the carport. Both men sat for a moment in silence.

"If you're richer than God," Seth asked, "why are you living in this building?"

Joe ruminated on this question for a few seconds before replying: "That's really not your concern. If I told you that, I'd have to kill you." He chuckled.

More questions then tumbled around Seth's brain: Who is this man? What is he doing here? What does he want? Everything he had said, about working for a publishing firm in New York, about his investments, about his wealth — was this all just invention? Then the questions became even more existential: Does he even exist, or is he just a figment, a phantom?

Joe extended his hand to Seth across the car. Seth grasped it, and they shook hands firmly.

"Thank you," Joe said. "That was a pleasure. A revelation."

"Fontana?" Seth asked. "Are you kidding?"

"Agamemnon," replied Joe. "You should rename him Cyclops. He's quite magnificent. You're feeling distressed about the circumstances of your profession, and maybe even your life. But these birds you brought into the world — you're like Zeus who fathered gods and demigods, among them Helen of Troy. These creatures should give you the deepest comfort and pride. Your devotion to them is as glorious as they are. They're not just chickens. They are God's creatures. Their powers are divine. Trust me. And they will care for you through your life as you have cared for them through theirs. I don't say this idly. I say this as somebody who crosses between worlds. I say this as your counselor, and as your friend."

Joe clasped Seth's hand throughout this entire speech, which left Seth thunderstruck. In Joe's grip, Seth felt his own hand turn icy, and then boil. At the moment when Seth was about to scream from what felt like blisters forming on his own palm, Joe let go of his hand and smiled. With his other hand, he opened the passenger door, walked out into the carport and slipped away behind the building.

Seth remained in the Honda for a moment, struggling to comprehend what had just transpired.

He had no recollection of walking from the carport to his apartment. It was as though he had been beamed up, his cells slightly rearranged by the transport.

Cassandra greeted him with a serenade of squawking and a leap from the rim of her playpen wall directly to his right shoulder. There she perched, contented, loving, preening his hair while he hand-fed her blueberries from his fridge. One of the berries dropped to the kitchen floor and she instantly dove off his shoulder to retrieve it, before jumping back up to his shoulder.

He gazed into the hollow of her eye. He'd read that chickens are dead behind the eyes, but in Cassandra's eyes, he saw depths. She clung to him now as though to life. She perched on his shoulder like a parrot as he jogged down the stairwell to open his vault in the recently installed bank of mailboxes with one of his new, shiny copper keys.

Amidst the usual detritus of newspaper coupons, glossy paper advertisements and "pre-sorted" applications for credit cards, he found what was clearly a greeting card. His name and address were on the envelope, but there was no return address.

Still standing near the mailboxes, he slid his finger through the envelope seam and withdrew the card. Now stretching tall on his shoulder, Cassandra puffed up her feathers and shook herself off, before settling into a seated position and preening a wing feather that was bothering her.

The "card" was actually a cutout from a children's crayon picture book. It depicted the plucked, uncooked carcass of a chicken that still had its head attached. Around its neck had been tied a thin, red cotton ribbon that dangled down and away from the rest of the paper. The card contained no writing.

Cassandra continued to preen the feather that so irritated her, oblivious to the conspicuous threat to her existence contained in the card her owner was holding.

Seth thought about showing it to Joe, but Seth wasn't, at this point, entirely convinced that Joe actually existed. Instead, he returned to his apartment to contemplate a rational response to this latest provocation by the Angelis duo. He thought about showing it to Winston, but would Winston argue, once again, that there was no proof that this harassment came from them?

To his pleasant surprise, Seth discovered later that evening in Winston's living room that Winston agreed that this latest aggression had come from Eddie as a warning related to their pending small claims trial. He was so convinced of this that he agreed to accompany Seth to the Hollywood division of the LAPD in order to determine whether or not, in light of the recent incident of assault investigated by officers Simpson and Crandall, the police regarded this "card" as a serious threat to Seth.

Behind the front desk, Winston explained to the slightly bemused desk clerk the history of aggression, starting with Seth's "pets," transitioning to the mailbox crisis and the dead rat.

The front-desk clerk stared at the paper cutout of the chicken carcass for almost a minute, shook his head, and said he'd have to refer it to a detective. He then slipped away into a hidden area partitioned from the lobby, and was gone for about two minutes.

He returned to the lobby with a stocky short man with thick features, a gun in a leather holster, slacks and a striped shirt. With his shaved head, he bore a striking resemblance to Telly Savalas. Like Savalas, he spoke with a New Jersey dialect.

Detective Savalas held the paper cutout of the dead chicken between his thumb and his forefinger, upside down by its feet, so that the red ribbon around its neck dangled down toward the floor. He stared at it intensely.

"The red ribbon is like blood coming from a slit throat, don't you think?" Seth remarked. "Does that constitute a threat to my personal safety — in your opinion?"

Detective Savalas continued to stare at the paper he held between his fingers.

Finally he spoke: "I'd say this is definitely a threat to your chicken." This was followed by a long pause.

"As for you," he continued, ". . . I'm not so sure."

BACK AT WINSTON'S APARTMENT, Seth remained upset by the paper cutout. Seeing this, Winston made a phone call. Moments later, Joe appeared in Winston's apartment.

"Show him," Winston said to Seth.

Seth handed Joe the paper cutout of the naked, dead chicken. Joe held it upside down so the red ribbon dangled from its neck. Joe understood everything, what it meant, and where it had come from. Once again, Joe strained to contain his rage. His cheeks flushed. His breathing became labored so that he sucked air through his clenched teeth.

Finally, after the rage had subsided, Joe uttered five words in a voice so deep, it was hardly recognizable as his own.

"I'll take care of it," Joe said.

FOUR DAYS LATER, A SCREAM WAS HEARD coming from JoJo's apartment within moments of her arrival home in the evening, after having visited her brother in Riverside. Seth wasn't home at the time, but JoJo's scream was heard by Timothy Rowland upstairs, by Ruby Malholtra in the apartment two doors down from Seth's, and by Melvin Channing in the building to the east. Chuck and Svetlana in the bungalow to the east also said they heard something strange but figured it was simply McCaw trying out a new bird call.

They each had slightly different accounts of what JoJo's scream sounded like, but their points of agreement converged on a squealing, gurgling sound that vaguely resembled a death rattle, even though it wasn't that. The last time anybody had heard an expression of terror with that magnitude from anybody in any building nearby was during the Northridge earthquake when all the buildings shook, cabinets slid around the floors and glass shattered.

It took a considerable time for JoJo to report the cause of her scream, because she was considering not mentioning it, and disposing of the evidence that had prompted her howl of horror.

That evidence was somebody's ghostly, pale blue, severed left arm that had been deposited on her bed. When the blood returned to her face after her near faint, JoJo observed that the arm had been recently washed, it was perfumed, with a light coating of dark brown hair on the forearm, and was defined on one end by a meticulously clean butcher-shop pork-chop slice near what would have been the shoulder if the piece of arm had extended another six inches. Upon closer inspection, JoJo observed that the hand, slightly clenched, contained fingernails that had been recently clipped. It was 9:06 p.m. when JoJo observed this, so she reported to the LAPD, the L.A. County Sheriff, the L.A. County Health Department, the L.A. County Coroner, the FBI and the CIA, all of whom paid visits to her, and to her son, Eddie.

The reason they visited Eddie was actually the cause of a different scream, coming from his girlfriend Jolene, upon their return to Eddie's apartment at approximately 9:55 that same night. The reason for her scream, and of her faint from which she regained consciousness a full forty-five minutes later (when a Fire Department paramedic brought her to with smelling salts), was the presence of the matching severed right arm on their bed.

Both JoJo and Eddie had received text messages that afternoon, with the cryptic words: "Hands off."

On linking the text message to the body parts on their beds, as was clearly intended by whoever thought up this ghastly prank, they couldn't discern whether "hands off" was telling them not to touch the severed arms, or whether they were being instructed to remove the hands from the arms, or whether there was some larger meaning.

Seth immediately understood from these messages that this work had been instigated by Joe, through whatever connections he may still have to Russia.

Joe's strategy worked perfectly. Normally, after targets are killed by the Russian Mafia, their fingertips are removed in order to preclude identification. Not so here, and that decision was strategic, because it implicated the Angelis duo in the crimes of murder and dismemberment.

The victim was quickly identified as a thirty-one-year-old immigrant from Loyno in Kirov Oblast, Russia, named Anton Antonovich Borovsky, whose testimony against a human trafficking ring was largely responsible for the arrest and conviction in Chicago of one Olga Vladimirovna Vragova of Moscow, who organized the ring. Olga headed a fiefdom that smuggled impoverished young men and women, such as Anton Antonovich Borovsky, who was sixteen years old at that time, and who were seeking a better life. This, to them, meant legitimate and gainful employment. Many, such as Anton Antonovich Borovsky, were simply sold by their parents to the traffickers for cash. Olga's network transported her victims from rural Russia and the Balkans into the United States and Canada. Upon landing on Western shores, they found themselves without documents, which were held by their enslavers. The documents would not be returned until their owners had paid the costs of their transport through indentured servitude, laboring as house cleaners and/or prostitutes for ten years, or even more.

When abducted at sixteen years old, Anton Antonovich Borovsky was already an illustrator of comic books. He wound up as a sex slave in a suburb outside Minneapolis — a brutal, terrible existence. By the time he was approaching thirty, he was far too old to be a sex slave. Instead, he accepted Olga's offer of recruiting youth from his home region and escorting them to the West. That's how these things sometimes go.

He was arrested by the FBI upon landing at San Francisco International Airport three years before his arms showed up in Bronson Canyon without the rest of him. In San Francisco, he spent two months in the Federal Detention Center as he awaited his arraignment on multiple charges ranging from human trafficking to aiding and abetting various crimes, including prostitution and fraud.

Borovsky denied nothing. He had been scribbling cartoons on a large, lined yellow notepad as he told his story to U.S. attorney Michael (The Spike) Fallbrook, who arranged to place Borovsky in a federal witness protection program where he could live with a new identity in Phoenix, Arizona, if he would help direct the FBI to Olga Vladimirovna Vragova the next time she was in the United States. Vragova was really the main target of their investigation.

And that is what Borovsky did. He submitted himself to surgery that altered the contours of his face; he adopted the new name Zeke Quincy Swilling. They gave him a new birth certificate with a new birthplace, Akron, Ohio; a new high school diploma; and all the attendant documents to verify on federal data sources that he and his Phoenix, Arizona home were as far removed from Kirov Oblast, Russia as Jupiter is from the sun. Clearly, even this was not sufficient to protect him from his former enslavers.

Zeke found work in Phoenix — named for an earlier creature who also, more famously, rose from the ashes — as an illustrator for video games. He married a pretty redheaded high school English teacher named Darlene Flemming, who, being from Buffalo, New York, complained bitterly about the desert heat, and what it was doing to her skin. Zeke and Darlene celebrated the birth of their beautiful daughter, Irma Leanne Swilling, who was barely a year old when Zeke disappeared while at a gaming conference in Tarzana, California.

Darlene presumed that Zeke had simply run off; she knew nothing of his tortured past. Those were the terms of his being in the witness protection program, and Anton/Zeke obeyed those terms dutifully. Nonetheless, shamed by having been abandoned, a week after Anton/Zeke's disappearance, Darlene reluctantly reported her husband missing to the Phoenix Police Department. She heard nothing for about a week and a half, until Anton/Zeke's severed left and right arms were discovered in Hollywood, California, placed respectively on two different beds. Darlene was not called in to identify these remains because Anton/Zeke sported no identifying tattoos, and the feds got all they needed from the fingerprints. The question for Darlene, and for the FBI, was whether Zeke was now walking around armless, which would certainly have put a crimp in his career as an illustrator, or whether the rest of him had been dumped with cement attachments into the L.A. River.

The L.A. Sheriff's Department's Search and Rescue division sent its elite Aquatics Retrieval Forensics Squad (ARFS) into the L.A. River, where they swam the river's length, from far below the downtown industrial zone all the way to Canoga Park in the San Fernando Valley.

"Swam" is probably a misrepresentation of what the divers did through much of their survey. Since the river has graffiti-enhanced concrete banks and merely trickles through a narrow cement ditch for miles, they actually waddled in their bodysuits with flippers and goggles through two-thirds of their assignment.

True, they admired the willow trees and marsh grasses and herons and geese in one large swath of the river where it runs expansively and deeply between Los Feliz and Atwater Village. Still, they found no remains belonging to Zeke Quincy Swilling that day, or any day after.

Joe's masterful scheme worked perfectly, because for weeks, JoJo and Eddie were visited by a cornucopia of agents from various government departments investigating the crime, for which JoJo and

Eddie were now suspects. Their prolonged travail began shortly after the county coroner removed the severed arms from their respective apartments — each arm in a blue plastic twist-top baggie — and drove them away in a large van to the county's Eastside morgue.

In visit after visit, JoJo and Eddie were compelled for their own defense to keep expressing their shock and amazement that these body parts were placed in their apartments. After all their groundless accusations against others, the tables had finally turned.

Seth realized he had Joe to thank, though he also tried to distance himself from the prank, which he had never countenanced. For his part, Joe kept repeating how shocked he was, and what a terrible thing had transpired, that he hoped they caught whoever was responsible.

Meanwhile, JoJo and Eddie found themselves subjected to relentless questioning by the authorities, sometimes in their apartments, sometimes in the offices of the FBI, about any connection they might have to the Russian Mafia. JoJo, in particular, employed her well-practiced technique of portraying herself as the wrongly injured party. This time, she was right.

Eddie merely trembled with anger and indignation while spouting half-sentences that kept crashing into each other, leaving in their wake belligerent verbal impressions and attitudes, rather than lucid thoughts.

The NSA pulled up records of every phone call, and every text message and email they'd sent and received over the past five years from all of their I.P. addresses. The Angelises were questioned in person, sometimes abusively, on connections to the Mafia that could be inferred from their correspondence. Even in their sleep, they found themselves blurting out: "I don't know!" "I have no idea!" "I just found it there!" "I don't *know* how it got there!!!"

Shortly after Jolene recovered from her fainting spell upon the initial discovery of Anton's right arm on the bed, she moved out. Eddie insisted to anybody who cared that they had not broken up, but that she could no longer sleep in that room. As for having sex there, that was now completely out of the question. This was a comfort to Winston and Suki, who lived next door and who could finally enjoy some repose in their own bedroom.

Meanwhile, the incident sent Joe into a state of apoplectic dismay, or such was his portrayal. From his drama critic's point of view, Seth found Joe's performance convincing and compelling. Joe kept saying that his main concern was property values, and nothing could be worse for property values than having the building associated with the Russian Mafia, with one of the suspects on the HOA Board!

Joe pleaded with JoJo to resign. JoJo had to remind him of the principle still viable in American law, "innocent until proven guilty," which Seth found somewhat ironic. Joe reminded her of the principle still viable where *he* came from, "guilt by association." JoJo then asked Joe *where* he came from, and Joe simply demurred with a dismissive wave of his hand.

Four weeks after the terrible discovery, Joe called an emergency meeting of all the homeowners to discuss what had come to be known as the Bronson Canyon Arms Crisis.

It was a somber meeting, held in Joe's apartment that now contained cardboard boxes on the floor, all around the couches and chairs on which the assembled homeowners sat. The telescope that Seth recalled seeing on the enclosed back patio was now gone, as well as the banks of computers behind Joe's curtains. The atmosphere was filled with dark broodings and suspicion. JoJo and Eddie acted as though they were on trial, and in a way they were, for bringing shame on the building — even if they were entirely victims of circumstance.

The most striking aspect of the meeting was Joe's costume, the same Soviet military uniform and boots in which he'd arrived on that auspicious day when he crashed through Winston's roof, a day that nobody except Seth even remembered. Joe's medals and ribbons gleamed like never before, though nobody commented on Joe's uniform, not even Seth. Also, Joe had allowed his moustache to grow back. He was Joseph Stalin once again, or some extraordinary mirror image of the tyrant.

Joe mentioned his recommendation that JoJo tender her resignation from the Board, and that JoJo had refused.

"I didn't do anything wrong!" JoJo protested.

This was met with a stony, embarrassed silence.

Seth's initial impulse was to stand up for the persecuted, as was his guiding principle, to defend JoJo, just as he had done years ago when JoJo was misidentified by Winston as the social worker responsible for a patient's suicide. This time, however, Seth thought it prudent to just stay out of it. There was now too much sordid history for such unfettered morality. His conscience was now a dream that had been driven to its knees by experience, expedience, and weariness.

Joe then rose and stood in front of the cloth-covered folding chair he'd been using. He told the homeowners that he had considered a petition for the impeachment of JoJo that needed to be signed by two-thirds of the owners prior to a special meeting to remove an officer, but he thought it would be more dignified and constructive if JoJo simply offered to resign.

"Because that hasn't happened . . ." Joe rumbled in a basso profundo. There was a dramatic pause after which Joe repeated, "Because that hasn't happened . . . I am announcing my decision to step down as your president and accept employment in Washington, DC with the National Security Agency."

This was followed by a long silence, during which Ruby Malholtra coughed after taking a sip from the wine that Joe had served to everybody in attendance. Ruby hacked heartily, gasping for breath, until she stepped into the kitchen for a glass of water while offering apologies.

"What kind of job is it?" Suki asked.

"I'm not at liberty to say," Joe replied tenderly.

"When will you be leaving?" Sam Rowland asked.

"That's classified information," Joe replied.

"Will you be selling your apartment, or leasing it?" Winston inquired.

"I'm afraid that's something I can't disclose at this time, for security reasons," Joe said.

JoJo spoke up once more, asking Joe, "I've always been curious, where exactly did you come from? And how have you been supporting yourself all this time?"

"These are excellent questions," Joe replied, and Seth agreed. "Unfortunately, the answer is classified."

"Do you *want* to leave us?" Ruby Malholtra asked woefully, as though imploring him to stay.

"I'd love to answer that question," Joe said. "Unfortunately, I'm bound by the Official Secrets Act to remain silent on that issue, and any issue related to it."

For a reason that Seth found incomprehensible, Ruby Malholtra, who had been Joe's other next-door neighbor, started sobbing. Then, dabbing her eyes with a Kleenex from a box on the black oak dining room table, she rushed toward Joe and embraced him. The two held each other for an entire minute, and kissed each other gently, repeatedly, directly on the lips, like lovers reuniting after some torturous absence. Ruby even ran her fingers through Joe's hair before, to Seth's amazement and disgust, she started licking his mustache as a dog grooms the face of its mate, over and over, in tongue-strokes up and down then side to side. Once his mustache was sufficiently soggy, Ruby then kissed Joe passionately on the mouth, occasionally raising her point of attack to suck on his moustache, while Joe snorted through his nose in erotic abandon. Seth wasn't the only one who imagined what a good thing it was that Ruby's longtime boyfriend, Bill Jackson — whom she'd initially picked up months ago at the Music Box for a one-night stand — wasn't there to see this appalling display.

Joe then tenderly eased Ruby away from him in order to deliver what was clearly a prepared speech:

"Ladies and gentlemen. I feel we've made great progress in the time I've been here as your leader. And I want to thank you for the support and confidence you've shown me. I don't have words to express what an honor it's been to serve you, of the pride I feel for the strides we've all made together, working as a team, in harmony, with grace and cooperation and even love, yes, I can use that word. Without that love, we'd never have come this far."

Ruby was now sniffling into a handkerchief. But Joe wasn't finished.

"I'll remember you all with gratitude and warmth, wherever I am in this cruel and acrimonious world. I'll cherish this community of neighbors, for your kindness, for your unspoken acknowledgement that we're all in this together, and that without each other, each of us is nowhere, and nobody. Even in a world filled with and fueled by hatred, as a community we can govern ourselves to our highest advantage. With our community and its laws as our guide, with our common dedication to the values we hold dear, with our compassion, with our soaring and noble wisdom, we can transcend the darkest recesses of our own characters, we can access the love that will propel us to greatness."

After a moment's pause, Winston started to applaud, but stopped after realizing that nobody else was joining him. Most were simply weeping from the emotional impact of Joe's speech, which Seth, on the other hand, found windy and pointless, as did Sam Rowland.

"Can somebody pass the guacamole," Sam asked. But nobody did — out of respect for Joe.

The room then shook. Plaster fell from the cottage-cheese ceiling. Dust tumbled onto the couches, table and floor. A crack appeared in the ceiling; chips of lumber fell into the room. The crack slowly opened to a length of about three feet by two feet wide, allowing Joseph Stalin, in full military attire, to ascend through it, smiling and waving to those below. Many waved back lovingly with tears streaming down their faces, as Stalin rose up, and up, and up, into the sky, until his image shrank into a tiny dot that eventually disappeared into the smog of history.

ACT III, SCENE 3: SMALL CLAIMS

T wo days after Joe's enigmatic departure, Seth's divorce finally came through. It had been snagged in the bureaucracy of the L.A. Superior Court for over two years, and had been an arduous, maddening process for Seth and for Katerina, given the terms were uncontested by both parties and there were no custody issues. The principle for the court came down to the manner in which Katerina had been originally served papers over two years earlier. Seth had simply FedExed them to her, and she signed them and then had them notarized at the U.S. Embassy in Moscow by a U.S. consular official. It took the court two years and three hearings to accept the legality of that process.

And this is why Seth now had an intuitive, toxic reaction to the hallways of the L.A. Superior Court — the same hallways where Eddie's small claims case against Seth was slated to be heard.

Seth had anticipated that by July 17, the date of the small claims hearing, some atrocity might befall one or both of the Angelis duo, thanks to the higher powers of Joe. However, the Bronson Canyon Arms Crisis had now passed on, as had Joe, whose apartment remained vacant. Seth realized that he would now need to rely on empirical evidence rather than mystical intervention.

News that this case was actually going to court was a source of entertainment and anticipation within two apartment buildings in Bronson Canyon, as well as the Craftsman house rented by Chuck and Svetlana. In the building to the east of Seth's, Melvin Channing set up a betting pool on who would prevail. The stakes of the bet grew to quintuple the amount that could be collected in the verdict.

Seth carried his backpack in one hand as he and Winston, who was there to testify on his behalf, showed up in the hallway outside the Small Claims Division in the Stanley Mosk Courthouse of the Los Angeles Superior Court at 8:15 a.m. on July 17. Eddie was already sitting outside the courtroom on a bench. They were fifteen minutes early for the trial and the courtroom door was locked. Seth and Winston sat on a bench by the opposing wall so that the adversaries glared at each other from across the hallway. Eddie was rifling through a stack of papers he'd brought as evidence. When he saw Winston and Seth, Eddie smiled as he bent the fingers on his right hand into the shape of a pistol, which he aimed directly at Winston before using his thumb to pull the "trigger."

Seth watched Winston's face sink and flush at this gesture, through which Eddie continued to smile. Seth found it strange that Eddie was dressed so shoddily for a court presentation — he wore a green T-shirt with wrinkled green jeans and tired sneakers, while Seth and Winston came attired in sport jackets and trousers. Seth was also struck by the absence of JoJo, or any other supporters for Eddie.

Suddenly, the courtroom door was flung open by a bailiff, who ordered everybody for small claims into the gallery. About two dozen people filed onto the audience benches of the courtroom, which looked to Seth shudderingly similar to the Family Law courtroom upstairs — the oak-walnut décor, the flags, the judge's podium, the separation of church and state, the clerks, the bailiff's desk.

The bailiff, a squatty county sheriff with a buzzcut, then barked orders that everyone was required to go directly back outside into the hall, to meet with their adversaries, and show them all written evidence about to be presented to the judge.

"If any of you has any sense," he shouted in a world-weary tone, "you'll use this opportunity to work out a settlement so you don't waste any more of the court's time and resources."

Two dozen litigants filed back out into the hallway. Eddie approached Seth and flung his stack of papers onto a bench near where they stood. That's when Seth noticed that Eddie was trembling. Seth withdrew a manila folder from his backpack and gave it to Eddie, who rifled with his shaking hands through the contents. Seeing the photographs of open mailboxes cluttered with papers and one open mailbox on a post, Eddie snapped, "What's this got to do with anything?"

"Community standards," Seth said. "How are these more secure than ours? You really want to go ahead with this? You really think it's worth the trouble? We could do this, or we could go 'round the corner and all have a beer."

Eddie thought about it for a moment. "Thanks," he said, nodding. "But I need to do this."

The bailiff shouted from the courtroom door for everyone to return. Seth and Winston sat together on one side of the courtroom, Eddie, alone, on the other.

"All rise!" the bailiff bellowed.

To Seth's dismay, there on high at the front of the courtroom appeared Joe, in black judicial robes. Joe settled behind his raised podium.

"You may be seated," Joe intoned.

Seth looked at Winston for some expression of shock that Joe should be the judge, but Winston sat complacent and unmoved.

"Does he look . . . familiar?" Seth whispered.

"Who?"

"The judge!"

"Quiet in the back!" the bailiff shouted.

Winston shrugged, appearing not to recognize the same man he'd invited so often into his own apartment.

Seth turned to Eddie for some telltale sign that the judge of their case was the former president of their HOA. But after looking at the judge, Eddie simply continued to flip through his papers nervously.

Seth's mind turned into a blur as Joe presided over seven cases.

Somebody's eucalyptus tree had fallen into a neighbor's yard and crashed onto a motorcycle. The tree owner was trying to prove that the motorcycle had never worked, that it wasn't worth the $3,000 in repairs that its owner was demanding.

A woman had bought a used car from some guy, only to discover that one of the tires was throwing the car's balance off. He'd advertised that the car had "all new tires" at the time he was selling it. Was it fraud if the "new tires" weren't all the same size?

Another woman claimed her dry cleaner had ruined her daughter's prom dress, that it was returned after a month two sizes smaller than when it was brought in. The dry cleaner countered that the daughter had actually swelled two sizes in that same time. He presented a time-stamped photograph of the young woman scarfing down a cream-filled chocolate napoleon as evidence.

Though he should have been at least somewhat amused by these disputes, as others in the courtroom clearly were, Seth merely found the entire spectacle dispiriting.

An hour or so later, Seth was standing in front of Joe; Eddie stood about six feet away. They all had their right hands raised and swore to tell the truth, so help them God.

At that moment, Reginald McCallister, dressed in work boots and a car mechanic's overalls, burst into the courtroom — the same Reginald McCallister who was Vera's boyfriend and apartment repairman, the same Reginald McCallister who had been cuffed by the LAPD after being charged by JoJo with "breaking and entering" Julia's apartment, which was now Joe's apartment.

"I'm here for this case, to testify, Your Honor!" Reginald shouted from the back.

"Take a place in the witness dock," Joe shouted back.

Reginald took his place in a waiting area, in front of the audience gallery and behind the litigants, where Winston was already standing. Winston and Reginald shook hands amiably. Though Vera had sold her apartment to Joe, she remained Suki's friend. And because Vera remained Suki's friend, and Winston remained Suki's husband, the debacle over the sliding glass door — in which Reginald had played such an unseemly role — had been long forgotten.

"So this is a case about . . . oh, I see," Joe said, "this is quite serious, mail tampering. Yes, federal offense. This is not a joke. I've read the complaint."

Joe turned to Seth: "So you lost your mailbox key."

"Yes, Your Honor." Once again, Seth had no intention of explaining that it had been eaten by his pet chicken, having no idea whether Judge Joe was the same Joe who had stood up for Cassandra or whether he was a clone.

"Do you deny jimmying open the mailbox?" Joe asked.

"No, Your Honor."

"And this went on for . . . ?"

"Well over a year," Eddie blurted out. "I have statements from witnesses."

"I see," Joe said with a solemnity that troubled Seth.

"There's a subpoena here," Joe said, rifling through his case file. "Is Mr. Pendleton here?"

"Here, Your Honor," Winston said from the witness dock.

"Step forward, please."

Winston approached the bench and was sworn in by a clerk.

"Your story?" Joe said.

"Mr. Jacobson requested a replacement key from the HOA right after he discovered it was broken."

"What do you mean, 'discovered it was broken'?" Joe asked. "Was it open when he first discovered it was broken?" Joe turned to Seth. "Mr. Jacobson?"

"I was able to pop it open with one finger, Your Honor. There was a crack in the frame. That's how I discovered it was broken."

"So you pried it open."

"It popped right open, Your Honor," Seth explained.

"After you pried it."

"A little tug."

"Without that tug," Joe continued, "it would never have opened. Is that correct?"

"I suppose so, Your Honor."

Winston spoke up: "The postmaster inspected the mailbox, Your Honor. He said that it was overdue to be replaced, that the lock was worn out."

Joe continued glaring at Seth, "But you pried it open nonetheless; for over a year, you continued prying it open, a mailbox that belongs to a community."

"I had the written permission of the HOA," Seth said, "until they either provided me a new key or replaced the unit, which they finally did."

"Over a year later," Joe added. "With or without their permission," Joe continued, "you still continued to pry open everybody's mailboxes. This is a serious offense."

Eddie had now finally stopped shaking. He stood just a little bit straighter, his confidence rising.

Joe perused the photographs that Seth had provided. "What's this?"

"Mailboxes within one block, Your Honor. Mailboxes in far worse shape than ours ever was."

Joe dismissively dropped them onto his desk and sighed. "This has nothing to do with anything. I've also noted that you gave a negative review to *War Horse*."

Seth was speechless.

Joe continued, "*War Horse*. What's wrong with *War Horse*?

"Nothing, Your Honor."

"That's not what you wrote. 'Sentimental drivel,' you called it. I'll have you know I wept for two days after that show. It was the most profound, soul-stirring, technically masterful, inspiring homage to the dignity of human and equine relations. You should be ashamed of yourself! I saw it five times!"

"I'm glad you enjoyed it, Your Honor."

"No you're not! Don't dissemble! Remember, you're under oath! And yet, you gave a positive review to that piece of shit, *Animal Farm*. Tell me what's inspiring about *that*? Pigs who take over the farm? One pig, the oppressive monster, based on *Stalin*? You have something against *Stalin*?! What did *Stalin* ever do to *you*?!!!"

Joe was almost hyperventilating with fury. His face was burgundy, until he took a sip of water.

He then turned to Reginald. "Sir, what do you have to add? Step forward, state your name and be sworn in."

After he was sworn in, Reginald engaged in a five-minute semi-coherent diatribe against the Angelis duo, about their history of persecuting their neighbors and of the misery they had inflicted over the years. It was a rage-fueled soliloquy filled with digressions and anecdotes, all wrapped in a tone that artfully blended pathos and indignation. Joe listened attentively as Reginald rounded the final turn of his speech into what might have been called a summation, had Reginald not simply, gaspingly run out of words, by which time his clothes and his head were saturated in sweat.

Though he believed Reginald's monologue to be largely beside the point, Seth found it quite well performed. It was better than many solo shows he'd seen in theaters large and small, and, for personal reasons, Seth was deeply grateful for it.

"Thank you, Mr. McCallister," Joe said respectfully, before rendering his verdict. "The demand is for the cost of a post office box during the time of the vandalism. I don't find that to be unreasonable."

"But Your Honor," Seth interjected, "if you would please just look at the receipts, at the dates. The date of the lease and the date of the repair. They're six days apart and he's charging me for a year!"

Joe did precisely that: He studied the two receipts. He stared at Eddie. He stared at Seth.

"Yes," Joe said, looking back at Eddie. "I'm sorry, I have no choice but to rule for the defendant."

"But he was vandalizing the mailboxes for over a year!" Eddie said imploringly.

"So why didn't you file your case when he started?" asked Joe calmly.

Both Seth and Winston thought of declaring that Eddie's lawsuit was tit-for-tat revenge against Seth for his summoning the police on Eddie, but given the case was now tilting in their favor, they each, independently, thought it more prudent to stay quiet.

"Why did you wait?" Joe continued plaintively to Eddie. "I can't make him pay your bill for a whole year when your complaint is only valid for a week. That's just not fair. That's just not right! Case dismissed. Next!"

When Seth and Winston and Reginald left the courtroom to celebrate with beers at a downtown bar, the last thing they saw was Eddie, still at the bench, pleading with Joe.

In a dark tavern with six huge plasma-screen TVs blaring a base-ball game between the Baltimore Orioles and the New York Yan-kees, Winston, Reginald, and Seth drank Samuel Adams lagers. They embraced and wept with joy, as though they had actually accom-plished something significant.

ACT III, SCENE 4: PEACE IN OUR TIME

Not two weeks had passed since Seth's small claims court victory over Eddie when he received a letter from the county Health Department responding to an anonymous complaint about a hen, also observed by a county inspector, housed inside his apartment. The hen violated the distance requirements set forth by the county for the housing of fowl. The letter requested Seth to attend an informal hearing at the Department of Health on Wilshire Boulevard on August 23, 1 p.m. The complainant, it said, would not be there.

Seth had presumed that this matter had already been resolved in his favor by the city's Department of Animal Services. He still had the full city report, which unambiguously granted Cassandra the right to live in his apartment because she was a pet. It was evident to Seth, to Winston and to everyone else in Bronson Canyon that the Angelis duo was trying the county as a new avenue for prosecution.

The county shared jurisdiction over the property with the city. Seth checked the county distance requirements, and the wording in their law was identical to that used by the city. It had probably been drafted by the same attorney, Seth surmised.

While Cassandra parked precariously on his head inside Seth's apartment, Winston, now incensed by the Angelis duo's obvious campaign of harassment, agreed to join Seth at the hearing as a sympathetic witness.

On August 23, Winston accompanied Seth to the field office of the L.A. County Health Department on Wilshire Boulevard for the hearing concerning Cassandra.

For reasons having to do as much with Seth's innate sense of theatricality as with fatigue from the government's endless intrusions into his private life, Seth decided to bring Cassandra to the hearing. He didn't transport her in a cage; rather, he held her in his left hand, when she wasn't perching on his shoulder.

The hearing office was surprisingly opulent, carpeted and with polished wood furniture and wall moldings. The two men, both in suits and ties and shined shoes, sat in upholstered chairs behind the hearing officer's oak desk. Cassandra sat on a towel that Seth had brought and placed over his lap. Seth spent most of the meeting rubbing the top of Cassandra's head, while she sat on his knees. On one occasion, she clucked in satisfaction. Seth figured there was no better way to demonstrate that she was a pet, since her being a pet was the crux of the city's argument.

The hearing officer was named Francine Blumenfeld. She was an elegant redheaded woman attired in a tailored, smoke-grey business suit, who appeared to be about forty. She showed some strain maintaining her decorum at the sight of two grown men and a chicken seated across from her, all of whom, including Cassandra, seemed to approach this case with dour reverence. Francine revealed more than she should after Seth told her he was fully aware that the complainant was either JoJo or Eddie Angelis, or both. Francine studied the paperwork associated with the complaint and nodded.

This gave both Seth and Winston license to expound on the history of the civil dispute in the building, and of the identical wording in both city and county law concerning the distance requirements for chickens to human dwellings. They spoke of how the city's ruling on Cassandra being a "pet" had resolved the matter with finality. Seth gave Francine a copy of the entire case file from the city's Department of Animal Services.

Before he rose to do so, Seth transferred Cassandra to Winston.

Cassandra took a quick jump to Winston's right shoulder. Winston slipped his right hand under her feet. Cassandra flapped her wings to keep her balance as Winston lowered her to his lap. Seth picked up a few papers that had fallen from Francine's desk from the breeze Cassandra had created.

"We apologize," Seth said, respectfully returning Francine's papers and showing her the city report.

"But we aren't the city," Francine replied with a tone straddling irritation and sympathy. "I've heard your point of view, and there is merit to what you're saying, but we will have to refer this matter to our legal department."

Seth thought this over for a moment.

"If the city and the county interpret the same law, written with exactly the same language, as applied to the same creature on the same slice of real estate, if they interpret this law in opposite ways, then the law is meaningless, don't you think?" Seth asked.

"That's not for me to say," Francine replied.

"Is it for a judge to say?" Seth asked.

"That may well be, if that's what our legal department determines," Francine added.

Seth leaned back in his chair and sighed.

Asked Winston, "And you believe that prosecuting a pet chicken, in defiance of the city, is a prudent use of county resources?"

"I, personally, don't," Francine said. This was her biggest concession. "But, as I said, that determination is for our legal department to make."

As he rose, Seth cradled Cassandra against his ribs with his left arm while he shook Francine's hand with his right hand. After this, Winston thanked her and also shook her hand. The two men and one chicken entered an elevator, already occupied by a man in a dress suit. Together, the quartet descended in stoic silence the seven flights to the garage, where Winston had parked. The only sound that broke the silence was that of three clucks, emitted by Cassandra between the fourth and third floors.

Seven days later, on the last day of August, Seth received a voicemail from Francine that the county had decided "not to pursue this matter any further," and she wished him well for the remainder of the summer.

THIS LATEST IN A SERIES OF administrative triumphs felt to Seth like a hollow victory — yet another victorious battle that never deserved a battlefield. On the next Saturday morning, Seth sat on his couch listening to a Bach cantata, drifting into a reverie while Cassandra occupied herself jumping to and fro, from her playpen floor to its wall, and back, up and down, as though she didn't quite know where she wanted to be. Normally, she would have settled onto Seth's shoulder, but she sensed his agitation and possessed the sensitivity to maintain some distance.

Seth did wonder when or if Joe would appear again in his life. Seth tried to reconcile himself to what was now the mystifying reality that nobody except Seth who had come into proximity, sometimes even intimate proximity, with Joe seemed to recognize or even remember him, or the bizarre, disruptive way he floated in and out of the building's roof. It cost the HOA a considerable sum to repair the roof on the two occasions Joe crashed it, but even that, too, was a distant and ever more fleeting memory to the building's community of neighbors. Like the petty assault by Eddie upon Seth, Joe had somehow vanished from the record, which reduced Seth's recollection of him to a figure in some incongruent scenes of a fiction novel.

Seth's crisis was no longer just professional. It was existential.

He was having an increasingly difficult time differentiating between what was real and what wasn't.

He had spent the larger part of his life analyzing and encouraging an art form in which people pretended to be who they weren't, to live in places and eras they didn't, to act in ways they otherwise wouldn't, and everyone, including audiences, went along with this. They even paid money to observe these charades, as though these fantasies were real and worthy of discussing in public forums, as though these "plays" and the discussions that stemmed from them might even enhance a common understanding of what was real and entertaining and truthful, and what wasn't.

Seth's role as a drama critic was to distinguish between what was real and what wasn't, between what *seemed* real and what didn't, between what might be popular and what might be valuable. In short, he was a professional arbiter of truth, who was at this moment swiftly losing confidence in his own capacity to know what, if anything, was truthful, or even true.

As these thoughts rolled around Seth's brain, Cassandra froze in place atop her playpen. Noises outside the open kitchen window set her on high alert — noises like chickens in the driveway.

"B-CAW-buk-buk-buk. B-CAW-buk-buk-buk."

Cassandra tilted her head and held it at an angle. She believed there was a chicken outside.

Seth understood differently. Then again, he was a drama critic professionally trained to differentiate between truth and pretense. The sound was Eddie, and maybe one or two of Eddie's friends, making chicken noises directly outside his open kitchen window as a taunt. Then he heard them laughing, and continuing the clucking.

Seth crossed over to the kitchen window and closed it. He then crossed to his stereo system and turned up the Bach cantata. He felt not only marginalized, but like a prisoner in his own home.

He played the cantata's closing chorale at full volume, sealing off the outside world and all of its taunts with a wall of music.

"*Wie ein Vogel des Stricks kömmt ab,*

Ist unsre Seel entgangen:

Strick ist entzwei, und wir sind frei . . ."

Seth understood the German, and the passage seemed apt:

"As a bird that escapes the snare,

So our soul is delivered:

The trap is broken, and we are free . . . "

Seth understood what he needed to do next: He prepared and packed a cheese and tomato sandwich, fed Cassandra some spinach before packing her into her portable carrier, and, after checking that Eddie and his cohorts had left the driveway, he carted her to his Honda Civic. Together they drove through the foothills to Fontana.

Before pulling out of his own driveway, Seth called Susan, leaving her a message that he was coming by to take Agamemnon for a ride.

It was noon when Seth and Cassandra pulled in next to Susan's front yard. She wasn't home. Seth placed Cassandra's carrier on the top of her front wall, before hopping over and landing on a gopher mound. Agamemnon raced over, wings flapping, then circled Seth, clucking excitedly and showing Seth a few fresh blades of grass from where Susan had been watering. Agamemnon bobbed his head, scraped the ground with his beak, to and fro, then looked up at Seth through his one eye before repeating the rite. Seth bent forward, hands on his knees and had an amiable discussion with Agamemnon. He then removed Cassandra's carrier from the wall, placed it on the ground and let her out.

On seeing his nestmate for the first time in many months, Agamemnon danced around Cassandra, bobbing his head up and down and clucking out his delight. For her part, Cassandra watched him warily and remained still, finally talking to him in the kind of caw-caws that were a staple of her verbal repertoire. After ten minutes or so, Agamemnon was showing her with his beak and feet the best places to dig for grubs, and she was following him with interest, so that they were both pecking and kicking the soil, side by side, clucking contentedly.

After the birds had finished running around for half an hour, he packed them both into the carrier, and drove east along Interstate 10 toward Arizona. He drove beyond the eucalyptus windbreaks of Rialto and San Bernardino, up over the oaken meadowlands of Yucaipa and Calimesa, past the strip malls of Beaumont and down into the small town of Banning, some eighty miles southeast of downtown L.A. Seth followed a highway he'd remembered from his college years.

Highway 243 snakes up Mount San Jacinto, past a junk-cluttered landscape of sandy ground and abandoned industrial parks at its base, slowly rising from the desert at the base of the mountains.

On this particular Saturday afternoon, the chaparral and tumbleweed had a tinge of soft-lime green. At the lower elevations, the plants were no more than four feet high, shrubs really, dotting the parched desert floor. But as he climbed the winding mountain road, the chaparral yielded to groves of black oak, until he found himself engulfed in the thickly planted, green contours of pine and cedar, deep in the San Bernardino National Forest.

At an elevation of about 5,000 feet, the air was thinner than below. Around one curve was Lake Fulmor, hidden behind a railing, an expansive mountain lake with a walking path encircling it. There were also any number of wooden benches, and a jetty where people might fish.

Seth parked and took the carrier and a blanket he'd brought and settled on a sandy bank. He opened the carrier, releasing Agamemnon and Cassandra. Both man and fowl were awestruck by the power of the silence. They were the lake's only visitors at that time. Footsteps and breathing, all the sounds of being alive, were muted by the pine needles and mulch and looming canopies of the sequoias and ponderosas. The chickens eventually started to dig for grubs in the nearby grasses while Seth ate his sandwich, then lay back to take in the vista of forest and sky.

Lake Fulmor had been closed during a federal government shutdown brought on by partisan squabbling in Washington, DC. Somebody there had determined that the park's caretakers were "non-essential." Just like in the schools, when budgets get tight, the first subjects cut are music, theater and painting, despite all the empirical evidence that these subjects measurably contribute to reading skills, cognitive development and even to intelligence.

Seth couldn't imagine a place more essential than Lake Fulmor, where you could be embraced by nature's majesty in order to better determine who you are, where you come from, and where you're going.

That determination, Seth figured, was also among the more enduring purposes of the arts. And Lake Fulmor also exemplified for Seth what was a critic's calling — to distinguish between what was popular and what was valuable. Lake Fulmor wasn't popular. Its value lay in its tranquility, far from the bustling boutiques and eateries in the desert cities below.

And yet a kid who worked at the Carl's Jr. in Beaumont for $10 an hour could easily afford to spend a day at Lake Fulmor. That was Teddy Roosevelt's vision when he created the National Forest and Park systems, to preserve natural treasures and keep them accessible for subsequent generations. Good luck if that same kid tried to get into *The Lion King* revival at the Pantages in Hollywood on his or her own dime. The kind of theater Seth enjoyed was like this forest. Both may be rarefied, but at least they were available to anyone with sufficient curiosity to seek them out. His fantasy, though, was to take something valuable and help make it popular.

As a drama critic, Seth had been marginalized. At Lake Fulmor, he came to understand that he had been professionally marginalized because the theater itself had become marginalized. Even in its most commercial forms, it was struggling to reach the largest market share, where popularity is confused with value. Something about the altitude, the craggy peaks, the crisp, clean air, made the value of what he believed in all so clear. He loved this place.

It was long past sundown when Seth got home, after having delivered Agamemnon back to Fontana. Carrying Cassandra up the rear stairwell, Seth noticed that all of his horse-trough planters had been removed from the railings. They weren't in the dumpsters behind the laundry room, as the last garden had been. They had simply vanished.

The prior week, Seth had cleaned out the tired marigolds and calendulas from the planters, replaced the soil, and planted daffodil, hyacinth, and tulip bulbs along with sprinklings of alyssum seeds that would sprout in two to four weeks, and bloom in the spring.

Seth checked his computer that was connected to the security camera trained on the garden, and there was no image. Somebody had placed a piece of cardboard or some other object in front of his living room window by the camera lens in order to block the image. This left Seth with no evidence as to who had stolen his property. He understood that he had no recourse and found it vexing that a man of his age and station couldn't even grow a tulip outside his front door.

"Denmark's a prison/Then is the world one."

By this time, Winston, who had been re-elected as president, tried to console him with the view that though he could have no garden of his own, at least he had won the battle for Cassandra, and that was no small victory.

But even that victory turned out to be more elusive than Winston presumed.

Eddie had been following reports of a new administrative head at the county Health Department, and he seized on this opportunity to re-open the case against Cassandra.

Almost a year after Francine Blumenfeld had left her message on Seth's voicemail, reporting the County's decision to drop the complaint against Cassandra on August 23rd of the prior year, Winston forwarded to Seth a new email from the Health Department, now advising Winston, in his capacity as president, of the distance requirements for chickens. The Health Department's new department head, Pablo Reissling, had listened sympathetically to a litany of complaints voiced by both JoJo and Eddie Angelis about the housing of Cassandra inside Seth's apartment, and the health threat she posed to the occupants of the building, including Seth. This led to a phone call between Pablo Reissling and Winston during which Pablo expressed his outrage that a chicken, i.e. Cassandra, should be a co-occupant in an urban apartment. Pablo Reissling was not going to let this situation continue one month longer, he warned Winston.

As it turns out, the chairman of the L.A. County Board of Supervisors had attended the L.A. Observer Theater Awards which Seth had hosted and in which Cassandra had put in her appearance, perched on the wrist of a prominent theater producer.

Seth sent an email to Nick Wettlaufer, the press attaché for that Supervisor. Nick had not only attended with his boss on the evening of Cassandra's performance, he was responsible for setting up the Supervisor's appearance.

Seth explained the entire situation, that he was now being compelled to fight the same battle with the county that he had fought the prior year and had prevailed in. Seth asked if there was anything Nick could do on behalf of Cassandra.

There are many arduous challenges in the field of a Supervisor representing one of the most populous counties in the nation, but standing up on behalf of a pet chicken is rarely among them. It was partly because the cause was so exotic and comical that Nick embraced it, partly to redress what he perceived as an injustice within his domain, but mostly to amuse himself.

Seth never saw what Nick wrote, or said, but its impact was palpable.

A week later, Winston called the Health Department to follow up. He found Pablo Reissling happy to chat with him once more. Reissling's point of view had taken a sharp turn. He told Winston that neither he nor his department would be going anywhere near the Angelis complaint, or the chicken that was its subject. As far as he was concerned, the matter was closed.

Winston expected Seth to be delighted by this news, but Seth felt mostly worn down by the belief that the Angelis duo would continue to be relentless in their pursuit of his personal misery. As it turned out, that also wasn't entirely true.

A GENERAL MEETING OF THE homeowners that Winston had called for November was filled with the usual acrimony. Most of the homeowners were sick of the nastiness of the past two years. It was, therefore, a sparsely populated meeting during which, through discussions of landscaping, roofing and other issues of deferred maintenance, the Angelis duo was uncharacteristically quiet. Eddie, in particular, looked at Seth without the contempt that had become so familiar. It certainly wasn't replaced by kindness. There was no smile to be found. But nor was it overtly hostile, and Seth took note of that.

Despite the stream of administrative rulings against JoJo and Eddie, at least they had prevailed in vanquishing Seth's railing garden. They could count at least one victory in their campaign, and that was enough for them. Short of aggravated assault or homicide, there was little more damage they could inflict. Perhaps they too had become war-weary.

When the meeting concluded with the usual pointless self-congratulations by the officers, Seth took what he imagined to be a risk, though it really wasn't. At the close of the meeting, he extended his hand in friendship to Eddie, who took it.

"Wanna get a beer?" Seth asked him. "It's on me."

Seth didn't fully understand why he made this offer. It was just an intuition that he was following.

"When?" Eddie replied.

"I don't care. Anytime."

"What for?

"Clear the air."

Eddie thought this over a moment before replying, "Okay."

The following Thursday, Seth and Eddie sat in semi-darkness facing each other across a high-top bar table at an eatery on Franklin Avenue. Struggling to contain years of pent-up rage, Eddie spoke in measured though at times wavering cadences, pouring out an exegesis of complaints about various actions and betrayals committed by Seth, who listened, as he promised he would, to Eddie's versions of events that frequently had no point of connection with his own recollections of the same incidents.

In one story, Seth and Katerina were about to leave for a month in Moscow. Because Seth and the Angelis duo were on good terms at that time, Seth knocked on JoJo's door and told her they were leaving, and that Reginald McCallister had agreed to care for their two dogs in their absence. This got twisted into a rendition in which, according to Eddie, Seth simply abandoned the dogs, and Reginald had stepped in rather than allowing the dogs to starve, alone and fouling the apartment. Eddie worked himself into a fury over what he called Seth's cavalier disregard for his own responsibilities.

"But that wasn't what happened," Seth said, calmly. "Your story has no bearing on what actually happened. You honestly think I'd abandon my animals in my own apartment? I was telling your mom about my travel plans as a courtesy. This has all gotten twisted into some venal knot."

But Eddie was having none of it.

"Your history," Eddie said, "is a history of revised stories to suit your needs at any given moment."

"Okay," Seth replied, vowing not to lose his temper or engage in a style of argumentation that would demean either of them. "We can continue to seethe for the rest of our lives. We can agree to hate each other and to block each other's every move. We can connive against each other and commit ourselves to making each other as miserable as possible. That's definitely one approach."

Seth noticed that Eddie was actually listening respectfully, which he appreciated.

"I have an alternative proposal," Seth continued. "Let's start with the reality: Your version of the past is now cemented in your brain. I don't happen to agree with it, but that's beside the point. It's obviously not going to change. My version of the past is equally cemented in my brain. There's no persuasion here. We believe what we believe. We've both turned the past into a fortress. The larger question is what happened — what is *true*. Neither of us can know for sure."

Amazingly to Seth, Eddie was still listening. He wasn't interjecting, or shaking. This was the first actual discussion he'd had with Eddie since they'd built the chicken coop together in the back garden.

"I propose," Seth continued, ". . . well, we don't have to be friends, we don't even have to like each other, but what needs to stop is the way we demonize each other. So here's what I propose: I will stop treating you as the resident demon who's out to make as many people as miserable as possible, because that's the way I've been seeing you, and I'll stop that. In exchange, you'll stop seeing me as this selfish jerk out to destroy the building for my own advantage, because it sounds like that's how you've been viewing me. I'm willing to suspend my long-held view of you, if you'll do the same for me. So we can pass each other on the stairway and just nod without a scowl. It's better that way, for us, and for everyone else. If I do my part, will you do yours?"

Eddie took a swig from his mug of beer, he reflected for a moment, and then he said, "Okay."

They shook hands on it, and finished their beers. Both honored their pact. There were no more complaints about Cassandra, there was no more violence, nor threats of violence. And that was that.

EPILOGUE: THE FOREST OF ARDEN

Despite the Truce of Bronson Canyon, Seth had grown to loathe the building, and coming home to it. It was now like an allergic reaction he had no control over. He still couldn't grow a tulip outside his front door, or anywhere else on the property in which he had a share of ownership, and this still seemed absurd to him.

At some point between Christmas and New Year's, Seth drove by himself to Lake Fulmor, but this time he kept driving past the lake, over the summit of Pine Cove, and descended into an enchanted fairy-tale town he'd remembered from long ago.

He stopped the car at a nature preserve at the rim of the village, and he started to hike down a trail into the thick of the woods. He sat on a tree stump for a good hour when it started to snow, at first in little sprinkles and then more thickly, silently. The air was still, and the forest was resonant. A coyote crossed below, so that the sound of the creature snapping twigs underfoot echoed through the woods. And when he looked up into the crowns of the ponderosas and cedars and the occasional sequoia in the biting, crisp air, he saw entire trees laced in white. The trails and the streets and the rooftops of the village were also painted white.

Seth had not seen snow since Moscow, and this place resembled the outskirts of that city. And this thought filled him with nostalgia, and a kind of sadness.

And when he walked around the snow-coated village, and saw the wood smoke slithering up and out from chimneys, he understood how this place could be enchanted. He understood that this was where he wanted, needed to be.

His intuition was given further support that night, when he was watching a production of *As You Like It* at Antaeus Company, a classical repertory troupe in North Hollywood.

The usurped Duke Senior opens the play's Act II. He's referring to the Forest of Arden, where he now lives with some contentment.

Perhaps it was the actor's calm resolve and the pleasure he took from the speech, or perhaps the pleasure he took from life itself. But the words, their unfettered truth, and the way this actor wrapped them around himself, sent Seth into something resembling a trance:

"Now, my co-mates and duo in exile, hath not old custom made this life
more sweet than that of painted pomp? Are not these woods more free from peril
than the envious court?

"Here feel we but the penalty of Adam, the seasons' difference, as the icy fang
and churlish chiding of the winter's wind, which, when it bites and blows upon my
body, even till I shrink with cold, I smile and say 'This is no flattery: these are
counselors that feelingly persuade me what I am.'

"Sweet are the uses of adversity, which, like the toad, ugly and venomous,
wears yet a precious jewel in his head; And this our life exempt from public haunt
finds tongues in trees, books in the running brooks, sermons in stones and good in
every thing.
"I would not change it."

IT WAS EARLY MAY WHEN SETH CAME to collect Agamemnon from Susan's Fontana home, to reclaim him. He feared Susan would be upset, because of her deep attachment to her "guard rooster," but that wasn't so.

A U-Haul van was parked in her driveway, half loaded with cardboard boxes, a distressed table and chest of drawers from Ikea, and a twin bed with a rusty frame.

Seth had attended the trial of *Epps v. Epps* two months earlier at the San Bernardino Superior Court in Fontana, where Susan's lawyer faced off against that of her brother, Dwayne, over the question of who owned the house. The judge cemented his earlier injunction, ruling that the intra-family transaction in which Susan had signed over the house to Dwayne, was fraudulent. Even if she had signed it, the judge said — and there was considerable suspicion about that, given how indecipherable the signature was — it had not been notarized, and the judge had reason to believe she'd signed it under duress.

Dwayne's case was further impeded by the numerous notices of eviction he had served upon his own sister. The judge believed that Dwayne had good reason to believe that Susan would be rendered destitute by Dwayne seizing her property. The judge didn't like that at all.

In exchange for a one-year supply of crystal meth from Dwayne, Melissa testified against her own sister, claiming that despite a court order forbidding Susan from owning or caring for any more cats, she had nonetheless acquired at least a dozen new felines. But Melissa's testimony was of no consequence, and her one-year promise of meth from Dwayne got shortened to two months.

Full title to the property was restored to Susan, who quickly sold it to a real estate agent from Rialto named Paco Fernandez. Susan used the money to buy a two-bedroom, two-bathroom property set back five hundred feet from Route 51 in southern Idaho, where she was headed, with her battered furniture and twelve cats in tow.

On this chilly Sunday afternoon, in the middle of Susan's detritus-strewn front yard in Fontana, Agamemnon stood with the proud posture of a weathervane, wheezing. Susan said that a few minutes earlier, he'd been obsessed with chasing a wind-blown leaf. This endeavor had left him out of breath. Brisk breezes ruffled his feathers and caused him to shake his head, as he felt the gusts rubbing against his one eye.

Seth and Susan hugged before Seth picked up Agamemnon, gently, with one hand beneath each wing. Agamemnon raised no objection, now nestled against Seth's stomach. He cackled deeply. Seth told him that he'd soon be joining Cassandra in a soundproof chicken coop nestled in the mountains. Agamemnon stared at Seth through his single eye, which was surrounded by pillows of red flesh, and Agamemnon, for once, had no comment.

TWO MONTHS LATER, IN JULY, A HOT sun blazed down on Seth as he sat in a large rocking chair on an expansive redwood deck, high in the San Bernardino National Forest not far from the peak of Mount San Jacinto.

Seth had scraped together every last penny from the sale of his apartment in Bronson Canyon for the down payment on a bank-owned, abandoned 1936 two-story home in this same enchanted, mile-high mountain town he'd visited earlier.

It was called Idyllwild.

THE HOUSE CAME WITH A SMALL REDWOOD deck, on which Seth now sat. It was attached to the back of the house.

On a banister around the rim of the deck, Seth attached six horse-trough railing planters, just like the ones he'd had in Bronson Canyon. His planters overflowed with flowering vincas, carnations and marigolds.

It was home. The forests recalled those in Sonoma County where Seth grew up. The same kind of blackberry bushes lined the ditches. When he bicycled along the village's empty roads, the air smelled of fresh pine.

FROM IDLE CURIOSITY, SETH USED the Internet to catch up on several developments that unfolded in the aftermath of the Bronson Canyon Arms Crisis.

In September, Seth learned that Anton Antonovich Borovsky a.k.a. Zeke Quincy Swilling was speaking to high school students in the Phoenix, Arizona area. He had been fitted with two prosthetic arms and hands. The surgery was paid for by his wife's medical insurance.

Zeke's wife, Darlene Flemming-Swilling, stood by him throughout his ordeal. Doing so was a role in life that gratified her, since her position teaching English grammar and literature to disinterested high school students in the Phoenix desert environs was eroding both her personal dignity and reason for living, and her prescriptions for Xanax and Wellbutrin were doing nothing to stem that collapse. Caring for her Zeke as though he were a wounded bird transformed her into a woman with a purpose.

Anton/Zeke spoke gratis at the schools, a project his wife had instigated, and he spoke with a newfound and almost evangelical fervor about both the cruelty of his parents for selling him to the Mafia, and for the subsequent mistakes he'd made in his life and of the terrible dangers of being in a gang. He turned out to be a persuasive speaker. His lectures brought tears to the eyes of many teenagers. It was a show he could easily have taken on the road, if he'd wanted. But he didn't. He preferred spending time with his infant daughter, whom he cherished.

Meanwhile, 357 miles away in Los Angeles, the FBI dropped its investigation of Eddie and JoJo Angelis in connection to the mutilation of Anton/Zeke. The government found no credible evidence linking them to the crime.

Across the globe in Moscow, Russia, Katerina Pavlova was becoming increasingly financially self-sufficient. Katerina was eventually able to show her own knitwear to the CEO of a high-end Italian design company, one Nikita Obromsky. The man was impressed by the quality of Katerina's designs. He offered to display a collection of Katerina's knitwear, on consignment, in one of his downtown boutiques, and Katerina found deep satisfaction in being able to run her own business in a place she could call home.

All of this seemed, felt real enough, despite Seth's eroding confidence in his abilities, as a critic as well as citizen, to determine what was plausible, to differentiate between what was real and what seemed real.

Seth was now settling on the reality and plausibility that the visage of Joseph Stalin who had so oddly crashed through the ceiling of Winston Pendleton's apartment, only to exit just as oddly through the ceiling of the apartment he later purchased, could, in the reality he had grown to know and believe, only have been an apparition, like the ghost of Hamlet's father, like the ghost of Seth's own father he once saw appear on a computer monitor at the *L.A. Observer* –- the manifestations of extreme stress.

Fine. But how then does one explain the two severed arms that appeared, in reality, on the respective beds of Eddie and JoJo Angelis, in their respective apartments? If that wasn't the work of the Joseph Stalin who had descended into the building in Bronson Canyon, then who else could have been responsible for the Bronson Canyon Arms Crisis?

A realization hit Seth like a lightning bolt: Katerina Pavlova.

She knew many people, and she certainly knew people in the Russian Mafia.

High in the forests of Riverside County, Seth called Katerina from his cellphone.

"Two severed arms appeared in the building, in different apartments," he told her. "Did you have anything to do with that?"

After a brief pause, Katerina burst into laughter, the laughter of recognition and delight, laughter that echoed through the tallest pines.

THE FOLLOWING MAY, UP IN IDYLLWILD, Seth hired a contractor to eradicate termites swarming below his kitchen. The worker, Jacob, noted that a ponderosa pine adjoining the balcony, soaring some two hundred feet into the sky, was being "blown out" by beetles. Jacob was a thin, eloquent guy with a silver goatee. He sported overalls and boots and spoke with a Southern twang. He squinted when he peered high in the sky to the top of the tree. He showed Seth how 25% of the needles at the very top were brown — probably from an invasion of the Ips beetle.

Furthermore, at the tree's base, Jacob ran his finger into a recess within the thick bark and scooped out sawdust.

"See this? This is also from beetles, probably turpentines. This tree isn't drinking. If the tree was drinking, this would be sap, but it's sawdust. It's the drought. These giants can't take the dry. They're parched."

Seth hadn't before noticed the die-back in the tree's mid-section, the straggling branches, some with thin clusters of browning needles, some bare, like skeletons.

"The beetles go after the stressed trees," Jacob continued. "There's nothing you can do. Edison will take out the tree for free, and you can use the firewood for two or three winters. I've seen giant trees completely blow out in less than a month once the beetles get in there."

After Jacob drove away in his flatbed pickup, Seth pored through Internet articles on the various varieties of beetles attacking the western forests. There were reports from the Forest Service confirming that once beetles had invaded a tree, it could not be saved. There were also reports saying just the opposite, that with a combination of injected insecticide and heavy watering, some trees — pines in particular — were resilient enough to bounce back.

In the evening, from his upstairs bathroom window, Seth looked outside to see in the half-light the four-foot-wide, marbled, majestic bark of the ponderosa. In addition to being a living sculpture, it nestled his new home in its embrace. Seth figured he'd call the local arborist and try to save the ponderosa, which he named Henry Thoreau.

What had Henry endured in his two hundred years on the mountain? How many forest fires had he seen? How many times had he watched the Big Dipper dance across a clear night sky?

He'd obviously seen the clear-cutting of his companions — the forestry equivalent of a pogrom. Had he seen the Gold Rush? Had he seen the Chinese immigrants build the American railroads? Had he seen the Roaring '20s and the Great Depression? Had he seen impoverished migrants from dust bowl Oklahoma trekking west like refugees? Had he seen them stopped at the California border, and placed into work camps? All those people crossing the land, fleeing home, seeking home. Had he seen any of that from his canopy, looking out over the mighty Mojave?

Beetles had savaged his crown. He was King Lear, being dethroned by pests, who thrived by preying on the vulnerable, the distressed. This is the shape of history. Pestilence.

There are only two impulses for human action: cruelty and kindness. Everything else is nonsense.

SETH LOOKED AT HENRY'S TATTERED CROWN. He saw that even a ponderosa as great and as regal as Henry was still fighting for his place in this world, fighting for his life, as we all do, until we don't.

He sat enshrouded by looming cedar and ponderosa pines that possessed rugged, thick bark being pounded on by woodpeckers. From across the expanse of a sandy side garden, he observed a crested blue jay scuttle to a nearby manzanita. The jay flew down from a lighting fixture attached to the front portal of a nearby garage — his garage. Thrushes twittered overhead. A brisk gust caused the trees to whir, as though the woods had been suddenly tossed into a blender. A raven squawked high, high in the giant ponderosa to his left, sending down a shower of pine needles and an auspicious chunk of branch.

Upon seeing the branch crash-land onto the parched sand beyond the deck, Agamemnon rushed to the wood fragment from across the yard, followed by Cassandra. Agamemnon sent up an alarm call — "b-CAW-buk-buk-buk, b-CAW-buk-buk-buk" — urging Cassandra to stand back. She didn't. She approached the now motionless piece of wood, and pecked at it. Agamemnon did the same. It rolled half an inch, causing both birds to dance backwards in fright and warn every living creature in earshot — "b-CAW-buk-buk-buk, b-CAW-buk-buk-buk."

Everybody who could hear, heard. Nobody complained. This was the forest. The sky was always falling.

CPSIA information can be obtained
at www.ICGtesting.com
Printed in the USA
FSOW01n1453180316
18168FS